KT-381-059

Please return/renew this item by the last date shown

Herefordshire
Libraries

Herefordshire
Council

MEMORIES OF MIDNIGHT

In *The Other Side of Midnight* Sidney Sheldon created one of his most unforgettable characters: Constantin Demiris, billionaire, art lover, womanizer . . . and killer. To Noelle, the woman who betrayed him, and Larry, the man who stole her, Demiris brought a chilling retribution. Now, in *Memories of Midnight*, he confronts the problem of someone else he believes has stayed alive too long.

Greece, 1948. In the seclusion of a remote convent a young woman emerges from the trauma of memory loss. To Catherine Alexander, Larry's widow, Demiris seems a benefactor, the man who helps her build a life again. She knows that Larry and Noelle are dead but not who was responsible. Nor that Demiris' desire for revenge is unquenched; that there is a last, unsilenced victim.

In this atmosphere of deception, Catherine's move to London seems just another example of Demiris' good nature. Set down in a strange and unsettling environment she cannot guess the fate her benefactor has in store, or that her life is inextricably bound up with other victims of his mighty ego.

Moving from the exotic shores of the Mediterranean to post-war London, *Memories of Midnight* is the compelling portrayal of one woman's fight against a terrifying destiny. Sidney Sheldon's genius as a master storyteller has never been more powerfully displayed.

By the same author

IF TOMORROW COMES
MASTER OF THE GAME
RAGE OF ANGELS
BLOODLINE
A STRANGER IN THE MIRROR
THE OTHER SIDE OF MIDNIGHT
THE NAKED FACE
WINDMILLS OF THE GODS
THE SANDS OF TIME

SIDNEY SHELDON

MEMORIES OF MIDNIGHT

COLLINS
London
1990

William Collins Sons & Co. Ltd
London · Glasgow · Sydney · Auckland
Toronto · Johannesburg

An overseas edition first published 1990
This edition first published in Great Britain 1990

BRITISH LIBRARY CATALOGUING IN PUBLICATION DATA

Sheldon, Sidney, *1917–*
Memories of midnight.
I. Title
813.54[F]

ISBN 0-00-223638-9

Photoset in Linotron Times Roman by
Rowland Phototypesetting Ltd,
Bury St Edmunds, Suffolk
Printed and bound in Great Britain by
William Collins Sons & Co. Ltd, Glasgow

For Alexandra
with Love

Sing me no songs of daylight,
For the sun is the enemy of lovers
Sing instead of shadows and darkness,
And memories of midnight

SAPPHO

Prologue

———◆———

Kowloon – May 1949

'It must look like an accident. Can you arrange that?'

It was an insult. He could feel the anger rising in him. That was a question you asked some amateur you picked up from the streets. He was tempted to reply with sarcasm: *Oh, yes, I think I can manage that. Would you prefer an accident indoors? I can arrange for her to break her neck falling down a flight of stairs.* The dancer in Marseilles. *Or she could get drunk and drown in her bath.* The heiress in Gstaad. *She could take an overdose of heroin.* He had disposed of three that way. *Or, she could fall asleep in bed with a lighted cigarette.* The Swedish detective at L'Hôtel on the Left Bank in Paris. *Or perhaps you would prefer something outdoors? I can arrange a traffic accident, a plane crash, or a disappearance at sea.*

But he said none of those things, for in truth he was afraid of the man seated across from him. He had heard too many chilling stories about him, and he had reason to believe them.

So all he said was, 'Yes, sir, I can arrange an accident. No one will ever know.' Even as he said the words, the thought struck him: *He knows that I'll know.* He waited.

They were on the second floor of a building in the walled city of Kowloon that had been built in 1840 by a group of Chinese to protect themselves from the British barbarians. The walls had been torn down in the Second World War, but there were other walls that kept outsiders away: Gangs of cut-throats and drug addicts and rapists roaming through the rabbit warren of crooked, narrow streets and dark stairways leading into gloom.

1

Tourists were warned to stay away, and not even the police would venture inside past Tung Tau Tsuen Street, on the outskirts. He could hear the street noises outside the window, and the shrill and raucous polyglot of languages that belonged to the residents of the walled city.

The man was studying him with cold, obsidian eyes. Finally he spoke. 'Very well. I will leave the method to you.'

'Yes, sir. Is the target here in Kowloon?'

'London. Her name is Catherine. Catherine Alexander.'

A limousine, followed by a second car with two armed body-guards, drove the man to the Blue House on Lascar Row, in the Tsim Sha Tsui area. The Blue House was open to special patrons only. Heads of state visited there, and movie stars, and presidents of corporations. The management prided itself on discretion. Half a dozen years earlier, one of the young girls who worked there had discussed her customers with a newspaperman, and she was found the next morning in Aberdeen Harbor with her tongue cut out. Everything was for sale in the Blue House: virgins, boys, lesbians who satisfied themselves without the 'jade stalks' of men, and animals. It was the only place he knew of where the tenth-century art of Ishinpo was still practiced. The Blue House was a cornucopia of forbidden pleasures.

The man had ordered the twins this time. They were an exquisitely matched pair with beautiful features, incredible bodies, and no inhibitions. He remembered the last time he had been there . . . the metal stool with no bottom and their soft caressing tongues and fingers, and the tub filled with fragrant warm water that overflowed onto the tiled floor and their hot mouths plundering his body. He felt the beginning of an erection.

'We're here, sir.'

Three hours later, when he had finished with them, sated and content, the man ordered the limousine to head for Mody Road. He looked out the window of the limousine at the sparkling lights of the city that never slept. The Chinese had named it

2

Gau-lung – nine dragons, and he imagined them lurking in the mountains above the city, ready to come down and destroy the weak and the unwary. He was neither.

They reached Mody Road.

The Taoist priest waiting for him looked like a figure from an ancient parchment, with a classic faded oriental robe and a long, wispy white beard.

'*Jou sahn.*'

'*Jou sahn.*'

'*Gei do chin?*'

'*Yat-chihn.*'

'*Jou.*'

The priest closed his eyes in a silent prayer and began shaking the *chim*, the wooden cup filled with numbered prayer sticks. A stick fell out and the shaking ceased. In the silence, the Taoist priest consulted his chart and turned to his visitor. He spoke in halting English. 'The gods say you will soon be rid of dangerous enemy.'

The man felt a pleasant jolt of surprise. He was too intelligent not to realize that the ancient art of *chim* was merely a superstition. And he was too intelligent to ignore it. Besides, there was another good luck omen. Today was Agios Constantinous Day, his birthday.

'The gods have blessed you with good *fung shui*.'

'*Do jeh.*'

'*Hou wah.*'

Five minutes later, he was in the limousine, on his way to Kai Tak, the Hong Kong airport, where his private plane was waiting to take him back to Athens.

3

Chapter 1

—◆—

Ioannina, Greece – July 1948

She woke up screaming every night and it was always the same dream. She was in the middle of a lake in a fierce storm and a man and a woman were forcing her head under the icy waters, drowning her. She awakened each time, panicky, gasping for breath, soaked with perspiration.

She had no idea who she was and she had no memory of the past. She spoke English – but she did not know what country she was from or how she had come to be in Greece, in the small Carmelite convent that sheltered her.

As time went by, there were tantalizing flashes of memory, glimpses of vague, ephemeral images that came and went too quickly for her to grasp them, to hold them and examine them. They came at unexpected moments, catching her off-guard, and filling her with confusion.

In the beginning, she had asked questions. The Carmelite nuns were kind and understanding, but theirs was an order of silence, and the only one permitted to speak was Sister Theresa, the elderly and frail Mother Superior.

'Do you know who I am?'

'No, my child,' Sister Theresa said.

'How did I get to this place?'

'At the foot of these mountains is a village called Ioannina. You were in a small boat in the lake during a storm last year. The boat sank, but by the grace of God, two of our sisters saw you and rescued you. They brought you here.'

'But . . . where did I come from before that?'

'I'm sorry, child. I do not know.'

She could not be satisfied with that. 'Hasn't anyone inquired about me? Hasn't anyone tried to find me?'

Sister Theresa shook her head. 'No one.'

She wanted to scream with frustration. She tried again. 'The newspapers . . . they must have had a story about my being missing.'

'As you know, we are permitted no communication with the outside world. We must accept God's will, child. We must thank Him for all His mercies. You are alive.'

And that was as far as she was able to get. In the beginning, she had been too ill to be concerned about herself, but slowly, as the months went by, she had regained her strength and her health.

When she was strong enough to move about, she spent her days tending the colorful gardens in the grounds of the convent, in the incandescent light that bathed Greece in a celestial glow, with the soft winds carrying the pungent aroma of lemons and vines.

The atmosphere was serene and calm and yet she could find no peace. *I'm lost*, she thought, *and no one cares. Why? Have I done something evil? Who am I? Who am I? Who am I?*

The images continued to come, unbidden. One morning she awakened suddenly with a vision of herself in a room with a naked man undressing her. Was it a dream? Or was it something that had happened in her past? Who was the man? Was it someone she had married? Did she have a husband? She wore no wedding ring. In fact she had no possessions other than the black Order of the Carmelite habit that Sister Theresa had given her, and a pin, a small golden bird with ruby eyes and outstretched wings.

She was anonymous, a stranger living among strangers. There was no one to help her, no psychiatrist to tell her that her mind had been so traumatized it could stay sane only by shutting out the terrible past.

And the images kept coming, faster and faster. It was as though her mind had suddenly turned into a giant jigsaw puzzle, with odd pieces tumbling into place. But the pieces made no

6

sense. She had a vision of a huge studio filled with men in army uniform. They seemed to be making a motion picture. *Was I an actress?* No, she seemed to be in charge. *But in charge of what?*

A soldier handed her a bouquet of flowers. *You'll have to pay for these yourself*, he laughed.

Two nights later, she had a dream about the same man. She was saying goodbye to him at the airport, and she woke up sobbing because she was losing him.

There was no more peace for her after that. These were not mere dreams. They were pieces of her life, her past. *I must find out who I was. Who I am.*

And unexpectedly, in the middle of the night, without warning, a name was dredged up out of her subconscious. *Catherine. My name is Catherine Alexander.*

Chapter 2

Athens, Greece

The empire of Constantin Demiris could not be located on any map, yet he was the ruler of a fiefdom larger and more powerful than many countries. He was one of the two or three wealthiest men in the world and his influence was incalculable. He had no title or official position but he regularly bought and sold prime ministers, cardinals, ambassadors and kings. Demiris' tentacles were everywhere, woven through the woof and warp of dozens of countries. He was a charismatic man, with a brilliantly incisive mind, physically striking, well above medium height, with a barrel chest and broad shoulders. His complexion was swarthy and he had a strong Greek nose and olive-black eyes. He had the face of a hawk, a predator. When he chose to take the trouble, Demiris could be extremely charming. He spoke eight languages and was a noted raconteur. He had one of the most important art collections in the world, a fleet of private planes and a dozen apartments, chateaus and villas scattered around the globe. He was a connoisseur of beauty, and he found beautiful women irresistible. He had the reputation of being a powerful lover, and his romantic escapades were as colorful as his financial adventures.

Constantin Demiris prided himself on being a patriot – the blue and white Greek flag was always on display at his villa in Kolonaki and on Psara, his private island – but he paid no taxes. He did not feel obliged to conform to the rules that applied to ordinary men. In his veins ran *ichor* – the blood of the gods.

*

8

Nearly every person Demiris met wanted something from him: financing for a business project; a donation to a charity; or simply the power that his friendship could bestow. Demiris enjoyed the challenge of figuring out what it was that people were really after, for it was rarely what it appeared to be. His analytical mind was skeptical of surface truth, and as a consequence he believed nothing he was told and trusted no one. His motto was 'Keep your friends close, but your enemies closer'. The reporters who chronicled his life were permitted to see only his geniality and charm, the sophisticated, urbane man of the world. They had no reason to suspect that beneath the amiable façade, Demiris was a killer, a gutter fighter whose instinct was to go for the jugular vein.

He was an unforgiving man who never forgot a slight. To the ancient Greeks the word *dikaiosini*, justice, was often synonymous with *ekdikisis*, vengeance, and Demiris was obsessed with both. He remembered every affront he had ever suffered, and those who were unlucky enough to incur his enmity were paid back a hundred fold. They were never aware of it, for Demiris' mathematical mind made a game of exacting retribution, patiently working out elaborate traps and spinning complex webs that finally caught and destroyed his enemies.

He enjoyed the hours he spent devising pitfalls for his adversaries. He would study his victims carefully, analyzing their personalities, assessing their strengths and their weaknesses.

At a dinner party one evening, Demiris had overheard a motion picture producer refer to him as 'that oily Greek'. Demiris bided his time. Two years later, the producer signed a glamorous internationally known actress to star in his new big-budget production in which he put in his own money. Demiris waited until the picture was half finished and then charmed the leading lady into walking out on it and joining him on his yacht.

'It will be a honeymoon,' Demiris told her.

She got the honeymoon but not the wedding. The movie finally had to shut down and the producer went bankrupt.

*

There were a few players in Demiris' game with whom he had not yet evened the score, but he was in no hurry. He enjoyed the anticipation, the planning and the execution. These days he made no enemies, for no man could afford to be his enemy, so his quarry was limited to those who had crossed his path in the past.

But Constantin Demiris' sense of *dikaiosini* was double-edged. Just as he never forgave an injury, neither did he forget a favor. A poor fisherman who had given the young boy shelter found himself the owner of a fishing fleet. A prostitute who had fed and clothed the young man when he was too poor to pay her, mysteriously inherited an apartment building, without any idea of who her benefactor was.

Demiris had started life as the son of a stevedore in Piraeus. He had fourteen brothers and sisters and there was never enough food on the table.

From the very beginning, Constantin Demiris showed an uncanny gift for business. He earned extra money doing odd jobs after school, and at sixteen, he had saved enough money to open a food stand on the docks with an older partner. The business flourished and the partner cheated Demiris out of his half. It took Demiris ten years to destroy the man. The young boy was burning with a fierce ambition. He would lie awake at night, his eyes bright in the darkness. *I'm going to be rich. I'm going to be famous. Some day everyone will know my name.* It was the only lullaby that could put him to sleep. He had no idea how it was going to happen. He knew only that it would.

On Demiris' seventeenth birthday, he came across an article about the oil fields in Saudi Arabia, and it was as though a magic door to the future had suddenly opened for him.

He went to his father. 'I'm going to Saudi Arabia. I'm going to work in the oil fields.'

'*Too-sou!* What do you know about oil fields?'

'Nothing, father. I'm going to learn.'

One month later, Constantin Demiris was on his way.

*

10

It was company policy for the overseas employees of the Trans-Continental Oil Corporation to sign a two-year employment contract, but Demiris felt no qualms about it. He planned to stay in Saudi Arabia for as long as it took him to make his fortune. He had envisioned a wonderful Arabian nights adventure, a glamorous, mysterious land with exotic-looking women, and black gold gushing up out of the ground. The reality was a shock.

On an early morning in summer, Demiris arrived at Fadili, a dreary camp in the middle of the desert, consisting of an ugly stone building surrounded by *barastis*, small brushwood huts. There were a thousand lower-bracket workers there, mostly Saudis. The women who trudged through the dusty, unpaved streets were heavily veiled.

Demiris entered the building where J. J. McIntyre, the personnel manager, had his office.

McIntyre looked up as the young man came in. 'So. The home office hired you, eh?'

'Yes, sir.'

'Ever work the oil fields before, son?'

For an instant, Demiris was tempted to lie. 'No, sir.'

McIntyre grinned. 'You're going to love it here. You're a million miles from nowhere, bad food, no women that you can touch without getting your balls chopped off, and not a goddamned thing to do at night. But the pay is good, right?'

'I'm here to learn,' Demiris said earnestly.

'Yeah? Then I'll tell you what you better learn fast. You're in Moslem country now. That means no alcohol. Anyone caught stealing gets his right hand cut off. Second time, left hand. The third time, you lose a foot. If you kill anyone you're beheaded.'

'I'm not planning to kill anyone.'

'Wait,' McIntyre grunted. 'You just got here.'

The compound was a Tower of Babel, people from a dozen different countries all speaking their native languages. Demiris had a good ear and picked up languages quickly. The men were

11

there to make roads in the middle of an inhospitable desert, construct housing, install electrical equipment, put in telephone communications, build workshops, arrange food and water supplies, design a drainage system, administer medical attention and, it seemed to young Demiris, to do a hundred other tasks. They were working in temperatures over one hundred degrees Fahrenheit, suffering from flies, mosquitoes, dust, fever and dysentery. Even in the desert there was a social hierarchy. At the top were the men engaged in locating oil, and below, the construction workers called 'stiffs', and the clerks known as 'shiny pants'.

Nearly all the men involved in the actual drilling – the geologists, surveyors, engineers and oil chemists – were Americans, for the new rotary drill had been invented in the United States and the Americans were more familiar with its operation. The young man went out of his way to make friends with them.

Constantin Demiris spent as much time as he could around the drillers and he never stopped asking questions. He stored away the information, absorbing it the way the hot sands soaked up water. He noticed that two different methods of drilling were being used.

He approached one of the drillers working near a giant 130-foot derrick. 'I was wondering why there are two different kinds of drilling going on.'

The driller explained. 'Well, son, one's cable tool and one's rotary. We're going more to rotary now. They start out exactly the same.'

'They do?'

'Yeah. For either one you have to erect a derrick like this one to hoist up the pieces of equipment that have to be lowered into the well.' He looked at the eager face of the young man. 'I'll bet you have no idea why they call it a derrick.'

'No, sir.'

'That was the name of a famous hangman in the seventeenth century.'

'I see.'

'Cable tool drilling goes way back. Hundreds of years ago, the Chinese used to dig water wells that way. They punched a hole

12

into the earth by lifting and dropping a heavy cutting tool hung from a cable. But today about eighty-five percent of all wells are drilled by the rotary method.' He turned to go back to his drilling.

'Excuse me. How does the rotary method work?'

The man stopped. 'Well, instead of slammin' a hole in the earth, you just bore one. You see here? In the middle of the derrick floor is a steel turntable that's rotated by machinery. This rotary table grips and turns a pipe that extends downward through it. There's a bit fastened to the lower end of the pipe.'

'It seems simple, doesn't it?'

'It's more complicated than it looks. You have to have a way to excavate the loosened material as you drill. You have to prevent the walls from caving in and you have to seal off the water and gas from the well.'

'With all that drilling, doesn't the rotary drill ever get dull?'

'Sure. Then we have to pull out the whole damned drill string, screw a new bit to the bottom of the drill pipe and lower the pipe back into the hole. Are you planning to be a driller?'

'No, sir. I'm planning to own oil wells.'

'Congratulations. Can I get back to work now?'

One morning, Demiris watched as a tool was lowered into the well, but instead of boring downward, he noticed that it cut small circular areas from the sides of the hole and brought up rocks.

'Excuse me. What's the point of doing that?' Demiris asked.

The driller paused to mop his brow. 'This is side wall coring. We use these rocks for analysis, to see whether they're oil-bearing.'

'I see.'

When things were going smoothly, Demiris would hear drillers cry out 'I'm turning to the right,' which meant they were making a hole. Demiris noticed that there were dozens of tiny holes drilled all over the field, with diameters as small as two or three inches.

13

'Excuse me. What are those for?' the young man asked.

'Those are prospect wells. They tell us what's underneath. Saves the company a lot of time and money.'

'I see.'

It was all utterly fascinating to the young man and his questions were endless.

'Excuse me. How do you know *where* to drill?'

'We got a lot of geologists – pebble pups – who take measurements of the strata and study the cuttings from wells. Then the rope chokers . . .'

'Excuse me, what's a rope choker?'

'A driller. When they . . .'

Constantin Demiris worked from early morning until sundown, hauling rigs through the burning desert, cleaning equipment, and driving trucks past the streamers of flame rising from the rocky peaks. The flames burned day and night, carrying off the poisonous gases.

J. J. McIntyre had told Demiris the truth. The food was bad, living conditions were horrible, and at night there was nothing to do. Worse, Demiris felt as though every pore in his body were filled with grains of sand. The desert was alive and there was no way to escape it. The sand filtered into the hut and through his clothes and into his body until he thought he would go crazy. And then it got worse.

The *shamal* struck. The sandstorms blew every day for a month, driven by a howling wind with an intensity strong enough to drive men mad.

Demiris stared out the door of his *barasti* at the swirling sand. 'Are we going out to work in that?'

'You're fucking right, Charlie. This ain't a health spa.'

Oil discoveries were being made all around them. There was a new find at Abu Hadriyah and another at Qatif and at Harad, and the workers were kept busier than ever.

*

14

There were two new arrivals, an English geologist and his wife. Henry Potter was in his late sixties and his wife, Sybil, was in her early thirties. In any other setting, Sybil Potter would have been described as a plain-looking, obese woman with a high, unpleasant voice. In Fadili, she was a raving beauty. Since Henry Potter was constantly away prospecting for new oil fields, his wife was left alone a great deal.

Young Demiris was assigned to help her move into their quarters and to assist her in getting settled.

'This is the most miserable place I've ever seen in my life,' Sybil Potter complained in her whining voice. 'Henry's always dragging me off to terrible places like this. I don't know why I put up with it.'

'Your husband is doing a very important job,' Demiris assured her.

She eyed the attractive young man speculatively. 'My husband isn't doing all the jobs he should be doing. Do you know what I mean?'

Demiris knew exactly what she meant. 'No, ma'am.'

'What's your name?'

'Demiris, ma'am. Constantin Demiris.'

'What do your friends call you?'

'Costa.'

'Well, Costa, I think you and I are going to become very good friends. We certainly have nothing in common with these wogs, have we?'

'Wogs?'

'You know. These foreign people.'

'I have to go back to work,' Demiris said.

Over the next few weeks, Sybil Potter constantly found excuses to send for the young man.

'Henry left again this morning,' she told him. 'He's off to do his silly drilling.' She added archly, 'He should do more drilling at home.'

Demiris had no answer. The geologist was a very important man in the company hierarchy and Demiris had no intention of getting involved with Potter's wife, and jeopardizing his own job. He was not sure exactly how, but he knew without question

15

that one way or another this job was going to be his passport to everything he dreamed of. Oil was the future and he was determined to be a part of it.

One midnight, Sybil Potter sent for Demiris. He walked into the compound where she lived, and knocked at the door.

'Come in.' Sybil was wearing a thin nightgown that unfortunately concealed nothing.

'I – did you want to see me, ma'am?'

'Yes, come in, Costa. This bedside lamp doesn't seem to be working.'

Demiris averted his eyes and walked over to the lamp. He picked it up to examine it. 'There's no bulb in . . .' And he felt her body pressing against his back and her hands groping him. 'Mrs Potter . . .'

Her lips were on his and she was pushing him onto the bed. And he had no control over what happened next.

His clothes were off and he was plunging into her and she was screaming with joy. 'That's it! Oh, yes, that's it. My God, it's been so long!'

She gave a final gasp and shuddered. 'Oh, darling, I love you.'

Demiris lay there panicky. *What have I done? If Potter ever finds out I'm finished.*

As though reading his mind, Sybil Potter giggled. 'This will be our little secret, won't it, darling?'

Their little secret went on for the next several months. There was no way Demiris could avoid her and, since her husband was away for days at a time on his explorations, Demiris could think of no excuse to keep from going to bed with her. What made it worse was that Sybil Potter had fallen madly in love with him.

'You're much too good to be working in a place like this, darling,' she told him. 'You and I are going back to England.'

'My home is Greece.'

'Not anymore.' She stroked his long, lean body. 'You're going

16

to come back home with me. I'll divorce Henry and we'll get married.'

Demiris felt a sudden sense of panic. 'Sybil, I . . . I have no money. I . . .'

She ran her lips down his chest. 'That's no problem. I know how you can make some money, sweetheart.'

'You do?'

She sat up in bed. 'Last night, Henry told me he's just discovered some big new oil field. He's very clever at that, you know. Anyway, he seemed terribly excited about it. He wrote out his report before he left and he asked me to send it out in the morning pouch. I have it here. Would you like to see it?'

Demiris' heart began to beat faster. 'Yes. I . . . I would.' He watched her get out of bed and lumber over to a small battered table in the corner. She picked up a large manila envelope and returned to the bed with it.

'Open it.'

Demiris hesitated for only an instant. He opened the envelope and took out the papers inside. There were five pages. He scanned through them quickly, then went back to the beginning and read every word.

'Is that information worth anything?'

Is that information worth anything? It was a report on a new field that could possibly turn out to be one of the richest oil fields in history.

Demiris swallowed. 'Yes. It . . . it could be.'

'Well there you are,' Sybil said happily. 'Now we have money.'

He sighed. 'It's not that simple.'

'Why not?'

Demiris explained. 'This is valuable to someone who can afford to buy up options on the land around this area. But that takes money.' He had three hundred dollars in his bank account.

'Oh, don't worry about that. Henry has money. I'll write a check. Will five thousand dollars be enough?'

Constantin Demiris could not believe what he was hearing. 'Yes. I . . . I don't know what to say.'

'It's for us, darling. For our future.'

17

He sat up in bed thinking hard. 'Sybil, do you think you could hold on to that report for the next day or two?'

'Of course. I'll keep it till Friday. Will that give you enough time, darling?'

He nodded slowly. 'That will give me enough time.'

With the five thousand dollars that Sybil gave him – *no, it's not a gift, it's a loan*, he told himself – Constantin Demiris bought up options on acres of land around the new potential strike. Some months later, when the gushers began to come in in the main field, Constantin Demiris was an instant millionaire.

He repaid Sybil Potter the five thousand dollars, sent her a new nightgown, and returned to Greece. She never saw him again.

Chapter 3

There is a theory that nothing in nature is ever lost – that every sound ever made, every word ever spoken, still exists somewhere in space and time, and may one day be recalled.

Before radio was invented, they say, who would have believed that the air around us was filled with the sounds of music and news and voices from around the world? One day we will be able to travel back in time and listen to Lincoln's Gettysburg Address, the voice of Shakespeare, the Sermon on the Mount . . .

Catherine Alexander heard voices from her past, but they were muffled and fragmented, and they filled her with confusion . . .

'Do you know you're a very special girl, Cathy? I felt it from the first time I saw you.'

'It's over, I want a divorce. I'm in love with someone else . . .'

'I know how badly I've behaved . . . I'd like to make it up to you . . .'

'He tried to kill me.'

'Who tried to kill you?'

'My husband.'

The voices would not stop. They were a torment. Her past became a kaleidoscope of shifting images that kept racing through her mind.

The convent should have been a wonderful, peaceful haven, but it had suddenly become a prison. *I don't belong here. But where do I belong?* She had no idea.

There were no mirrors in the convent, but there was a reflecting pool outside, near the garden. Catherine had carefully avoided it, afraid of what it might reveal to her. But on this morning, she walked over to it, slowly knelt, and looked down. The pool reflected a lovely-looking, suntanned woman with black hair, flawless features and solemn, grey eyes that seemed filled with pain . . . but perhaps that was merely a trick of the water. She saw a generous mouth that looked ready to smile, and a nose that was slightly turned up – a beautiful woman in her early thirties. But a woman with no past and no future. A woman lost. *I need someone to help me*, Catherine thought desperately, *someone I can talk to*. She went into Sister Theresa's office.

'Sister . . .'

'Yes, child?'

'I . . . think I would like to see a doctor. Someone who can help me find out who I am.'

Sister Theresa looked at her a long moment. 'Sit down.'

Catherine sat on the hard chair across from the ancient, scarred desk.

Sister Theresa said quietly: 'My dear, God is your doctor. In due time He will let you know what He wishes you to know. Besides, no outsiders are ever permitted within these walls.'

Catherine had a sudden flash of memory . . . a vague image of a man talking to her in the garden of the convent – handing her something . . . but then it was gone.

'I don't belong here.'

'Where do you belong?'

And that was the problem. 'I'm not sure. I'm searching for something. Forgive me, Sister Theresa, but I know it isn't here.'

Sister Theresa was studying her, her face thoughtful. 'I see. If you left here, where would you go?'

'I don't know.'

'Let me think about this, child. We will talk again soon.'

'Thank you, Sister.'

When Catherine left, Sister Theresa sat at her desk for a long time, staring at nothing. It was a difficult decision that she had to make. Finally she reached for a piece of paper and a pen, and began to write.

'Dear sir,' she began. 'Something has happened that I feel I should call to your attention. Our mutual friend has informed

20

me that she wishes to leave the convent. Please advise me what to do.'

He read the note once, and then sat back in his chair, analyzing the consequences of the message. *So! Catherine Alexander wants to come back from the dead. Too bad. I'll have to get rid of her. Carefully. Very carefully.*

The first step was to remove her from the convent. Demiris decided it was time to pay Sister Theresa a visit.

The following morning, Demiris had his chauffeur take him to Ioannina. Driving through the countryside, Constantin Demiris thought about Catherine Alexander. He remembered how beautiful she had been when he had first met her. She had been bright and funny and high-spirited, excited about being in Greece. *She had had everything*, Demiris thought. And then the gods had taken their vengeance. Catherine had been married to one of his pilots, and their marriage had become a living hell. Almost overnight, she had aged ten years and become a fat, blowsy drunk. Demiris sighed. *What a waste.*

Demiris was seated in Sister Theresa's office.

'I hated to bother you about this,' Sister Theresa apologized, 'but the child has nowhere to go and . . .'

'You did the right thing,' Constantin Demiris assured her. 'Does she remember anything of her past?'

Sister Theresa shook her head. 'No. The poor dear . . .' She walked over to the window where several nuns were working in the garden. 'She's out there now.'

Constantin Demiris moved to her side and looked out the window. There were three nuns, their backs to him. He waited. One of them turned, and he could see her face, and his breath caught in his throat. She was beautiful. What had happened to that fat, ravaged woman?

'She's the one in the middle,' Sister Theresa said.

21

Demiris nodded. 'Yes.' Sister Theresa's words were truer than she knew.

'What do you want me to do with her?'

Careful. 'Let me think about it,' Demiris said. 'I'll be in touch with you.'

Constantin Demiris had a decision to make. Catherine Alexander's appearance had caught him by surprise. She had changed so completely. *No one would know it's the same woman*, he thought. And the idea that came into his head was so diabolically simple that he almost laughed aloud.

That evening he dispatched a note to Sister Theresa.

It's a miracle, Catherine thought. *A dream come true.* Sister Theresa had stopped by her tiny cell after matins.

'I have some news for you, child.'

'Yes?'

Sister Theresa chose her words carefully. 'Good news. I have written to a friend of the convent about you, and he wishes to help you.'

Catherine could feel her heart leap. 'Help me – how?'

'That is something he will have to tell you. But he is a very kind and generous man. You will be leaving the convent.'

And the words sent a sudden, unexpected chill through Catherine. She would be going out into a strange world she could not even remember. *And who was her benefactor?*

All Sister Theresa would say was: 'He is a very caring man. You should be grateful. His car will be here for you Monday morning.'

Catherine was unable to sleep for the next two nights. The idea of leaving the convent and going into the world outside was suddenly terrifying. She felt naked and lost. *Perhaps I'm better off not knowing who I am. Please God, keep an eye on me.*

*

On Monday, the limousine arrived outside the convent gate at seven o'clock in the morning. Catherine had been awake all night thinking about the unknown future that lay ahead of her.

Sister Theresa walked her to the gate that led to the world outside.

'We will pray for you. Remember, if you decide to come back to us you will always have a place here.'

'Thank you, Sister. I'll remember.'

But in her heart, Catherine was sure that she was never going to return.

The long drive from Ioannina to Athens filled Catherine with a series of conflicting emotions. It was tremendously exciting to be outside the gates of the convent, and yet there was something ominous about the world beyond. Was she going to learn what terrible thing had happened in her past? Did it have anything to do with her recurring dream that someone was trying to drown her?

In the early afternoon, the countryside gave way to small villages and finally they reached the outskirts of Athens, and soon were in the middle of the bustling city. It all seemed strange and unreal to Catherine – and yet oddly familiar. *I've been here before*, Catherine thought excitedly.

The driver headed east, and fifteen minutes later they reached an enormous estate high on a hill. They drove through a tall iron gate and a stone gatehouse, up a long driveway lined with majestic cypress trees, and stopped before a large white Mediterranean villa framed by half a dozen magnificent statues.

The chauffeur opened the car door for Catherine and she stepped out. A man was waiting at the front door.

'*Kalimehra.*' The word for good morning sprang to Catherine's lips unbidden.

'*Kalimehra.*'

'Are you . . . are you the person I've come to see?'

'Oh no. Mr Demiris is waiting for you in the library.'

Demiris. It was a name she had never heard before. Why was he interested in helping her?

Catherine followed the man through an enormous rotunda, with a domed roof set in plaques of Wedgwood. The floors were of creamy Italian marble.

The living room was huge, with a high-beamed ceiling, and large, low comfortable couches and chairs everywhere. A huge canvas, a dark and glowering Goya, covered one entire wall. As they approached the library, the man stopped.

'Mr Demiris is waiting for you inside.'

The walls of the library were white and gold boiserie, and the shelves lining the walls were filled with leather books embossed in gold. A man was seated behind a huge desk. He looked up as Catherine entered, and rose. He searched for a sign of recognition on her face, but there was none.

'Welcome. I am Constantin Demiris. What is your name?' He made the question sound casual. *Did she remember her name?*

'Catherine Alexander.'

He showed no reaction. 'Welcome, Catherine Alexander. Please sit down.' He took a seat opposite her, on a black leather couch. She was even lovelier close up. *She's magnificent*, Demiris thought. *Even dressed in that black habit. It's a shame to destroy anything that beautiful. At least she will die happy.*

'It's . . . it's very kind of you to see me,' Catherine said. 'I don't understand why you . . .'

He smiled, genially. 'It's really quite simple. From time to time I help out Sister Theresa. The convent has very little money, and I do what I can. When she wrote me about you and asked if I could be helpful, I told her that I would be happy to try.'

'That's very . . .' She stopped, not knowing how to continue. 'Did Sister Theresa tell you that I . . . that I've lost my memory?'

'Yes, she did mention something about that.' He paused and asked off-handedly, 'How much do you remember?'

'I know my name, but I don't know where I came from, or who I really am.' She added, hopefully, 'Perhaps I can find someone here in Athens who knows me.'

Constantin Demiris felt a sudden *frisson* of alarm. That was the last thing in the world he wanted. 'That's possible of course,'

24

he said carefully. 'Why don't we discuss it in the morning? Unfortunately I have to attend a meeting now. I've arranged to have a suite prepared for you here. I think you'll be comfortable.'

'I . . . I really don't know how to thank you.'

He waved a hand. 'That isn't necessary. You will be well taken care of here. Just make yourself at home.'

'Thank you, Mr . . .'

'My friends call me Costa.'

A housekeeper led Catherine into a fantastic bedroom suite, done in soft shades of white, furnished with an oversized bed with a silk canopy, white couches and armchairs, antique tables and lamps and Impressionist paintings on the walls. Pale shutters of sea-green kept the glaring sun at bay. Through the windows, Catherine could see the turquoise sea below in the distance.

The housekeeper said, 'Mr Demiris has arranged to have some clothes sent here for your approval. You are to select whatever you like.'

Catherine was conscious, for the first time, that she was still wearing the habit given her at the convent.

'Thank you.' She sank down in the soft bed, feeling as though she were in a dream. Who was this stranger, and why was he being so kind to her?

An hour later a van pulled up, filled with clothes. A couturière was ushered into Catherine's bedroom.

'I'm Madame Dimas. Let's see what we have to work with. Would you get undressed, please?'

'I . . . I beg your pardon?'

'Will you get undressed? I can't tell much about your figure under those clothes.'

How long had it been since she had been naked in front of another person?

Catherine began to take off her clothes, moving slowly, feeling self-conscious. When she stood nude in front of the woman,

25

Madame Dimas looked her over with a practiced eye. She was impressed.

'You have a fine figure. I think we're going to be able to do very well for you.'

Two female assistants walked in with boxes of dresses, underwear, blouses, skirts, shoes.

'Select whatever you like,' the couturière said, 'and we'll try them on.'

'I . . . I can't afford any of these,' Catherine protested. 'I have no money.'

The couturière laughed. 'I don't think money will be a problem. Mr Demiris is taking care of it.'

But why?

The fabrics brought back tactile memories of clothes she must have once worn. There were silks and tweeds and cottons, in an array of exquisite colors.

The three women were quick and efficient, and two hours later Catherine had half a dozen beautiful outfits. It was overwhelming. She sat there, not knowing what to do with herself.

I'm all dressed up, she thought, *with no place to go*. But there *was* some place to go – into the city. The key to whatever had happened to her was in Athens. She was convinced of it. She stood up. *Come on, stranger. We're going to try to find out who you are.*

Catherine wandered out into the front hall, and a butler approached her. 'May I help you, miss?'

'Yes. I . . . I would like to go into the city. Could you call a taxi for me?'

'I'm sure that won't be necessary, miss. We have limousines at your disposal. I will arrange a driver for you.'

Catherine hesitated. 'Thank you.' Would Mr Demiris be angry if she went into the city? He had not said not to.

A few minutes later she was seated in the back of a Daimler limousine, headed for downtown Athens.

*

26

Catherine was dazzled by the noisy, bustling city, and the poignant succession of ruins and monuments that appeared all around her.

The driver pointed ahead and said proudly, 'That is the Parthenon, miss, on top of the Acropolis.'

Catherine stared up at the familiar white marble building. 'Dedicated to Athena, the goddess of wisdom,' she heard herself saying.

The driver smiled approvingly. 'Are you a student of Greek history, miss?'

Tears of frustration blurred Catherine's vision. 'I don't know,' she whispered. 'I don't know.'

They were passing another ruin. 'That is the theatre of Herodes Atticus. As you can see, parts of the walls are still standing. It once seated more than five thousand people.'

'Six thousand, two hundred and fifty-seven,' Catherine said softly.

Modern hotels and office buildings were everywhere amid the timeless ruins, an exotic mixture of the past and present. The limousine passed a large park in the center of the city, with sparkling, dancing fountains in the middle. Dozens of tables with green and orange poles lined the park, and the air above them was carpeted with blue awnings.

I've seen this before, Catherine thought, her hands growing cold. *And I was happy.*

There were outdoor cafés on almost every block, and on the corners men were selling freshly caught sponges. Everywhere, flowers were being sold by vendors, their booths a rage of violently colored blossoms.

The limousine had reached Syntagma Square.

As they passed a hotel on the corner, Catherine called out: 'Stop, please!'

The driver pulled over to the curb. Catherine was finding it difficult to breathe. *I recognize this hotel. I've stayed here.*

When she spoke, her voice was shaky. 'I'd like to get out here. I wonder if you could pick me up in – in two hours?'

'Of course, miss.' The chauffeur hurried to open the door for her, and Catherine stepped outside into the hot summer air. Her legs were trembling. 'Are you all right, miss?' She had no answer. She felt as though she were on the edge of a precipice, about to fall into an unknown, terrifying abyss.

She moved through the crowds, marvelling at the hordes of people hurrying through the streets, creating a roaring din of conversation. After the silence and solitude of the convent, everything seemed unreal. Catherine found herself moving toward the Plaka, the old section of Athens in the heart of the city, with its twisted alleys and crumbling, worn-down stairways that led to tiny houses, coffee shops, and whitewashed, rambling structures. She found her way by some instinct she did not understand nor try to control. She passed a *taverna* on top of a roof, overlooking the city, and stopped, staring. *I've sat at that table. They handed me a menu in Greek. There were three of us.*

What would you like to eat? they had asked.

Would you mind ordering for me? I'm afraid I might order the proprietor.

They had laughed. But who were 'they'?

A waiter approached Catherine. '*Boro na sas voithiso?*'

'*Ochi efharisto.*'

Can I help you? No, thank you. How did I know that? Am I Greek?

Catherine hurriedly moved on, and it was as though someone were guiding her. She seemed to know exactly where to go.

Everything seemed familiar. And nothing. *My God*, she thought. *I'm going crazy. I'm hallucinating.* She passed a café that said 'Treflinkas'. A memory was nagging at the corners of her mind. Something had happened to her here, something important. She could not remember what.

She walked through the busy, winding streets and turned left at Voukourestiou. It was filled with smart stores. *I used to shop here.* She started to cross the street, and a blue sedan raced around the corner, barely missing her.

She could recall a voice saying, *The Greeks haven't made the transition to automobiles. In their hearts they're still driving donkeys. If you want insight into the Greeks, don't read the guidebooks; read the old Greek tragedies. We're filled with grand passions, deep joys and great sorrows, and we haven't learned how to cover them up with a civilized veneer.*

Who had said that to her?

A man was hurrying down the street, walking toward her, staring at her. He slowed, a look of recognition on his face. He was tall and dark and Catherine was sure she had never seen him before. And yet . . .

'Hello.' He seemed very pleased to see her.

'Hello.' Catherine took a deep breath. 'Do you know me?'

He was grinning. 'Of course I know you.'

Catherine felt her heart leap. She was finally going to learn the truth about the past. But how do you say 'who am I' to a stranger in a crowded street?

'Could . . . could we talk?' Catherine asked.

'I think we'd better.'

Catherine was on the edge of panic. The mystery of her identity was about to be solved. And yet she felt a terrible fear. *What if I don't want to know? What if I've done something dreadful?*

The man was leading her toward a small open-air *taverna*. 'I'm so glad I ran into you,' he said.

Catherine swallowed. 'So am I.'

A waiter led them to a table.

'What would you like to drink?' the man asked.

She shook her head. 'Nothing.'

There were so many questions to ask. *Where do I begin?*

'You're very beautiful,' the man said. 'This is fate. Don't you agree?'

'Yes.' She was almost trembling with excitement. She took a deep breath. 'I – where did we meet?'

He grinned. 'Is that important, *koritsimon*? Paris, or Rome, at the races, at a party.' He reached forward and pressed her

29

hand. 'You're the prettiest one I've seen around here. How much do you charge?'

Catherine stared at him, not understanding for a moment, then shocked, she sprang to her feet.

'Hey! What's the matter? I'll pay you whatever . . .'

Catherine turned and fled, running down the street. She turned a corner and slowed down, her eyes filled with tears of humiliation.

Ahead was a small *taverna* with a sign in the window that read, 'Madame Piris – Fortune Teller'. Catherine slowed, then stopped. *I know Madame Piris. I've been here before.* Her heart began to race. She sensed that here, through the darkened doorway, was the beginning of the end of the mystery. She opened the door and stepped inside. It took her several moments to get used to the cavernous darkness of the room. There was a familiar bar in the corner, and a dozen tables and chairs. A waiter walked up to her and addressed her in Greek.

'*Kalimehra.*'

'*Kalimehra. Pou ineh* Madame Piris?'

'Madame Piris?'

The waiter gestured toward an empty table in the corner of the room, and Catherine walked over and sat down. Everything was exactly as she remembered it.

An incredibly old woman, dressed in black, with a face desiccated into angles and planes, was moving toward the table.

'What can I . . . ?' She stopped, peering into Catherine's face. Her eyes opened wide. 'I knew you once but your face . . .' She gasped. 'You've come back!'

'You know who I am?' Catherine asked eagerly.

The woman was staring, her eyes filled with horror. 'No! You're dead! Get out!'

Catherine moaned faintly and felt the hair on her scalp begin to rise. 'Please – I just . . .'

'Go, Mrs Douglas!'

'I have to know . . .'

The old woman made the sign of the cross, turned, and fled.

Catherine sat there for a moment, trembling, then rushed out into the street. The voice in her head followed her. *Mrs Douglas!*

30

And it was as though a floodgate opened up. Dozens of brightly lighted scenes suddenly poured into her head, a brilliant series of kaleidoscopes out of control. *I'm Mrs Larry Douglas.* She could see her husband's handsome face. She had been madly in love with him, but something had gone wrong. Something . . .

The next image was of herself trying to commit suicide, and waking up in a hospital.

Catherine stood in the street, afraid her legs would not carry her, letting the pictures come tumbling into her mind.

She had been drinking a lot, because she had lost Larry. But then he had come back to her. They were at her apartment, and Larry was saying, 'I know how badly I've behaved. I'd like to make it up to you, Cathy. I love you. I've never really loved anyone else. I want another chance. How would you like to go away on a second honeymoon? I know a wonderful little place we can go. It's called Ioannina.'

And then the horror had begun.

The pictures that came into her mind now were terrifying.

She was on a mountain top with Larry, lost in a swirling grey mist, and he was moving toward her, his arms outstretched, ready to push her off the edge. At that moment, some tourists arrived and saved her.

And then the caves.

'The hotel clerk told me about some caves near here. All the honeymooners go there.'

And they had gone to the caves, and Larry had taken her deep into the bowels of them, and left her there to die.

She put her hands over her ears as if to shut out the terrible thoughts that were rushing at her.

She had been rescued and taken back to the hotel, and a doctor had given her a sedative. But in the middle of the night she had awakened and heard Larry and his mistress in the kitchen, planning her murder, the wind whipping away their words.

– no one will ever –

– I told you I'd take care of –

– went wrong. There's nothing they can –

– now, while she's asleep.

31

And she remembered running away in that terrible storm – being pursued by them – getting into the rowboat, the wind lashing the boat into the middle of the stormy lake. The boat had started to sink, and she had lost consciousness.

Catherine sank onto a street bench, too exhausted to move. So her nightmares had been real. Her husband and his mistress had tried to kill her.

She thought again about the stranger who had come to visit her at the convent shortly after her rescue. He had handed her an exquisitely made golden bird, its wings poised for flight. 'No one will harm you now. The wicked people are dead.' She could still not see his face clearly.

Catherine's head began to throb.

Finally, she rose and slowly walked toward the street where she was to meet the driver who would take her back to Constantin Demiris where she would be safe.

Chapter 4

'Why did you let her leave the house?' Constantin Demiris demanded.

'I'm sorry, sir,' the butler replied. 'You didn't say anything about her not leaving, so . . .'

Demiris forced himself to appear calm. 'It's not important. She'll probably be back soon.'

'Is there anything else, sir?'

'No.'

Demiris watched the butler go. He walked over to a window and stared out at the impeccably manicured garden. It was dangerous for Catherine Alexander to appear in the streets of Athens, where someone might recognize her. *It's too bad I can't afford to let her live. But first – my vengeance. She'll stay alive until I take my revenge. I'm going to enjoy myself with her. I'll send her away from here, somewhere where no one will know her. London will be safe. We can keep an eye on her. I'll give her a job at my offices there.*

An hour later, when Catherine returned to the house, Constantin Demiris could sense instantly the change in her. It was as though some dark curtain had been lifted and Catherine had suddenly come alive. She was wearing an attractive white silk suit, with a white blouse – and Demiris was taken aback by how much her appearance had changed. *Nostimi*, he thought. *Sexy*

'Mr Demiris . . .'

'Costa.'

'I . . . I know who I am, and – and what happened.'

His face revealed nothing. 'Really? Sit down, my dear, and tell me.'

33

Catherine was too excited to sit. She began to pace jerkily on the carpet, back and forth, the words tumbling out of her. 'My husband and his – his mistress, Noelle, tried to kill me.' She stopped, looking at him anxiously. 'Does that sound crazy? I – I don't know. Maybe it is.'

'Go on, my dear,' he said soothingly.

'Some nuns from the convent saved me. My husband worked for you, didn't he?' she blurted out.

Demiris hesitated, carefully weighing his answer. 'Yes.' How much should he tell her? 'He was one of my pilots. I felt a sense of responsibility toward you. That's only . . .'

She faced him. 'But you knew who I was. Why didn't you tell me this morning?'

'I was afraid of the shock,' Demiris said smoothly. 'I thought it better to let you discover things for yourself.'

'Do you know what happened to my husband and that – that woman? Where are they?'

Demiris looked into Catherine's eyes. 'They were executed.'

He watched the blood drain from her face. She made a small sound. She suddenly felt too weak to stand and sank into a chair.

'I don't . . .'

'They were executed by the State, Catherine.'

'But . . . why?'

Careful. Danger. 'Because they tried to murder you.'

Catherine frowned. 'I don't understand. Why would the State execute them? I'm alive . . .'

He broke in. 'Catherine, Greek laws are very strict. And justice here is swift. They had a public trial. A number of witnesses testified that your husband and Noelle Page attempted to kill you. They were convicted, and sentenced to death.'

'It's hard to believe.' Catherine sat there, dazed. 'The trial . . .'

Constantin Demiris walked over to her and put his hand on her shoulder. 'You must put the past out of your mind. They tried to do an evil thing to you, and they paid for it.' He struck a more buoyant tone. 'I think you and I should discuss the future. Do you have any plans?'

She did not hear him. *Larry*, she thought. *Larry's handsome face, laughing. Larry's arms, his voice . . .*

'Catherine . . .'

She looked up. 'I'm sorry?'

'Have you had any thoughts about your future?'

'No, I . . . I don't know what I'm going to do. I suppose I could stay in Athens . . .'

'No,' Demiris said firmly. 'That wouldn't be a good idea. It would bring back too many unpleasant memories. I would suggest that you leave Greece.'

'But I have nowhere to go.'

'I've given it some thought,' Demiris told her. 'I have offices in London. You once worked for a man named William Fraser in Washington. Do you remember that?'

'William . . . ?' And suddenly she did remember it. That had been one of the happiest times of her life.

'You were his administrative assistant, I believe.'

'Yes, I . . .'

'You could do the same job for me in London.'

She hesitated. 'I don't know. I don't want to seem ungrateful, but . . .'

'I understand. I know everything seems to be happening very quickly,' Demiris said sympathetically. 'You need some time to think about all this. Why don't you have a nice quiet dinner in your room, and in the morning we'll discuss it further.'

Asking her to have dinner in her room was a last-minute inspiration. He could not afford to have his wife run into her.

'You're very thoughtful,' Catherine said. 'And very generous. The clothes are . . .'

He patted her hand and held it a fraction longer than necessary. 'It's my pleasure.'

She sat in her bedroom watching the blazing sun set over the blue Aegean in an explosion of color. *There is no point in reliving the past. There is the future to think about. Thank God for Constantin Demiris.* He was her lifeline. Without him, she would have had no one to turn to. And he had offered her a job in

35

London. *Am I going to take it?* Her thoughts were interrupted by a knock on the door. 'We've brought your dinner, miss.'

Long after Catherine had gone, Constantin Demiris sat in the library, thinking about their conversation. *Noelle.* Only once in his life had Demiris permitted himself to lose control of his emotions. He had fallen deeply in love with Noelle Page, and she had become his mistress. He had never known a woman like her. She was knowledgeable about art, and music, and business, and she had become indispensable. Nothing about Noelle surprised him. Everything about Noelle surprised him. He was obsessed with her. She was the most beautiful, the most sensual woman Demiris had ever known. She had given up stardom to be at his side. Noelle had stirred emotions in him that he had never felt before. She was his lover, his confidante, his friend. Demiris had trusted her completely and she had betrayed him with Larry Douglas. It was a mistake Noelle had paid for with her life. Constantin Demiris had arranged with the authorities for her body to be buried on the grounds of the cemetery on Psara, his private island in the Aegean. Everyone had remarked on what a beautiful, sentimental gesture it was. In fact, Demiris had arranged for the burial plot to be there so that he could have the exquisite pleasure of walking over the bitch's grave. At Demiris' bedside in his own bedroom was a photograph of Noelle at her loveliest, looking up at him and smiling. Forever smiling, frozen in time.

Even now, more than a year later, Demiris was unable to stop thinking about her. She was an open wound that no doctor could ever heal.

Why, Noelle, why? I gave you everything. I loved you, you bitch. I loved you. I love you.

And then there was Larry Douglas. He had paid with his life. But that was not enough for Demiris. He had another vengeance in mind. A perfect one. He was going to take his pleasure with Douglas' wife as Douglas had done with Noelle. Then he would send Catherine to join her husband.

*

36

'Costa . . .'

It was his wife's voice.

Melina walked into the library.

Constantin Demiris was married to Melina Lambrou, an attractive woman from an old, aristocratic Greek family. She was tall and regal-looking, with an innate dignity.

'Costa, who is the woman I saw in the hall?' Her voice was tense.

The question caught him off-guard. 'What? Oh. She's a friend of a business associate,' Demiris said. 'She's going to work for me in London.'

'I caught a glimpse of her. She reminds me of someone.'

'Really?'

'Yes.' Melina hesitated. 'She reminds me of the wife of the pilot who used to work for you. But that's impossible, of course. They murdered her.'

'Yes,' Constantin Demiris agreed. 'They murdered her.'

He watched Melina as she walked away. He would have to be careful. Melina was no fool. *I never should have married her*, Demiris thought. *It was a bad mistake . . .*

Ten years earlier, the wedding of Melina Lambrou and Constantin Demiris had sent shock waves through business and social circles from Athens to the Riviera to Newport. What had made it so titillating was that only one month before the wedding the bride had been engaged to marry another man.

As a child, Melina Lambrou had dismayed her family by her willfulness. When she was ten, she decided she wanted to be a sailor. The family chauffeur found her at the harbor, trying to sneak aboard a ship, and brought her home in disgrace. At twelve, she tried to run away with a travelling circus.

By the time Melina was seventeen, she was resigned to her fate – she was beautiful, fabulously wealthy and the daughter of

37

Mihalis Lambrou. The newspapers loved to write about her. She was a fairy-tale figure whose playmates were princesses and princes, and through it all, by some miracle, Melina had managed to remain unspoiled. Melina had one brother, Spyros, who was ten years older than she, and they adored each other. Their parents had died in a boating accident when Melina was thirteen, and it was Spyros who had reared her.

Spyros was extremely protective of her – too much so, Melina thought. As Melina reached her late teens, Spyros became even more wary about Melina's suitors, and he carefully examined each candidate for his sister's hand. Not one of them proved to be good enough.

'You have to be careful,' he constantly counseled Melina. 'You're a target for every fortune hunter in the world. You're young and rich and beautiful, and you bear a famous name.'

'Bravo, my dear brother. That will be of immense comfort to me, when I'm eighty years old and die an old maid.'

'Don't worry, Melina. The right man will come along.'

His name was Count Vassilis Manos, and he was in his middle forties, a successful businessman from an old and distinguished Greek family. The Count had fallen instantly in love with the beautiful young Melina. His proposal came only a few weeks after they met.

'He's perfect for you,' Spyros said happily. 'Manos has his feet on the ground, and he's crazy about you.'

Melina was less enthusiastic. 'He's not exciting, Spyros. When we're together, all he talks about is business, business, business. I wish he were more – more romantic.'

Her brother said firmly, 'There's more to marriage than romance. You want a husband who is solid and stable, someone who will devote himself to you.'

And finally Melina was persuaded to accept Count Manos' proposal.

The Count was thrilled. 'You've made me the happiest man in the world,' he declared. 'I've just formed a new company. I'm going to name it Melina International.'

38

She would have preferred a dozen roses. The wedding date was set, one thousand invitations were sent out, and elaborate plans were made.

It was then that Constantin Demiris entered Melina Lambrou's life.

They met at one of the dozen or so engagement parties that were being given for the betrothed pair.

The hostess introduced them. 'This is Melina Lambrou – Constantin Demiris.'

Demiris stared at her with his brooding black eyes. 'How long will they let you stay?' he asked.

'I beg your pardon?'

'Surely you've been sent from the heavens to teach us mortals what beauty is.'

Melina laughed. 'You're very flattering, Mr Demiris.'

He shook his head. 'You're beyond flattery. Nothing I could say would do you justice.'

At that moment Count Manos approached and interrupted the conversation.

That night, just before falling asleep, Melina thought about Demiris. She had heard about him, of course. He was wealthy, he was a widower, and he had the reputation of being a ruthless businessman and a compulsive womanizer. *I'm glad I'm not involved with him*, Melina thought.

The gods were laughing.

The morning after the party, Melina's butler walked into the breakfast room. 'A package has arrived for you, Miss Lambrou. It was delivered by Mr Demiris' chauffeur.'

'Bring it in, please.'

So Constantin Demiris thinks he's going to impress me with his wealth. Well, he's in for a big disappointment. Whatever he's sent . . . whether it's an expensive piece of jewelry, or some priceless antique . . . I'm going to send it right back to him.

The package was small and oblong, and beautifully wrapped.

39

Curious, Melina opened it. The card read, simply: 'I thought you might enjoy this. Constantin.'

It was a leather-bound copy of *Toda Raba* by Nikos Kazantzakis, her favorite author. *How could he have known?*

Melina wrote a polite thank-you note, and thought: *That's that*.

The following morning, another package arrived. This time it was a recording by Delius, her favorite composer. The note read: 'You might enjoy listening to this while reading *Toda Raba*.'

From that day on there were gifts every day. Her favorite flowers, and perfume, and music, and books. Constantin Demiris had taken the trouble to find out what Melina's tastes were, and she could not help but be flattered by his attention.

When Melina telephoned to thank Demiris, he said: 'There's nothing I could ever give you that would do you justice.'

How many women had he said that to before?

'Will you have lunch with me, Melina?'

She started to say no, and then thought: *It can't hurt to have lunch with the man. He's been very thoughtful.*

'Very well.'

When she mentioned to Count Manos that she was having lunch with Constantin Demiris he objected.

'What's the point, my dear? You have nothing in common with that terrible man. Why are you going to see him?'

'Vassilis, he's been sending me little gifts every day. I'm going to tell him to stop.' And even as Melina said it, she thought: *I could have told him that over the telephone.*

Constantin Demiris had made reservations at the popular Floca restaurant on Panepistimiou Street and he was waiting for Melina when she arrived.

He rose. 'You're here. I was so afraid you might change your mind.'

'I always keep my word.'

He looked at her and said solemnly: 'And I keep mine. I'm going to marry you.'

40

Melina shook her head, half amused, half annoyed. 'Mr Demiris, I'm engaged to marry someone else.'

'Manos?' He waved a hand in dismissal. 'He's not right for you.'

'Oh, really? And why is that?'

'I've checked on him. Insanity runs in his family, he's a hemophiliac, he's wanted by the police on a sex charge in Brussels, and he plays a dreadful game of tennis.'

Melina could not help laughing. 'And you?'

'I don't play tennis.'

'I see. And that's why I should marry you?'

'No. You'll marry me because I'm going to make you the happiest woman who ever lived.'

'Mr Demiris . . .'

He covered her hand with his. 'Costa.'

She withdrew her hand. 'Mr Demiris, I came here today to tell you that I want you to stop sending me gifts. I don't intend to see you again.'

He studied her for a long moment. 'I'm sure you are not a cruel person.'

'I hope not.'

He smiled. 'Good. Then you won't want to break my heart.'

'I doubt if your heart is that easily broken. You have quite a reputation.'

'Ah, that was before I met you. I've dreamed about you for a long time.'

Melina laughed.

'I'm serious. When I was a very young man, I used to read about the Lambrou family. You were very rich and I was very poor. I had nothing. We lived from hand to mouth. My father was a stevedore who worked on the docks of Piraeus. I had fourteen brothers and sisters, and we had to fight for everything we wanted.'

In spite of herself, she was touched. 'But now you are rich.'

'Yes. Not as rich as I am going to be.'

'What made you rich?'

'Hunger. I was always hungry. I'm still hungry.'

41

She could read the truth in his eyes. 'How did you . . . how did you get started?'

'Do you really want to know?'

And Melina found herself saying, 'I really want to know.'

'When I was seventeen, I went to work for a small oil company in the Middle East. I was not doing very well. One night I had dinner with a young geologist who worked for a large oil company. I ordered a steak that night, and he ordered only soup. I asked him why he didn't have a steak, and he said it was because he had no back teeth, and he couldn't afford to buy dentures. I gave him fifty dollars to buy new teeth. A month later he telephoned me in the middle of the night to tell me he had just discovered a new oil deposit. He hadn't told his employer about it yet. In the morning, I started borrowing every cent I could, and by evening I had bought options on all the land around the new discovery. It turned out to be one of the biggest oil deposits in the world.'

Melina was hanging on his every word, fascinated.

'That was the beginning. I needed tankers to ship my oil in, so in time I acquired a fleet. Then a refinery. Then an airline.' He shrugged. 'It went on from there.'

It was not until long after they were married that Melina learned that the story about the steak was pure fiction.

Melina Lambrou had had no intention of seeing Constantin Demiris again. But, by a series of carefully arranged coincidences, Demiris invariably managed to appear at the same party, or theater, or charity event that Melina was attending. And each time, she felt his overpowering magnetism. Beside him, Vassilis Manos seemed – she hated to admit it, even to herself – boring.

Melina Lambrou was fond of the Flemish painters, and when Bruegel's *Hunters in the Snow* came on the market, before she could purchase it, Constantin Demiris sent it to her as a gift.

Melina was fascinated by his uncanny knowledge of her tastes. 'I can't accept such an expensive gift from you,' she protested.

'Ah, but it's not a gift. You must pay for it. Dinner with me tonight.'

42

And she had finally agreed. The man was irresistible.

A week later Melina broke off her engagement to Count Manos.

When Melina told her brother the news he was stunned.

'Why, in heaven's name?' Spyros asked. '*Why?*'

'Because I'm going to marry Constantin Demiris.'

He was aghast. 'You must be crazy. You can't marry Demiris. He's a monster. He'll destroy you. If . . .'

'You're wrong about him, Spyros. He's wonderful. And we're in love. It's . . .'

'*You're* in love,' he snapped. 'I don't know what he's after, but it has nothing to do with love. Do you know what his reputation is with women? He . . .'

'That's all in the past, Spyros. I'm going to be his wife.'

And there was nothing he could do to talk his sister out of the wedding.

A month later Melina Lambrou and Constantin Demiris were married.

In the beginning it seemed to be a perfect marriage. Constantin was amusing and attentive. He was an exciting and passionate lover, and he constantly surprised Melina with lavish gifts and trips to exotic places.

On the first night of their honeymoon, he said, 'My first wife was never able to give me a child. Now we'll have many sons.'

'No daughters?' Melina teased.

'If you wish. But a son first.'

The day Melina learned she was pregnant, Constantin was ecstatic.

'He will take over my empire,' he declared happily.

In her third month, Melina miscarried. Constantin Demiris was out of the country when it happened. When he returned and heard the news he reacted like a madman.

'What did you do?' he screamed. 'How could it happen?'

'Costa, I . . .'

43

'You were careless!'

'No, I swear . . .'

He took a deep breath. 'All right. What's done is done. We'll have another son.'

'I . . . I can't.' She could not meet his eyes.

'What are you saying?'

'They had to perform an operation. I can't have another child.'

He stood there, frozen, then turned and stalked out without a word.

From that moment on, Melina's life became a hell. Constantin Demiris carried on as though his wife had deliberately killed his son. He ignored her, and began seeing other women.

Melina could have borne that, but what made the humiliation so painful was the pleasure he took in publicly flaunting his liaisons. He openly had affairs with movie stars, opera singers, and the wives of some of his friends. He took his lovers to Psara and on cruises on his yacht, and to public functions. The press gleefully chronicled Constantin Demiris' romantic adventures.

They were at a dinner party at the house of a prominent banker.

'You and Melina must come,' the banker had said. 'I have a new Oriental chef who makes the best Chinese food in the world.'

The guest list was prestigious. At the dinner table was a fascinating collection of artists, politicians and industrialists. The food was indeed wonderful. The chef had prepared shark-fin soup, shrimp rolls, *mu shu* pork, Peking duck, spareribs, Canton noodles and a dozen other dishes.

Melina was seated near the host, at one end of the table, her husband next to the hostess at the other end. To Demiris' right was a pretty young film star. Demiris was concentrating on her, ignoring everyone else at the table. Melina could hear snatches of his conversation.

'When you finish your picture, you must come on my yacht. It will be a lovely vacation for you. We'll cruise along the Dalmatian coast . . .'

44

Melina tried not to listen, but it was impossible. Demiris made no effort to keep his voice down. 'You've never been to Psara, have you? It's a lovely little island, completely isolated. You'll enjoy it.' Melina wanted to crawl under the table. But the worst was yet to come.

They had just finished the sparerib course, and the butlers were bringing silver finger bowls.

As a finger bowl was placed in front of the young star, Demiris said, 'You won't need that.' And, grinning, he lifted her hands in his and began slowly licking the sauce from her fingers, one by one. The other guests averted their eyes.

Melina rose to her feet and turned to her host. 'If you'll excuse me, I – I have a headache.'

The guests watched as she fled from the room. Demiris did not come home that night, or the next.

When Spyros heard about the incident, he was livid. 'Just give me the word,' Melina's brother fumed, 'and I'll kill the son-of-a-bitch.'

'He can't help it,' Melina defended him. 'It's his nature.'

'His nature? He's an animal! He should be put away. Why don't you divorce him?'

It was a question Melina Demiris had asked herself often in the still of the long, lonely nights she spent by herself. And it always came down to the same answer. *I love him.*

At five thirty in the morning, Catherine was awakened by an apologetic maid.

'Good morning, miss . . .'

Catherine opened her eyes and looked around in confusion. Instead of her tiny cell at the convent, she was in a beautiful bedroom in . . . Her memory came flooding back. *The trip into Athens . . . You're Catherine Douglas . . . They were executed by the State . . .*

'Miss . . .'

'Yes?'

45

'Mr Demiris asked if you would join him for breakfast on the terrace.'

Catherine stared up at her sleepily. She had been awake until four o'clock, her mind in a turmoil.

'Thank you. Tell Mr Demiris I'll be right there.'

Twenty minutes later a butler escorted Catherine to an enormous terrace facing the sea. There was a low stone wall that overlooked the gardens twenty feet below. Constantin Demiris was seated at a table, waiting. He studied Catherine as she walked toward him. There was an exciting innocence about her. He was going to take it, possess it, make it his. He imagined her naked in his bed, helping him punish Noelle and Larry again. Demiris rose.

'Good morning. Forgive me for awakening you so early, but I must leave for my office in a few minutes, and I wanted the opportunity for us to have a little chat first.'

'Yes, of course,' Catherine said.

She sat down at the large marble table opposite him, facing the sea. The sun was just rising, showering the sea with a thousand sparkles.

'What would you like for breakfast?'

She shook her head. 'I'm not hungry.'

'Some coffee perhaps?'

'Thank you.'

The butler was pouring hot coffee into a Belleek cup.

'Well, Catherine,' Demiris began. 'Have you thought about our conversation?'

Catherine had thought of nothing else all night. There was nothing left for her in Athens, and she had nowhere else to go. *I won't go back to the convent*, she vowed. The invitation to work for Constantin Demiris in London sounded intriguing. *In fact*, Catherine admitted to herself, *it sounds exciting. It could be the beginning of a new life*.

'Yes,' Catherine said, 'I have.'

'And?'

'I – I think I would like to try it.'

46

Constantin Demiris managed to conceal his relief. 'I'm delighted. Have you ever been to London?'

'No. That is – I don't think so.' *Why don't I know for sure?* There were still so many frightening gaps in her memory. *How many more surprises am I going to get?*

'It's one of the few civilized cities left in the world. I'm sure you'll enjoy it very much.'

Catherine hesitated. 'Mr Demiris, why are you going to all this trouble for me?'

'Let's just say it's because I feel a sense of responsibility.' He paused. 'I introduced your husband to Noelle Page.'

'Ah,' Catherine said slowly. *Noelle Page.* The name sent a small shiver through her. The two of them had died for each other. *Larry must have loved her so much.*

Catherine forced herself to ask a question that had been tormenting her all night long. 'How . . . how were they executed?'

There was a small pause. 'They were shot by a firing squad.'

'Oh.' She could feel the bullets tearing into Larry's flesh, ripping apart the body of the man she had once loved so much. She was sorry she had asked.

'Let me give you some advice. Don't think about the past. It can only be hurtful. You must put all that behind you.'

Catherine said slowly, 'You're right. I'll try.'

'Good. I happen to have a plane flying to London this morning, Catherine. Can you be ready to leave in a little while?'

Catherine thought of all the trips she had taken with Larry, the excited preparations, the packing, the anticipation.

This time, there would be no one to go with, little to pack, and nothing to prepare for. 'Yes. I can be ready.'

'Excellent. By the way,' Demiris said casually, 'now that your memory has returned, perhaps there's someone you'd like to get in touch with, someone from your past whom you would like to let know that you're all right.'

The name that instantly sprang to her mind was William Fraser. He was the only one in the world who remained from her past. But she knew she was not ready to face him yet. *When*

I get settled, Catherine thought. *When I start working again, I'll get in touch with him.*

Constantin Demiris was watching her, waiting for her answer.

'No,' Catherine said finally. 'There's no one.'

She had no idea that she had just saved William Fraser's life.

'I'll arrange a passport for you.' He handed her an envelope. 'This is an advance on your salary. You won't have to worry about a place to live. The company has a flat in London. You'll stay there.'

It was overwhelming. 'You're much too generous.'

He took her hand in his. 'You'll find that I'm . . .' He changed what he was going to say. *Handle her carefully*, he thought. *Slowly. You don't want to scare her away.* '. . . that I can be a very good friend.'

'You *are* a very good friend.'

Demiris smiled. *Wait.*

Two hours later, Constantin Demiris helped Catherine into the back seat of the Rolls-Royce that was to take her to the airport.

'Enjoy London,' he said. 'I'll be in touch with you.'

Five minutes after the car had departed, Demiris was on the telephone to London. 'She's on her way.'

Chapter 5

The plane was scheduled to leave from Hellenikon Airport at 9.00 a.m. It was a Hawker Siddeley, and to Catherine's surprise, she was the only passenger. The pilot, a pleasant-faced, middle-aged Greek named Pantelis, saw to it that Catherine was comfortably seated and buckled in.

'We'll be taking off in just a few minutes,' he informed her.

'Thank you.'

Catherine watched him walk into the cockpit to join the co-pilot, and her heart suddenly began to beat faster. *This is the plane that Larry flew. Had Noelle Page sat in the seat I am now sitting in?* Catherine suddenly felt as though she were going to faint; the walls began to close in on her. She shut her eyes and took a deep breath. *That's all over*, she thought. *Demiris is right. That's the past and nothing can change it.*

She heard the roar of the engines, and opened her eyes. The plane was lifting off, heading northwest toward London. *How many times had Larry made this flight? Larry.* She was shaken by the mixture of emotions that his name brought. And the memories. The wonderful, terrible memories . . .

It was the summer of 1940, the year before America got into the war. She had been fresh out of Northwestern University, and had gone from Chicago to Washington, DC, for her first job.

Her roommate had said: 'Hey, I heard about a job opening that might interest you. One of the girls at the party said she's quitting to go back to Texas. She works for Bill Fraser. He's in charge of public relations for the State Department. I just heard about it last night, so if you get over there now, you should beat all the other girls to it.'

Catherine had raced over, only to find Fraser's reception office already packed with dozens of applicants for the job. *I haven't*

49

a chance, Catherine thought. The door to the inner office opened and William Fraser emerged. He was a tall, attractive man, with curly, blond hair, greying at the temples, bright blue eyes, and a strong, rather forbidding jawline.

He said to the receptionist, 'I need a copy of *Life*. The issue that came out three or four weeks ago. It has a picture of Stalin on the cover.'

'I'll order it, Mr Fraser,' the receptionist said.

'Sally, I have Senator Borah on the line. I want to read him a paragraph from that issue. You have two minutes to find a copy for me.' He went into his office and closed the door.

The applicants looked at one another and shrugged.

Catherine stood there, thinking hard. She turned and pushed her way out of the office. She heard one of the women say, 'Good. That's one down.'

Three minutes later, Catherine returned to the office with the old copy of *Life* with a picture of Stalin on the cover. She handed it to the receptionist. Five minutes later Catherine found herself seated in William Fraser's office.

'Sally tells me that you came up with the *Life* magazine.'

'Yes, sir.'

'I assume you didn't just happen to have a three-week-old issue in your purse.'

'No, sir.'

'How did you find it so quickly?'

'I went down to the barber shop. Barber shops and dentists' offices always have old issues lying around.'

'Are you that bright about everything?'

'No, sir.'

'We'll find out,' William Fraser said. She was hired.

Catherine enjoyed the excitement of working for Fraser. He was a bachelor, wealthy and social, and he seemed to know everyone in Washington. *Time* magazine had called him: 'The most eligible bachelor of the year'.

Six months after Catherine started to work for William Fraser, they fell in love.

50

In his bedroom, Catherine said, 'I have to tell you something. I'm a virgin.'

Fraser shook his head in wonder. 'That's incredible. How did I wind up with the only virgin in the city of Washington?'

One day William Fraser said to Catherine, 'They've asked our office to supervise an Army Air Corps recruiting film they're shooting at MGM studios in Hollywood. I'd like you to handle the picture while I'm in London.'

'Me? Bill, I can't even load a Brownie. What do I know about making a training film?'

Fraser grinned. 'About as much as anyone else. You don't have to worry. They have a director. His name is Allan Benjamin. The Army plans to use actors in the film.'

'Why?'

'I guess they feel that soldiers won't be convincing enough to play soldiers.'

'That sounds like the Army.'

And Catherine had flown to Hollywood to supervise the training film.

The soundstage was filled with extras, most of them in ill-fitting army uniforms.

'Excuse me,' Catherine said to a man passing by. 'Is Mr Allan Benjamin here?'

'The little corporal?' He pointed. 'Over there.'

Catherine turned and saw a slight, frail-looking man in a uniform with corporal's stripes. He was screaming at a man wearing a general's stars.

'Fuck what the casting director said. I'm up to my ass in generals. I need non-coms.' He raised his hands in despair. 'Everybody wants to be a chief, nobody wants to be an Indian.'

'Excuse me,' Catherine said. 'I'm Catherine Alexander.'

'Thank God!' the little man said. 'You take over. I don't know what I'm doing here. I had a thirty-five-hundred-dollar-a-year

51

job in Dearborn editing a furniture trade magazine, and I was drafted into the Signal Corps and sent to write training films. What do I know about producing or directing? This is all yours.' He turned and hurried toward the exit, leaving Catherine standing there.

A lean, grey-haired man in a sweater moved toward her, an amused smile on his face. 'Need any help?'

'I need a miracle,' Catherine said. 'I'm in charge of this, and I don't know what I'm supposed to be doing.'

He grinned at her. 'Welcome to Hollywood. I'm Tom O'Brien, the assistant director.'

'Do you think you could direct this?'

She saw the corner of his lips twist. 'I could try. I've done six pictures with Willie Wyler. The situation isn't as bad as it looks. All it needs is a little organization. The script's written, and the set's ready.'

Catherine looked around the soundstage. 'Some of these uniforms look terrible. Let's see if we can't do better.'

O'Brien nodded approvingly. 'Right.'

Catherine and O'Brien walked over to the group of extras. The din of conversation on the enormous stage was deafening.

'Let's hold it down, boys,' O'Brien yelled. 'This is Miss Alexander. She's going to be in charge here.'

Catherine said, 'Let's line up, so we can take a good look at you, please.'

O'Brien formed the men into a ragged line. Catherine heard laughter and voices nearby and turned in annoyance. One of the men in uniform stood in a corner, paying no attention, talking to some girls who were hanging on his every word and giggling. The man's manner irritated Catherine.

'Excuse me. Would you mind joining the rest of us?'

He turned and asked, lazily: 'Are you talking to me?'

'Yes. We'd like to go to work.'

He was extraordinarily handsome, tall and wiry, with blue-black hair and stormy dark eyes. His uniform fitted perfectly. On his shoulders were the bars of a captain, and across his breast he had pinned on a splash of brightly colored ribbons. Catherine stared at them. 'Those medals . . .'

'Are they impressive enough, boss?' His voice was deep and filled with insolent amusement.

'Take them off.'

'Why? I thought I'd give this film a little color.'

'There's one little thing you forgot. America's not at war yet. You'd have had to have won those at a carnival.'

'You're right,' he admitted sheepishly. 'I didn't think of that. I'll take some of them off.'

'Take them *all* off,' Catherine snapped.

After the morning's shooting, while Catherine was having lunch at the commissary, he walked up to her table. 'I wanted to ask you how I did this morning. Was I convincing?'

His manner infuriated her. 'You enjoy wearing that uniform and strutting around the girls, but have you thought about enlisting?'

He looked shocked. 'And get shot at? That's for suckers.'

Catherine was ready to explode. 'I think you're contemptible.'

'Why?'

'If you don't know why, I could never explain it to you.'

'Why don't you try? At dinner tonight. Your place. Do you cook?'

'Don't bother coming back to the set,' Catherine snapped. 'I'll tell Mr O'Brien to send you your check for this morning's work. What's your name?'

'Douglas. Larry Douglas.'

The experience with the arrogant young actor rankled Catherine, and she was determined to put it out of her mind. For some reason, she found it difficult to forget him.

When Catherine returned to Washington, William Fraser said, 'I missed you. I've been doing a lot of thinking about you. Do you love me?'

53

'Very much, Bill.'

'I love you too. Why don't we go out tonight and celebrate?'

Catherine knew that that was the night he was going to propose.

They went to the exclusive Jefferson Club. In the middle of dinner, Larry Douglas walked in, still wearing his Army Air Corps uniform with all the medals. Catherine watched unbelievingly as he walked over to their table and greeted not her, but Fraser.

Bill Fraser rose: 'Cathy, this is Captain Lawrence Douglas. Larry, this is Miss Alexander – Catherine. Larry's been flying with the RAF. He was the leader of the American squadron over there. They talked him into heading up a fighter base in Virginia to get some of our boys ready for combat.'

Like the re-run of an old movie, Catherine remembered how she had ordered him to take off his bars and his medals, and how he had cheerfully obliged. She had been smug, overbearing – and she had called him a coward! She wanted to crawl under the table.

The next day, Larry Douglas telephoned Catherine at her office. She refused to take his calls. When she finished work he was outside, waiting for her. He had taken off his medals and ribbons and was wearing the bars of a second lieutenant.

He smiled and walked up to her. 'Is this better?'

Catherine stared at him. 'Isn't . . . isn't wearing the wrong insignia against regulations?'

'I don't know. I thought you were in charge of all that.'

She looked into his eyes and knew that she was lost. There was a magnetic force about him that was irresistible.

'What do you want from me?'

'Everything. I want you.'

They had gone to his apartment and made love. And it was an exquisite joy that Catherine had never dreamed possible, a fantastic coming together that rocked the room and the universe

54

– until there was an explosion that became a delirious ecstasy, an unbelievable shattering journey, an arriving and a departing, an ending and a beginning. And she had lain there, spent and numb, holding him tightly, never wanting to let him go, never wanting this feeling to stop.

They were married five hours later, in Maryland.

Now, seated in the plane, on her way to London to begin a new life, Catherine thought: *We were so happy. Where did it all go wrong? The romantic movies and the love songs tricked us all into believing in happy endings and knights in shining armor and love that never, never died. We really believed that James Stewart and Donna Reed had A Wonderful Life and we knew that Clark Gable and Claudette Colbert would be together forever after It Happened One Night, and we shed tears when Fredric March returned to Myrna Loy for The Best Years of Our Lives, and we were sure that Joan Fontaine found happiness in the arms of Laurence Olivier in* Rebecca. *And they were lies. All lies. And the songs.* I'll Be Loving You, Always. *How do men figure always? With an egg timer?* How Deep Is The Ocean? *What did Irving Berlin have in mind? One foot? Two feet? And . . .* Forever and a Day. *I'm leaving. I want a divorce.* Some Enchanted Evening. *Come on. We're going to climb Mount Tzoumerka . . .* You and the Night and the Music. *The hotel manager told me about some caves near here . . .* I Love You For Sentimental Reasons. *No one will ever . . . now while she's asleep.* Be My Love. *And we listened to the songs, and we watched the movies and really thought that was what life was going to be like. I believed in my husband so much. Can I ever believe in anyone again? What did I do to make him want to murder me?*

'Miss Alexander . . .'

Catherine looked up, startled, unfocused.

The pilot was standing over her. 'We've landed. Welcome to London.'

There was a limousine waiting for Catherine at the airport. The chauffeur said, 'I'll arrange for your luggage, Miss Alexander. My name is Alfred. Would you like to go directly to your flat?'

My flat. 'Yes, that will be fine.'

Catherine sank back in her seat. Unbelievable. Constantin Demiris had arranged a private plane for her, and a place to live. He was either the most generous man in the world, or . . . She simply could not think of any alternative. No. *He's the most generous man in the world. I'll have to find a suitable way to show my appreciation.*

The flat, on Elizabeth Street off Eaton Square, was utterly luxurious. It consisted of a large entrance hall, a beautifully furnished drawing room, with a crystal chandelier, a panelled library, a kitchen stocked with food, three attractively furnished bedrooms, and servants quarters.

Catherine was greeted at the door by a woman in her forties, wearing a black dress. 'Good afternoon, Miss Alexander. I am Anna. I am your housekeeper.'

Of course. My housekeeper. Catherine was beginning to take it all in stride. 'How do you do?'

The chauffeur brought Catherine's suitcases in and placed them in her bedroom. 'The limousine is at your disposal,' he told her. 'Just tell Anna when you're ready to go to the office, and I will pick you up.'

The limousine is at my disposal. Naturally. 'Thank you.'

Anna said, 'I'll unpack your bags. If there's anything else you need, just let me know.'

'I can't think of a thing,' Catherine said honestly.

Catherine wandered around the flat until Anna had finished unpacking. She went into the bedroom and looked at the beautiful new dresses that Demiris had bought her, and thought: *All this is like a wonderful dream.* There was a feeling of total unreality about it. Forty-eight hours ago, she had been watering rose bushes at the convent. Now she was living the life of a duchess. She wondered what the job would be like. *I'll work*

56

hard. I don't want to let him down. He's been so wonderful. She felt suddenly tired. She lay down on the soft, comfortable bed. *I'll just rest a minute,* she thought. She closed her eyes.

She was drowning, and screaming for help. And Larry was swimming toward her, and when he reached her he pushed her under water. And she was in a dark cave, and bats were coming at her, tearing at her hair, beating their clammy wings against her face. Catherine awakened with a shuddering start and sat up in bed, trembling.

She took deep breaths to steady herself. *That's enough,* she thought. *It's over. That was yesterday. This is today. No one's going to hurt you. No one. Not any more.*

Outside Catherine's bedroom, Anna, the housekeeper, had been listening to the screams. She waited a moment, and when there was silence she walked down the hall and picked up the telephone to report to Constantin Demiris.

The Hellenic Trade Corporation was located at 217 Bond Street, off Piccadilly, in an old government building that had been converted years earlier to offices. The exterior of the building was a masterpiece of architecture, elegant and graceful.

When Catherine arrived, the office staff was waiting for her. There were half a dozen people near the door to greet her.

'Welcome, Miss Alexander. I'm Evelyn Kaye. This is Carl . . . Tucker . . . Matthew . . . Jennie . . .'

The names and faces became a blur.

'How do you do?'

'Your office is ready for you. I'll show you the way.'

'Thank you.'

The reception room was tastefully furnished, with a large chesterfield sofa, flanked by two Chippendale chairs and a tapestry. They walked down a long carpeted corridor and passed a conference room with heavy pine panelling, and leather chairs along a highly polished table.

Catherine was ushered into an attractive office, with worn, comfortable furniture and a leather couch.

'It's all yours.'

'It's lovely,' she murmured.

There were fresh flowers on the desk.

'From Mr Demiris.'

He's so thoughtful.

Evelyn Kaye, the woman who had shown her into the office, was a stocky, middle-aged woman with a pleasant face and a comfortable manner. 'It will take you a few days to get used to the place, but the operation is really quite simple. We're one of the nerve centers of the Demiris empire. We coordinate the reports from the overseas divisions, and send them on to headquarters in Athens. I'm the office manager. You'll be my assistant.'

'Oh.' *So I'm the assistant to the office manager.* Catherine had no idea what was expected of her. She had been thrown into a fantasy world. Private planes, limousines, a beautiful flat with servants . . .

'Wim Vandeen is our resident mathematical genius. He computes all the statements and puts them into a master financial analysis chart. His mind works faster than most calculating machines. Come along to his office and meet him.'

They walked down the corridor to an office at the end of the hall. Evelyn opened the door without knocking.

'Wim, this is my new assistant.'

Catherine stepped into the office and stood there, riveted. Wim Vandeen appeared to be in his early thirties, a thin man with a slack-jawed mouth, and a dull, vacant expression. He was staring out the window.

'Wim. Wim! This is Catherine Alexander.'

He turned around. 'Catherine the First's real name was Marta Skowronka she was a servant girl born in 1684 who was captured by the Russians she married Peter the First and was empress of Russia from 1725 to 1727, Catherine the Great was the daughter of a German prince she was born in 1729 and she married Peter, who became Emperor Peter the Third in 1762, and she succeeded to his throne that same year after she had him murdered. Under her reign there were three divisions of Poland and two wars against Turkey . . .' The information poured out like a fountain, in a monotone.

58

Catherine was listening, stunned. 'That's . . . that's very interesting,' she managed.

Wim Vandeen looked away.

Evelyn said, 'Wim is shy when he meets people.'

Shy? Catherine thought. *The man is weird. And he's a genius? What kind of job is this going to be?*

In Athens, in his offices on Aghiou Geronda Street, Constantin Demiris was listening to a telephone report from Alfred in London.

'I drove Miss Alexander directly from the airport to the flat, Mr Demiris. I asked her if she wished me to take her anywhere else, as you suggested, and she said no.'

'She's had no outside contacts at all?'

'No, sir. Not unless she made some telephone calls from the flat, sir.'

Constantin Demiris was not worried about that. Anna, the housekeeper, would report to him. He replaced the receiver, satisfied. She presented no immediate danger to him and he would see that she was watched. She was alone in the world. She had no one to turn to except her benefactor, Constantin Demiris. *I must make arrangements to go to London soon*, Demiris thought happily. *Very soon.*

Catherine Alexander found her new job interesting. Daily reports came in from Constantin Demiris' far-flung empire. There were bills of lading from a steel mill in Indiana, audits from an automobile factory in Italy, invoices from a newspaper chain in Australia, a gold mine, an insurance company. Catherine collated the reports and saw to it that the information went directly to Wim Vandeen. Win glanced at the reports once, put them through the incredible computer that was his brain, and almost instantly calculated the percentages of profit or loss to the company.

Catherine enjoyed getting to know her new colleagues and she was awed by the beauty of the old building she worked in.

She mentioned it to Evelyn Kaye once in front of Wim and Wim said, 'This was a government custom house designed by Sir Christopher Wren in seventeen twenty-one. After the great fire of London, Christopher Wren redesigned fifty churches including St Paul's, St Michael's, and St Bride's He designed the Royal Exchange and Buckingham House He died in seventeen twenty-three and is buried in St Paul's This house was converted to an office building in nineteen seven, and in the Second World War during the Blitz, the government declared it an official air-raid shelter.'

The air-raid shelter was a large, bomb-proof room located through a heavy iron door adjoining the basement. Catherine looked into the heavily fortified room, and thought about the brave British men and women and children who had found shelter here during the terrible bombing by Hitler's Luftwaffe.

The basement itself was huge, running the entire length of the building. It had a large boiler for heating the building, and was filled with electronic and telephone equipment. The boiler was a problem. Several times, Catherine had escorted a repair-man down to the basement to take a look at it. Each one would tinker with it, pronounce it cured of whatever had ailed it, and leave.

'It looks so dangerous,' Catherine said. 'Is there any chance that it might explode?'

'Bless your heart, miss, of course not. See this safety valve here? Well, if the boiler should ever get too hot, the safety valve releases all the excess steam, and Bob's your uncle. No problem.'

After the work day was over, there was London. London . . . a cornucopia of wonderful theatre, ballet and music concerts. There were interesting old bookstores like Hatchards, and Foyles – and dozens of museums, and little antique shops, and res-taurants. Catherine visited the lithograph shops in Cecil Court and shopped at Harrods, Fortnum & Mason, and Marks & Spencer and had Sunday tea at the Savoy.

From time to time, unbidden thoughts came into Catherine's mind. There were so many things to remind her of Larry. A

60

voice . . . a phrase . . . a cologne . . . a song. *No. The past is finished. The future is what's important.* And each day she became stronger.

Catherine and Evelyn Kaye became friends and occasionally went out together. One Sunday they visited the open-air art exhibition on the Thames embankment. There were dozens of artists there, young and old, displaying their paintings, and they all had one thing in common: they were failures who had been unable to have their works exhibited in any gallery. The paintings were terrible. Catherine bought one out of sympathy.

'Where are you going to put it?' Evelyn asked.

'In the boiler room,' Catherine said.

As they walked along the London streets, they came across the pavement artists, men who used colored chalks to paint on the stone of the pavement. Some of their work was amazing. Passersby would stop to admire them and then toss a few coins to the artists. One afternoon on her way back from lunch, Catherine stopped to watch an elderly man working on a beautiful landscape in chalk. As he was finishing it, it began to rain and the old man stood there watching his work being washed away. *That's a lot like my past life*, Catherine thought.

Evelyn took Catherine to Shepherd Market. 'This is an interesting area,' Evelyn promised.

It was certainly colorful. There was a three-hundred-year-old restaurant called Tiddy Dols, a magazine stand, a market, a beauty parlor, a bakery, antique shops and several two- and three-story residences.

The name plates on the mailboxes were odd. One read 'Helen' and below it 'French lessons'. Another read 'Rosie' and, below that, 'Greek taught here'.

'Is this an educational area?' Catherine asked.

Evelyn laughed aloud. 'In a way I guess it is. Only the

kind of education these girls give can't be taught in school.'

Evelyn laughed even louder when Catherine blushed.

Catherine was alone most of the time, but she kept herself too busy to be lonely. She plunged into her days as though trying to make up for the precious moments of her life that had been stolen from her. She refused to worry about the past or the future. She visited Windsor Castle, and Canterbury with its beautiful cathedral, and Hampton Court. On weekends, she went into the country and stayed at quaint little inns and took long walks through the countryside.

I'm alive, she thought. *No one is born happy. Everyone has to make his own happiness. I'm a survivor. I'm young and I'm healthy and wonderful things are going to happen.*

On Monday she would go back to work. Back to Evelyn and the girls and Wim Vandeen.

Wim Vandeen was an enigma.

Catherine had never met anyone like him. There were twenty employees in the office, and without even bothering to use a calculator, Wim Vandeen remembered every employee's salary, national insurance number and deductions. Although all of this was on file, he kept all the company records in his head. He knew the monthly cash flow from each division and how it compared with the previous months, going back five years when he had started with the company.

Wim Vandeen remembered everything he had ever seen or heard or read. The range of his knowledge was incredible. The simplest questions on any subject would trigger a stream of information, yet he was anti-social.

Catherine discussed him with Evelyn. 'I don't understand Wim at all.'

'Wim is an eccentric,' Evelyn said. 'You just have to take him as he is. All he's interested in is numbers. I don't think he cares about people.'

'Does he have friends?'

'No.'

'Does he ever date? I mean – go out with girls?'

'No.'

It seemed to Catherine that Wim was isolated and lonely, and she felt a kinship with him.

Wim's range of knowledge amazed Catherine. One morning, she developed an earache.

Wim said gruffly, 'This weather's not going to help it much. You'd better go and see an ear doctor.'

'Thanks, Wim. I . . .'

'The parts of the ear are the auricle, auditory meatus, tympanic membrane, the chain of ossicles – hammer, anvil and stirrup – tympanic cavity, the semicircular duct, oval window, the eustachian tube, auditory nerve, and the cochlear duct.' And he walked away.

On another day, Catherine and Evelyn took Wim to lunch at the Ram's Head, a local pub. In the back room, customers were throwing darts.

'Are you interested in sports, Wim?' Catherine asked. 'Have you ever seen a baseball game?'

'Baseball,' Wim said. 'A baseball is nine and a quarter inches in circumference. It's made of yarn, wound on a hard rubber cone and covered with white leather. The bat is usually made of ash, not more than two and three quarter inches in the greatest diameter, and not more than forty-two inches in length.'

He knows all the statistics, Catherine thought, *but has he ever felt the excitement of actually doing it?*

'Have you ever *played* any sports? Basketball, for instance?'

'Basketball is played on a wooden or concrete floor. The ball has a spherical leather cover thirty-one inches in circumference, inflated by a rubber bladder to thirteen pounds of pressure. It weighs twenty to twenty-two ounces. Basketball was invented by James Naismith in eighteen ninety-one.'

Catherine had her answer.

*

Sometimes Wim could be an embarrassment in public. One Sunday, Catherine and Evelyn took Wim to Maidenhead, on the Thames. They stopped at the Compleat Angler for lunch. The waiter came up to their table. 'We have fresh clams today.'

Catherine turned to Wim. 'Do you like clams?'

Wim said, 'There are long clams, quahog, or round clams, razor clams, surf clams, single shells, and blood clams.'

The waiter was staring at him. 'Would you care to order some, sir?'

'I don't like clams,' Wim snapped.

Catherine liked the people she was working with, but Wim became special to her. He was brilliant beyond her comprehension, and at the same time, he seemed withdrawn and lonely.

Catherine said to Evelyn one day: 'Isn't there some chance that Wim might lead a normal life? Fall in love and get married?'

Evelyn sighed. 'I told you. He has no emotions. He'll never get attached to anyone.'

But Catherine did not believe it. Once or twice she had caught a flash of interest – of affection – of laughter – in Wim's eyes, and she wanted to draw him out, to help him. Or had it been her imagination?

One day, the office staff received an invitation to a charity ball being held at the Savoy.

Catherine walked into Wim's office. 'Wim, do you dance?'

He stared at her. 'A bar and a half of four-four time music completes one rhythmic unit in a foxtrot. The man starts the basic step with his left foot and takes two steps forward. The woman starts with her right foot and takes two steps backward. The two slow steps are followed by a quick step at right angles to the slow steps. To dip, the man steps forward on his left foot and dips – slow – then he moves forward on his right foot – slow. Then he moves to the left with his left foot – quick. Then closes his right foot to his left foot – quick.'

Catherine stood there, not knowing what to say. *He knows all the words, but he doesn't understand their meaning.*

Constantin Demiris telephoned. It was late at night and Catherine was preparing to go to bed.

'I hope I didn't disturb you. It's Costa.'

'No, of course not.' She was glad to hear his voice. She had missed talking to him, asking his advice. After all, he was the only one in the world who really knew about her past. She felt as though he were an old friend.

'I've been thinking about you, Catherine. I was concerned that you might find London a lonely place. After all, you don't know anyone there.'

'I do get a little lonely sometimes,' Catherine admitted. 'But I'm coping. I keep remembering what you said. Forget about the past, live for the future.'

'That's right. Speaking of the future, I'm going to be in London tomorrow. I would like to take you to dinner.'

'I would enjoy that very much,' Catherine said warmly. She was looking forward to it. She would have a chance to tell him how grateful she was to him.

When Constantin Demiris replaced the receiver, he smiled to himself. *The chase is on.*

They had dinner at the Ritz. The dining room was elegant and the food was delicious. But Catherine was too excited to pay attention to anything except the man who was sitting opposite her. There was so much she had to tell him.

'You have a wonderful office staff,' Catherine said. 'Wim is amazing. I've never seen anyone who can . . .'

But Demiris was not listening to the words. He was studying her, thinking how beautiful she was, and how vulnerable. *But I mustn't rush her*, Demiris decided. *No, I'll play the game slowly and savor the victory. This one will be for you, Noelle, and for your lover.*

'Are you going to be in London long?' Catherine was asking.

65

'Just a day or two. I had some business to take care of.' That was true. But he knew he could have handled it by telephone. No, he had come to London to begin his campaign to draw Catherine closer to him, to make her emotionally dependent on him. He leaned forward.

'Catherine, did I ever tell you about the time I worked in the oil fields in Saudi Arabia . . . ?'

Demiris took Catherine to dinner the following night.

'Evelyn told me what a wonderful job you're doing at the office. I'm going to give you a raise.'

'You've been so generous already,' Catherine protested. 'I . . .'

Demiris looked into her eyes. 'You don't know how generous I can be.'

Catherine was embarrassed. *He's only being kind*, she thought. *I mustn't imagine things*.

The following day, Demiris was ready to leave. 'Would you like to ride out to the airport with me, Catherine?'

'Yes.'

She found him fascinating, almost spellbinding. He was amusing and brilliant and she was flattered by his attention.

At the airport, Demiris kissed Catherine lightly on the cheek. 'I'm glad we could spend some time together, Catherine.'

'So am I. Thank you, Costa.'

She stood there watching his plane take off. *He's very special*, Catherine thought. *I'm going to miss him*.

Chapter 6

Everyone had always been amazed by the apparent close friendship of Constantin Demiris and his brother-in-law, Spyros Lambrou.

Spyros Lambrou was almost as rich and powerful as Demiris. Demiris owned the largest fleet of cargo ships in the world; Spyros Lambrou owned the second largest. Constantin Demiris controlled a chain of newspapers and airlines, oil fields, steel mills, and gold mines; Spyros Lambrou had insurance companies, banks, enormous amounts of real estate, and a chemical plant. They seemed friendly competitors; better than that, buddies.

'Isn't it wonderful,' people said, 'that two of the most powerful men in the world are such great friends?'

In reality, they were implacable rivals who despised each other. When Spyros Lambrou bought a 100-foot yacht, Constantin Demiris immediately commissioned a 150-foot yacht that had four GM diesels, a crew of 13, two speedboats and a freshwater swimming pool.

When Spyros Lambrou's fleet reached a total of twelve tankers, with a tonnage of 200,000, Constantin Demiris increased his own fleet to twenty-three tankers, with a tonnage of 650,000. Spyros Lambrou acquired a string of race horses, and Demiris bought a larger stable to run against him, and consistently won.

The two men saw each other frequently, for they served together on charity committees, sat on the boards of various corporations, and occasionally attended family gatherings.

They were exactly opposite in temperament. Where Constantin Demiris had come from the gutter and fought his way to the top, Spyros Lambrou was born an aristocrat. He was a lean and elegant man, always impeccably dressed, with courtly, old-world manners. He could trace his family tree back to Otto of Bavaria, who had once ruled as King of Greece. During the early political uprisings in Greece, a small minority, the oligarchy, amassed fortunes in trade, shipping and land. Spyros Lambrou's father was one of them, and Spyros had inherited his empire.

Over the years, Spyros Lambrou and Constantin Demiris had carried on their charade of friendship. But each was determined that, in the end, he would destroy the other, Demiris because of his instinct for survival, Lambrou because of his brother-in-law's treatment of Melina.

Spyros Lambrou was a superstitious man. He appreciated his good fortune in life, and he was anxious not to antagonize the gods. From time to time he consulted psychics for guidance. He was intelligent enough to recognize the frauds, but there was one psychic whom he had found to be uncanny. She had predicted his sister Melina's miscarriage and what would happen to the marriage, and a dozen other things that had come to pass. She lived in Athens.

Her name was Madame Piris.

Constantin Demiris made it a habit to arrive at his offices in Aghiou Geronda Street every morning punctually at six o'clock. By the time his rivals went to work, Demiris had already conducted several hours of business with his agents in a dozen countries.

Demiris' private office was spectacular. The view was magnificent, with picture windows putting the city of Athens at his feet. The floor was black granite. The furniture was steel and leather. On the walls was a Cubist art collection, with Légers, Braques, and half a dozen Picassos. There was an enormous glass and steel desk and a leather throne-chair. On the desk was a death mask of Alexander the Great, set in crystal. The inscription under it read: *Alexandros. The defender of man*.

On this particular morning, Constantin Demiris' private phone was ringing when he entered his office. There were only half a dozen people who had access to the telephone number.

Demiris picked up the telephone. '*Kalimehra.*'

'*Kalimehra.*' The voice at the other end belonged to Spyros

Lambrou's private secretary, Nikos Veritos. He sounded nervous.

'Forgive me for disturbing you, Mr Demiris. You told me to call when I had some information that you might . . .'

'Yes. What is it?'

'Mr Lambrou is planning to acquire a company called Aurora International. It is listed on the New York Stock Exchange. Mr Lambrou has a friend on the board of directors who told him that a big government contract is going to be given to the company to build bombers. This is, of course, very confidential. The stock will have a big rise when the announcement . . .'

'I'm not interested in the stock market,' Demiris snapped. 'Don't bother me again unless you have something important to tell me.'

'I'm sorry, Mr Demiris. I thought . . .'

But Demiris had hung up.

At eight o'clock, when Demiris' assistant, Giannis Tcharos, walked in, Constantin Demiris looked up from his desk. 'There's a company on the New York Stock Exchange, Aurora International. Notify all our newspapers that the company is being investigated for fraud. Use an anonymous source, but spread the word. I want them to keep hammering at the story until the stock drops. Then start buying until I have control.'

'Yes, sir. Is that all?'

'No. After I've acquired control, announce that the rumors were unfounded. Oh, yes. See that the New York Stock Exchange is notified that Spyros Lambrou bought his stock on insider information.'

Giannis Tcharos said delicately, 'Mr Demiris, in the United States, that is a criminal offense.'

Constantin Demiris smiled. 'I know.'

A mile away, at Syntagma Square, Spyros Lambrou was working in his office. His work place reflected his eclectic taste. The furniture consisted of rare antiques, a mixture of French and

Italian. Three of the walls were covered with the works of French Impressionists. The fourth wall was devoted to an array of Belgian artists, from Van Rysselberghe to De Smet. The sign on the outer office door read: 'Lambrou and Associates', but there had never been any associates. Spyros Lambrou had inherited a successful business from his father, and over the years he had built it into a worldwide conglomerate.

Spyros Lambrou should have been a happy man. He was rich and successful, and he enjoyed excellent health. But it was impossible for him to be truly happy as long as Constantin Demiris was alive. His brother-in-law was anathema to him. Lambrou despised him. To him, Demiris was *polymichanos*, a man fertile in devices, a scoundrel without morals. Lambrou had always hated Demiris for his treatment of Melina, but the savage rivalry between them had its own terrible nexus.

It had begun ten years earlier, at a lunch Spyros Lambrou had with his sister. She had never seen him so excited.

'Melina, did you know that every single day the world consumes all the fossil fuel it took a thousand years to create?'

'No, Spyros.'

'There's going to be a tremendous demand for oil in the future, and there aren't going to be enough oil tankers to handle it.'

'You're going to build some?'

He nodded. 'But not just ordinary tankers. I'm going to build the first fleet of large tankers. They'll be twice as large as the present ones.' His voice was filled with enthusiasm. 'I've spent months going over the figures. Listen to this. A gallon of crude petroleum hauled from the Persian Gulf to an east-coast port of the United States costs seven cents. But on a big tanker, the cost would come down to three cents a gallon. Do you have any idea what that could mean?'

'Spyros – where are you going to get the money to build a fleet like that?'

He smiled. 'That's the beautiful part of my plan. It won't cost me a cent.'

'*What?*'

He leaned forward. 'I'm going to America next month to talk to the heads of the big oil companies. With these tankers, I can carry their oil for them for half the price they can carry it.'

'But . . . you don't have any big tankers.'

His smile turned into a grin. 'No, but if I can get long-term charter contracts from the oil companies, the banks will loan me the money I need to build them. What do you think?'

'I think you're a genius. It's a brilliant plan.'

Melina was so excited about her brother's idea that she mentioned it to Demiris that evening at dinner.

When she had finished explaining it, Melina said, 'Isn't that a wonderful idea?'

Constantin Demiris was silent for a moment. 'Your brother's a dreamer. It could never work.'

Melina looked at him in surprise. 'Why not, Costa?'

'Because it's a hare-brained scheme. In the first place, there's not going to be that big a demand for oil, so those mythical tankers of his will run empty. Secondly, the oil companies aren't about to turn their precious oil over to a phantom fleet that doesn't even exist. And third, those bankers he's going to will laugh him out of their offices.'

Melina's face clouded with disappointment. 'Spyros was so enthusiastic. Would you mind discussing it with him?'

Demiris shook his head. 'Let him have his dream, Melina. It would be better if he didn't even know about our conversation.'

'All right, Costa. Whatever you say.'

Early the following morning Constantin Demiris was on his way to the United States to discuss large tankers. He was aware that the world petroleum reserves outside the United States and the Soviet-bloc territories were controlled by the seven sisters: Standard Oil Company of New Jersey, Standard Oil Company of California, Gulf Oil, the Texas Company, Socony-Vacuum, Royal Dutch-Shell and Anglo-Iranian. He knew that if he could get just one of them, the others were sure to follow.

*

71

Constantin Demiris' first visit was to the executive offices of Standard Oil of New Jersey. He had an appointment with Owen Curtiss, a fourth vice-president.

'What can I do for you, Mr Demiris?'

'I have a concept that I think could be of great financial benefit to your company.'

'Yes, you mentioned that over the telephone.' Curtiss glanced at his wristwatch. 'I have a meeting in a few minutes. If you could be brief . . .'

'I'll be very brief. It costs you seven cents to haul a gallon of crude petroleum from the Persian Gulf to the eastern coast of the United States.'

'That's correct.'

'What would you say if I told you that I can guarantee to carry your oil for three cents a gallon?'

Curtiss smiled patronizingly. 'And just how would you perform that miracle?'

Demiris said quietly, 'With a fleet of large tankers that will have twice the carrying capacity of the present ones. I can transport your oil as fast as you can pump it out of the ground.'

Curtiss was studying him, his face thoughtful. 'Where would you get a fleet of large tankers?'

'I'm going to build them.'

'I'm sorry. We wouldn't be interested in investing in . . .'

Demiris interrupted. 'It won't cost you a penny. All I'm asking from you is a long-term contract to carry your oil at half the price you're paying now. I'll get my financing from the banks.'

There was a long, pregnant silence. Owen Curtiss cleared his throat. 'I think I had better take you upstairs to meet our president.'

That was the beginning. The other oil companies were just as eager to make deals for Constantin Demiris' new tankers. By the time Spyros Lambrou learned what was happening, it was too late. He flew to the United States and was able to make a few deals for large tankers with some independent companies, but Demiris had skimmed off the cream of the market.

72

'He's your husband,' Lambrou stormed, 'but I swear to you, Melina, some day I'm going to make him pay for what he's done.'

Melina felt miserable about what had happened. She felt she had betrayed her brother.

But when she confronted her husband, he shrugged. 'I didn't go to them, Melina. They came to me. How could I refuse them?'

And that was the end of the discussion.

But business considerations were unimportant compared to Lambrou's feelings about how Demiris treated Melina.

He could have shrugged off the fact that Constantin Demiris was a notorious philanderer – after all, a man had to have his pleasure. But Demiris' being so blatant about it was an insult not only to Melina but to the whole Lambrou family. Demiris' affair with the actress, Noelle Page, had been the most egregious example. It had made headlines all over the world. *One day*, Spyros Lambrou thought. *One day . . .*

Nikos Veritos, Lambrou's assistant, walked into the office. Veritos had been with Spyros Lambrou for fifteen years. He was competent, but unimaginative, a man with no future, grey and faceless. The rivalry between the two brothers-in-law presented Veritos with what he considered a golden opportunity. He was betting on Constantin Demiris to win, and from time to time he passed on confidential information to him, hoping for a suitable reward.

Veritos approached Lambrou. 'Excuse me. There's a Mr Anthony Rizzoli here to see you.'

Lambrou sighed. 'Let's get it over with,' he said. 'Send him in.'

Anthony Rizzoli was in his mid-forties. He had black hair, a thin aquiline nose, and deep-set brown eyes. He moved with the grace of a trained boxer. He wore an expensive beige tailored suit, a yellow silk shirt and soft leather shoes. He was soft-spoken and polite, and yet there was something oddly menacing about him.

73

'Pleasure to meet you, Mr Lambrou.'

'Sit down, Mr Rizzoli.'

Rizzoli took a seat.

'What can I do for you?'

'Well, as I explained to Mr Veritos here, I'd like to charter one of your cargo ships. You see, I have a factory in Marseilles and I want to ship some heavy machinery to the United States. If you and me can work out a deal, I can throw a lot of business your way in the future.'

Spyros Lambrou leaned back in his chair and studied the man seated in front of him. *Unsavory.* 'Is that all you're planning to ship, Mr Rizzoli?' he asked.

Tony Rizzoli frowned, 'What? I don't understand.'

'I think you do,' Lambrou said. 'My ships are not available to you.'

'Why not? What are you talkin' about?'

'Drugs, Mr Rizzoli. You're a drug dealer.'

Rizzoli's eyes narrowed. 'You're crazy! You've been listenin' to a lot of rumors.'

But they were more than rumors. Spyros Lambrou had carefully checked out the man. Tony Rizzoli was one of the top drug smugglers in Europe. He was Mafia, part of the Organization, and the word was out that Rizzoli's transportation sources had dried up. That was why he was so anxious to make a deal.

'I'm afraid you'll have to go elsewhere.'

Tony Rizzoli sat there, staring at him, his eyes cold. Finally he nodded. 'Okay.' He took a business card from his pocket and threw it on the desk. 'If you change your mind, here's where you can reach me.' He rose to his feet and a moment later he was gone.

Spyros Lambrou picked up the card. It read *Anthony Rizzoli – Import-Export*. There was an Athens hotel address and a telephone number at the bottom of the card.

Nikos Veritos had sat there wide-eyed, listening to the conversation. When Tony Rizzoli walked out the door he said, 'Is he really . . . ?'

'Yes. Mr Rizzoli deals in heroin. If we ever let him use one

74

of our ships, the government could put our whole fleet out of business.'

Tony Rizzoli walked out of Lambrou's office in a fury. *That fucking Greek treating me like I'm some peasant off the street! And how had he known about the drugs? The shipment was an unusually large one, with a street value of at least ten million dollars. But the problem was in getting it to New York. The Goddamned narcs are swarming all over Athens. I'll have to make a phone call to Sicily and stall.* Tony Rizzoli had never lost a shipment, and he did not intend to lose this one. He thought of himself as a born winner.

He had grown up in Hell's Kitchen in New York. Geographically, it was located in the middle of the West Side of Manhattan, between 8th Avenue and the Hudson River, and its northern and southern boundaries ran from 23rd to 59th Streets. But psychologically and emotionally Hell's Kitchen was a city within a city, an armed enclave. The streets were ruled by gangs. There were the Gophers, the Parlor Mob, the Gorillas, and the Rhodes gang. Murder contracts retailed at a hundred dollars, with mayhem a little less.

The occupants of Hell's Kitchen lived in dirty tenements, overrun by lice, rats and roaches. There were no bathtubs, and the youths solved the shortage in their own way; they plunged naked into the water off the Hudson River docks, where the sewers from the Kitchen's streets emptied into the river. The docks stank of the stagnant mass of dead, swollen cats and dogs.

The street scene provided an endless variety of action. A fire engine answering an alarm . . . a gang fight on one of the tenement roofs . . . a wedding procession . . . a stickball game on the sidewalk . . . a chase after a runaway horse . . . a shooting . . . The only playgrounds the children had were the streets, the tenement roofs, the rubbish-strewn vacant lots and – in the summer time – the noisome waters of the river. And over everything, the acrid smell of poverty. That was the atmosphere in which Tony Rizzoli had grown up.

*

75

Tony Rizzoli's earliest memory was of being knocked down, and having his milk money stolen. He was seven years old. Older and bigger boys were a constant threat. The route to school was a no-man's-land, and the school itself was a battleground. By the time Rizzoli was fifteen years old he had developed a strong body and considerable skill as a fighter. He enjoyed fighting, and because he was good at it, it gave him a feeling of superiority. He and his friends put on boxing matches at Stillman's Gym.

From time to time, some of the mobsters dropped in to keep an eye on the fighters they owned. Frank Costello appeared once or twice a month, along with Joe Adonis and Lucky Luciano. They were amused by the boxing matches that the youngsters put on, and as a form of diversion they began to bet on their fights. Tony Rizzoli was always the winner, and he quickly became a favorite of the mobsters.

One day while Rizzoli was changing in the locker room the young boy overheard a conversation between Frank Costello and Lucky Luciano. 'The kid's a gold mine,' Luciano was saying. 'I won five grand on him last week.'

'You going to put a bet on his fight with Lou Domenic?'

'Sure. I'm betting ten big ones.'

'What odds do you have to lay?'

'Ten to one. But what the hell? Rizzoli's a shoo-in.'

Tony Rizzoli was not certain what the conversation meant. He went to his older brother, Gino, and told him about it.

'Jesus!' his brother exclaimed. 'Those guys are bettin' big money on you.'

'But why? I'm not a professional.'

Gino thought for a moment. 'You've never lost a fight, have you, Tony?'

'No.'

'What probably happened is that they made a few small bets for kicks, and then when they saw what you could do they began betting for real.'

The younger boy shrugged. 'It don't mean nothin' to me.'

Gino took his arm and said earnestly, 'It could mean a lot to you. To both of us. Listen to me, kid . . .'

*

76

The fight with Lou Domenic took place at Stillman's Gym on a Friday afternoon and all the big boys were there – Frank Costello, Joe Adonis, Albert Anastasia, Lucky Luciano and Meyer Lansky. They enjoyed watching the young boys fight, but what they enjoyed even more was the fact that they had found a way to make money on the kids.

Lou Domenic was seventeen, a year older than Tony and five pounds heavier. But he was no match for Tony Rizzoli's boxing skills and killer instinct.

The fight was five rounds. The first round went easily to young Tony. The second round also went to him. And the third. The mobsters were already counting their money.

'The kid's going to grow up to be a world champion,' Lucky Luciano crowed. 'How much did you bet on him?'

'Ten grand,' Frank Costello replied. 'The best odds I could get was fifteen to one. The kid's already got a reputation.'

And suddenly, the unexpected happened. In the middle of the fifth round, Lou Domenic knocked out Tony Rizzoli with an upper cut. The referee began to count . . . very slowly, looking apprehensively out at the stony-faced audience.

'Get to your feet, you little bastard,' Joe Adonis screamed. 'Get up and fight!'

The counting went on, and even at that slow pace, it finally reached ten. Tony Rizzoli was still on the mat, out cold.

'Son-of-a-bitch. *One* lucky punch!'

The men began to add up their losses. They were substantial. Tony Rizzoli was carried to one of the dressing rooms by Gino. Tony kept his eyes tightly closed, afraid that they would find out he was conscious and do something terrible to him.

It was not until Tony was safely home that he began to relax.

'We did it!' his brother yelled excitedly. 'Do you know how much fucking money we made? Almost one thousand dollars.'

'I don't understand. I . . .'

'I borrowed money from their own shylocks to bet on Domenic, and got fifteen to one odds. We're rich.'

'Won't they be mad?' Tony asked.

Gino smiled. 'They'll never know.'

*

The following day when Tony Rizzoli got out of school there was a long black limousine waiting at the curb. Lucky Luciano was in the back seat. He waved the boy over to the car. 'Get in.'

Tony Rizzoli's heart began to pound. 'I can't, Mr Luciano, I'm late for . . .'

'Get in.'

Tony Rizzoli got into the limousine. Lucky Luciano said to the driver, 'Go around the block.'

Thank God he wasn't being taken for a ride!

Luciano turned to the boy. 'You took a dive,' he said flatly.

Rizzoli flushed. 'No, sir. I . . .'

'Don't shit me. How much did you make on the fight?'

'Nothing, Mr Luciano. I . . .'

'I'll ask you once more. How much did you make by taking that dive?'

The boy hesitated. 'A thousand dollars.'

Lucky Luciano laughed. 'That's chicken feed. But I guess for a . . . how old are you?'

'Almost sixteen.'

'I guess for a sixteen-year-old kid, that ain't bad. You know you cost me and my friends a lot of money.'

'I'm sorry. I – '

'Forget it. You're a bright boy. You've got a future.'

'Thank you.'

'I'm going to keep quiet about this, Tony, or my friends will cut your nuts off and feed them to you. But I want you to come and see me Monday. You and me are going to work together.'

A week later, Tony Rizzoli was working for Lucky Luciano. Rizzoli started as a numbers runner, and then became an enforcer. He was bright and quick and in time he worked himself up to being Luciano's lieutenant.

When Lucky Luciano was arrested, convicted and sent to prison, Tony Rizzoli stayed on with Luciano's organization.

The Families were into gambling, shylocking, prostitution, and anything else in which there was an illegal profit to be made.

Dealing drugs was generally frowned on, but some of the members insisted on being involved, and the Families reluctantly gave them permission to set up drug trafficking on their own.

The idea became an obsession with Tony Rizzoli. From what he had seen, the people who were in drug trafficking were completely disorganized. *They're all spinning their wheels. With the right brains and muscle behind it . . .*

He made his decision.

Tony Rizzoli was not a man to go into anything haphazardly. He began by reading everything he could find out about heroin.

Heroin was fast becoming the king of narcotics. Marijuana and cocaine provided a 'high', but heroin created a state of complete euphoria, with no pain, no problems, no cares. Those enslaved by heroin were willing to sell anything they possessed, steal anything within their reach, commit any crime. Heroin became their religion, their reason for being.

Turkey was one of the leading growers of the poppy from which heroin was derived.

The Family had contacts in Turkey, so Rizzoli had a talk with Pete Lucca, one of the capos.

'I'm going to get involved,' Rizzoli said. 'But anything I do will be for the Family. I want you to know that.'

'You're a good boy, Tony.'

'I'd like to go to Turkey to look things over. Can you set it up?'

The old man hesitated. 'I'll send word. But they're not like us, Tony. They have no morals. They're animals. If they don't trust you, they'll kill you.'

'I'll be careful.'

'You do that.'

Two weeks later, Tony Rizzoli was on his way to Turkey.

He travelled to Izmir, Afyon, and Eskisehir, the regions where the poppies were grown, and in the beginning, he was greeted with deep suspicion. He was a stranger, and strangers were not welcome.

'We're going to do a lot of business together,' Rizzoli said. 'I'd like to take a look at the poppy fields.'

A shrug. 'I don't know nothin' about no poppy fields. You're wastin' your time. Go home.'

But Rizzoli was determined. Half a dozen phone calls were made and coded cables were exchanged. Finally, in Kilis, on the Turkish-Syrian border, he was allowed to watch the opium being harvested at the farm of Carella, one of the large landowners.

'I don't understand it,' Tony said. 'How can you get heroin from a fuckin' flower?'

A white-coated scientist explained it to him. 'There are several steps, Mr Rizzoli. Heroin is synthesized from opium, which is made by treating morphine with acetic acid. Heroin is derived from a particular strain of poppy plant called *Papaver somniferum*, the flower of sleep. Opium gets its name from the Greek word *opos*, meaning juice.'

'Got you.'

At harvesting time, Tony was invited to visit Carella's main estate. Each member of Carella's family was equipped with a *cizgi bicak*, a scalpel-shaped cutting knife, to make a precise incision into the plant. Carella explained, 'The poppies have to be harvested within a twenty-four-hour period or the crop is ruined.'

There were nine members in the family and each one worked frantically to make sure the crop was in on time. The air was filled with fumes that induced drowsiness.

Rizzoli felt groggy. 'Be careful,' Carella warned. 'Stay awake. If you lie down in the field, you will never get up again.'

The farmhouse windows and doors were kept tightly closed during the twenty-four-hour period of harvest.

When the poppies had been picked, Rizzoli watched the sticky white gum transformed from a morphine base into heroin, at a 'laboratory' in the hills.

'So, that's it, huh?'

Carella shook his head. 'No, my friend. That's only the beginning. Making the heroin is the easiest part. The trick is to transport it without getting caught.'

Tony Rizzoli felt an excitement building in him. This was where his expertise was going to take over. Up until now, the business had been run by bunglers. Now he was going to show them how a professional operated.

'How do you move this stuff?'

'There are many ways. Truck, bus, train, car, mule, camel . . .'

'Camel?'

'We used to smuggle heroin in cans in the camel's belly – until the guards started using metal detectors. So we switched to rubber bags. At the end of the trip we kill the camels. The problem is that sometimes the bags burst inside the camels, and the animals stagger up to the border like drunks. So the guards caught on.'

'What route do you use?'

'Sometimes the heroin is routed from Aleppo, Beirut and Istanbul, and on to Marseilles. Sometimes the drugs go from Istanbul to Greece, then on to Sicily through Corsica and Morocco and across the Atlantic.'

'I appreciate your cooperation,' Rizzoli said. 'I'll tell the boys. I have another favor to ask of you.'

'Yes?'

'I'd like to go along with the next shipment.'

There was a long pause. 'That could be dangerous.'

'I'll take my chances.'

The following afternoon, Tony Rizzoli was introduced to a large, hulking bandit of a man, with a grandiose, flowing mustache, and the body of a tank. 'This is Mustafa from Afyon. In Turkish, *afyon* means opium. Mustafa is one of our most skilled smugglers.'

'One has to be skilled,' Mustafa said modestly. 'There are many dangers.'

Tony Rizzoli grinned. 'But it's worth the risk, eh?'

Mustafa said with dignity, 'You are speaking of money. To

81

us, opium is more than a money crop. There is a mystique about it. It is the one crop that is more than food alone. The white sap of the plant is a God-given elixir which is a natural medicine if taken in small quantities. It can be eaten, or applied directly to the skin, and it will cure most of the common ailments – upset stomachs, colds, fever, aches, pains, sprains. But you must be careful. If you take it in large amounts, not only will it cloud the senses, it will rob you of your sexual prowess, and nothing in Turkey could more destroy a man's dignity than impotence.'

'Sure. Anything you say.'

The journey from Afyon began at midnight. A group of farmers, walking single file through the black night, rendezvoused with Mustafa. The mules were loaded with opium, 350 kilos, more than 700 pounds, strapped to the backs of seven stout mules. The sweet pungent odor of the opium, like wet hay, hovered in the air about the men. There were a dozen farmers who had come to guard the opium in the transaction with Mustafa. Each farmer was armed with a rifle.

'We have to be careful these days,' Mustafa told Rizzoli. 'We have Interpol and many police looking for us. In the old days, it was more fun. We used to transport opium through a village or the city in a casket draped in black. It was a heart-warming sight to see the people and the police on the street, lifting their hats and saluting in respect as a coffin of opium went by.'

The province of Afyon lies in the center of the western third of Turkey at the foot of the Sultan Mountains on a high plateau, remote and virtually isolated from the nation's leading cities.

'This terrain is very good for our work,' Mustafa said. 'We are not easy to find.'

The mules moved slowly through the desolate mountains, and at midnight, three days later, they reached the Turkish-Syrian border. There they were met by a woman dressed in black. She was leading a horse carrying an innocent sack of flour, and there was a hemp rope knotted loosely on its saddle horn. The rope trailed behind the horse, but it never touched the ground. It was a long rope, two hundred feet in length. The other end was held up by Mustafa and his fifteen hired runners behind him. They walked in a crouch, each bent over close to the ground, one hand holding the rope line, and the other clutching a gunny sack of opium. Each sack weighed thirty-five pounds. The woman and her horse walked through a stretch booby-trapped with anti-personnel mines, but there was a path that had been cleared by a small herd of sheep driven through the area earlier. If the rope fell to the earth, the slack was a signal to Mustafa and the others that there were gendarmes up ahead. If the woman was taken in for questioning, then the smugglers would safely move on ahead across the border.

They crossed at Kilis, the border point, which was heavily mined. Once past the area controlled by the gendarme patrols, the smugglers moved into the buffer zone three miles wide, until they reached their rendezvous, where they were greeted by Syrian smugglers. They put their sacks of opium on the ground and were presented with a bottle of *raki* which the men passed from one to the other. Rizzoli watched as the opium was weighed, stacked, tied and secured upon the sway-backs of a dozen dirty Syrian donkeys. The job was done.

All right, Rizzoli thought. *Now let's see how the boys in Thailand do it.*

Rizzoli's next stop was Bangkok. When his bona fides had been established he was allowed on a Thai fishing vessel that carried drugs wrapped in polyethylene sheeting packed into empty kerosene drums, with rings attached to the top. As the shipping boats approached Hong Kong they jettisoned the drums in a neat row in shallow water around Lima and the Ladrone Islands, where it was simple for a Hong Kong fishing boat to pick them up with a grappling hook.

'Not bad,' Rizzoli said. *But there has to be a better way.*

The growers referred to heroin as 'H' and 'horse', but to Tony Rizzoli, heroin was gold. The profits were staggering. The peasants who grew the raw opium were paid three hundred fifty dollars for ten kilos but by the time the opium was processed and sold on the streets of New York, its value had increased to two hundred fifty thousand dollars.

It's so easy, Rizzoli thought. *Carella was right. The trick is not to get caught.*

That had been in the beginning, ten years ealier. But now it was more difficult. Interpol, the international police force, had recently put drug smuggling at the top of its list. All vessels leaving the key smuggling ports that looked even slightly suspicious were boarded and searched. That was why Rizzoli had gone to Spyros Lambrou. His fleet was above suspicion. It was unlikely that the police would search one of his cargo ships. But the bastard had turned him down. *I'll find another way*, Tony Rizzoli thought. *But I'd better find it fast.*

'Catherine – am I disturbing you?'

It was midnight. 'No, Costa. It's nice to hear your voice.'

'Is everything going well?'

'Yes – thanks to you. I'm really enjoying my job.'

'Good. I'll be coming to London in a few weeks. I'll look forward to seeing you.' *Careful. Don't push too fast.* 'I want to discuss some of the company's personnel.'

'Fine.'

'Good night, then.'

'Good night.'

This time she was calling him. 'Costa – I don't know what to say. The locket is beautiful. You shouldn't have . . .'

'It's a small token, Catherine. Evelyn told me what a big help you are to her. I just wanted to express my appreciation.'

It's so easy, Demiris thought. Little gifts and flattery.

Later: My wife and I are separating.

Then the 'I'm so lonely' stage.

A vague talk of marriage and an invitation to travel on his

yacht to his island. The routine never failed. *This is going to be particularly exciting*, Demiris thought, *because it's going to have a different ending. She's going to die.*

He telephoned Napoleon Chotas. The lawyer was delighted to hear from him. 'It's been a while, Costa. Everything goes well?'

'Yes, thank you. I need a favor.'

'Of course.'

'Noelle Page owned a little villa in Rafina. I want you to buy it for me, under someone else's name.'

'Certainly. I'll have one of the lawyers in my office . . .'

'I want you to handle it personally.'

There was a pause. 'Very well. I'll take care of it.'

'Thank you.'

Napoleon Chotas sat there, staring at the phone. The villa was the love nest where Noelle Page and Larry Douglas had carried on their affair. What could Constantin Demiris possibly want with it?

Chapter 7

The Arsakion Courthouse in downtown Athens is a large, grey stone building that takes up the entire square block at University Street and Strada. Of the thirty courtrooms in the building, only three rooms are reserved for criminal trials: rooms 21, 30 and 33.

Because of the enormous interest generated by the murder trial of Anastasia Savalas, it was being held in room 33. The courtroom was forty feet wide and three hundred feet long, and the seats were divided into three blocks, six feet apart, with nine wooden benches to each row. At the front of the courtroom was a raised dais behind a six-foot mahogany partition, with high-backed chairs for the three presiding judges.

In front of the dais was a witness stand, a small raised platform on which was fixed a reading lectern, and against the far wall was a jury box, filled now with its ten jurors. In front of the defendant's box was the lawyers' table.

The murder trial was spectacular enough in itself, but the *pièce de résistance* was the fact that the defense was being conducted by Napoleon Chotas, one of the preeminent criminal lawyers in the world. Chotas tried only murder cases, and he had a remarkable record of success. His fees were rumored to be in the millions of dollars. Napoleon Chotas was a thin, emaciated-looking man with the large sad eyes of a bloodhound in a corrugated face. He dressed badly, and his physical appearance did nothing to inspire confidence. But behind his vaguely baffled manner was hidden a brilliant, trenchant mind.

The press had speculated furiously about why Napoleon Chotas had agreed to defend the woman on trial. There was no way he could possibly win the case. Wagers were being made that it would be Chotas' first defeat.

Peter Demonides, the Prosecuting Attorney, had come up

against Chotas before, and – though he would never admit it, even to himself – he was in awe of Chotas' skill. This time, however, Demonides felt that he had little to worry about. If ever there was a classic open-and-shut murder case, the Anastasia Savalas trial was it.

The facts were simple: Anastasia Savalas was a beautiful young woman married to a wealthy man named George Savalas, who was thirty years her senior. Anastasia had been having an affair with their young chauffeur, Josef Pappas, and, according to witnesses, her husband had threatened to divorce Anastasia and write her out of his will. On the night of the murder, she had dismissed the servants and prepared dinner for her husband. George Savalas had had a cold. During dinner, he had suffered a coughing spell. His wife had brought him his bottle of cough medicine. Savalas had taken one swallow and dropped dead.

An open-and-shut case.

Room 33 was crowded with spectators on this early morning. Anastasia Savalas was seated at the defendant's table dressed in a simple black skirt and blouse, with no jewelry and very little make-up. She was stunningly beautiful.

The prosecutor, Peter Demonides, was addressing the jury.

'Ladies and gentlemen. Sometimes, in a murder case, a trial takes up to three or four months. But I don't think any of you are going to have to worry about being here for that length of time. When you hear the facts in this case, I'm sure you will agree without question that there is only one possible verdict – murder in the first degree. The State will prove that the defendant willfully murdered her husband because he threatened to divorce her when he found out she was having an affair with the family chauffeur. We will prove that the defendant had the motive, the opportunity, and the means to carry out her cold-blooded scheme. Thank you.' He returned to his seat.

The Chief Justice turned toward Chotas: 'Is the counsel for the defense prepared to make his opening statement?'

Napoleon Chotas rose slowly to his feet. 'Yes, Your Honor.'

He moved toward the jury box in an uncertain, shuffling gait. He stood there blinking at them, and when he spoke it was almost as though he were speaking to himself. 'I've lived a long time, and I've learned that no man or woman can hide an evil nature. It always shows. A poet once said that the eyes are the windows of the soul. I believe that's true. I want you ladies and gentlemen to look into the eyes of the defendant. There is no way she could have found it in her heart to murder anyone.' Napoleon Chotas stood there a moment as though trying to think of something else to say, then shuffled back to his seat.

Peter Demonides was filled with a sudden sense of triumph. *Jesus Christ. That's the weakest opening I have ever heard in my life! The old man's lost it.*

'Is the Prosecuting Attorney prepared to call his first witness?'

'Yes, Your Honor. I would like to call Rosa Lykourgos.'

A middle-aged, heavy-set woman rose from the spectators' bench and sailed determinedly toward the front of the court-room. She was sworn in.

'Mrs Lykourgos, what is your occupation?'

'I am the housekeeper . . .' Her voice choked up, 'I *was* the housekeeper to Mr Savalas.'

'Mr George Savalas?'

'Yes, sir.'

'And would you tell us how long you were employed by Mr Savalas?'

'Twenty-five years.'

'My, that's a long time. Were you fond of your employer?'

'He was a saint.'

'Were you employed by Mr Savalas during his first marriage?'

'Yes, sir. I was at the graveside with him when his wife was buried.'

'Would it be fair to say that they had a good relationship?'

'They were madly in love with each other.'

Peter Demonides looked over at Napoleon Chotas, waiting for his objection on the line of questioning. But Chotas remained in his seat, apparently lost in thought.

Peter Demonides went on. 'And were you in Mr Savalas'

employ during his second marriage, to Anastasia Savalas?'

'Oh, yes, sir. I certainly was.' She spat the words out.

'Would you say that it was a happy marriage?' Again he glanced at Napoleon Chotas, but there was no reaction.

'Happy? No, sir. They fought like cats and dogs.'

'Did you witness any of these fights?'

'A person couldn't help it. You could hear them all over the house – and it's a big house.'

'I take it these fights were verbal, rather than physical? That is, Mr Savalas never struck his wife?'

'Oh, it was physical all right. But it was the other way around, it was the madam who struck *him*. Mr Savalas was getting on in years, and the poor man had become frail.'

'You actually saw Mrs Savalas strike her husband?'

'More than once.' The witness looked over at Anastasia Savalas, and there was grim satisfaction in her voice.

'Mrs Lykourgos, on the night Mr Savalas died, which members of the staff were working in the house?'

'None of us.'

Peter Demonides let his voice register surprise. 'You mean in a house that you say was so large, not one member of the staff was there? Didn't Mr Savalas employ a cook, or a maid . . . a butler . . . ?'

'Oh, yes, sir. We had all of those. But the madam told everyone to take that night off. She said she wanted to cook dinner for her husband herself. It was going to be a second honeymoon.' The last remark was said with a snort.

'So Mrs Savalas got rid of everybody?'

This time it was the Chief Justice who looked over at Napoleon Chotas, waiting for him to object. But the attorney sat there, preoccupied.

The Chief Justice turned to Demonides. 'The Prosecutor will stop leading the witness.'

'I apologize, Your Honor. I'll rephrase the question.'

Demonides moved closer to Mrs Lykourgos. 'What you are saying is that on a night when members of the staff ordinarily would be in the house, Mrs Savalas ordered everyone to leave so that she could be alone with her husband?'

'Yes, sir. And the poor man was suffering from a terrible cold.'

'Did Mrs Savalas often cook dinner for her husband?'

Mrs Lykourgos sniffed. 'Her? No, sir. Not her. She never lifted a finger around the house.'

And Napoleon Chotas sat there, listening as though he were merely a spectator.

'Thank you, Mrs Lykourgos. You've been very helpful.'

Peter Demonides turned to Chotas, trying to conceal his satisfaction. Mrs Lykourgos' testimony had had a perceptible effect on the jury. They were casting disapproving glances at the defendant. *Let's see the old man try to get around that.* 'Your witness.'

Napoleon Chotas glanced up. 'What? Oh, no questions.'

The Chief Justice looked at him in surprise. 'Mr Chotas . . . you don't wish to cross-examine this witness?'

Napoleon Chotas rose to his feet. 'No, Your Honor. She seems like a perfectly honest woman.' He sat down again.

Peter Demonides could not believe his good fortune. *My God*, he thought, *he's not even putting up a fight. The old man's finished.* Demonides was already savoring his victory.

The Chief Justice turned to the Prosecuting Attorney. 'You may call your next witness.'

'The State would like to call Josef Pappas.'

A tall, good-looking, dark-haired young man rose from the spectators' bench and walked toward the witness box. He was sworn in.

Peter Demonides began. 'Mr Pappas, would you please tell the court your occupation?'

'I'm a chauffeur.'

'Are you employed at the moment?'

'No.'

'But you were employed until recently. That is, you were employed until the death of George Savalas.'

'That's right.'

'How long were you employed by the Savalas family?'

'A little over a year.'

'Was it a pleasant job?'

90

Josef Pappas had one eye on Chotas, waiting for him to come to his rescue. There was only silence.

'Was it a pleasant job, Mr Pappas?'

'It was okay, I guess.'

'Did you get a good salary?'

'Yes.'

'Then wouldn't you say the job was more than okay? I mean, weren't there some extras that went along with it? Weren't you going to bed regularly with Mrs Savalas?'

Josef Pappas looked toward Napoleon Chotas for help. But there was none.

'I . . . Yes, sir. I guess I was.'

Peter Demonides was withering in his scorn. 'You *guess* you were? You're under oath. You either had an affair with her or you didn't. Which is it?'

Pappas was squirming in his seat. 'We had an affair.'

'Even though you were working for her husband – being paid generously by him, and living under his roof?'

'Yes, sir.'

'It didn't bother you, to take Mr Savalas' money week after week while you were having an affair with his wife?'

'It wasn't just an affair.'

Peter Demonides baited the trap carefully. 'It wasn't just an affair? What do you mean by that? I'm afraid I don't understand.'

'I mean – me and Anastasia were planning to get married.'

There was a surprised murmur from the courtroom. The jurors were staring at the defendant.

'Was the marriage your idea, or Mrs Savalas'?'

'Well, we both wanted to.'

'Who suggested it?'

'I guess she did.' He looked over toward where Anastasia Savalas was seated. She returned his look without flinching.

'Frankly, Mr Pappas, I'm puzzled. How did you expect to get married? Mrs Savalas already had a husband, hadn't she? Did you plan to wait for him to die of old age? Or have a fatal accident of some kind? What exactly did you have in mind?'

The questions were so inflammatory that the Prosecutor and the three judges looked toward Napoleon Chotas, waiting for him to thunder an objection. But the defense lawyer was busily doodling, paying no attention. Anastasia Savalas, too, was beginning to look concerned.

Peter Demonides pressed his advantage. 'You haven't answered my question, Mr Pappas.'

Josef Pappas shifted uncomfortably in his chair. 'I don't know, exactly.'

Peter Demonides' voice was a whiplash. 'Then let me tell you, *exactly*. Mrs Savalas planned to murder her husband to get him out of the way. She knew that her husband was going to divorce her and cut her out of his will, and that she would be left with nothing. She . . .'

'Objection!' It came not from Napoleon Chotas, but from the Chief Justice. 'You're asking the witness to speculate.' He looked over at Napoleon Chotas, surprised at the silence of the lawyer. The old man was sitting back on the bench, his eyes half-closed.

'Sorry, Your Honor.' But he knew he had made his point. Peter Demonides turned to Chotas. 'Your witness.'

Napoleon Chotas rose. 'Thank you, Mr Demonides. No questions.'

The three Justices turned to look at one another, puzzled. One of them spoke up: 'Mr Chotas, you are aware that this will be your only opportunity to cross-examine this witness?'

Napoleon Chotas blinked. 'Yes, Your Honor.'

'In view of his testimony, you don't wish to ask him any questions?'

Napoleon Chotas waved a hand in the air and said, vaguely, 'No, Your Honor.'

The judge sighed, 'Very well. The Prosecutor may call his next witness.'

The next witness was Mihalis Haritonides, a burly man in his sixties.

When Haritonides was sworn in, the Prosecutor asked: 'Would you tell the court your occupation, please?'

'Yes, sir. I manage a hotel.'

'Would you tell us the name of the hotel?'

'The Argos.'

'And this hotel is located where?'

'In Corfu.'

'I'm going to ask you, Mr Haritonides, whether any of the people in this room have ever stayed at your hotel.'

Haritonides looked around and said, 'Yes, sir. Him and her.'

'Let the record show that the witness is pointing to Josef Pappas and Anastasia Savalas.' He turned back to the witness. 'Did they stay at your hotel more than once?'

'Oh, yes, sir. They were there half a dozen times, at least.'

'And they spent the night there, together, in the same room?'

'Yes, sir. They usually came for the weekend.'

'Thank you, Mr Haritonides.' He looked at Napoleon Chotas. 'Your witness.'

'No questions.'

The Chief Justice turned to the other two Justices, and they whispered among themselves for a moment.

The Chief Justice looked toward Napoleon Chotas. 'You have no questions for this witness, Mr Chotas?'

'No, Your Honor. I believe his testimony. It's a nice hotel. I've stayed there myself.'

The Chief Justice stared at Napoleon Chotas for a long moment. Then he turned to the Prosecutor. 'The State may call its next witness.'

'The State would like to call Dr Vassilis Frangescos.'

A tall, distinguished-looking man rose and moved toward the witness box. He was sworn in.

'Dr Frangescos, would you be good enough to tell the court what kind of medicine you practice?'

'I'm a general practitioner.'

'Is that equivalent to a family doctor?'

'It's another way of putting it, yes.'

'How long have you been in practice, Doctor?'

'Almost thirty years.'

'And you are licensed by the State, of course.'

'Of course.'

'Dr Frangescos, was George Savalas a patient of yours?'

'Yes, he was.'

'For what period of time?'

'A little more than ten years.'

93

'And were you treating Mr Savalas for any specific problem?'

'Well, the first time I saw him, he came to me because he had high blood pressure.'

'And you treated him for that.'

'Yes.'

'But you saw him after that?'

'Oh, yes. He would come to see me from time to time – when he had bronchitis, or a liver ailment – nothing serious.'

'When was the last time you saw Mr Savalas?'

'In December of last year.'

'That was shortly before he died.'

'That's right.'

'Did he come to your office, Doctor?'

'No. I went to see him at his home.'

'Do you usually make house calls?'

'Not usually, no.'

'But in this case you made an exception.'

'Yes.'

'Why?'

The doctor hesitated. 'Well, he wasn't in any shape to come to the office.'

'What shape was he in?'

'He had lacerations, some bruised ribs, and a concussion.'

'Was he in some kind of accident?'

Dr Frangescos hesitated. 'No. He told me he had been beaten by his wife.'

There was an audible gasp from the courtroom.

The Chief Justice said, angrily, 'Mr Chotas, aren't you going to object to putting hearsay testimony into the record?'

Napoleon Chotas looked up and said mildly, 'Oh, thank you, Your Honor. Yes, I object.'

But, of course, the damage had already been done. The jurors were now looking at the defendant with overt hostility.

'Thank you, Dr Frangescos. No more questions.' Peter Demonides turned to Chotas and said smugly, 'Your witness.'

'No questions.'

*

94

There followed a steady flow of witnesses: a maid who testified that she had seen Mrs Savalas going into the chauffeur's quarters on several occasions . . . a butler who testified that he had heard George Savalas threaten to divorce his wife and change his will . . . neighbors who had heard the noisy arguments between the Savalases . . .

And still Napoleon Chotas had no questions for any of the witnesses.

The net was fast closing in on Anastasia Savalas.

Peter Demonides could already feel the glow of victory. In his mind's eye he could see the headlines in the newspapers. This trial was going to be the fastest murder trial in history. *This trial could even end today*, he thought. *The great Napoleon Chotas is a beaten man.*

'I would like to call Mr Niko Mentakis to the stand.'

Mentakis was a thin, earnest young man, with a slow and careful manner of speech.

'Mr Mentakis, would you tell the court your occupation please?'

'Yes, sir. I work at a nursery.'

'You take care of children?'

'Oh no, sir. It's not that kind of nursery. We have trees and flowers, and all kinds of plants.'

'Oh, I see. So you are an expert on growing things.'

'I should be. I've been at it for a long time.'

'And I presume that a part of your job is to make sure that the plants you have for sale stay healthy?'

'Oh, yes, sir. We take very good care of them. We wouldn't sell any ailing plants to our customers. Most of them are regulars.'

'By that, you mean the same customers keep coming back to you?'

'Yes, sir.' His voice was proud. 'We give good service.'

'Tell me, Mr Mentakis, was Mrs Savalas one of your regular customers?'

'Oh, yes, sir. Mrs Savalas loves plants and flowers.'

The Chief Justice said impatiently, 'Mr Demonides, the court does not feel that this line of questioning is pertinent. Would you move on to something else, or . . .'

'If the court will let me finish, Your Honor, this witness has a very important bearing on the case.'

The Chief Justice looked toward Napoleon Chotas. 'Mr Chotas, do you have any objection to this line of questioning?'

Napoleon Chotas looked up and blinked. 'What? No, Your Honor.'

The Chief Justice stared at him in frustration, and then turned to Peter Demonides. 'Very well. You may proceed.'

'Mr Mentakis, did Mrs Savalas come to you one day in December and tell you that she was having problems with some of her plants?'

'Yes, sir. She did.'

'In fact, didn't she say that there was an infestation of insects that was destroying her plants?'

'Yes, sir.'

'And didn't she ask you for something to get rid of them?'

'Yes, sir.'

'Would you tell the court what it was?'

'I sold her some antimony.'

'And would you tell the court exactly what that is?'

'It's a poison, like arsenic.'

There was an uproar from the courtroom.

The Chief Justice slammed down his gavel. 'If there's another outburst, I'm going to order the bailiff to clear this court.' He turned to Peter Demonides. 'You may continue the questioning.'

'So you sold her a quantity of antimony.'

'Yes, sir.'

'And would you say it's a deadly poison? You compared it to arsenic.'

'Oh, yes, sir. It's deadly, all right.'

'And you entered the sale in your record book, as you are required to do by law when you sell any poison?'

'Yes, sir.'

'And did you bring those records with you, Mr Mentakis?'

'I did.' He handed Peter Demonides a ledger.

The Prosecuting Attorney walked over to the judges. 'Your Honors, I would like this to be labelled Exhibit A.' He turned to the witness. 'I have no more questions.' He looked over at Napoleon Chotas.

Napoleon Chotas looked up and shook his head. 'No questions.'

Peter Demonides took a deep breath. It was time for his bombshell. 'I would like to introduce Exhibit B.' He turned toward the back of the room, and said to a bailiff standing near the door, 'Would you bring it in now, please?'

The bailiff hurried out and a few moments later he returned carrying a bottle of cough syrup on a tray. There was a noticeable amount missing. The spectators watched, fascinated, as the bailiff handed the bottle to the Prosecutor. Peter Demonides placed it on a table in front of the jurors.

'Ladies and gentlemen, you are looking at the murder weapon. This is the weapon that killed George Savalas. This is the cough syrup that Mrs Savalas administered to her husband on the night he died. It is loaded with antimony. As you can see, the victim swallowed some – and twenty minutes later he was dead.'

Napoleon Chotas rose to his feet, and said mildly, 'Objection. There is no way the Prosecuting Attorney has of knowing that it was from that particular bottle that the deceased was medicated.'

And Peter Demonides slammed the trap shut. 'With all due respect to my learned colleague, Mrs Savalas has admitted that she gave her husband this syrup during a coughing spell on the night he died. It has been kept under lock and key by the police until it was brought into this court a few minutes ago. The coroner has testified that George Savalas died of antimony poisoning. This cough syrup is loaded with antimony.' He looked at Napoleon Chotas challengingly.

Napoleon Chotas shook his head in defeat. 'Then I guess there's no doubt.'

Peter Demonides said triumphantly, 'None at all. Thank you, Mr Chotas. The prosecution rests its case.'

The Chief Justice turned to Napoleon Chotas. 'Is the defense ready for its summation?'

Napoleon Chotas rose. 'Yes, Your Honour.'

He stood there for a long moment. Then he slowly ambled forward. He stood in front of the jury box, scratching his head as though trying to figure out what he was going to say. When he finally began, he spoke slowly, searching for words.

'I suppose some of you must be wondering why I haven't cross-examined any of the witnesses. Well, to tell you the truth, I thought Mr Demonides here did such a fine job that it wasn't necessary for me to ask them any questions.'

The fool is pleading my case for me, Peter Demonides thought gleefully.

Napoleon Chotas turned to look at the bottle of cough syrup for a moment, then turned back to the jurors. 'All the witnesses seemed very honest. But they didn't really prove anything, did they? What I mean is . . .' He shook his head. 'Well, when you add everything up that those witnesses said, it comes down to just one thing: a pretty young girl is married to an old man who probably couldn't satisfy her sexually.' He nodded toward Josef Pappas. 'So she found a young man who could. But we all knew that much from the newspapers, didn't we? There's nothing secret about their affair. The whole world knew about it. It's been written up in every trashy magazine in the world. Now, you and I might not approve of her behavior, ladies and gentlemen, but Anastasia Savalas is not on trial here for adultery. She's not in this court because she has normal sexual urges that any young woman might have. No, she's being tried in this court for murder.'

He turned to look at the bottle again, as though fascinated by it.

Let the old man rave on, Peter Demonides thought. He glanced up at the clock on the courtroom wall. It was five minutes to twelve. The judges always called a recess at noon. *The old fool won't be able to finish his summation*. He wasn't even smart enough to wait until court was recessed again. *Why was I ever afraid of him?* Peter Demonides wondered.

Napoleon Chotas was rambling on. 'Let's examine the evidence together, shall we? Some plants of Mrs Savalas were ailing and she cared enough about them to want to save them. She went to Mr Mentakis, a plant expert, who advised her to use antimony. So she followed his advice. Do you call that murder? I certainly don't. And then there's the testimony of the housekeeper, who said that Mrs Savalas sent all the servants away so she could have a honeymoon dinner with her husband that she was going to prepare for him. Well, I think the truth is that the housekeeper was probably half in love with Mr Savalas herself. You don't work for a man for twenty-five years unless you have pretty deep feelings for him. She resented Anastasia Savalas. Couldn't you tell that from her tone?' Chotas coughed slightly and cleared his throat. 'So, let us assume that the defendant, deep in her heart, really loved her husband, and she was trying desperately to make the marriage work. How does any woman show love for a man? Well, one of the most basic ways, I guess, is to cook for him. Isn't that a form of love? I think it is.' He turned to look at the bottle again. 'And isn't another to tend to him when he's ill – in sickness and in health?'

The clock on the wall showed one minute to twelve.

'Ladies and gentlemen, I told you when this trial began to look into the face of this woman. That's not the face of a murderess. Those aren't the eyes of a killer.'

Peter Demonides watched the jurors as they stared at the defendant. He had never seen such open hostility. He had the jury in his pocket.

'The law is very clear, ladies and gentlemen. As you will be informed by our honorable judges, in order to return a verdict of guilty, you must have no doubt at all about the guilt of the defendant. None.'

As Napoleon Chotas talked, he coughed again, drawing a handkerchief from his pocket to cover his mouth. He walked over to the bottle of syrup on the table in front of the jury.

'When you come right down to it, the Prosecutor hasn't proved anything, really, has he? Except that this is the bottle Mrs Savalas handed to her husband. The truth is, the State has no case at all.' As he finished the sentence, he had a coughing spell. Unconsciously, he reached for the bottle of cough medicine, unscrewed the cap, raised the bottle to his lips and took a large swallow. Everyone in the courtroom stared, mesmerized, and there was a gasp of horror.

The courtroom was in an uproar.

The Chief Justice said in alarm, 'Mr Chotas . . .'

99

Napoleon Chotas took another swallow. 'Your Honor, the Prosecutor's case is a mockery of justice. George Savalas did not die at the hands of this woman. The defense rests its case.'

The clock struck twelve. A bailiff hurried up to the Chief Justice and whispered.

The Chief Justice pounded his gavel. 'Order! Order! We are going to recess. The jury will retire and try to reach a verdict. Court will reconvene at two o'clock.'

Peter Demonides was standing there, transfixed. Someone had switched bottles! But no, that was impossible. The evidence had been guarded every moment. Could the pathologist have been that wrong? Demonides turned to speak to his assistant, and when he looked around for Napoleon Chotas, he had disappeared.

At two o'clock, when the court reconvened, the jury slowly filed into the courtroom and took their seats. Napoleon Chotas was missing.

The son-of-a-bitch is dead, Peter Demonides thought.

And even as he was thinking it, Napoleon Chotas walked through the door, looking perfectly healthy. Everyone in the courtroom turned around to stare at him as he walked to his seat.

The Chief Justice said, 'Ladies and gentlemen of the jury, have you reached a verdict?'

The foreman of the jury stood up. 'We have, Your Honor. We find the defendant not guilty.'

There was a spontaneous burst of applause from the spectators.

Peter Demonides felt the blood drain from his face. *The bastard has done it to me again*, he thought. He glanced up and Napoleon Chotas was watching him, grinning.

Chapter 8

The firm of Tritsis and Tritsis was without question the most prestigious law firm in Greece. The founders had long since retired, and the firm belonged to Napoleon Chotas. There were half a dozen partners, but Chotas was the guiding genius.

Whenever people of wealth were accused of murder, their thoughts invariably turned to Napoleon Chotas. His record was phenomenal. In his years of defending people accused of capital crimes, Chotas had scored success after success. The recent trial of Anastasia Savalas had made headlines all over the world. Chotas had defended a client in what everyone thought was a clear-cut case of murder, and he had won a spectacular victory. He had taken a big risk with that one, but he had known that it was the only way he could save his client's life.

He smiled to himself as he recalled the faces of the jurors when he had taken a swallow of the syrup loaded with a deadly poison. He had carefully timed his summation so that he would be interrupted at exactly twelve o'clock. That was the key to everything. If the judges had changed their fixed routine and gone past twelve o'clock . . . He shuddered to think what would have happened.

As it was, an unexpected occurrence had arisen that had nearly cost him his life. After the recess, Chotas was hurrying down the corridor when a group of reporters blocked his path.

'Mr Chotas, how did you know the cough syrup wasn't poisoned . . . ?'

'Can you explain how . . . ?'

'Do you think someone switched bottles . . . ?'

'Did Anastasia Savalas have . . . ?'

'Please, gentlemen. I'm afraid I have to answer a call of nature. I'll be happy to answer your questions later.'

He hurried on to the men's room at the end of the corridor. A sign on the knob read: 'Out of Order'.

A reporter said, 'I guess you'll have to find another men's room.'

Napoleon Chotas grinned. 'I'm afraid I can't wait.' He pushed the door open, walked in and locked it behind him.

The team was inside, waiting for him. The doctor complained, 'I was beginning to get worried. Antimony works fast.' He snapped at his assistant. 'Get the stomach pump ready.'

'Yes, Doctor.'

The doctor turned to Napoleon Chotas. 'Lie on the floor. I'm afraid this is going to be unpleasant.'

'When I consider the alternative,' Napoleon Chotas grinned, 'I'm sure I won't mind.'

Napoleon Chotas' fee for saving Anastasia Savalas' life was one million dollars, deposited in a Swiss bank account. Chotas had a palatial home in Kolonarai – a lovely residential section of Athens – a villa on the island of Corfu, and an apartment in Paris on Avenue Foch.

All in all, Napoleon Chotas had excellent reason to be pleased with his life. There was only one cloud on his horizon.

His name was Frederick Stavros, and he was the newest member of Tritsis and Tritsis. The other lawyers in the firm were constantly complaining about Stavros.

'He's second-rate, Napoleon. He doesn't belong in a firm like this . . .'

'Stavros almost bungled my case. The man's a fool . . .'

'Did you hear what Stavros did yesterday in court? The judge almost threw him out . . .'

'Damn it, why don't you fire that Stavros fellow? He's a fifth wheel here. We don't need him, and he's hurting our reputation.'

Napoleon Chotas was only too well aware of that. And he was almost tempted to blurt out the truth. *I can't fire him.* But all he said was, 'Give him a chance. Stavros will work out fine.'

And that was all his partners could get out of him.

*

A philosopher once said, 'Be careful what you wish for; you might get it.'

Frederick Stavros, the junior member of Tritsis and Tritsis, had gotten his wish, and it had made him one of the most miserable men on earth. He was unable to sleep or eat, and his weight had dropped alarmingly.

'You must see a doctor, Frederick,' his wife insisted. 'You look terrible.'

'No, I . . . it wouldn't do any good.'

He knew that what was wrong with him was something no doctor could cure. His conscience was killing him.

Frederick Stavros was an intense young man, eager, ambitious, and idealistic. For years he had worked out of a shabby office in the poor Monastiraki section of Athens, fighting for indigent clients, often working without fees. When he had met Napoleon Chotas, his life changed overnight.

A year earlier, Stavros had defended Larry Douglas, on trial with Noelle Page for the murder of Douglas' wife, Catherine. Napoleon Chotas had been hired by the powerful Constantin Demiris to defend his mistress. From the beginning, Stavros had been happy to let Chotas take charge of both defenses. He was in awe of the brilliant lawyer.

'You should see Chotas in action,' he would say to his wife. 'The man is incredible. I wish I could join his firm some day.'

As the trial was nearing its end, it took an unexpected turn. A smiling Napoleon Chotas assembled Noelle Page, Larry Douglas and Frederick Stavros in a private chamber.

Chotas said to Stavros, 'I have just had a conference with the judges. If the defendants are willing to change their pleas to guilty, the judges have agreed to give each of them a five-year sentence, four years of which will be suspended. In reality they will never have to serve more than six months.' He turned to Larry. 'Because you are an American, Mr Douglas, you will be deported. You will never be permitted to return to Greece.'

Noelle Page and Larry Douglas had eagerly agreed to change

103

their pleas. Fifteen minutes later, as the defendants and their lawyers stood in front of the bench, the Chief Justice said, 'The Greek courts have never given the death penalty in a case where a murder has not been definitely proven to have been committed. My colleagues and I were, for that reason, frankly surprised when the defendants changed their pleas to guilty in mid-trial . . . I pronounce that the sentence on the two defendants, Noelle Page and Lawrence Douglas, shall be execution by a firing squad . . . to be carried out within ninety days from this date.'

And that was the moment when Stavros knew that Napoleon Chotas had tricked them all. There had never been a deal. Chotas had been hired by Constantin Demiris not to defend Noelle Page, but to make sure she was convicted. This was Demiris' revenge on the woman who had betrayed him. Stavros had been an unwitting party to a cold-blooded frame-up.

I can't let this happen, Stavros thought. *I'll go tell the Chief Justice what Chotas did and the verdict will be overturned.*

And then Napoleon Chotas had come up to Stavros and said, 'If you're free tomorrow, why don't you come and have lunch with me, Frederick? I'd like you to meet my partners . . .'

Four weeks later, Frederick Stavros was a full partner in the prestigious firm of Tritsis and Tritsis, with a large office and a generous salary. He had sold his soul to the devil. But he had come to the realization that it was a bargain too terrible to keep. *I can't go on like this.*

He could not shake off his deep feelings of guilt. *I'm a murderer*, he thought.

Frederick Stavros agonized over his dilemma, and finally came to a decision.

He walked into Napoleon Chotas' office early one morning. 'Leon –.'

'My God, man, you look terrible,' Napoleon Chotas said. 'Why don't you take a little vacation, Frederick? It will do you good.'

104

But Stavros knew that this was not the answer to his problem. 'Leon, I'm very grateful for what you've done for me, but I . . . I can't stay here.'

Chotas looked at him in surprise. 'What are you talking about? You're doing fine.'

'No. I – I'm being torn apart.'

'Torn apart? I don't understand what's bothering you.'

Frederick Stavros stared at him incredulously. 'What . . . what you and I did to Noelle Page and Larry Douglas. Don't you . . . don't you feel any guilt?'

Chotas' eyes narrowed. *Careful.* 'Frederick, sometimes justice must be served by devious means.' Napoleon Chotas smiled. 'Believe me, we have nothing to reproach ourselves with. They were guilty.'

'*We* convicted them. We tricked them. I can't live with it any longer. I'm sorry. I'm giving you my notice. I'll stay here until the end of the month.'

'I won't accept your resignation,' Chotas said firmly. 'Why don't you do as I suggest – take a vacation and . . . ?'

'No. I could never be happy here, knowing what I know. I'm sorry.'

Napoleon Chotas studied him, his eyes hard. 'Do you have any idea what you're doing? You're throwing away a brilliant career . . . your life.'

'No. I'm saving my life.'

'So you've definitely made up your mind?'

'Yes. I'm really sorry, Leon. But you don't have to worry, I won't ever discuss – what happened.' He turned and walked out of the office.

Napoleon Chotas sat at his desk for a long time, lost in thought. Finally, he made a decision. He picked up the telephone and dialed a number. 'Would you tell Mr Demiris I must meet with him this afternoon? Tell him it's urgent.'

At four o'clock that afternoon, Napoleon Chotas was seated in Constantin Demiris' office.

'What's the problem, Leon?' Demiris asked.

105

'There may not be a problem,' Chotas replied carefully, 'but I thought I should inform you that Frederick Stavros came in to see me this morning. He's decided to quit the firm.'

'Stavros? Larry Douglas' lawyer? So?'

'It seems that his conscience is bothering him.'

There was a heavy silence.

'I see.'

'He promised not to discuss what . . . what occurred that day in court.'

'Do you believe him?'

'Yes. As a matter of fact, I do, Costa.'

Constantin Demiris smiled. 'Well, then. We have nothing to worry about, have we?'

Napoleon Chotas rose, relieved. 'I suppose not. I just thought you should know.'

'You were right to tell me. Are you free for dinner next week?'

'Of course.'

'I'll give you a call, and we'll arrange something.'

'Thank you, Costa.'

On Friday, in the late afternoon, the ancient Kapnikarea Church in downtown Athens was filled with the sound of silence, peaceful and hushed. In a corner next to the altar, Frederick Stavros knelt before Father Konstantinou. The priest placed a cloth over Stavros' head.

'I have sinned, Father. I am beyond redemption.'

'Man's great trouble, my son, is that he thinks he is only human. What are your sins?'

'I am a murderer.'

'You have taken lives?'

'Yes, Father. I don't know what to do to atone.'

'God knows what to do. We will ask Him.'

'I let myself be led astray, out of vanity and greed. It happened a year ago. I was defending a man accused of murder. The trial was going well. But then Napoleon Chotas . . .'

*

106

When Frederick Stavros left the church half an hour later, he felt like a different man. It was as though a tremendous burden had been lifted from his shoulders. He felt cleansed by the centuries-old ritual of confession. He had told the priest everything, and for the first time since that terrible day, he felt whole again.

I'll start a new life. I'll move to another city and begin fresh. I'll try to make up somehow for the terrible thing I've done. Thank you, Father, for giving me another chance.

Darkness had fallen and the center of Ermos Square was almost deserted. As Frederick Stavros reached the street corner, the light turned green, and he started to cross. When he reached the middle of the intersection, a black limousine started down the hill, its headlights out, hurtling toward him like a giant, mindless monster. Stavros stared, frozen. It was too late to jump out of the way. There was a thundering roar and Stavros felt his body being smashed and split open. There was an instant of excruciating pain, and then darkness.

Napoleon Chotas was an early riser. He enjoyed his moments of solitude before the pressures of the day began to engulf him. He always breakfasted alone, and read the morning newspapers with his meal. On this particular morning there were several items of interest. Premier Themistocles Sophoulis had formed a new five-party coalition cabinet. *I must send him a note of congratulation.* Chinese communist forces were reported to have reached the north bank of the Yangtze River. Harry Truman and Alben Barkley were inaugurated as President and Vice-President of the United States. Napoleon Chotas turned to page two, and his blood froze. The item that caught his eye read:

> Mr Frederick Stavros, a partner in the prestigious law firm of Tritsis and Tritsis, was struck and killed last evening by a hit-and-run driver as he was leaving Kapnikarea Church. Witnesses report that the vehicle was a black limousine with no license plates. Mr Stavros was a major figure in the sensational murder trial of Noelle Page and Larry Douglas. He was the attorney for Larry Douglas and . . .

107

Napoleon Chotas stopped reading. He sat in his chair, rigid, his breakfast forgotten. An accident. *Was it an accident?* Constantin Demiris had told him there was nothing to worry about. But too many people had made the mistake of taking Demiris at face value.

Chotas reached for the telephone and called Constantin Demiris. A secretary put him through.

'Have you read the morning papers yet?' Chotas asked.

'No, I haven't. Why?'

'Frederick Stavros is dead.'

'*What?*' It was an exclamation of surprise. 'What are you talking about?'

'He was killed last night by a hit-and-run driver.'

'My God. I'm sorry, Leon. Have they caught the driver?'

'No, not yet.'

'Maybe I can put a little extra pressure on the police. Nobody's safe these days. By the way, how is Thursday for you for dinner?'

'Fine.'

'It's a date.'

Napoleon Chotas was an expert at reading between the lines. *Constantin Demiris was genuinely surprised. He had nothing to do with Stavros' death*, Chotas decided.

The following morning, Napoleon Chotas drove into the private garage of his office building and parked his car. As he moved toward the elevator, a young man appeared out of the shadows.

'Do you have a match?'

An alarm in Chotas' mind went off. The man was a stranger, and he had no business being in this garage.

'Certainly.' Without thinking, Chotas slammed his briefcase into the man's face.

The stranger screamed out in pain. 'You son-of-a-bitch!' He reached into his pocket and pulled out a gun with a silencer attached.

'Hey! What's going on here?' a voice called. A uniformed guard was running toward them.

The stranger hesitated for an instant, then ran for the open door.

The guard reached Chotas' side. 'Are you all right, Mr Chotas?'

'Ah . . . yes.' Napoleon Chotas found himself struggling for breath. 'I'm fine.'

'What was he trying to do?'

Napoleon Chotas said slowly, 'I'm not sure.'

It could have been a coincidence, Chotas told himself, as he sat at his desk. *It's possible that the man was simply trying to rob me. But you don't use a gun with a silencer to rob people. No, he intended to kill me.* And Constantin Demiris would have professed to have been as shocked by the news as he had pretended to have been about the death of Frederick Stavros.

I should have known, Chotas thought. *Demiris is not a man to take risks. He can't afford to leave any loose ends. Well, Mr Demiris is in for a surprise.*

Napoleon Chotas' secretary's voice came over the intercom: 'Mr Chotas, you're due in court in thirty minutes.'

Today was his summation in a serial murder case, but Chotas was too shaken to appear in a courtroom. 'Call the judge and explain that I'm ill. Have one of the partners cover for me. No more calls.'

He took a tape recorder from a desk drawer and sat there, thinking. Then he began to speak.

Early that afternoon, Napoleon Chotas appeared at the office of the State Prosecuting Attorney, Peter Demonides, carrying a manila envelope. The receptionist recognized him at once.

'Good afternoon, Mr Chotas. May I help you?'

'I want to see Mr Demonides.'

'He's in a meeting. Do you have an appointment?'

'No. Would you please tell him I'm here, and that it's urgent.'

'Yes, of course.'

Fifteen minutes later, Napoleon Chotas was ushered into the office of the Prosecuting Attorney.

'Well,' Demonides said. 'Mohammed comes to the mountain. What can I do for you? Are we going to do a little plea bargaining this afternoon?'

'No. This is a personal matter, Peter.'

'Sit down, Leon.'

When the two men were seated, Chotas said, 'I want to leave an envelope with you. It's sealed, and it is to be opened only in the event of my accidental death.'

Peter Demonides was studying him, curious. 'Are you expecting something to happen to you?'

'It's a possibility.'

'I see. One of your ungrateful clients?'

'It doesn't matter who. You're the only one I can trust. Can you put this away in a safe where no one can get to it?'

'Of course.' He leaned forward. 'You look frightened.'

'I am.'

'Would you like my office to give you some protection? I could send a policeman along with you.'

Chotas tapped the envelope. 'This is the only protection I need.'

'All right. If you're sure.'

'I'm sure.' Chotas rose and held out his hand. '*Efharisto*. I can't tell you how much I appreciate this.'

Peter Demonides smiled. '*Parakalo*. You owe me one.'

One hour later, a uniformed messenger appeared at the offices of the Hellenic Trade Corporation. He approached one of the secretaries.

'I have a package for Mr Demiris.'

'I'll sign for it.'

'I have orders to deliver it to Mr Demiris personally.'

'I'm sorry, I can't interrupt him. Who is the package from?'

'Napoleon Chotas.'

'You're sure you can't just leave it?'

'Yes, ma'am.'

110

'I'll see if Mr Demiris will accept it.'

She pushed down an intercom switch. 'Excuse me, Mr Demiris. A messenger has a package for you from Mr Chotas.'

Demiris' voice came over the intercom. 'Bring it in, Irene.'

'He says he has orders to deliver it to you personally.'

There was a pause. 'Come in with him.'

Irene and the messenger entered the office.

'Are you Constantin Demiris?'

'Yes.'

'Will you sign for this, please?'

Demiris signed a slip of paper. The messenger laid the envelope on Demiris' desk. 'Thank you.'

Constantin Demiris watched his secretary and the messenger leave. He studied the envelope for a moment, his face thoughtful, then opened it. There was a tape player inside, with a tape in it. Curious, he pressed a button and the tape began to play.

Napoleon Chotas' voice came into the office.

'My dear Costa: Everything would have been so much simpler if you had believed that Frederick Stavros did not intend to reveal our little secret. I regret even more that you did not believe that I had no intention of discussing that unfortunate affair. I have every reason to think that you were behind the death of poor Stavros, and that it is now your intention to have me killed. Since my life is as precious to me as yours is to you, I must respectfully decline to be your next victim . . . I have taken the precaution of writing out the details of the part that you and I played in the trial of Noelle Page and Larry Douglas, and have placed it in a sealed envelope and given it to the Prosecuting Attorney to be opened only in the event of my accidental death. So now it is very much in your interest, my friend, to see that I stay alive and well.'

The tape ended.

Constantin Demiris sat there, staring into space.

*

111

When Napoleon Chotas returned to his office that afternoon, the fear had left him. Constantin Demiris was a dangerous man, but he was far from a fool. He was not going to harm anyone at the risk of putting himself in jeopardy. *He's made his move*, Chotas thought, *and I have checkmated him*. He smiled to himself. *I suppose I had better make other plans for dinner Thursday.*

During the next few days, Napoleon Chotas was busy getting ready for a new murder trial involving a wife who had killed her husband's two mistresses. Chotas rose early each morning and worked until late at night, preparing his cross-examinations. His instincts told him that – against all odds – he had another winner.

On Wednesday night, he worked at the office until midnight, and then drove home. He reached his villa at 1.00 a.m.

His butler greeted him at the door. 'Would you care for anything, Mr Chotas? I can prepare some *mezedes* if you're hungry, or . . . ?'

'No, thank you. I'm fine. Go on to bed.'

Napoleon Chotas went up to his bedroom. He spent the next hour going over the trial in his mind, and finally at two o'clock he fell asleep. He had dreams.

He was in court, cross-examining a witness, when the witness suddenly started to tear off his clothes.

'Why are you doing that?' Chotas demanded.

'I'm burning up.'

Chotas looked around the crowded courtroom and saw that all the spectators were undressing.

He turned to the judge. 'Your Honor, I must object to . . .'

The judge was taking off his robe. 'It's too hot in here,' he said.

It is hot in here. And noisy.

Napoleon Chotas opened his eyes. Flames were licking at the bedroom door and smoke was pouring into the room.

Napoleon sat up, instantly wide awake.

The house is on fire. Why didn't the alarm go off?

The door was beginning to buckle from the intense heat.

112

Chotas hurried to the window, choking on the smoke. He tried to force the window open but it was jammed shut. The smoke was getting thicker, and it was becoming more difficult to breathe. There was no escape.

Burning embers started dropping from the ceiling. A wall collapsed and a sheet of flames engulfed him. He screamed. His hair and pajamas were on fire. Blindly, he threw himself at the closed window and crashed through it, his blazing body hurtling to the ground sixteen feet below.

Early the following morning, State Prosecutor Peter Demonides was ushered into Constantin Demiris' study by a maid.

'*Kalimehra*, Peter,' Demiris said. 'Thank you for coming. Have you brought it?'

'Yes, sir.' He handed Demiris the sealed envelope that Napoleon Chotas had given him. 'I thought you might like to keep this here.'

'That's thoughtful of you, Peter. Would you care for some breakfast?'

'*Efharisto*. That's very kind of you, Mr Demiris.'

'Costa. Call me Costa. I've had my eye on you for some time, Peter. I think you have an important future. I'd like to find a suitable position for you in my organization. Would you be interested?'

Peter Demonides smiled. 'Yes, Costa. I would be very interested.'

'Good. We'll have a nice chat about it over breakfast.'

Chapter 9

London

Catherine spoke to Constantin Demiris at least once a week and it became a pattern. He kept sending gifts and when she protested he assured her that they were merely small tokens of his appreciation. 'Evelyn told me how well you handled the Baxter situation.' Or, 'I heard from Evelyn that your idea is saving us a lot of money in shipping charges.'

As a matter of fact, Catherine was proud of how well she was doing. She had found half a dozen things in the office that could be improved. Her old skills had come back, and she knew that the efficiency of the office had increased a great deal because of her.

'I'm very proud of you,' Constantin Demiris told her.

And Catherine felt a glow. He was such a wonderful, caring man.

It's almost time to make my move, Demiris decided. With Stavros and Chotas safely out of the way, the only person who could link him with what had happened was Catherine. The danger of that was slight but, as Napoleon Chotas had found out, Demiris was not a man to take chances. *It's a pity*, Demiris thought, *that she has to go. She's so beautiful. But first, the villa in Rafina.*

He had bought the villa. He would take Catherine there and make love to her just as Larry Douglas had made love to Noelle. After that . . .

*

From time to time, Catherine was reminded of the past. She read in the London *Times* the news of the deaths of Frederick Stavros and Napoleon Chotas, and the names would have meant nothing to her except for the mention that they had been the attorneys for Larry Douglas and Noelle Page.

That night she had the dream again.

One morning, Catherine saw a newspaper item that jolted her:

> William Fraser, Assistant to US President Harry Truman, has arrived in London to work out a new trade agreement with the British Prime Minister.

She put down the paper, feeling foolishly vulnerable. *William Fraser.* He had been such an important part of her life. *What would have happened if I hadn't left him?*

Catherine sat at her desk, smiling tremulously, staring at the item in the newspaper. William Fraser was one of the dearest men she had ever known. Just the memory of him made her feel warm and loved. And he was here in London. *I have to see him*, she thought. According to the newspaper, he was staying at Claridge's.

Catherine dialed the number of the hotel, and her fingers were trembling. She had a feeling that the past was about to become the present. She found herself thrilled at the thought of seeing Fraser. *What will he say when he hears my voice? When he sees me again?*

The operator was saying, 'Good morning, Claridge's.'

Catherine took a deep breath. 'Mr William Fraser, please.'

'I'm sorry, madam. Did you say Mr or *Mrs* William Fraser?'

Catherine felt as though she had been struck. *What a fool I am. Why didn't I think of that? Of course he could be married by now.*

'Madam . . .'

'I . . . Never mind. Thank you.' She slowly replaced the receiver.

I'm too late. It's over. Costa was right. Let the past remain the past.

*

115

Loneliness can be a corrosive, eating away at the spirit. Everyone needs to share joy and glory and pain. Catherine was living in a world full of strangers, watching the happiness of other couples, hearing the echo of the laughter of lovers. But she refused to feel sorry for herself.

I'm not the only woman in the world who's alone. I'm alive! I'm alive!

There was never a shortage of things to do in London. The London cinemas were filled with American films and Catherine enjoyed going to them. She saw *The Razor's Edge* and *Anna and the King of Siam*. *Gentleman's Agreement* was a disturbing film, and Cary Grant was wonderful in *The Bachelor and the Bobby Soxer*.

Catherine went to concerts at the Albert Hall and attended the ballet at Sadler's Wells. She went to Stratford-upon-Avon to see Anthony Quayle in *The Taming of the Shrew*, and to see Sir Laurence Olivier in *Richard III*. But it was not as much fun going alone.

And then Kirk Reynolds came along.

It was in the office that a tall, attractive man walked up to Catherine and said, 'I'm Kirk Reynolds. Where have you been?'

'I beg your pardon?'

'I've been waiting for you.'

That was how it began.

Kirk Reynolds was an American attorney, working for Constantin Demiris on international mergers. He was in his forties, serious-minded, intelligent and attentive.

When she discussed Kirk Reynolds with Evelyn, Catherine said, 'Do you know what I like about him most? He makes me feel like a woman. I haven't felt that way in a long time.'

'I don't know,' Evelyn demurred. 'I'd be careful if I were you. Don't rush into anything.'

'I won't,' Catherine promised.

*

116

Kirk Reynolds took Catherine on a legal journey through London. They went to the Old Bailey, where criminals had been tried over the centuries, and they wandered through the main hall of the law courts, past grave-looking barristers in wigs and gowns. They visited the site of Newgate Prison, built in the eighteenth century. Just in front of where the prison had been, the road widened, then unexpectedly narrowed again.

'That's odd,' Catherine said. 'I wonder why they built the road like that?'

'To accommodate the crowds. This is where they used to hold public executions.'

Catherine shuddered. It hit too close to home.

One evening, Kirk Reynolds took Catherine to East India Dock Road, along the piers.

'Not too long ago, this was a place where policemen walked in pairs,' Reynolds said. 'It was the hangout for criminals.'

The area was dark and forbidding, and it still looked dangerous to Catherine.

They had dinner at the Prospect of Whitby, one of England's oldest pubs, seated on a balcony built over the Thames, watching the barges move down the river past the big ships that were on their way to sea.

Catherine loved the unusual names of London pubs. Ye Olde Cheshire Cheese and the Falstaff and the Goat In Boots. On another night they went to a colorful old public house in City Road, called The Eagle.

'I'll bet you used to sing about this place when you were a child,' Kirk said.

Catherine stared at him. 'Sing about it? I've never even heard of this place.'

'Yes, you have. The Eagle is where an old nursery rhyme comes from.'

'What nursery rhyme?'

'Years ago, City Road used to be the heart of the tailoring trade and toward the end of the week, the tailors would find

117

themselves short of money, and they'd put their pressing iron –
or weasel – into pawn until payday. So someone wrote a nursery
rhyme about it:
   Up and down the city road
   In and out The Eagle
   That's the way the money goes
   Pop goes the weasel.'
Catherine laughed, 'How in the world did you know that?'
'Lawyers are supposed to know everything. But there's one
thing I don't know. Do you ski?'
'I'm afraid not. Why . . . ?'
He was suddenly serious. 'I'm going to St Moritz. They
have wonderful ski instructors there. Will you come with me,
Catherine?'
The question caught her completely off-guard.
Kirk was waiting for an answer.
'I . . . I don't know, Kirk.'
'Will you think about it?'
'Yes.' Her body was trembling. She was remembering how
exciting it had been to make love with Larry, and she wondered
whether she could ever feel anything like that again. 'I'll think
about it.'

Catherine decided to introduce Kirk to Wim.
They picked Wim up at his flat and took him to The Ivy for
dinner. During the entire evening, Wim never once looked
directly at Kirk Reynolds. He seemed completely withdrawn.
Kirk looked askance at Catherine. She mouthed, *Talk to him.*
Kirk nodded and turned to Wim.
'Do you like London, Wim?'
'It's all right.'
'Do you have a favorite city?'
'No.'
'Do you enjoy your job?'
'It's all right.'
Kirk looked at Catherine, shook his head and shrugged.
Catherine mouthed: *Please.*

118

Kirk sighed, and turned back to Wim. 'I'm playing golf Sunday, Wim. Do you play?'

Wim said, 'In golf the iron-headed clubs are a driving iron midiron mid mashie mashie iron mashie spade mashie mashie niblick niblick shorter niblick and putter. Wooden-headed clubs are the driver brassie spoon and baffy.'

Kirk Reynolds blinked, 'You must be pretty good.'

'He's never played,' Catherine explained. 'Wim just . . . knows things. He can do anything with mathematics.'

Kirk Reynolds had had enough. He had hoped to spend an evening alone with Catherine, and she had brought along this nuisance.

Kirk forced a smile. 'Really?' He turned to Wim and asked innocently, 'Do you happen to know the fifty-ninth power of two?'

Wim sat there in silence for thirty seconds studying the tablecloth, and, as Kirk was about to speak, Wim said, '576,460,752,303,423,488.'

'Jesus!' Kirk said. 'Is that for real?'

'Yeah,' Wim snarled. 'That's for real.'

Catherine turned to Wim. 'Wim, can you extract the sixth root of . . .' She picked a number at random. '24,137,585?'

They both watched Wim as he sat there, his face expressionless. Twenty-five seconds later he said, 'Seventeen; the remainder is sixteen.'

'I can't believe this,' Kirk exclaimed.

'Believe it,' Catherine told him.

Kirk looked at Wim. 'How did you do that?'

Wim shrugged.

Catherine said, 'Wim can multiply two four-digit numbers in thirty seconds, and memorize fifty phone numbers in five minutes. Once he's learned them, he never forgets them.'

Kirk Reynolds was looking at Wim Vandeen in astonishment. 'My office could certainly use someone like you,' he said.

'I've got a job,' Wim snapped.

*

119

When Kirk Reynolds dropped Catherine off at the end of the evening, he said, 'You won't forget about St Moritz, will you?'

'No. I won't forget.' *Why can't I just say 'yes'?*

Constantin Demiris phoned late that night. Catherine was tempted to tell him about Kirk Reynolds, but at the last moment she decided not to.

Chapter 10

—◆—

Athens

Father Konstantinou was perturbed. From the moment he had seen the newspaper report of Frederick Stavros' hit-and-run death, he had been haunted by it. The priest had heard thousands of confessions since he had been ordained, but the dramatic confession of Frederick Stavros, followed by his death, had left an indelible impression.

'Hey, what's bothering you?'

Father Konstantinou turned to look at the beautiful young man lying naked in bed beside him. 'Nothing, love.'

'Don't I make you happy?'

'You know you do, Georgios.'

'Then what's the problem? You're acting like I'm not here, for Christ's sake.'

'Don't use profanity.'

'I don't like being ignored.'

'I'm sorry, darling. It's just that . . . one of my parishioners was killed in an automobile accident.'

'We all have to go some time, right?'

'Yes, of course. But this was a very troubled man.'

'You mean he was sick in the head?'

'No. He had a terrible secret, and it was too large a burden for him to carry.'

'What kind of secret?'

The priest stroked the young man's thigh. 'You know I can't discuss that. It was told to me in the confessional.'

'I thought we didn't have no secrets from each other.'

'We don't, Georgios, but . . .'

'*Gamoto!* We either do, or we don't. Anyway, you said the guy's dead. What difference can it make now?'

'None, I suppose, but . . .'

Georgios Lato wrapped his arms around his bed partner, and whispered in his ear, 'I'm curious.'

'You're tickling my ear.'

Lato began stroking Father Konstantinou's body.

'Oh . . . don't stop . . .'

'Then tell me.'

'Very well. I suppose it can't really do any harm now . . .'

Georgios Lato had come up in the world. He was born in the slums of Athens, and when he was twelve years old he became a male prostitute. In the beginning Lato had walked the streets, picking up a few dollars for servicing drunks in alleys and tourists in their hotel rooms. He was gifted with dark good looks and a strong, firm body.

When he was sixteen, a pimp said to him: 'You're a *poulaki*, Georgios. You're giving it away. I can set you up to make a lot of money.'

And he kept his promise. From that moment on Georgios Lato serviced only important, wealthy men, and he was handsomely rewarded for it.

When Lato met Nikos Veritos, the personal assistant to the great tycoon, Spyros Lambrou, Lato's life changed.

'I'm in love with you,' Nikos Veritos told the young boy. 'I want you to stop whoring around. You belong to me now.'

'Sure, Niki. I love you, too.'

Veritos was constantly pampering the boy with gifts. He bought his clothes, paid for a small apartment for him and gave him spending money. But he fretted about what Lato was doing when he was away from him.

Veritos solved the problem one day by announcing, 'I've gotten you a job with Spyros Lambrou's company, where I work.'

'So you can keep a fucking eye on me? I won't . . .'

122

'Of course that's not it, sweetheart. I just like to have you near me.'

Georgios Lato had protested at first, but he finally gave in. He found that he actually enjoyed working for the company. He worked in the mail room, and as a delivery boy, and that gave him the freedom to pick up extra money outside, from appreciative clients like Father Konstantinou.

When Georgios Lato left Father Konstantinou's bed that afternoon, his mind was in a turmoil. The secret that the priest had confided to him was a stunning piece of news, and Georgios Lato's mind immediately turned to how he could make money out of it. He could have confided it to Nikos Veritos, but he had bigger plans. *I'm going right to the big boss with this*, Lato told himself. *That's where the real payoff will be.*

The following morning, Lato walked into Spyros Lambrou's reception office.

The secretary behind the desk looked up. 'Oh. The mail's early today, Georgios.'

Georgios Lato shook his head. 'No, ma'am. I have to see Mr Lambrou.'

She smiled. 'Really? What do you want to see him about? Do you have a business proposition for him?' she teased.

Lato said seriously, 'No, it's nothing like that. I just got word that my mother is dying, and I . . . I have to go back home. I just wanted to thank Mr Lambrou for giving me a job here. It would only take a minute, but if he's too busy . . .' He started to turn away.

'Wait. I'm sure he won't mind.'

Ten minutes later, Georgios Lato was standing in Spyros Lambrou's office. He had never been inside before, and the opulence overwhelmed him.

'Well, young man. I'm sorry to hear your mother is dying. Perhaps a small bonus would . . .'

'Thank you, sir. But that's not really why I'm here.'

123

Lambrou frowned at him. 'I don't understand.'

'Mr Lambrou, I have some important information that I think might be valuable to you.'

He could see the skepticism on Lambrou's face. 'Oh really? I'm afraid I'm rather busy, so if you'll . . .'

'It's about Constantin Demiris.' The words tumbled out. 'I have a good friend who's a priest. He heard a confession from a man who was killed right afterward in a car accident, and what the man told him is about Constantin Demiris. Mr Demiris did an awful thing. Really awful. He could go to prison for it. But if you're not interested . . .'

Spyros Lambrou suddenly found himself very interested. 'Sit down . . . what's your name?'

'Lato, sir. Georgios Lato.'

'All right, Lato. Suppose you start at the beginning . . .'

The marriage of Constantin Demiris and Melina had been disintegrating for years, but there had never been any physical violence until recently.

It had started in the middle of a heated argument over an affair Constantin Demiris was having with Melina's closest friend.

'You turn every woman into a whore,' she screamed. 'Everything you touch turns to dirt.'

'*Skaseh!* Shut your fucking mouth.'

'You can't make me,' Melina said defiantly. 'I'm going to tell the whole world what a *pousti* you are. My brother was right. You're a monster.'

Demiris raised his arm and slapped Melina hard across the face. She ran from the room.

The following week they had another argument, and Constantin struck her again. Melina packed her bags and took a plane to Atticos, the private island owned by her brother. She stayed there for a week, miserable and lonely. She missed her husband, and she began to make excuses for what he had done.

It was my fault, Melina thought. *I shouldn't have antagonized Costa.* And: *He didn't mean to hit me. He just lost his temper and didn't know what he was doing.* And: *If Costa didn't care so much about me, he wouldn't have hit me, would he?*

But in the end, Melina knew they were simply excuses, because she could not bear to dissolve her marriage. The following Sunday she returned home.

Demiris was in the library.

He looked up as Melina entered. 'So you decided to come back.'

'This is my home, Costa. You're my husband, and I love you. But I want to tell you something. If you ever touch me again, I will kill you.'

And he looked into her eyes and knew that she meant it.

In an odd way, their marriage seemed to improve after that episode. For a long time after that, Constantin was careful never to lose his temper with Melina. He continued to have his affairs, and Melina was too proud to plead with him to stop. *One day he'll get tired of all his whores*, Melina thought, *and he'll realize that he needs only me.*

On a Saturday evening, Constantin Demiris was putting on a dinner jacket, preparing to go out. Melina came into the room.

'Where are you going?'

'I have an engagement.'

'Have you forgotten? We're having dinner at Spyros' tonight.'

'I haven't forgotten. Something more important has come up.'

Melina stood there watching him, furious. 'And I know what it is – your *poulaki*! And you're going to one of your whores to satisfy it.'

'You should watch your tongue. You're becoming a fishwife, Melina.' Demiris examined himself in the mirror.

'I won't let you do this!' What he was doing to her was bad enough, but to insult her brother deliberately on top of everything that had gone before was too much. She had to find a way to hurt him, and there was only one way she knew. 'We both really should stay home tonight,' Melina said.

125

'Oh, really?' he asked indifferently. 'And why is that?'

'Don't you know what today is?' she taunted him.

'No.'

'It's the anniversary of the day I killed your son, Costa. I had an abortion.'

He stood stock-still, and she could see the pupils of his eyes darken.

'I told the doctors to fix it so I could never have another one of your children,' she lied.

He completely lost control. '*Skaseh!*' And he punched her in the face, and kept hitting.

Melina screamed and turned and ran down the hall, Constantin right behind her.

He caught her at the head of the stairs.

'I'll kill you for that,' he roared. As he hit her again, Melina lost her balance and fell, crashing down the long staircase.

She lay at the bottom, whimpering in pain. 'Oh, God. Help me. I've broken something.'

Demiris stood there, staring down at her, his eyes cold.

'I'll have one of the maids call a doctor. I don't want to be late for my engagement.'

The telephone call came shortly before dinnertime.

'Mr Lambrou? This is Dr Metaxis. Your sister asked me to call you. She's here in my private hospital. I'm afraid she's been in an accident . . .'

When Spyros Lambrou walked into Melina's hospital room, he walked over to her bed, and stared down at her, appalled. Melina had a broken arm, a concussion, and her face was badly swollen.

Spyros Lambrou said one word, 'Constantin.' His voice was trembling with rage.

Melina's eyes filled with tears. 'He didn't mean it,' she whispered.

'I'm going to destroy him. I swear it on my life.' Spyros Lambrou had never felt such rage.

He could not bear the thought of what Constantin Demiris

126

was doing to Melina. There had to be a way to stop him, but how? He was at a loss. He needed advice. As he had so often in the past, Spyros Lambrou decided to consult Madame Piris. Perhaps there was some way in which she would be able to help him.

On the way to see her, Lambrou thought wryly, *My friends would laugh at me if they thought I was consulting a psychic.* But the fact was that in the past, Madame Piris had told him some extraordinary things that had come to pass. *She's got to help me now.*

They were seated at a table in a dark corner of the dimly lit café. She seemed older than when he had last seen her. She sat there, her eyes fastened on him.

'I need some help, Madame Piris,' Lambrou said.

She nodded.

Where to start? 'There was a murder trial about a year and a half ago. A woman named Catherine Douglas was . . .'

The expression on Madame Piris' face changed. 'No,' she moaned.

Spyros Lambrou stared at her, puzzled. 'She was murdered by . . .'

Madam Piris rose. 'No! The spirits told me she would die!'

Spyros Lambrou was confused. 'She *did* die,' he said. 'She was killed by . . .'

'She's alive!'

He was completely bewildered. 'She can't be.'

'She was here. She came to see me three months ago. They kept her at the convent.'

He stared at her, stock still. And suddenly all the pieces fell into place. *They kept her at the convent.* One of Demiris' favorite charitable acts was to give money to the convent at Ioannina, the town where Catherine Douglas was supposed to have been murdered. The information Spyros had received from Georgios Lato fitted in perfectly. Demiris had sent two innocent people

127

to their deaths for Catherine's murder while she had been very much alive, hidden away by the nuns.

And Lambrou knew how he was going to destroy Constantin Demiris.

Tony Rizzoli.

Chapter 11

Tony Rizzoli's problems were multiplying. Everything that could go wrong was going wrong. What had happened was certainly not his fault, but he knew that the Family would hold him responsible. They were not tolerant of excuses.

What made it particularly frustrating was that the first part of the drug operation had gone perfectly. He had smuggled the shipment into Athens with no problems and had it temporarily stored at a warehouse. He had bribed an airline steward to smuggle it out on a flight from Athens to New York. And then, just twenty-four hours before the flight, the idiot had been arrested for drunk driving, and the airline had fired him.

Tony Rizzoli had turned to an alternate plan. He had arranged for a mule – in this case, a seventy-year-old tourist named Sara Murchison who was visiting her daughter in Athens – to take a suitcase back to New York for him. She had no idea what she would be carrying.

'It's some souvenirs I promised to send my mother,' Tony Rizzoli explained, 'and because you're nice enough to do this, I want to pay for your ticket.'

'Oh, that's not necessary,' Sara Murchison protested, 'I'm happy to do it for you. I live not far from your mother's apartment. I look forward to meeting her.'

'And I'm sure she'd like to meet you, too,' Tony Rizzoli said glibly. 'The problem is, she's pretty sick. But there will be someone there to take the suitcase.'

She was perfect for the job – a sweet, all-American grandmother. The only thing customs would be worrying about her smuggling would be knitting needles.

Sara Murchison was to leave for New York the following morning.

129

'I'll pick you up and drive you to the airport.'

'Why, thank you. What a thoughtful young man you are. Your mother must be very proud of you.'

'Yes. We're very close.' His mother had been dead for ten years.

The following morning, as Rizzoli was about to leave his hotel for the warehouse to pick up the package, his telephone rang.

'Mr Rizzoli?' It was a stranger's voice.

'Yes?'

'This is Dr Patsaka at the Athens Hospital Emergency Ward. We have a Mrs Sara Murchison here. She tripped and fell last night and broke her hip. She was very anxious for me to tell you how sorry . . .'

Tony Rizzoli slammed the phone down. '*Merda!*' That was two in a row. Where was he going to find another mule?

Rizzoli knew he had to be careful. There was a rumor that a hot-shot American narcotics agent was in Athens working with the Greek authorities. They were watching all exits from Athens, and planes and ships were routinely being searched.

As if that weren't enough, there was another problem. One of his gowsters – a thief who was an addict – had informed him that the police were beginning to search warehouses, looking for stored drugs and other contraband. The pressure was mounting. It was time to explain the situation to the Family.

Tony Rizzoli left his hotel and walked down Patission Street toward the City Telephone Exchange. He was not sure whether his hotel phone was being bugged, but he did not want to risk the chance.

Number 85 Patission was a large brown stone building with a row of pillars in front, and a plaque that read: O.T.E. Rizzoli walked into the entry and looked around. Two dozen telephone booths lined the walls, each one numbered. Shelves were filled with telephone directories from all over the world. In the center of the room was a desk where four clerks were taking orders for calls to be placed. People were lined up waiting to be put through.

130

Tony Rizzoli approached one of the women behind the desk. 'Good morning,' he said.

'Can I help you?'

'I'd like to place an overseas call.'

'There will be a thirty-minute wait, I'm afraid.'

'No problem.'

'Would you give me the country and the number, please?'

Tony Rizzoli hesitated. 'Sure.' He handed a piece of paper to the woman. 'I'd like to make the call collect.'

'Your name?'

'Brown. Tom Brown.'

'Very well, Mr Brown. I will call you when it comes through.'

'Thank you.'

He went over to one of the benches across the room, and sat down. *I could try to hide the package in an automobile, and pay someone to drive it across the border. But that's risky; cars are searched. Maybe if I could find another . . .*

'Mr Brown . . . Mr Tom Brown . . .' The name was repeated twice before Rizzoli realized it was for him. He rose and hurried over to the desk.

'Your party is accepting the call. Booth seven, please.'

'Thank you. By the way, could I have the piece of paper back that I gave you? I'll need the number again.'

'Certainly.' She handed him back the slip.

Tony Rizzoli walked into booth seven and closed the door.

'Hello.'

'Tony? Is that you?'

'Yeah. How are you, Pete?'

'To tell you the truth, we're a little concerned, Tony. The boys expected the package to be on its way by now.'

'I've had some problems.'

'Has the package been sent?'

'No. It's still here.'

There was a silence. 'We wouldn't want anything to happen to it, Tony.'

'Nothing's going to happen to it. I just have to find another way of getting it out of here. There are goddamned narcs all over the place.'

131

'We're talking ten million dollars, Tony.'
'I know. Don't worry, I'll figure out something.'
'You do that, Tony. You figure out something.'
The line went dead.

A man in a grey suit watched as Tony Rizzoli moved toward the exit. He approached the woman behind the desk.
'*Signomi*. Do you see that man who's just leaving?'
The woman looked up. '*Ochi?*'
'I want to know what number he called.'
'I'm sorry. We're not allowed to give out that information.'
The man reached into his back pocket and took out a wallet. There was a gold shield pinned to it. 'Police. I'm Inspector Tinou.'
Her expression changed. 'Oh. He handed me a slip of paper with a number on it, and then he took it back.'
'But you made a copy for your records?'
'Oh, yes, we always do that.'
'Would you give me the number, please?'
'Of course.'
She wrote a number on a piece of paper and handed it to the inspector. He studied it a moment. The country code was 39, and the exchange was 91. *Italy. Palermo.*
'Thank you. Do you happen to remember what name the man gave you?'
'Yes. It was Brown. Tom Brown.'

The telephone conversation had made Tony Rizzoli nervous. He had to go to the bathroom. *Damn Pete Lucca!* Ahead, on the corner of Kolonaki Square, Rizzoli saw a sign: *Apohoritirion*, WC. Men and women alike were walking through the doorway to use the same facilities. *And the Greeks call themselves civilized*, Rizzoli thought. *Disgusting*.

*

132

There were four men seated around the conference table in the villa in the mountains above Palermo.

'The stuff should've been sent already, Pete,' one of them complained. 'What's the problem?'

'I'm not sure. The problem may be Tony Rizzoli.'

'We've never had no trouble with Tony before.'

'I know – but sometimes people get greedy. I think maybe we better send someone to Athens to check things out.'

'Too bad. I always liked Tony.'

At Number 10 Stadiou Street, police headquarters in downtown Athens, a conference was being held. In the room were Chief of Police Livreri Dmitri, Inspector Tinou and an American, Lieutenant Walt Kelly, an agent with the Customs Division of the US Treasury Department.

'We have word,' Kelly was saying, 'that a big drug deal is going to take place. The shipment is going out of Athens. Tony Rizzoli is involved.'

Inspector Tinou sat silent. The Greek police department did not welcome interference from other countries in their affairs. Particularly Americans. *They are always* too-sou, *so sure of themselves.*

The chief of police spoke up. 'We are already working on it, Lieutenant. Tony Rizzoli made a phone call to Palermo a little while ago. We're tracing the number now. When we have that, we'll have his source.'

The telephone on his desk rang. Dmitri and Inspector Tinou looked at each other.

Inspector Tinou picked up the phone. 'Did you get it?' He listened a moment, his face expressionless, then replaced the receiver.

'Well?'

'They traced the number.'

'And?'

'The call was made to a public telephone booth in the town square.'

'*Gamoto!*'

133

'Our Mr Rizzoli is very *ineh eksipnos*.'

Walt Kelly said impatiently, 'I don't speak Greek.'

'Sorry, Lieutenant. It means he's cunning.'

Kelly said, 'I'd like you to increase the surveillance on him.'

The arrogance of the man. Chief Dmitri turned to Inspector Tinou. 'We really don't have enough evidence to do more, do we?'

'No, sir. Only strong suspicions.'

Chief Dmitri turned to Walt Kelly. 'I'm afraid I can't spare enough men to follow everyone we suspect of being involved in narcotics.'

'But Rizzoli – '

'I assure you, we have our own sources, Mr Kelly. If we get any further information, we know where to reach you.'

Walt Kelly started at him, frustrated. 'Don't wait too long,' he said. 'That shipment will be gone.'

The villa at Rafina was ready. The realtor had said to Constantin Demiris, 'I know you bought it furnished, but if I might suggest some new furniture . . .'

'No. I want everything exactly as it is.'

Exactly as it was when his faithless Noelle and her lover, Larry, were there betraying him. He walked through the living room. *Did they make love here in the middle of the floor? In the den? In the kitchen?* Demiris walked into the bedroom. There was a large bed in the corner. *Their* bed. Where Douglas had caressed Noelle's naked body, where he had stolen what belonged to Demiris. Douglas had paid for his treachery and now he was going to pay again. Demiris looked at the bed. *I'll make love to Catherine here first*, Demiris thought. *Then the other rooms. All of them.* He telephoned Catherine from the villa.

'Hello.'

'I've been thinking about you.'

Tony Rizzoli had two unexpected visitors from Sicily. They walked into his hotel room unannounced, and Rizzoli instantly

134

smelled trouble. Alfredo Mancuso was big. Gino Laveri was bigger.

Mancuso came straight to the point. 'Pete Lucca sent us.'

Rizzoli tried to sound casual. 'That's great. Welcome to Athens. What can I do for you?'

'You can cut the bullshit, Rizzoli,' Mancuso said. 'Pete wants to know what kind of games you're playin'.'

'Games? What are you talking about? I explained to him that I'm having a little problem.'

'That's why we're here. To help you solve it.'

'Wait a minute, fellows,' Rizzoli protested. 'I have the package stashed away, and it's safe. When . . .'

'Pete doesn't want it stashed away. He's got a lot of money invested in it.' Laveri put his fist against Rizzoli's chest, and pushed him into a chair. 'Lemme explain it to you, Rizzoli. If this stuff was out on the streets in New York now like it was supposed to be, Pete could take the money, launder it, and put it to work on the street. See what I mean?'

I could probably take these two gorillas, Rizzoli thought. But he knew he wouldn't be fighting them; he'd be fighting Pete Lucca.

'Sure, I understand exactly what you're saying,' Rizzoli said soothingly. 'But it's not as easy as it used to be. The Greek police are all over the place, and they've got a narc in from Washington. I have a plan . . .'

'So has Pete,' Laveri interrupted. 'Do you know what his plan is? He says to tell you if the stuff isn't on its way by next week you're going to have to come up with the cash yourself.'

'Hey!' Rizzoli protested. 'I don't have that kind of money. I . . .'

'Pete thought maybe you didn't. So he told us to find other ways to make you pay.'

Tony Rizzoli took a deep breath. 'Okay. Just tell him everything's under control.'

'Sure. Meanwhile we'll stick around. You've got one week.'

*

135

Tony Rizzoli made it a point of honor never to drink before noon, but when the two men left, he opened a bottle of Scotch and took two long gulps. He felt the warmth of the Scotch course through him, but it didn't help. *Nothing's going to help*, he thought. *How could the old man turn on me like this? I've been like a son to him and he gives me one week to find a way out of this. I need a mule, fast. The casino*, he decided. *I'll find a mule there.*

At ten o'clock that evening, Rizzoli drove to Loutraki, the popular casino fifty miles west of Athens. He wandered around the huge, busy gaming room, watching the action. There were always plenty of losers, ready to do anything for more gambling money. The more desperate the person, the easier the prey. Rizzoli spotted his target almost immediately at a roulette table. He was a small, birdlike man, grey-haired, in his fifties, who was constantly stabbing at his forehead with a handkerchief. The more he lost, the more he perspired.

Rizzoli watched him with interest. He had seen the symptoms before. This was a classic case of a compulsive gambler losing more than he could afford.

When the chips in front of the man were gone he said to the croupier, 'I . . . I would like to sign for another pile of chips.'

The croupier turned to look at the pit boss.

'Give it to him. That'll be the last.'

Tony Rizzoli wondered how much the pigeon was already hooked for. He took a seat next to the man, and bought into the game. Roulette was a sucker's game, but Rizzoli knew how to play the odds, and his pile of chips grew while that of the man next to him diminished. The loser was desperately spreading chips all over the table, playing the numbers, the colors, and taking odd-even bets. *He has no idea what the hell he's doing*, Rizzoli thought.

The last of the chips were swept away. The stranger sat there, rigid.

He looked up at the croupier hopefully. 'Could I . . . ?'

The croupier shook his head. 'Sorry.'

The man sighed, and rose.

136

Rizzoli stood up at the same time. 'Too bad,' he said sympathetically. 'I've had a little luck. Let me buy you a drink.'

The man blinked. His voice quavered. 'That's very kind of you, sir.'

I've found my mule, Rizzoli thought. The man obviously needed money. He would probably jump at the chance to fly a harmless package to New York for a hundred dollars or so and a free trip to the United States.

'My name is Tony Rizzoli.'

'Victor Korontzis.'

Rizzoli led Korontzis to the bar. 'What will you have?'

'I'm . . . I'm afraid I haven't any money left.'

Tony Rizzoli waved an expansive hand. 'Don't worry about it.'

'Then I'll have a retsina, thank you.'

Rizzoli turned to the waiter. 'And a Chivas Regal on the rocks.'

'Are you here as a tourist?' Korontzis asked politely.

'Yes,' Rizzoli replied. 'I'm on vacation. It's a beautiful country.'

Korontzis shrugged. 'I suppose so.'

'You don't like it here?'

'Oh, it's beautiful, all right. It's just that it's gotten so expensive. I mean, everything's gone up. Unless you're a millionaire, it's hard to put food on the table, especially when you have a wife and four children.' His tone was bitter.

Better and better. 'What do you do, Victor?' Rizzoli asked casually.

'I'm a curator at the Athens State Museum.'

'Yeah? What does a curator do?'

A note of pride crept into Korontzis' voice. 'I'm in charge of all the antiquities that are dug up in Greece.' He took a sip of his drink. 'Well, not *all* of them, of course. We have other museums. The Acropolis, and the National Archaeological Museum. But our museum has the most valuable artifacts.'

Tony Rizzoli found himself becoming interested. 'How valuable?'

Victor Korontzis shrugged. 'Most of them are priceless.

137

There's a law against taking any antiquities out of the country, naturally. But we have a little shop in the museum that sells copies.'

Rizzoli's brain was beginning to work furiously. 'Is that so? How good are the copies?'

'Oh, they're excellent. Only an expert could distinguish between a facsimile and the real thing.'

'Let me buy you another drink,' Rizzoli said.

'Thank you. That's very kind of you. I'm afraid I'm not in a position to reciprocate.'

Rizzoli smiled. 'Don't worry about it. As a matter of fact, there's something you *can* do for me. I'd like to see your museum. It sounds fascinating.'

'Oh, it is,' Korontzis assured him enthusiastically. 'It's one of the most interesting museums in the world. I'd be happy to show you around any time. When would you be free?'

'How about tomorrow morning?'

Tony Rizzoli had a feeling that he was onto something more profitable than a mule.

The Athens State Museum is located off the Platia Syntagma, in the heart of Athens. The museum itself is a beautiful building built in the style of an ancient temple, with four Ionian columns in front, a Greek flag flying on top, and four carved figures on the high roof.

Inside, the large marble halls contain antiquities from various periods of Greek history, and the rooms are crowded with cases of relics and artifacts. There are gold cups and gold crowns, inlaid swords and libation vessels. One case holds four gold burial masks, and another, fragments of centuries-old statues.

Victor Korontzis was giving Tony Rizzoli a personally conducted tour. Korontzis stopped in front of a case holding a figurine of a goddess with a crown of opium poppies. 'That's the poppy goddess,' he explained in a hushed voice. 'The crown is symbolic of her function as the bringer of sleep, dreams, revelation and death.'

'How much would that be worth?'

Korontzis laughed. 'If it were for sale? Many millions.'

138

'Really?'

The little curator was filled with obvious pride as he walked around, pointing out his priceless treasures. 'This is a head of kouros, five hundred and thirty BC . . . this is the head of Athena with a Corinthian helmet, circa fourteen fifty BC . . . and here's a fabulous piece. A gold mask of an Achaean from the royal tomb of the Acropolis of Mycenae, from the sixteenth century BC. It is believed to be Agamemnon.'

'You don't say?'

He led Tony Rizzoli to another case. In it was an exquisite amphora.

'This is one of my favorites,' Korontzis confessed, beaming. 'I know a parent shouldn't have a favorite child but I can't help it. This amphora . . .'

'It looks like a vase to me.'

'Er – yes. This vase was discovered in the throne room during the excavation in Knossos. You can see the fragments showing the capture of a bull with a net. In ancient times, of course, they captured bulls with nets to avoid the premature spilling of their sacred blood, so that . . .'

'How much is it worth?' Rizzoli interrupted.

'I suppose about ten million dollars.'

Tony Rizzoli frowned. 'For *that*?'

'Indeed! You must remember, it came from the Late Minoan period, around fifteen hundred BC.'

Tony was looking around at the dozens of glass cases, crammed with artifacts. 'Is all this stuff that valuable?'

'Oh my, no. Only the real antiquities. They're irreplaceable, of course, and they give us a clue as to how ancient civilizations lived. Let me show you something over here.'

Tony followed Korontzis to another chamber. They stopped in front of a case in the corner.

Victor Korontzis pointed to a vase. 'This is one of our greatest treasures. It's one of the earliest examples of the symbolism of phonetic signs. The circle with the cross that you see is the figure of Ka. The crossed circle is one of the very earliest forms inscribed by human beings to express the cosmos. There are only . . .'

139

Who gives a shit! 'How much is it worth?' Tony demanded.
Korontzis sighed. 'A king's ransom.'

When Tony Rizzoli left the museum that morning, he was counting riches beyond his wildest dreams. By a fantastic stroke of luck he had stumbled upon a gold mine. He had been looking for a mule, and instead, he had found the key to a treasure-house. The profits from the heroin deal would have to be split six ways. Nobody was stupid enough to double-cross the Family; but the antiques caper was something else again. If he smuggled artifacts out of Greece, it would be a side deal that belonged only to him; the mob would not expect anything from it. Rizzoli had every reason to be elated. *Now all I have to do*, Rizzoli thought, *is to figure out how to hook the fish. I'll worry about the mule later.*

That evening, Rizzoli took his new-found friend to the Mostrov Athena, a nightclub where the entertainment was lewd, and amorous hostesses were available after the show.

'Let's pick up a couple of broads and have some fun,' Rizzoli suggested.

'I should be getting home to my family,' Korontzis protested. 'Besides, I'm afraid I couldn't afford anything like that.'

'Hey, you're my guest. I'm on an expense account. It doesn't cost me anything.'

Rizzoli arranged for one of the girls to take Victor Korontzis back to her hotel.

'Aren't you coming?' Korontzis asked.

'I have a little business to handle,' Tony told him. 'You go ahead. Everything's taken care of.'

The following morning, Tony Rizzoli dropped in at the museum again. There was a large crowd of tourists walking through the various rooms, marvelling at the ancient treasures.

Korontzis took Rizzoli into his office. He was actually blushing. 'I . . . I don't know how to thank you for last night, Tony. She . . . it was wonderful.'

Rizzoli smiled. 'What are friends for, Victor?'

'But there's nothing I can do for you in return.'

'I don't expect you to,' Rizzoli said earnestly. 'I like you. I like your company. By the way, there's a little poker game in one of the hotels tonight. I'm going to play. Are you interested?'

'Thanks. I'd love to, but . . .' He shrugged. 'I don't think I'd better.'

'Come on. If it's money that's bothering you, don't worry about it. I'll stake you.'

Korontzis shook his head. 'You have been too kind already. If I lost, I couldn't pay you back.'

Tony Rizzoli grinned. 'Who said you're going to lose? It's a set-up.'

'A set-up? I . . . I don't understand.'

Rizzoli said quietly, 'A friend of mine named Otto Dalton is running the game. There are some big-money American tourists in town who love to gamble, and Otto and I are going to take them.'

Korontzis was looking at him, wide-eyed. 'Take them? You mean, you're . . . you're going to cheat?' Korontzis licked his lips. 'I . . . I've never done anything like that.'

Rizzoli nodded sympathetically. 'I understand. If it bothers you, you shouldn't do it. I just thought it would be an easy way for you to pick up two or three thousand dollars.'

Korontzis' eyes went wide. 'Two or three thousand dollars?'

'Oh, yes. At least.'

Korontzis licked his lips again. 'I . . . I . . . Isn't it dangerous?'

Tony Rizzoli laughed. 'If it were dangerous, I wouldn't be doing it, would I? It's a piece of cake. Otto's a mechanic . . . a dealer. He can deal a deck from the top, the bottom or the middle. He's been doing it for years and he's never been caught.'

Korontzis sat there, staring at Rizzoli.

'How . . . how much would I need, to get in the game?'

'About five hundred dollars. But I'll tell you what. This thing

141

is such a cinch that I'll loan you the five hundred, and if you lose it you don't even have to pay it back.'

'That's certainly very generous of you, Tony. Why . . . why are you doing this for me?'

'I'll tell you why.' Tony's voice filled with indignation. 'When I see a decent, hard-working man like you, with a responsible position like being curator of one of the greatest museums in the world, and the State doesn't appreciate you enough to give you a decent salary – and you're struggling to feed your family – well, to tell you the truth, Victor, it burns me up. How long since you've gotten a raise?'

'They . . . they don't give raises.'

'Well, there you are. Listen. You have a choice, Victor. You can let me do you a little favor tonight, so you can pick up a few thousand dollars and start living like you should. Or you go on living hand-to-mouth for the rest of your life.'

'I . . . I don't know, Tony. I shouldn't . . .'

Tony Rizzoli rose. 'I understand. I'll probably be coming back to Athens in a year or two, and maybe we can get together again. It was a pleasure knowing you, Victor.' Rizzoli started for the door.

Korontzis made his decision. 'Wait. I . . . I would like to go with you tonight.'

He had taken the bait. 'Hey, that's great,' Tony Rizzoli said. 'It really makes me feel good to be able to help you out.'

Korontzis hesitated. 'Forgive me, but I want to be sure I understood you correctly. You said that if I lose the five hundred dollars, I will not have to pay you back?'

'That's right,' Rizzoli said. 'Because you can't lose. The game is fixed.'

'Where is the game going to be?'

'Room four twenty at the Metropole Hotel. Ten o'clock. Tell your wife you're working late.'

142

Chapter 12

There were four men in the hotel room besides Tony Rizzoli and Victor Korontzis.

'I want you to meet my friend Otto Dalton,' Rizzoli said. 'Victor Korontzis.'

The two men shook hands.

Rizzoli looked at the others quizzically. 'I don't believe I've met these other gentlemen.'

Otto Dalton made the introductions.

'Perry Breslauer from Detroit . . . Marvin Seymour from Houston . . . Sal Prizzi from New York.'

Victor Korontzis nodded to the men, not trusting his voice.

Otto Dalton was in his sixties, thin, grey-haired, affable. Perry Breslauer was younger, but his face was drawn and pinched. Marvin Seymour was a thin, mild-looking man. Sal Prizzi was a huge man, built like an oak tree, with powerful limbs for arms. He had small, mean eyes, and his face had been badly scarred with a knife.

Rizzoli had briefed Korontzis before the game. *These guys have a lot of money. They can afford to lose big. Seymour owns an insurance company. Breslauer has auto dealerships all over the United States, and Sal Prizzi is head of a big union in New York.*

Otto Dalton was speaking. 'All right, gentlemen. Shall we get started? The white chips are five dollars, the blue are ten, the red are twenty-five, and the black ones are fifty. Let's see the color of your money.'

Korontzis pulled out the five hundred dollars that Tony Rizzoli had loaned him. *No*, he thought, *not loaned, given.* He looked over at Rizzoli and smiled. *What a wonderful friend Rizzoli is.*

143

The other men were taking out large bank rolls.

Korontzis felt a sudden sense of concern. What if something went wrong, and he lost the five hundred dollars? He shrugged it off. His friend Tony would take care of it. But if he *won*. Korontzis was filled with a sudden feeling of euphoria.

The game began.

It was dealer's choice. The stakes were small at first, and there were games of five-card stud, seven-card stud, draw poker, and high-low.

In the beginning the wins and losses were spread evenly, but slowly the tide began to turn.

It seemed that Victor Korontzis and Tony Rizzoli could do no wrong. If they had fair cards, the others had worse cards. If the others had good hands, Korontzis and Rizzoli had better hands.

Victor Korontzis could not believe his luck. At the end of the evening he had won almost two thousand dollars. It was like a miracle.

'You guys were sure lucky,' Marvin Seymour grumbled.

'I'll say,' Breslauer agreed. 'How about giving us another chance tomorrow?'

'I'll let you know,' Rizzoli said.

When they had gone, Korontzis exclaimed, 'I can't believe it. Two thousand dollars!'

Rizzoli laughed. 'That's chicken feed. I told you. Otto is one of the slickest mechanics in the business. Those guys are dying to get another crack at us. Are you interested?'

'You bet.' There was a broad grin on Korontzis' face. 'I think I just made a joke.'

The following night, Victor Korontzis won three thousand dollars.

'It's fantastic!' he told Rizzoli. 'Don't they suspect anything?'

'Of course not. I'll bet you they ask us to raise the stakes tomorrow. They think they're going to win their money back. Are you in?'

'Sure, Tony. I'm in.'

As they were sitting down to play, Sal Prizzi said, 'You know, we're the big losers so far. How about upping the stakes?'

Tony Rizzoli looked over at Korontzis and winked.

'It's all right with me,' Rizzoli said. 'How about you fellows?'

They all nodded agreement.

Otto Dalton set up piles of chips. 'The whites are fifty dollars, the blues are a hundred, reds five hundred, blacks a thousand.'

Victor Korontzis looked at Rizzoli uneasily. He had not planned on the stakes being so high.

Rizzoli nodded reassuringly.

The game began.

Nothing changed. Victor Korontzis' hands were magic. Whatever cards he held beat the others. Tony Rizzoli was also winning, but not as much.

'Fucking cards!' Prizzi grumbled. 'Let's change decks.'

Otto Dalton obligingly produced a fresh deck.

Korontzis looked over at Tony Rizzoli and smiled. He knew that nothing was going to change their luck.

At midnight they had sandwiches sent up. The players took a fifteen-minute break.

Tony Rizzoli took Korontzis aside. 'I told Otto to chum them a little,' he whispered.

'I don't understand.'

'Let them win a few hands. If they keep losing all the time, they'll get discouraged and quit.'

'Oh, I see. That's very smart.'

'When they think they're hot, we'll raise the stakes again and really nail them big.'

Victor Korontzis was hesitant. 'I've already won so much money, Tony. Don't you think maybe we should quit while we're . . . ?'

145

Tony Rizzoli looked him in the eye and said, 'Victor, how would you like to leave here tonight with fifty thousand dollars in your pocket?'

When the game resumed, Breslauer, Prizzi and Seymour began to win. Korontzis' hands were still good, but the others were better.

Otto Dalton is a genius, Korontzis thought. He had been watching him deal, and had not been able to detect one false move.

As the play went on, Victor Korontzis kept losing. He was not concerned. In a few minutes, when they had – what was the word? – *chummed* the others, he and Rizzoli and Dalton would move in for the kill.

Sal Prizzi was gloating. 'Well,' he said, 'it looks like you fellows have cooled off.'

Tony Rizzoli shook his head ruefully. 'Yes it sure does, doesn't it?' He gave Korontzis a knowing look.

'Your luck couldn't go on forever,' Marvin Seymour said.

Perry Breslauer spoke up. 'What do you say we increase the stakes again, and give us a real crack at you?'

Tony Rizzoli pretended to consider it. 'I don't know,' he said thoughtfully. He turned to Victor Korontzis. 'What do you think, Victor?'

How would you like to leave here tonight with fifty thousand dollars in your pocket? I'll be able to buy a house, and a new car. I can take the family on vacations . . . Korontzis was almost trembling with excitement. He smiled. 'Why not?'

'All right,' Sal Prizzi said. 'We'll play table stakes. The sky's the limit.'

They were playing five-card draw. The cards were dealt.

'It's my ante,' Breslauer said. 'Let's open for five thousand dollars.'

Each player put in his ante.

Victor Korontzis was dealt two queens. He drew three cards, and one of them was another queen.

Rizzoli looked at his hand and said, 'Up a thousand.'

146

Marvin Seymour studied his hand. 'I'll call, and raise you two thousand.'

Otto Dalton threw in his cards. 'Too rich for my blood.'

Sal Prizzi said, 'I'll call.'

The pot went to Marvin Seymour's straight.

In the next hand, Victor Korontzis was dealt an eight, nine, ten and jack of hearts. One card away from a straight flush!

'I'll call for a thousand dollars,' Dalton said.

'I'll call, and raise you a thousand.'

Sal Prizzi said, 'Let's bump it another thousand.'

It was Korontzis' turn. He was sure that a straight flush would beat whatever the others were holding. He was only one card away.

'I call.' He drew a card, and put it face down, not daring to look at it.

Breslauer laid his hand down. 'A pair of fours and a pair of tens.'

Prizzi put his hand down. 'Three sevens.'

They turned to look at Victor Korontzis. He took a deep breath, and picked up his hole card. It was black. 'Busted,' he said. He threw his hand in.

The pots kept growing larger.

Victor Korontzis' pile of chips had shrunk to almost nothing. He looked over at Tony Rizzoli, concerned.

Rizzoli smiled reassuringly, a smile that said, *There's nothing to worry about.*

Rizzoli opened the next pot.

The cards were dealt.

'We'll ante a thousand dollars.'

Perry Breslauer: 'I'll raise you a thousand.'

Marvin Seymour: 'And I'll bump you two.'

Sal Prizzi: 'You know something? I think you fellows are bluffing. Let's raise it five more.'

Victor Korontzis had not looked at his hand yet. *When is the damn chumming going to stop?*

'Victor?'

Korontzis picked up his hand slowly and fanned out the cards one by one. An ace, another ace, and a third ace, plus a king and a ten. His blood began to race.

'Are you in?'

He smiled to himself. The chumming had stopped. He knew that he was going to be dealt another king for a full house. He threw the ten away and tried to keep his voice casual. 'I'll call. One card please.'

Otto Dalton said, 'I'll take two.' He looked at his cards. 'I raise a thousand.'

Tony Rizzoli shook his head. 'Too rich for me.' He threw his hand in.

'I'm in,' Prizzi said, 'and I'll raise five thousand.'

Marvin Seymour threw in his hand. 'I'm out.'

It was between Victor Korontzis and Sal Prizzi.

'Are you calling?' Prizzi asked. 'It'll cost you five thousand more.'

Victor Korontzis looked at his pile of chips. Five thousand was all he had left. *But when I win this pot . . .* he thought. He looked at his hand again. It was unbeatable. He put the pile of chips in the center of the table and drew a card. It was a five. But he still had three aces. He laid down his hand. 'Three aces.'

Prizzi spread out his hand. 'Four deuces.'

Korontzis sat there, stunned, watching Prizzi rake in the pot. Somehow he felt as though he had failed his friend Tony. *If I could only have held out until we started to win.*

It was Prizzi's deal. 'Seven-card stud,' he announced. 'Let's put a thousand dollars in the pot.'

The other players threw in their antes.

Victor Korontzis looked over at Tony Rizzoli helplessly. 'I don't have . . .'

'It's all right,' Rizzoli said. He turned to the others. 'Look, fellows, Victor didn't have a chance to pick up much cash to bring tonight, but I can assure you all that he's good for it. Let's give him credit, and we'll settle up at the end of the evening.'

Prizzi said, 'Hold it. What is this – a fucking credit union? We don't know Victor Korontzis from Adam's ass. How do we know he'll pay up?'

'You have my word on it,' Tony Rizzoli assured him. 'Otto here will vouch for me.'

Otto Dalton spoke up. 'If Tony says Mr Korontzis is all right, then he's all right.'

Sal Prizzi shrugged. 'Well, I guess it's okay.'

'It's fine with me,' Perry Breslauer said.

Otto Dalton turned to Victor Korontzis. 'How much would you like?'

'Give him ten thousand,' Tony Rizzoli said.

Korontzis looked over at him in surprise. Ten thousand dollars was more money than he made in two years. But Rizzoli must have known what he was doing.

Victor Korontzis swallowed. 'That . . . that will be fine.'

A pile of chips was put in front of Korontzis.

The cards that night were Victor Korontzis' enemy. As the stakes went up, his new pile of chips kept diminishing. Tony Rizzoli was losing also.

At 2.00 a.m. they took a break. Korontzis got Tony Rizzoli in a corner.

'What's happening?' Korontzis whispered in a panic. 'My God, do you know how much money I'm behind?'

'Don't worry, Victor. So am I. I've given Otto the signal. When it's his turn to deal the game will turn around. We're going to hit them big.'

They took their seats again.

'Give my friend another twenty-five thousand dollars,' Rizzoli said.

Marvin Seymour frowned. 'Are you sure he wants to keep playing?'

Rizzoli turned to Victor Korontzis. 'It's up to you.'

Korontzis hesitated. *I've given Otto the signal. The game will turn around.* 'I'm in.'

'Okay.'

Twenty-five thousand dollars' worth of chips was placed in front of Korontzis. He looked at the chips and suddenly felt very lucky.

Otto Dalton was dealing. 'All right, gentlemen. The game is five-card stud. The initial bet is one thousand dollars.'

The players put their chips in the center of the table.

Dalton dealt out five cards to each player. Korontzis did not look at his hand. *I'll wait*, he thought. *It will be good luck.*

'Place your bets.'

Marvin Seymour, seated at Dalton's right, studied his hand for a moment. 'I'll fold.' He threw his cards in.

Sal Prizzi was next. 'I'll call, and raise a thousand.' He put his chips in the center of the table.

Tony Rizzoli looked at his hand and shrugged. 'I'll fold.' He threw his cards down.

Perry Breslauer was looking at his hand and grinning. 'I'll see the raise, and I'll raise you five thousand more.'

It would cost Victor Korontzis six thousand dollars to stay in the game. Slowly he picked up his hand and fanned out the cards. He could not believe what he saw. He was holding a pat straight flush – a five, six, seven, eight, and nine of hearts. A perfect hand! So Tony had been right. *Thank God!* Korontzis tried to hide his excitement. 'I'll see the raise, and I'll raise you five thousand.' This was the hand that was going to make him rich.

Dalton threw in his hand. 'Not for me. Pass.'

'It's up to me,' Sal Prizzi said. 'I think you're bluffing, pal. I'll call, and raise you another five.'

Victor Korontzis felt a little thrill of excitement go through him. He had been dealt the hand of a lifetime. This would be the biggest jackpot of the game.

Perry Breslauer was studying his hand. 'Well, I think I'll call, and raise another five, fellows.'

It was up to Victor Korontzis again. He took a deep breath. 'I'll see you, and raise another five.' He was almost trembling with excitement. It was all he could do to keep from reaching out and raking in the pot.

Perry Breslauer spread out his hand, a look of triumph on his face. 'Three kings.'

I've won! Victor Korontzis thought. 'Not good enough,' he

smiled. 'A straight flush.' He put down his cards, and reached eagerly for the pot.

'Hold it!' Sal Prizzi slowly laid down his hand. 'I beat you with a royal flush. The ten to the ace of spades.'

Victor Korontzis turned pale. He felt suddenly faint, and his heart began to palpitate.

'Jesus,' Tony Rizzoli said. 'Two goddamned straight flushes?' He turned to Korontzis. 'I'm sorry, Victor. I . . . I don't know what to say.'

Otto Dalton said, 'I think that's it for tonight, gentlemen.' He consulted a slip of paper and turned to Victor Korontzis. 'You owe sixty-five thousand dollars.'

Victor Korontzis looked over at Tony Rizzoli, stunned. Rizzoli shrugged helplessly. Korontzis pulled out a handkerchief and began to swab at his brow.

'How do you want to pay that?' Dalton asked. 'Cash or check?'

'I don't take checks,' Prizzi said. He looked at Victor Korontzis. 'I'll take the cash.'

'I . . . I . . .' The words would not come out. He found he was trembling. 'I . . . I don't have that . . .'

Sal Prizzi's face darkened. 'You *what*?' he barked.

Tony Rizzoli said quickly, 'Wait a minute. Victor means he doesn't have it *with* him. I told you he was good for it.'

'That doesn't put any bread on my table, Rizzoli. I want to see his money.'

'You will,' Rizzoli said reassuringly. 'You'll have it in the next few days.'

Sal Prizzi jumped to his feet. 'Fuck that. I'm not a charity. I want that money by tomorrow.'

'Don't worry. He'll deliver it.'

Victor Korontzis was caught in the middle of a nightmare and there was no way out. He sat there, unable to move, barely aware of the others leaving. Tony and Korontzis were alone.

Korontzis was in a daze. 'I . . . I can never raise that kind of money,' he moaned. 'Never!'

Rizzoli put a hand on Korontzis' shoulder. 'I don't know what to tell you, Victor. I don't know what went wrong. I guess I lost almost as much money as you did tonight.'

Victor Korontzis wiped his eyes. 'But . . . but you can afford it, Tony. I . . . I can't. I'm going to have to explain to them that I can't pay them.'

Tony Rizzoli said, 'I'd think about that if I were you, Victor. Sal Prizzi is the head of the East Coast Seamen's Union. I hear those boys play pretty rough.'

'I can't help it. If I haven't got the money, I haven't got the money. What can he do to me?'

'Let me explain what he can do to you,' Rizzoli said earnestly. 'He can have his boys shoot off your kneecaps. You'll never walk again. He can have them throw acid in your eyes. You'll never see again. And then, when you've had all the pain you can stand, he'll decide whether to let you live like that, or to kill you.'

Victor Korontzis was staring at him, his face ashen. 'You . . . you're joking.'

'I wish I was. It's my fault, Victor. I should never have let you get in a game with a man like Sal Prizzi. He's a killer.'

'Oh, my God. What am I going to do?'

'Do you have any way of raising the money?'

Korontzis began to laugh hysterically. 'Tony . . . I can barely support my family on what I make.'

'Well then, the only thing I can suggest is that you leave town, Victor. Maybe get out of the country. Go somewhere where Prizzi can't find you.'

'I can't do that,' Victor Korontzis wailed. 'I have a wife and four children.' He looked at Tony Rizzoli accusingly. 'You said it was going to be a set-up, that we couldn't lose. You told me . . .'

'I know. And I'm really sorry. It always worked before. The only thing I can think of is that Prizzi cheated.'

Korontzis' face filled with hope. 'Well then, if he cheated I don't have to pay him.'

'There's a problem with that, Victor,' Rizzoli said patiently. 'If you accuse him of cheating he'll kill you, and if you don't pay him he'll kill you.'

'Oh, my God,' Korontzis moaned. 'I'm a dead man.'

'I really feel terrible about this. Are you sure there's no way you could raise . . . ?'

'It would take me a hundred lifetimes. A thousand lifetimes. Everything I have is mortgaged. Where would I get . . . ?'

And at that moment, Tony Rizzoli had a sudden inspiration. 'Wait a minute, Victor! Didn't you say that those artifacts in the museum were worth a lot of money?'

'Yes, but what does that have to do with . . . ?'

'Just let me finish. You said that the copies were as good as the originals.'

'Of course they're not. Any expert could tell . . .'

'Whoa. Hold it. What if one of those artifacts was missing and a copy was put in its place? I mean, when I was in the museum there were a lot of tourists going through. Could they tell the difference?'

'No, but . . . I . . . I see what you mean. No, I could never do that.'

Rizzoli said, soothingly, 'I understand, Victor. I just thought maybe the museum could spare one little artifact. They've got so many.'

Victor Korontzis shook his head. 'I've been the curator at that museum for twenty years. I could never think of such a thing.'

'I'm sorry. I shouldn't have even suggested it. The only reason I thought of it was because it could save your life.' Rizzoli stood up and stretched. 'Well, it's getting late. I guess your wife will be wondering where you are.'

Victor Korontzis was staring at him. 'It could save my life? How?'

'It's simple. If you took one of those antiques . . .'

'Antiquities.'

'. . . antiquities . . . and gave it to me, I could get it out of the country and sell it for you, and give Prizzi the money you owe him. I think I could persuade him to hold off that long. And you'd be off the hook. I don't have to tell you that I'd be taking a big risk for you, because if I got caught I'd be in a lot of trouble. But I'm offering to do it because I feel I owe you one. It's my fault you got into this mess.'

'You're a good friend,' Victor Korontzis said. 'But I can't blame you. I didn't have to get in that game. You were trying to do me a favor.'

153

'I know. I just wish it had turned out differently. Well, let's get some sleep. I'll talk to you tomorrow. Good night, Victor.'

'Good night, Tony.'

The call came in to the museum early the following morning. 'Korontzis?'

'Yes?'

'This is Sal Prizzi.'

'Good morning, Mr Prizzi.'

'I'm callin' about that little matter of sixty-five thousand dollars. What time can I pick it up?'

Victor Korontzis began to perspire heavily. 'I . . . I don't have the money right now, Mr Prizzi.'

There was an ominous silence at the other end of the phone. 'What the hell kind of game are you playing with me?'

'Believe me, I'm not playing any games. I . . .'

'Then I want my fucking money. Is that clear?'

'Yes, sir.'

'What time does your museum close?'

'Six . . . six o'clock.'

'I'll be there. Have the money for me, or I'll break your face in. And after that, I'm *really* going to hurt you.'

The line went dead.

Victor Korontzis sat there in a panic. He wanted to hide. But where? He was engulfed by a feeling of total desperation, caught in a vortex of 'ifs': *if only I hadn't gone to the casino that night; if only I had never met Tony Rizzoli; if only I had kept my promise to my wife never to gamble again.* He shook his head to clear it. *I have to do something – now.*

And at that moment, Tony Rizzoli walked into his office. 'Good morning, Victor.'

It was six thirty. The staff had gone home, and the museum had been closed for half an hour. Victor Korontzis and Tony Rizzoli were watching the front door.

Korontzis was getting increasingly nervous. 'What if he says no? What if he wants his money tonight?'

'I'll handle him,' Tony Rizzoli said. 'Just let me do the talking.'

'What if he doesn't show up? What if he just . . . you know . . . sends someone to kill me? Do you think he would do that?'

'Not as long as he has a chance of getting his money,' Rizzoli said confidently.

At seven o'clock, Sal Prizzi finally appeared.

Korontzis hurried over to the door and opened it. 'Good evening,' he said.

Prizzi looked at Rizzoli. 'What the fuck are you doin' here?' He turned back to Victor Korontzis. 'This is just between us.'

'Take it easy,' Rizzoli said. 'I'm here to help.'

'I don't need your help.' Prizzi turned to Korontzis. 'Where's my money?'

'I . . . I don't have it. But . . .'

Prizzi grabbed him by the throat. 'Listen, you little prick. You'll give me that money tonight, or I'm going to feed you to the fish. Do you understand?'

Tony Rizzoli said, 'Hey, cool down. You're going to get your money.'

Prizzi turned on him. 'I told you to stay out of this. It's none of your business.'

'I'm making it my business. I'm Victor's friend. Victor doesn't have the cash right now, but he has a way to get it for you.'

'Has he got the money, or hasn't he?'

'He has, and he hasn't,' Rizzoli said.

'What the hell kind of answer is that?'

Tony Rizzoli's arm swept around the room. 'The money's there.'

Sal Prizzi scanned the room. 'Where?'

'In those cases. They're full of antiques . . .'

'Antiquities,' Korontzis said automatically.

'. . . that are worth a fortune. I'm talking about millions.'

'Yeah?' Prizzi turned to look at the cases. 'What good are they going to do me if they're locked away in a museum? I want cash.'

'You're going to get cash,' Rizzoli said soothingly. 'Twice what

155

our friend owes you. You just have to be a little patient, that's all. Victor's not a welsher. He just needs a little more time. I'll tell you his plan. Victor's going to take one of these antiques . . . antiquities . . . and arrange to sell it. As soon as he gets the money, he'll pay you.'

Sal Prizzi shook his head. 'I don't like it. I don't know nothing about this antique stuff.'

'You don't have to. Victor's one of the world's greatest experts.' Tony Rizzoli walked over to one of the cases and pointed to a marble head. 'What would you say that's worth, Victor?'

Victor Korontzis swallowed. 'That's the goddess Hygea, four-teenth century BC. Any collector would gladly pay two or three million dollars for it.'

Rizzoli turned to Sal Prizzi. 'There you are. See what I mean?'

Prizzi frowned. 'I don't know. How long would I have to wait?'

'You'll have double your money inside a month.'

Prizzi thought a moment, then nodded. 'Okay, but if I have to wait a month, I want more – say an extra couple of hundred grand.'

Tony Rizzoli looked over at Victor Korontzis.

Korontzis was nodding his head eagerly.

'Okay,' Rizzoli said. 'You have a deal.'

Sal Prizzi walked over to the little curator. 'I'm giving you thirty days. If I don't have my money by then, you're dog meat. Do I make myself clear?'

Korontzis swallowed. 'Yes, sir.'

'Remember . . . thirty days.'

He gave Tony Rizzoli a long hard look. 'I don't like you.'

They watched as Sal Prizzi turned and walked out the door.

Korontzis sank into a chair, wiping his brow.

'Oh, my God,' he said. 'I thought he was going to kill me. Do you think we can get him his money in thirty days?'

'Sure,' Tony Rizzoli promised. 'All you have to do is take one of those things out of the case and put a copy in its place.'

'How will you get it out of the country? You'll go to prison if they catch you.'

'I know,' Tony Rizzoli said stoutly. 'But it's a chance I'm going to have to take. I owe you that much, Victor.'

One hour later, Tony Rizzoli, Sal Prizzi, Otto Dalton, Perry Breslauer and Marvin Seymour were having drinks in Dalton's hotel suite.

'Smooth as silk,' Rizzoli boasted. 'The bastard pissed his pants.'

Sal Prizzi grinned. 'I scared him, huh?'

'You scared *me*,' Rizzoli said. 'You should be a fucking actor.'

'What's the deal now?' Marvin Seymour asked.

Rizzoli replied, 'The deal is, he gives me one of those antiques. I'll find a way to smuggle it out of the country and sell it. Then I'll give you each your cut.'

'Beautiful,' Perry Breslauer said. 'I love it.'

It's like having a gold mine, Rizzoli thought. *Once Korontzis goes along with this, he's hooked. There's no way he can ever back out. I'm going to make him clean out the whole goddamned museum.*

Marvin Seymour asked, 'How are you going to get the stuff out of the country?'

'I'll find a way,' Tony Rizzoli said. 'I'll find a way.'

He had to. And fast. Alfredo Mancuso and Gino Laveri were waiting.

157

Chapter 13

At police headquarters on Stadiou Street, an emergency meeting had been called. In the conference room were Chief of Police Dmitri, Inspector Tinou, Inspector Nicolino, Walt Kelly, the US Treasury agent, and half a dozen detectives. The atmosphere was far different than it had been at the previous meeting.

Inspector Nicolino was saying, 'We now have reason to believe your information was correct, Mr Kelly. Our sources tell us that Tony Rizzoli is trying to find a way to smuggle a very large shipment of heroin out of Athens. We have already begun a search of possible warehouses where he might have stored it.'

'Did you put a tail on Rizzoli?'

'We increased the number of men this morning,' Chief Dmitri said.

Walt Kelly sighed. 'I hope to God it isn't too late.'

Inspector Nicolino assigned two teams of detectives to handle the surveillance on Tony Rizzoli, but he underestimated his subject. By afternoon Rizzoli became aware that he had company. Whenever he left the little hotel he was staying at, he was followed, and when he returned, someone was always casually loitering in the background. They were real professionals. Rizzoli liked that. It was a sign of respect for him.

He now not only had to find a way to get the heroin out of Athens, but he was going to have a priceless antiquity to smuggle out. *Alfredo Mancuso and Gino Laveri are on my back, and the police are all over me like a wet blanket. I've got to make a contact fast.* The only name that immediately came to mind was Ivo Bruggi, a small-time ship owner in Rome. Rizzoli had done business with Bruggi in the past. It was a long-shot, but it was better than nothing.

*

158

Rizzoli was certain that the telephone in his hotel room was tapped. *I've got to have a set-up where I can receive calls at the hotel.* He sat there thinking for a long time. Finally, he rose and walked over to the room across the hall and knocked at the door. It was opened by an elderly, sour-faced man.

'Yeah?'

Rizzoli turned on the charm. 'Excuse me,' he said. 'I'm sorry to bother you. I'm your neighbor across the hall. I wonder if I could come in and talk to you for a minute?'

The man studied him suspiciously. 'Lemme see you open the door to your room.'

Tony Rizzoli smiled. 'Certainly.' He stepped across the hall, took out his key, and opened the door.

The man nodded. 'All right. Come in.'

Tony Rizzoli closed his door and went into the room across the hall.

'What do you want?'

'It's really a personal problem, and I hate to trouble you, but . . . Well, the truth is, I'm in the middle of getting a divorce, and my wife is having me followed.' He shook his head in disgust. 'She even had the phone in my room bugged.'

'Women!' his neighbor growled. 'God damn them. I divorced my wife last year. I should've done it ten years ago.'

'Really? Anyway, what I was wondering was if you would be good enough to let me give a couple of friends your room number so they can telephone me here. I promise you there won't be many calls.'

The man started to shake his head. 'I can't be bother – '

Rizzoli pulled a hundred-dollar bill from his pocket. 'This is for your trouble.'

The man licked his lips. 'Oh. Well, sure,' he said. 'I guess it'll be all right. I'm glad to do a fellow sufferer a favor.'

'That's certainly kind of you. Whenever there's a call for me, just knock at my door. I'll be here most of the time.'

'Right.'

*

159

Early the following morning, Rizzoli walked to a public pay station to telephone Ivo Bruggi. He dialed the operator and put in a call for Rome.

'*Signor Bruggi, per piacere.*'

'*Non c'è in casa.*'

'*Quando arriverà'?*'

'*Non lo so.*'

'*Gli dica, di chiamare il Signor Rizzoli.*'

Rizzoli left the telephone number of the switchboard at his hotel and the room number of his neighbor. He went back to his room. He hated the room. Someone had told him that the Greek word for hotel was *xenodochion*, meaning a container for strangers. *It's more like a fucking prison*, Rizzoli thought. The furniture was ugly: an old green sofa, two battered end tables with lamps, a little writing desk with a lamp and desk chair, and a bed designed by Torquemada.

For the next two days Tony Rizzoli stayed in his room, waiting for a knock on the door, sending a bellboy out for food. No call. *Where the fuck is Ivo Bruggi?*

The surveillance team was reporting to Inspector Nicolino and Walt Kelly. 'Rizzoli's holed up in his hotel. He hasn't budged for forty-eight hours.'

'Are you sure he's in there?'

'Yes, sir. The maids see him in the morning and night when they make up his room.'

'What about phone calls?'

'Not a one. What do you want us to do?'

'Sit tight. He'll make his move sooner or later. And make sure the tap on his phone is working.'

The following day, the telephone in Rizzoli's room rang. *Shit!* Bruggi shouldn't have been calling him in this room. He had left a message for the idiot to call him in his neighbor's room. He would have to be careful. Rizzoli picked up the telephone.

'Yes?'

A voice said, 'Is this Tony Rizzoli?'

It was not Ivo Bruggi's voice. 'Who is this?'

'You came to see me at my office the other day with a business proposition, Mr Rizzoli. I turned you down. I think perhaps you and I should discuss it again.'

Tony Rizzoli felt a sudden thrill of exaltation. *Spyros Lambrou! So the bastard has come around.* He could not believe his good luck. *All my problems are solved. I can ship the heroin and the antique at the same time.*

'Yeah. Sure. I'll be happy to discuss it. When would you like to meet?'

'Can you make it this afternoon?'

So, he's hungry to make a deal. The fucking rich are all the same. They never have enough. 'Fine. Where?'

'Why don't you come to my office?'

'I'll be there.' Tony Rizzoli replaced the receiver, elated.

In the lobby of the hotel, a frustrated detective was reporting to headquarters. 'Rizzoli just received a telephone call. He's going to meet someone at his office, but the man didn't give a name and we can't trace the call.'

'All right. Cover him when he leaves the hotel. Let me know where he goes.'

'Yes, sir.'

Ten minutes later, Tony Rizzoli was crawling out of a basement window leading to an alley behind the hotel. He changed taxis twice to make sure he was not being followed, and headed for Spyros Lambrou's office.

From the day Spyros Lambrou had visited Melina in the hospital, he had vowed to avenge his sister. But he had been unable to think of a punishment terrible enough for Constantin Demiris. Then, with the visit from Georgios Lato, and the startling news that Madame Piris had given him, a weapon had been put into his hands that was going to destroy his brother-in-law.

His secretary announced: 'A Mr Anthony Rizzoli is here to see you, Mr Lambrou. He has no appointment and I told him you couldn't . . .'

161

'Send him in.'

'Yes, sir.'

Spyros Lambrou watched as Rizzoli walked through the doorway, smiling and confident.

'Thank you for coming, Mr Rizzoli.'

Tony Rizzoli grinned. 'My pleasure. So, you've decided you and I are going to do business together, huh?'

'No.'

Tony Rizzoli's smile faded. 'What did you say?'

'I said "No." I have no intention of doing business with you.'

Tony Rizzoli stared at him, baffled. 'Then what the hell did you call me for? You said you had a proposition for me and . . .'

'I do. How would you like to have the use of Constantin Demiris' fleet of ships?'

Tony Rizzoli sank into a chair. 'Constantin Demiris? What are you talking about? He'd never . . .'

'Yes, he would. I can promise you that Mr Demiris will be happy to give you anything you want.'

'Why? What does he get out of it?'

'Nothing.'

'That doesn't make sense. Why would Demiris make a deal like that?'

'I'm glad you asked.' Lambrou pressed down the intercom button: 'Bring in some coffee, please.' He looked at Tony Rizzoli. 'How do you like yours?'

'Er – black, no sugar.'

'Black, no sugar, for Mr Rizzoli.'

When the coffee had been served, and his secretary had left the office, Spyros Lambrou said: 'I'm going to tell you a little story, Mr Rizzoli.'

Tony Rizzoli was watching him, wary. 'Shoot.'

'Constantin Demiris is married to my sister. A number of years ago he took on a mistress. Her name was Noelle Page.'

'The actress, right?'

'Yes. She cheated on him with a man named Larry Douglas. Noelle and Douglas went on trial for murdering Douglas' wife because she wouldn't give him a divorce. Constantin Demiris hired a lawyer named Napoleon Chotas to defend Noelle.'

162

'I remember reading something about the trial.'

'There are some things that were not in the newspapers. You see, my dear brother-in-law had no intention of saving his unfaithful mistress's life. He wanted vengeance. He hired Napoleon Chotas to see that Noelle was convicted. Near the end of the trial, Napoleon Chotas told the defendants he had made a deal with the judges if they pleaded guilty. It was a lie. They pleaded guilty. And they were executed.'

'Maybe this Chotas really thought that . . .'

'Let me finish, please. The body of Catherine Douglas was never found. The reason it was never found, Mr Rizzoli, is because she is alive. Constantin Demiris had her hidden away.'

Tony Rizzoli was staring at him. 'Wait a minute. Demiris *knew* she was alive, and he let his mistress and her boyfriend go to their deaths for killing her?'

'Exactly. I'm not sure precisely what the law is, but I am sure that if the facts were to come out, my brother-in-law would spend a good deal of time in prison. At the very least, he would certainly be ruined.'

Tony Rizzoli sat there, thinking about what he had just heard. There was something puzzling him. 'Mr Lambrou, why are you telling me this?'

Spyros Lambrou's lips moved in a beatific smile. 'Because I owe my brother-in-law a favor. I want you to go see him. I have a feeling he'll be very happy to let you use his ships.'

Chapter 14

There were storms raging in him over which he had no control, a cold center deep within him with no warm memories to dissolve it. They had begun a year ago with his act of revenge against Noelle. He had thought that that had ended it, that the past was buried. It had never occurred to him that there might be repercussions until, unexpectedly, Catherine Alexander had come back into his life. That had necessitated the removal of Frederick Stavros and Napoleon Chotas. They had played a deadly game against him, and he had won. But what surprised Constantin Demiris was how much he had enjoyed the risk, the cutting edge of excitement. Business was fascinating, but it paled compared to the game of life and death. *I'm a murderer*, Demiris thought. *No – not a murderer. An executioner*. And instead of being appalled by it, he found it exhilarating.

Constantin Demiris received a weekly report on Catherine Alexander's activities. So far, everything was working out perfectly. Her social activities were confined to the people she worked with. According to Evelyn, Catherine occasionally went out with Kirk Reynolds. But since Reynolds worked for Demiris, that presented no problem. *The poor girl must be desperate*, Demiris thought. Reynolds was boring. He could talk about nothing but the law. But that was all to the good. The more desperate Catherine was for companionship, the easier it would be for him. *I owe Reynolds a vote of thanks*.

Catherine was seeing Kirk Reynolds regularly, and she found herself drawn to him more and more. He was not handsome, but he was certainly attractive. *I learned my lesson about handsome with Larry*, Catherine thought wryly. *The old expression*

164

is true: Handsome is as handsome does. Kirk Reynolds was thoughtful and reliable. *He's someone I can count on*, Catherine thought. *I don't feel any great burning spark, but I probably never will again. Larry took care of that. I'm mature enough now to settle for a man I respect, who respects me as a companion, someone with whom I can share a nice, sane life without being worried about being thrown off mountain tops, or being buried in dark caves.*

They went to the theatre to see *The Lady's Not For Burning* by Christopher Fry, and, on another evening, *September Tide*, with Gertrude Lawrence. They went to nightclubs. The orchestras all seemed to be playing *The Third Man* theme and 'La Vie En Rose'.

'I'm going to St Moritz next week,' Kirk Reynolds told Catherine. 'Have you thought about it?'

Catherine had given it a great deal of thought. She was sure that Kirk Reynolds was in love with her. *And I love him*, Catherine thought. *But loving and being in love are two different things, aren't they? Or am I just being a dumb romantic? What am I looking for – another Larry? – someone who'll sweep me off my feet, fall in love with another woman, and try to kill me? Kirk Reynolds would make a wonderful husband. Why am I hesitating?*

That night Catherine and Kirk dined at the Mirabelle, and when they were having dessert, Kirk said, 'Catherine, in case you don't know, I'm in love with you. I want to marry you.'

She felt a sudden panic. 'Kirk . . .' And she was not sure what she was going to say. *My next words*, Catherine thought, *are going to change my life. It would be so simple to say yes. What's holding me back? Is it the fear of the past? Am I going to live my whole life being afraid? I can't let that happen.*

'Cathy . . .'

'Kirk – Why don't we go to St Moritz together?'

Kirk's face lit up. 'Does that mean . . . ?'

165

'We'll see. Once you see me ski you probably won't want to marry me.'

Kirk laughed. 'Nothing in the world could keep me from wanting to marry you. You've made me one very happy fellow. We'll go up on November fifth – Guy Fawkes Day.'

'What is Guy Fawkes Day?'

'It's a fascinating story. King James had a strict anti-Catholic policy, so a group of prominent Roman Catholics plotted to overthrow the government. A soldier named Guy Fawkes was brought over from Spain to lead the plot. He arranged for a ton of gunpowder, in thirty-six barrels, to be hidden in the basement of the House of Lords. But on the morning that they were to blow up the House of Lords, one of the conspirators told on them and they were all caught. Guy Fawkes was tortured, but he wouldn't talk. All the men were executed. Now, every year in England, the day of the discovery of the plot is celebrated by bonfires and fireworks, and small boys make effigies of "Guys".'

Catherine shook her head. 'That's a pretty grim holiday.'

He smiled at her, and said quietly, 'I promise you that ours won't be grim.'

The night before they were to leave, Catherine washed her hair, packed and unpacked twice and felt sick with excitement. She had only known two men carnally in her life, William Fraser and her husband. *Do they still use words like 'carnally'?* Catherine wondered. *My God, I hope I remember how. They say it's like riding a bicycle; once you do it, you never forget. Maybe he's going to be disappointed in me in bed. Maybe I'm going to be disappointed in me in bed. Maybe I should just stop worrying about it and go to sleep.*

'Mr Demiris?'

  'Yes.'

  'Catherine Alexander left this morning for St Moritz.'

There was a silence. 'St Moritz?'

  'Yes, sir.'

166

'Did she go alone?'

'No, sir. She went with Kirk Reynolds.'

This time the silence was longer. 'Thank you, Evelyn.'

Kirk Reynolds! It was impossible. What could she see in him? *I waited too long. I should have moved more quickly. I'll have to do something about this. I can't let her –* His secretary buzzed.

'Mr Demiris, there's a Mr Anthony Rizzoli here to see you. He does not have an appointment and . . .'

'Then why are you bothering me?' Demiris asked. He snapped down the intercom.

It buzzed again. 'I'm sorry to disturb you. Mr Rizzoli says he has a message for you from Mr Lambrou. He says it's very important.'

A message? Strange. Why wouldn't his brother-in-law deliver his own message? 'Send him in.'

'Yes, sir.'

Tony Rizzoli was ushered into Constantin Demiris' office. He looked around the office appreciatively. It was even more lavish than the offices of Spyros Lambrou. 'Nice of you to see me, Mr Demiris.'

'You have two minutes.'

'Spyros sent me. He thought you and I should have a talk.'

'Really? And what do we have to talk about?'

'Do you mind if I sit down?'

'I don't think you'll be staying that long.'

Tony Rizzoli settled himself in a chair facing Demiris. 'I have a manufacturing plant, Mr Demiris. I ship things to various parts of the world.'

'I see. And you want to charter one of my ships.'

'Exactly.'

'Why did Spyros send you to me? Why don't you charter one of his ships? He happens to have two of them idle at the moment.'

Tony Rizzoli shrugged. 'I guess he doesn't like what I ship.'

'I don't understand. What is it you ship?'

'Drugs,' Tony Rizzoli said delicately. 'Heroin.'

Constantin Demiris was staring at him in disbelief. 'And you expect me to . . . ? Get out of here, before I call the police.'

Rizzoli nodded toward the phone. 'Go right ahead.'

167

He watched Demiris reach for the phone. 'I'd like to speak to them, too. I'd like to tell them all about that trial of Noelle Page and Larry Douglas.'

Constantin Demiris froze. 'What are you talking about?'

'I'm talking about two people executed for the murder of a woman who's still alive.'

Constantin Demiris' face had gone white.

'Do you think maybe the police would be interested in that story, Mr Demiris? If they aren't, maybe the press would be, huh? I can see the headlines now, can't you? Can I call you Costa? Spyros told me all your friends call you Costa, and I think you and I are going to be good friends. Do you know why? Because good friends don't rat on each other. We'll keep that little stunt you pulled our secret, shall we?'

Constantin Demiris was sitting rigid in his chair. When he spoke his voice was hoarse. 'What is it you want?'

'I told you. I want to charter one of your ships – and, you and I being such good friends, I don't think you would want to charge me for the charter, would you? Let's say it's a favor traded for a favor.'

Demiris took a deep breath. 'I can't let you do this. If it ever got out that I allowed drugs to be smuggled on one of my ships, I could lose my whole fleet.'

'But it's not going to get out, is it? In my business, I don't advertise. We're going to do this very quietly.'

Constantin Demiris' expression hardened. 'You're making a big mistake. You can't blackmail me. Do you know who I am?'

'Yeah. You're my new partner. You and I are going to be doing business together for a long time, Costa baby, because, if you say no, I go right to the police and the newspapers and spill the whole story. And there goes your reputation and your fucking empire, right down the drain.'

There was a long, painful silence.

'How – how did my brother-in-law find out?'

Rizzoli grinned. 'That's not important. What's important is that I've got you by the balls. If I squeeze, you're a eunuch. You'll be singing soprano for the rest of your life, and you'll be singing it in a prison cell.' Tony Rizzoli looked at his watch. 'My

168

goodness, my two minutes are up.' He rose to his feet. 'I'm giving you sixty seconds to decide whether I walk out of here as your partner – or I just walk out.'

Constantin Demiris suddenly looked ten years older. His face was drained of color. He had no illusions about what would happen if the true story of the trial came out. The press would eat him alive. He would be portrayed as a monster, a murderer. They might even open an investigation into the deaths of Stavros and Chotas.

'Your sixty seconds are up.'

Constantin Demiris nodded slowly. 'All right,' he whispered, 'all right.'

Tony Rizzoli beamed down at him. 'You're smart.'

Constantin Demiris slowly rose to his feet. 'I'll let you get away with it this once,' he said. 'I don't want to know how you do it, or when. I'll put one of your men aboard one of my ships. That's as far as I'll go.'

'It's a deal,' Tony Rizzoli said. He thought, *Maybe you're not so smart. You smuggle one load of heroin and you're hooked, Costa baby. There's no way I will ever let you go*. Aloud, he repeated, 'Sure, it's a deal.'

On the way back to the hotel, Tony Rizzoli was exultant. *Jackpot. The narcs would never dream of touching Constantin Demiris' fleet. Christ, from now on I can load up every ship of his that sails out of here. The money will roll in. Horse and antiques – sorry, Victor*, he laughed aloud – *antiquities*.

Rizzoli went to a public telephone booth on Stadiou Avenue and made two calls. The first was to Pete Lucca in Palermo.

'You can get your two gorillas out of here, Pete, and put them back in the zoo where they belong. The stuff's ready to move. It's going by ship.'

'Are you sure the package is safe?'

Rizzoli laughed. 'It's safer than the Bank of England. I'll tell you about it when I see you. And I have more good news. From now on we're going to be able to make a shipment every week.'

169

'That's wonderful, Tony. I always knew I could count on you.'
The hell you did, you bastard.

The second call was to Spyros Lambrou. 'It went fine. Your brother-in-law and I are going into business together.'

'Congratulations. I'm delighted to hear it, Mr Rizzoli.'

When Spyros Lambrou replaced the receiver, he smiled. *The narcotics squad will be, too.*

Constantin Demiris stayed in his office past midnight, sitting at his desk, contemplating his new problem. He had avenged himself against Noelle Page, and now she was returning from the grave to haunt him. He reached inside a desk drawer and took out a framed photograph of Noelle. *Hello, bitch.* God, she was beautiful! *So you think you're going to destroy me. Well, we'll see. We'll see.*

Chapter 15

St Moritz was an enchantment. There were miles of downhill ski runs, hiking trails, bobsled and sleigh rides, polo tournaments and a dozen other activities. Curled around a sparkling lake in the Engadine Valley 6000 feet high on the southern slope of the Alps, between Celerina and Piz Nair, the little village made Catherine gasp with delight.

Catherine and Kirk Reynolds checked into the fabled Palace Hotel. The lobby was filled with tourists from a dozen countries.

Kirk Reynolds said to the reception clerk, 'A reservation for Mr and Mrs Reynolds,' and Catherine looked away. *I should have put on a wedding ring.* She was sure everyone in the lobby was staring at her, knowing what she was doing.

'Yes, Mr Reynolds. Suite two fifteen.' The clerk handed a bellboy the key, and the bellboy said, 'Right this way, please.'

They were escorted to a lovely suite, simply furnished, with a spectacular view of the mountains from each window.

When the bellboy left, Kirk Reynolds took Catherine in his arms. 'I can't tell you how happy you've made me, darling.'

'I hope I will,' Catherine replied. 'I . . . It's been a long time, Kirk.'

'Don't worry. I won't rush you.'

He's so dear, Catherine thought, *but how would he feel about me if I told him about my past?* She had never mentioned Larry to him, or the murder trial, or any of the terrible things that had happened to her. She wanted to feel close to him, to confide in him, but something held her back.

'I'd better unpack,' Catherine said.

She unpacked slowly – too slowly – and she suddenly realized

171

that she was stalling, afraid to finish what she was doing because she was afraid of what was going to happen next.

From the other room she heard Kirk calling, 'Catherine . . .'

Oh, my God, he's going to say let's get undressed and go to bed. Catherine swallowed and said in a small voice, 'Yes?'

'Why don't we go outside and look around?'

Catherine went limp with relief. 'That's a wonderful idea,' she said enthusiastically. *What's the matter with me? I'm in one of the most romantic places on earth, with an attractive man who loves me, and I'm panicky.*

Reynolds was looking at her strangely. 'Are you all right?'

'Fine,' Catherine said brightly. 'Just fine.'

'You look worried.'

'No. I . . . I was thinking about – about skiing. It's supposed to be dangerous.'

Reynolds smiled. 'Don't worry. We'll start you on a gentle slope, tomorrow. Let's go.'

They put on sweaters and lined jackets and walked outside into the crisp, clear air.

Catherine breathed deeply. 'Oh, it's wonderful, Kirk. I love it here.'

'You ain't seen nothin' yet,' he grinned. 'It's twice as beautiful in the summer.'

Will he still want to see me in the summer? Catherine wondered. *Or am I going to be a big disappointment to him? Why don't I stop worrying so much?*

The village of St Moritz was charming, a medieval marvel, filled with quaint shops and restaurants and chalets set among the majestic Alps.

They wandered around the shops, and Catherine bought presents for Evelyn and Wim. They stopped at a little café and had a fondue.

In the afternoon, Kirk Reynolds hired a sleigh driven by a bay, and they rode along the snow-covered path up into the hills, the snow crunching beneath the metal runners.

'Enjoying?' Reynolds asked.

172

'Oh, yes.' Catherine looked at him and thought, *I'm going to make you so happy. Tonight. Yes, tonight. I'm going to make you happy tonight.*

That evening, they dined in the hotel at the Stübli, a restaurant with the atmosphere of an old country inn.

'This room dates back to fourteen eighty,' Kirk said.

'Then we'd better not order the bread.'

'What?'

'Small joke. Sorry.'

Larry used to understand my jokes; why am I thinking about him? Because I don't want to think about tonight. I feel like Marie Antoinette going to her execution. I won't have cake for dessert.

The meal was superb, but Catherine was too nervous to enjoy it. When they had finished, Reynolds said, 'Shall we go upstairs? I've arranged an early ski lesson for you in the morning.'

'Sure. Fine. Sure.'

They started upstairs, and Catherine found that her heart was pounding. *He's going to say, 'Let's go right to bed.' And why shouldn't he? That's what I came here for, isn't it? I can't pretend I came for the skiing.*

They reached their suite, and Reynolds opened the door and turned on the lights. They walked into the bedroom and Catherine stared at the large bed. It seemed to take up the whole room.

Kirk was watching her. 'Catherine . . . are you worried about anything?'

'What?' A hollow little laugh. 'Of course not. I . . . I just . . .'

'Just what?'

She gave him a bright smile. 'Nothing. I'm fine.'

'Good. Let's get undressed and go to bed.'

Exactly what I knew he was going to say. But did he have to say it? We could have just gone ahead and done it. Putting it in words is so . . . so . . . crass.

'What did you say?'

Catherine had not realized that she had spoken aloud. 'Nothing.'

Catherine had reached the bed. It was the largest she had ever

173

seen. It was a bed that had been built for lovers, and lovers only. It was not a bed to sleep in. It was a bed to . . .

'Aren't you going to get undressed, darling?'

Am I? How long has it been since I slept with a man? More than a year. And he was my husband.

'Cathy . . . ?'

'Yes.' *I'm going to get undressed, and I'm going to get into bed, and I'm going to disappoint you. I'm not in love with you, Kirk. I can't sleep with you.*

'Kirk . . .'

He turned to her, half undressed. 'Yes?'

'Kirk, I . . . Forgive me. You're going to hate me, but I . . . I can't. I'm terribly sorry. You must think I'm . . .'

She saw the look of disappointment on his face. He forced a smile. 'Cathy, I told you I'd be patient. If you're not ready yet, I . . . I understand. We can still have a wonderful time here.'

She kissed his cheek gratefully. 'Oh, Kirk. Thank you. I feel so ridiculous. I don't know what's the matter with me.'

'There's nothing the matter with you,' he assured her. 'I understand.'

She hugged him. 'Thank you. You're an angel.'

'Meanwhile,' he sighed, 'I'll sleep on the couch in the living room.'

'No you won't,' Catherine declared. 'Since I'm the one responsible for this dumb problem, the least I can do is see that you're comfortable. I'll sleep on the couch. You take the bed.'

'Absolutely not.'

Catherine lay on the bed, wide awake, thinking about Kirk Reynolds. *Will I ever be able to make love with another man? Or has Larry burned that out of me? Maybe, in a way, Larry did manage to kill me after all.* Finally, Catherine slept.

Kirk Reynolds was awakened in the middle of the night by the screams. He sat straight up on the couch and, as the screams continued, he hurried into the bedroom.

174

Catherine was flailing about on the bed, her eyes tightly closed. 'No,' she was yelling. 'Don't! Don't! Leave me alone!'

Reynolds knelt down and put his arms around her and held her close. 'Shhh,' he said. 'It's all right. It's all right.'

Catherine's body was racked with sobs, and he held her close until they subsided.

'They – tried to drown me.'

'It was only a dream,' he said soothingly. 'You had a bad dream.'

Catherine opened her eyes and sat up. Her body was trembling. 'No, it wasn't a dream. It was real. They tried to kill me.'

Kirk was looking at her, puzzled. 'Who tried to kill you?'

'My . . . my husband and his mistress.'

He shook his head. 'Catherine, you had a nightmare, and . . .'

'I'm telling you the truth. They tried to murder me, and they were executed for it.'

Kirk's face was filled with disbelief. 'Catherine . . .'

'I didn't tell you before, because it's . . . it's painful for me to talk about it.'

He suddenly realized that she was serious. 'What happened?'

'I wouldn't give Larry a divorce, and he . . . he was in love with another woman, and they decided to murder me.'

Kirk was listening intently now. 'When was this?'

'A year ago.'

'What happened to them?'

'They were – they were executed by the State.'

He raised a hand. 'Wait a minute. They were executed for *attempting* to kill you?'

'Yes.'

Reynolds said, 'I'm not an expert on Greek law, but I'm willing to bet that there's no death sentence for *attempted* murder. There has to be some mistake. I know a lawyer in Athens. Actually, he works for the State. I'll give him a call in the morning, and clear this up. His name is Peter Demonides.'

Catherine was still asleep when Kirk Reynolds awakened. He dressed quietly and went into the bedroom. He stood there a

175

moment, looking down at Catherine. *I love her so much. I have to find out what really happened, and clear the shadows away for her.*

Kirk Reynolds went down to the hotel lobby and placed a phone call to Athens. 'I'd like to make it person to person, operator. I want to speak with Peter Demonides.'

The call came through half an hour later.

'Mr Demonides? This is Kirk Reynolds. I don't know whether you remember me, but . . .'

'Of course I do. You work for Constantin Demiris.'

'Yes.'

'What can I do for you, Mr Reynolds?'

'Forgive me for bothering you. I'm a bit puzzled about some information I just came across. It involves a point of Greek law.'

'I know a little bit about Greek law,' Demonides said jovially. 'I'll be happy to help you.'

'Is there anything in your law that allows someone to be executed for attempted murder?'

There was a long silence on the other end of the line. 'May I ask why you are inquiring?'

'I'm with a woman named Catherine Alexander. She seems to think that her husband and his mistress were executed by the State for trying to kill her. It doesn't sound logical. Do you see what I mean?'

'Yes.' Demonides' voice was thoughtful. 'I see what you mean. Where are you, Mr Reynolds?'

'I'm staying at the Palace Hotel in St Moritz.'

'Let me check this out, and I'll get back to you.'

'I would appreciate it. The truth is, I think Miss Alexander may be imagining things, and I'd like to straighten this out and relieve her mind.'

'I understand. You will hear from me. I promise.'

The air was bright and crisp, and the beauty of Catherine's surroundings dispelled her terrors of the night before.

The two of them breakfasted in the village, and when they had finished, Reynolds said, 'Let's go over to the ski slope and turn you into a snow bunny.'

He took Catherine over to the beginners' slope and hired an instructor for her.

Catherine got into her skis, and stood up. She looked down at her feet. 'This is ridiculous. If God had meant us to look like this, our fathers would have been trees.'

'What?'

'Nothing, Kirk.'

The instructor smiled. 'Don't worry. In no time at all you'll be skiing like a pro, Miss Alexander. We'll start out at Corviglia Sass Ronsol. That's the beginners' slope.'

'You'll be surprised at how quickly you'll get the hang of it,' Reynolds assured Catherine.

He looked over at a ski run in the distance, and turned to the instructor. 'I think I'll try Fuorcla Grischa today.'

'It sounds delicious. I'll have mine grilled,' Catherine said.

Not a smile. 'It's a ski run, darling.'

'Oh.' Catherine felt embarrassed to tell him it was a joke. *I mustn't do that around him*, Catherine thought.

The instructor said, 'The Grischa's a pretty steep run. You might start out on the Corviglia Standard Marguns to warm up, Mr Reynolds.'

'Good idea. I'll do that. Catherine, I'll meet you at the hotel for lunch.'

'Fine.'

Reynolds waved and walked away.

'Have a nice time,' Catherine called. 'Don't forget to write.'

'Well,' the instructor said. 'Let's go to work.'

To Catherine's surprise, the lessons turned out to be fun. She was nervous in the beginning. She felt awkward and moved up the small slope clumsily.

'Lean forward a little. Keep your skis pointed forward.'

'Tell *them*. They have a mind of their own,' Catherine declared.

177

'You're doing fine. Now we're going down the slope. Bend your knees. Get your balance. There you go!'

She fell.

'Once more. You're doing fine.'

She fell again. And again. And suddenly, she found her sense of balance. And it was as though she had wings. She sailed down the slope, and it was exhilarating. It was almost like flying. She loved the crunch of the snow beneath her skis and the feel of the wind batting at her face.

'I love it!' Catherine said. 'No wonder people get hooked on this. How soon can we do the big slope?'

The instructor laughed. 'Let's stay with this for today. Tomorrow, the Olympics.'

All in all, it was a glorious morning.

She was waiting for Kirk Reynolds in the Grill Room when he returned from skiing. His cheeks were ruddy and he looked animated. He walked up to Catherine's table and sat down.

'Well,' he asked. 'How did it go?'

'Great. I didn't break anything important. I only fell down six times. And you know something?' she said proudly. 'Toward the end I got pretty good. I think he's going to enter me in the Olympics.'

Reynolds smiled. 'Good.' He started to mention the phone call he had made to Peter Demonides, and then decided against it. He did not want to have Catherine upset again.

After lunch they went for a long walk in the snow, stopping in at some of the shops to browse. Catherine was beginning to feel tired.

'I think I'd like to go back to the room,' she said. 'I might take a little nap.'

'Good idea. The air's pretty thin here, and if you're not used to it you can get tired easily.'

'What are you going to do, Kirk?'

He looked up at a distant slope. 'I think I might ski down the Grischa. I've never done it before. It's a challenge.'

'You mean – "because it's there".'

178

'What?'

'Nothing. It looks so dangerous.'

Reynolds nodded. 'That's why it's a challenge.'

Catherine took his hand. 'Kirk, about last night. I'm sorry. I . . . I'll try to do better.'

'Don't worry about it. Go back to the hotel and get some sleep.'

'I will.'

Catherine watched him walk away and thought, *He's a wonderful man. I wonder what he sees in an idiot like me?*

Catherine slept during the afternoon, and this time there were no dreams. When she awakened it was almost six o'clock. Kirk would be returning soon.

Catherine bathed and dressed, thinking about the evening ahead of her. *No, not the evening*, she admitted to herself, *the night. I'll make it up to him.*

She went to the window and looked out. It was beginning to get dark. *Kirk must really be enjoying himself*, Catherine thought. She looked up at the huge slope in the distance. *Is that the Grischa? I wonder if I'll ever be able to ski down that.*

At seven o'clock Kirk Reynolds still had not returned. The twilight had turned to a deep blackness. *He can't be skiing in the dark*, Catherine thought. *I'll bet he's in the bar downstairs having a drink.*

She started for the door just as the phone rang.

Catherine smiled. *I was right. He's calling me to ask me to join him downstairs.*

She lifted the receiver and said brightly, 'Well, did you come across any Sherpas?'

A strange voice said, 'Mrs Reynolds?'

She started to say no, then remembered how Kirk had registered them. 'Yes. This is Mrs Reynolds.'

'I'm afraid I have some bad news for you. Your husband has been in a skiing accident.'

179

'Oh, no! Is it . . . is it serious?'

'I'm afraid it is.'

'I'll come right away. Where . . . ?'

'I'm sorry to tell you he's . . . he's dead, Mrs Reynolds. He was skiing the Lagalp and broke his neck.'

Chapter 16

Tony Rizzoli watched her come out of the bathroom, naked, and thought, *Why do Greek women have such big asses?*

She slid into bed beside him, put her arms around him and whispered, 'I'm so glad you chose me, *poulaki*. I wanted you from the first moment I saw you.'

It was all Tony Rizzoli could do to keep from laughing out loud. The bitch had seen too many B movies.

'Sure,' he said. 'I feel the same way, baby.'

He had picked her up at The New Yorker, a sleazy nightclub on Kallari Street, where she worked as a singer. She was what the Greeks contemptuously called a *gavyeezee skilo*, a barking dog. None of the girls who worked at the club had talent – not in their throats, anyway – but for a price, they were all available to be taken home. This one, Helena, was moderately attractive, with dark eyes, a sensuous face, and a full, ripe body. She was twenty-four, a little old for Rizzoli's taste, but he did not know any ladies in Athens, and he could not afford to be choosy.

'Do you like me?' Helena asked coyly.

'Yeah. I'm *pazzo* about you.'

He began to stroke her breasts, and felt her nipples get hard, and squeezed.

'Ouch!'

'Move your head down, baby.'

She shook her head. 'I don't do that.'

Rizzoli stared at her. 'Really?'

The next instant, he grabbed her hair, and pulled.

Helena screamed. '*Parakalo!*'

181

Rizzoli slapped her hard across the face. 'Make one more sound and I'll break your neck.'

Rizzoli dragged her face down between his legs. 'There he is, baby. Make him happy.'

'Let me go,' she whimpered. 'You're hurting me.'

Rizzoli tightened his grip on her hair. 'Hey – you're crazy about me – remember?'

He let go of her hair, and she looked up at him, her eyes blazing.

'You can go . . .'

The look on his face stopped her. There was something terribly wrong with this man. Why hadn't she seen it sooner?

'There's no reason for us to fight,' she said placatingly. 'You and me . . .'

His fingers dug into her neck. 'I'm not paying you for conversation.' His fist smashed into her cheek. 'Shut up and go to work.'

'Of course, sweetheart,' Helena whimpered. 'Of course.'

Rizzoli was insatiable, and by the time he was satisfied, Helena was exhausted. She lay at his side until she was sure he was asleep, and then she quietly slipped out of bed and got dressed. She was in pain. Rizzoli had not paid her yet, and ordinarily Helena would have taken the money from his wallet, plus a handsome tip for herself. But some instinct made her decide to leave without taking any money.

An hour later, Tony Rizzoli was awakened by a pounding on the door. He sat up and peered at his wristwatch. It was four o'clock in the morning. He looked around. The girl had gone.

'Who is it?' he called.

'It's your neighbor.' The voice was angry. 'There's a telephone call for you.'

Rizzoli rubbed a hand across his forehead. 'I'm coming.'

He put on a robe and walked across the room to where his trousers were draped on the back of a chair. He checked his wallet. His money was all there. *So, the bitch wasn't stupid.* He extracted a hundred-dollar bill, walked over to the door and opened it.

His neighbor was standing in the hallway in a robe and slippers. 'Do you know what time it is?' he asked indignantly. 'You told me . . .'

Rizzoli handed him the hundred-dollar bill. 'I'm terribly sorry,' he said apologetically. 'I won't be long.'

The man swallowed, his indignation gone. 'That's all right. It must be important for someone to wake people up at four o'clock in the morning.'

Rizzoli walked into the room across the hall and picked up the phone. 'Rizzoli.'

A voice said, 'You have a problem, Mr Rizzoli.'

'Who is this?'

'Spyros Lambrou asked me to call you.'

'Oh.' He felt a sudden sense of alarm. 'What's the problem?'

'It concerns Constantin Demiris.'

'What about him?'

'One of his tankers, the *Thele*, is in Marseilles. It's tied up at the pier in the Bassin de la Grande Joliette.'

'So?'

'We've learned that Mr Demiris has ordered the ship diverted to Athens. It will be docking there Sunday morning, and sailing Sunday night. Constantin Demiris plans to be on it when it sails.'

'*What?*'

'He's running.'

'But he and I have a . . .'

'Mr Lambrou said to tell you that Demiris is planning to hide out in the United States until he can find a way to get rid of you.'

The sneaky son-of-a-bitch! 'I see. Thank Mr Lambrou for me. Tell him thanks very much.'

'It's his pleasure.'

Rizzoli replaced the receiver.

'Is everything all right, Mr Rizzoli?'

'What? Yeah. Everything is great.' And it was.

*

The more Rizzoli thought about the phone call, the more pleased he was. He had Constantin Demiris running scared. That would make it a lot easier to handle him. *Sunday.* He had two days in which to lay his plans.

Rizzoli knew he had to be careful. He was being followed wherever he went. *Fucking Keystone Kops*, Rizzoli thought contemptuously. *When the time comes, I'll dump them.*

Early the following morning, Rizzoli walked to a public telephone booth on Kifissias Street and dialed the number of the Athens State Museum.

In the reflection in the glass Rizzoli could see a man pretending to look in a shop window, and across the street another man in conversation with a flower vendor. The two men were part of the surveillance team that was covering him. *Good luck to you*, Rizzoli thought.

'Office of the curator. Can I help you?'

'Victor? It's Tony.'

'Is anything wrong?' There was sudden panic in Korontzis' voice.

'No,' Rizzoli said soothingly. 'Everything's fine. Victor, you know that pretty vase with the red figures on it?'

'The Ka amphora.'

'Yeah. I'm going to pick it up tonight.'

There was a long pause. 'Tonight? I . . . I don't know, Tony.' Korontzis' voice was trembling. 'If anything should go wrong . . .'

'Okay, pal, forget it. I was trying to do you a favor. You just tell Sal Prizzi you don't have the money, and let him do whatever . . .'

'No, Tony. Wait. I . . . I . . .' There was another pause. 'All right.'

'You sure it's all right, Victor? Because if you don't want to do it, just say so, and I'll head back to the States, where I don't have problems like this. I don't need all this aggravation, you know. I can . . .'

'No, no. I appreciate everything you're doing for me, Tony. Really I do. Tonight will be fine.'

184

'Okay then. When the museum closes, all you have to do is substitute a copy for the real vase.'

'The guards check all packages out of here.'

'So what? Are the guards some kind of art experts?'

'No. Of course not, but . . .'

'All right, Victor, listen to me. You just get a bill of sale for one of the copies and stick it with the original in a paper bag. Do you understand?'

'Yes. I . . . I understand. Where will we meet?'

'We're not going to meet. Leave the museum at six o'clock. There will be a taxi in front. Have the package with you. Tell the driver to take you to Hotel Grande Bretagne. Tell him to wait for you. Leave the package in the cab. Go into the hotel bar and have a drink. After that, go home.'

'But the package . . .'

'Don't worry. It will be taken care of.'

Victor Korontzis was sweating. 'I've never done anything like this, Tony. I've never stolen anything. All my life . . .'

'I know,' Rizzoli said soothingly. 'Neither have I. Remember, Victor, I'm taking all the risks, and I don't get a thing out of it.'

Korontzis' voice broke. 'You're a good friend, Tony. The best friend I ever had.' He was wringing his hands. 'Do you have any idea when I will get my money?'

'Very soon,' Rizzoli assured him. 'Once we pull this off, you won't have any more worries.' *And neither will I*, Rizzoli thought exultantly. *Never again.*

Two cruise ships were in the port of Piraeus that afternoon and consequently the museum was filled with tourists. Usually Victor Korontzis enjoyed studying them, trying to guess what their lives were like. There were Americans and British, and visitors from a dozen other countries. Now, Korontzis was too panicky to think about them.

He looked over at the two showcases where copies of the antiquities were sold. There was a crowd around them, and the two saleswomen were busily trying to keep up with the demand.

185

Maybe they'll sell out, Korontzis thought hopefully, *and I won't be able to go through with Rizzoli's plan*. But he knew he was being unrealistic. There were hundreds of replicas stored in the basement of the museum.

The vase that Tony had asked him to steal was one of the museum's great treasures. It was from the fifteenth century BC, an amphora with red mythological figures painted on a black background. The last time Victor Korontzis had touched it had been fifteen years earlier when he had reverently placed it inside the case to be locked up forever. *And now I'm stealing it*, Korontzis thought miserably. *God help me*.

Dazedly, Korontzis went through the afternoon, dreading the moment when he would become a thief. He went back to his office, shut the door, and sat down at his desk, filled with despair. *I can't do it*, he thought. *There has to be some other way out. But what?* He could think of no way to raise that kind of money. He could still hear Prizzi's voice. *You'll give me that money tonight, or I'm going to feed you to the fish. Do you understand?* The man was a killer. No, he had no choice.

A few minutes before six, Korontzis came out of his office. The two women who sold replicas of the artifacts were beginning to lock up.

'*Signomi*,' Korontzis called. 'A friend of mine is having a birthday. I thought I'd get him something from the museum.' He walked over to the case and pretended to be studying it. There were vases and busts, chalices and books and maps. He looked them over as though trying to decide which to choose. Finally, he pointed to the copy of the red amphora. 'I think he'd like that one.'

'I'm sure he will,' the woman said. She removed it from the case and handed it to Korontzis.

'Could I have a receipt, please?'

'Certainly, Mr Korontzis. Would you like me to gift-wrap this for you?'

'No, no,' Korontzis said quickly. 'You can just throw it in a bag.'

186

He watched her place the replica in a paper bag and put the receipt inside. 'Thank you.'

'I hope your friend enjoys it.'

'I'm sure he will.' He took the bag, his hands trembling, and walked back to his office.

He locked the door, then removed the imitation vase from the bag and placed it on his desk. *It's not too late*, Korontzis thought. *I haven't committed any crime yet.* He was in an agony of indecision. A series of terrifying thoughts ran through his head. *I could run away to another country and abandon my wife and children. Or I could commit suicide. I could go to the police and tell them I'm being threatened. But when the facts come out I will be ruined.* No, there was no way out. If he did not pay the money he owed, he knew that Prizzi would kill him. *Thank God*, he thought, *for my friend Tony. Without him, I would be a dead man.*

He looked at his watch. Time to move. Korontzis rose to his feet, his legs unsteady. He stood there, taking deep breaths, trying to calm himself. His hands were wet with perspiration. He wiped them on his shirt. He put the replica back in the paper bag, and moved toward the door. There was a guard stationed at the front door who left at six, after the museum closed, and another guard who made the rounds, but he had half a dozen rooms to cover. He should be at the far end of the museum now.

Korontzis walked out of his office, and bumped into the guard. He gave a guilty start.

'Excuse me, Mr Korontzis. I didn't know you were still here.'

'Yes. I . . . I'm just getting ready to leave.'

'You know,' the guard said admiringly, 'I envy you.'

If he only knew. 'Really? Why?'

'You know so much about all these beautiful things. I walk around here and I look at them and they're all pieces of history, aren't they? I don't know much about them. Maybe some day you could explain them to me. I really . . .'

The damn fool would not stop talking. 'Yes, of course. Some day. I would be happy to.' At the other end of the room, Korontzis could see the cabinet containing the precious vase. He had to get rid of the guard.

'There . . . there seems to be a problem with the alarm circuit in the basement. Would you check it out?'

'Sure. I understand that some of the things here date back to . . .'

'Would you mind checking it out now? I don't want to leave before I know that everything is all right.'

'Certainly, Mr Korontzis. I'll be right back.'

Victor Korontzis stood there, watching the guard move through the hall, heading toward the basement. The moment he was out of sight, Korontzis hurried over to the case containing the red amphora. He took out a key, and thought, *I'm really going to do it. I'm going to steal it.* The key slipped out of his fingers, and clattered to the floor. *Is this a sign? Is God telling me something?* Perspiration was pouring out of him. He bent down and picked up the key, and stared at the vase. It was so utterly exquisite. It had been made with such loving care by his ancestors, thousands of years ago. The guard was right; it was a piece of history, something that could never be replaced.

Korontzis shut his eyes for an instant and shuddered. He looked around to make sure no one was watching, then unlocked the case and carefully lifted out the vase. He removed the replica from the paper bag and placed it in the case where the genuine one had stood.

Korontzis stood there, studying it a moment. It was an expert reproduction but to him it screamed *Fake*. It was so obvious. *But only to me*, Korontzis thought, *and to a few other experts*. No one else could ever tell the difference. And there would be no reason for anyone to examine it closely. Korontzis closed the case and locked it, and put the genuine vase in the paper bag with the receipt.

He took out a handkerchief and wiped his face and hands. It was done. He looked at his watch. Six ten. He had to hurry. He moved toward the door and saw the guard coming toward him.

'I couldn't find anything wrong with the alarm system, Mr Korontzis and . . .'

'Good,' Korontzis said. 'We can't be too careful.'

The guard smiled. 'You're right about that. Leaving now?'

'Yes. Good night.'

'Good night.'

The second guard was at the front door, getting ready to leave. He noticed the paper bag and grinned. 'I'm going to have to check that out. Your rules.'

'Of course,' Korontzis said quickly. He handed the bag to the guard.

The guard looked inside, took out the vase and saw the receipt.

'It's a gift for a friend,' Korontzis explained. 'He's an engineer.' *Why did I have to say that? What does he care! I must act natural.*

'Nice.' The guard tossed the vase back into the bag, and for one terrible instant Korontzis thought it was going to break.

Korontzis clutched the bag to his breast. '*Kalispehra.*'

The guard opened the door for him. '*Kalispehra.*'

Korontzis went out into the cool night air, breathing heavily and fighting nausea. He had something worth millions of dollars in his hands, but Korontzis did not think of it in those terms. What he was thinking was that he was betraying his country, stealing a piece of history from his beloved Greece and selling it to some faceless foreigner.

He started down the steps. As Rizzoli had promised, there was a taxi waiting in front of the museum. Korontzis moved toward it, and got in. 'Hotel Grande Bretagne,' he said.

He slumped back in his seat. He felt beaten and exhausted, as though he had just been through some terrible battle. But had he won or lost?

When the taxi pulled up in front of Hotel Grande Bretagne, Korontzis said to the driver, 'Wait here, please.' He took a last look at the precious package on the back seat, then got out and quickly walked into the lobby of the hotel. Inside the door he turned and watched. A man was entering the taxi. A moment later it sped away.

So. It was done. *I'll never have to do anything like this again,* Korontzis thought. *Not as long as I live. The nightmare is over.*

*

189

At three o'clock Sunday afternoon, Tony Rizzoli walked out of his hotel and strolled toward the Platia Omonia. He was wearing a bright red check jacket, green trousers and a red beret. Two detectives were trailing him. One of them said, 'He must have gone shopping for those clothes at a circus.'

At Metaxa Street, Rizzoli hailed a taxi. The detective spoke into his walkie-talkie. 'The subject is getting into a taxi heading west.'

A voice replied, 'We see him. We're following. Return to the hotel.'

'Right.'

An unmarked grey sedan pulled in behind the taxi, keeping a discreet distance. The taxi headed south, past Monastiraki. In the sedan the detective seated next to the driver picked up the hand microphone.

'Central. This is Unit Four. The subject is in a taxi. It's driving down Philhellinon Street . . . Wait. They just turned right at Peta Street. It looks like he's headed for the Plaka. We might lose him in there. Can you have a detail follow him on foot?'

'Just a minute, Unit Four.' A few seconds later, the radio crackled back to life. 'Unit Four. We have assistance available. If he gets off at the Plaka, he'll be kept under surveillance.'

'*Kala*. The subject is wearing a red check jacket, green trousers and a red beret. He's hard to miss. Wait a minute. The taxi is stopping. He's getting out at the Plaka.'

'We'll pass on the information. He's covered. You're clear. Out.'

At the Plaka, two detectives were watching as the man emerged from the taxi.

'Where the hell did he buy that outfit?' one of the detectives wondered aloud.

They closed in behind him and began to follow him through the crowded maze of the old section of the city. For the next hour he strolled aimlessly through the streets, wandering past tavernas, bars, souvenir shops and small art galleries. He walked

190

down Anaphiotika and stopped to browse at a flea market filled with swords, daggers, muskets, cooking pots, candlesticks, oil lamps and binoculars.

'What the hell is he up to?'

'It looks like he's just out for an afternoon stroll. Hold it. There he goes.'

They followed as he turned into Aghiou Geronda and headed for Xinos restaurant. The two detectives stood outside, at a distance, watching him order.

The detectives were beginning to get bored. 'I hope he makes a move soon. I'd like to go home. I could use a nap.'

'Stay awake. If we lose him, Nicolino will have our ass.'

'How can we lose him? He stands out like a beacon.'

The other detective was staring at him.

'What? What did you say?'

'I said . . .'

'Never mind.' There was a sudden urgency in his voice. 'Did you get a look at his face?'

'No.'

'Neither did I. *Tiflo!* Come on.'

The two detectives hurried into the restaurant and strode up to his table.

They were looking into the face of a complete stranger.

Inspector Nicolino was in a fury. 'I had three teams assigned to follow Rizzoli. How could you lose him?'

'He pulled a switch on us, Inspector. The first team saw him get into a taxi and . . .'

'And they lost the taxi?'

'No, sir. We watched him get out. Or at least we thought it was him. He was wearing a wild outfit. Rizzoli had another passenger hidden in the taxi, and the two men switched clothes. We followed the wrong man.'

'And Rizzoli rode away in the taxi.'

'Yes, sir.'

'Did you get the license number?'

'Well, no, sir. It – it didn't seem important.'

'What about the man you picked up?'

'He's a bellboy at Rizzoli's hotel. Rizzoli told him he was playing a joke on someone. He gave him a hundred dollars. That's all the boy knows.'

Inspector Nicolino took a deep breath. 'And I don't suppose anyone knows where Mr Rizzoli is at this moment?'

'No, sir. I'm afraid not.'

Greece has seven main ports – Thessaloniki, Patras, Volos, Igoumenitsa, Kavala, Iraklion and Piraeus.

Piraeus lies seven miles southwest of the center of Athens, and it serves not only as the main port of Greece, but as one of the major ports of Europe. The port complex consists of four harbors, three of them for pleasure boats and ocean-going vessels. The fourth harbor, Herakles, is reserved for freighters fitted with hatches opening directly onto the quay.

The *Thele* was lying at anchor at Herakles. It was a huge tanker, and lying still in the dark harbor, it resembled a giant behemoth ready to pounce.

Tony Rizzoli, accompanied by four men, drove up to the pier. Rizzoli looked up at the huge ship and thought, *So it is here. Now let's see if our friend Demiris is aboard.*

He turned to the men with him. 'I want two of you to wait here. The other two come with me. See that nobody gets off the ship.'

'Right.'

Rizzoli and two men walked up the gangplank. As they reached the top, a deck hand approached them. 'Can I help you?'

'We're here to see Mr Demiris.'

'Mr Demiris is in the owner's cabin. Is he expecting you?'

So the tip-off was right. Rizzoli smiled. 'Yeah. He's expecting us. What time is the ship sailing?'

'At midnight. I'll show you the way.'

'Thank you.'

They followed the sailor along the deck until they came to a ladder that led below. The three men trailed him down the ladder and along a narrow passageway, passing half a dozen cabins along the way.

When they arrived at the last cabin, the sailor started to knock. Rizzoli pushed him aside. 'We'll announce ourselves.' He shoved the door open and walked in.

The cabin was larger than Rizzoli had expected. It was furnished with a bed and a couch, a desk, and two easy chairs. Behind the desk sat Constantin Demiris.

When he looked up and saw Rizzoli, Demiris scrambled to his feet. His face paled. 'What . . . what are you doing here?' His voice was a whisper.

'My friends and I decided to pay you a little bon voyage visit, Costa.'

'How did you know I . . . ? I mean . . . I wasn't expecting you.'

'I'm sure you weren't,' Rizzoli said. He turned to the sailor. 'Thanks, pal.'

The sailor left.

Rizzoli turned back to Demiris. 'Were you planning on taking a trip without saying goodbye to your partner?'

Demiris said quickly, 'No. Of course not. I just . . . I just came to check out some things on the ship. She's sailing tomorrow morning.' His fingers were trembling.

Rizzoli moved closer to him. When he spoke, his voice was soft. 'Costa baby, you made a big mistake. There's no point in trying to run away, because you have no place to hide. You and I have a deal, remember? Do you know what happens to people who welsh on deals? They die bad – real bad.'

Demiris swallowed. 'I . . . I'd like to talk to you alone.'

Rizzoli turned to his men. 'Wait outside.'

When they were gone, Rizzoli sank into an armchair. 'I'm very disappointed in you, Costa.'

'I can't go through with this,' Demiris said. 'I'll give you money – more money than you've ever dreamed of.'

'In return for what?'

'For getting off this ship and leaving me alone.' There was desperation in Demiris' voice. 'You can't do this to me. The government will take my fleet away. I'll be ruined. Please. I'll give you anything you want.'

Tony Rizzoli smiled. 'I have everything I want. How many tankers do you have? Twenty? Thirty? We're going to keep them all busy, you and me. All you have to do is add an extra port of call or two.'

'You . . . you don't have any idea what you're doing to me.'

'I guess you should have thought of that before you pulled that little frame-up.' Tony Rizzoli rose to his feet. 'You're going to have a talk with the captain. Tell him we're going to make an extra stop, off the coast of Florida.'

Demiris hesitated. 'All right. When you come back in the morning . . .'

Rizzoli laughed. 'I'm not going any place. The games are over. You were planning to sneak away at midnight. Fine. I'm going to sneak away with you. We're bringing a load of heroin aboard, Costa, and just to sweeten the deal, we're taking along one of the treasures from the State Museum. And you're going to smuggle it into the United States for me. That's your punishment for trying to double-cross me.'

There was a dazed look in Demiris' eyes. 'I – isn't there anything,' he pleaded, 'anything I can do to . . . ?'

Rizzoli patted him on the shoulder. 'Cheer up. I promise you're going to enjoy being my partner.'

Rizzoli walked over to the door and opened it. 'All right, let's load the stuff on board,' he said.

'Where do you want us to put it?'

There are hundreds of hiding places on any ship, but Rizzoli did not feel the need to be clever. Constantin Demiris' fleet was above suspicion.

'Put it in a sack of potatoes,' he said. 'Mark the sack and stow it in the rear of the galley. Bring the vase to Mr Demiris. He's going to take care of it personally.' Rizzoli turned to Demiris, his eyes filled with contempt. 'Do you have any problem with that?'

Demiris tried to speak, but no words came out.

'All right, boys,' Rizzoli said. 'Let's move.'

Rizzoli settled back in the armchair. 'Nice cabin. I'm going to let you keep it, Costa. My boys and I will find our own quarters.'

'Thank you,' Demiris said miserably. 'Thank you.'

*

At midnight, the huge tanker sailed away from the wharf with two tugboats guiding it out to sea. The heroin had been hidden aboard, and the vase had been delivered to Constantin Demiris' cabin.

Tony Rizzoli called one of his men aside. 'I want you to go to the radio room and tear out the wireless. I don't want Demiris sending any messages.'

'Gotcha, Tony.'

Constantin Demiris was a broken man, but Rizzoli was taking no chances.

Rizzoli had been afraid up until the moment of sailing that something might go wrong, for what was happening was beyond his wildest dreams. Constantin Demiris, one of the richest, most powerful men in the world, was his partner. *Partner, hell*, Rizzoli thought. *I own the bastard. His whole goddamned fleet belongs to me. I can ship as much stuff as the boys can deliver. Let the other guys break their asses trying to figure out how to smuggle the stuff into the States. I've got it made. And then there's all the treasures from the museum. That's another real gold mine. Only it all belongs to me. What the boys don't know won't hurt them.*

Tony Rizzoli fell asleep dreaming of a fleet of golden ships and palaces and nubile serving girls.

When Rizzoli awoke in the morning, he and his men went to the dining room for breakfast. Half a dozen crew members were already there. A steward approached the table. 'Good morning.'

'Where's Mr Demiris?' Rizzoli asked. 'Isn't he having breakfast?'

'He's staying in his cabin, Mr Rizzoli. He gave us instructions to give you and your friends anything you want.'

'That's very nice of him,' Rizzoli smiled. 'I'll have some orange juice, and bacon and eggs. What about you, boys?'

'Sounds good.'

When they had ordered, Rizzoli said, 'I want you boys to play

195

it cool. Keep your pieces out of sight. Be nice and polite. Remember, we're Mr Demiris' guests.'

Demiris did not appear for lunch that day. Nor did he show up for dinner.

Rizzoli went up to have a talk with him.

Demiris was in his cabin, staring out of a porthole. He looked pale and drawn.

Rizzoli said, 'You gotta eat to keep your strength up, partner. I wouldn't want you to get sick. We have a lot to do. I told the steward to send in some dinner here.'

Demiris took a deep breath. 'I can't – all right. Get out, please.'

Rizzoli grinned. 'Sure. After dinner, get some sleep. You look terrible.'

In the morning, Rizzoli went to see the captain.

'I'm Tony Rizzoli,' he said. 'I'm a guest of Mr Demiris.'

'Ah, yes. Mr Demiris told me you would be coming to see me. He mentioned that there might be a change of course?'

'Right. I'll let you know. When will we be arriving off the coast of Florida?'

'In approximately three weeks, Mr Rizzoli.'

'Good. I'll see you later.'

Rizzoli left and strolled around the ship – *his* ship. The whole goddamned fleet was his. The world was his. Rizzoli was filled with a euphoria such as he had never known.

The crossing was smooth, and from time to time, Rizzoli dropped into Constantin Demiris' cabin.

'You should have some broads on board,' Rizzoli said. 'But I guess you Greeks don't need broads, do you?'

Demiris refused to rise to the bait.

*

The days passed slowly, but every hour brought Rizzoli closer to his dreams. He was in a fever of impatience. A week passed, then another week, and they were nearing the North American continent.

On Saturday evening Rizzoli was standing at the ship's rail looking out at the ocean when there was a flash of lightning.

The first mate came up to him. 'We might be in for some rough weather, Mr Rizzoli. I hope you're a good sailor.'

Rizzoli shrugged. 'Nothing bothers me.'

The sea began its swell. The ship started to dip into the sea and then buck upwards as it ploughed through the waves.

Rizzoli began to feel queasy. *So I'm not a good sailor*, he thought. *What's the difference?* He owned the world. He returned to his cabin early and got into bed.

He had dreams. This time, there were no golden ships or beautiful naked girls. They were dark dreams. There was a war going on, and he could hear the roar of cannons. An explosion woke him up.

Rizzoli sat up in bed, wide awake. The cabin *was* rocking. The ship was in the middle of a goddamned storm. He could hear footsteps running through the corridor. What the hell was going on?

Tony Rizzoli hurried out of bed and went into the corridor. The floor suddenly listed to one side and he almost lost his balance.

'What's happening?' he called to one of the men running past him.

'An explosion. The ship's on fire. We're sinking. You'd better get up on deck.'

'*Sinking* . . . ?' Rizzoli could not believe it. Everything had gone so smoothly. *But it doesn't matter*, Rizzoli thought. *I can afford to lose this shipment. There will be plenty more. I've got to save Demiris. He's the key to everything. We'll send out a call for help.* And then he remembered that he had ordered the wireless destroyed.

Fighting to keep his balance, Tony Rizzoli made his way toward the companionway and climbed up to the deck. To his surprise, he saw that the storm had cleared. The sea was smooth.

A full moon had come out. There was another loud explosion, and another, and the ship started to list farther. The stern was in the water, going down rapidly. Sailors were trying to lower the lifeboats, but it was too late. The water around the ship was a mass of burning oil. Where was Constantin Demiris?

And then Rizzoli heard it. It was a whirring sound, pitched high above the thunder of the explosions. He looked up. There was a helicopter poised ten feet above the ship.

We're saved, Rizzoli thought jubilantly. He waved frantically at the helicopter.

A face appeared at the window. It took Rizzoli a moment to realize that it was Constantin Demiris. He was smiling, and in his raised hand he was holding up the priceless amphora.

Rizzoli stared, his brain trying to put together what was happening. How had Constantin Demiris found a helicopter in the middle of the night to . . . ?

And then Rizzoli knew, and his bowels turned to water. Constantin Demiris had never had any intention of doing business with him. The son-of-a-bitch had planned the whole thing from the beginning. The phone call telling him that Demiris was running away – that phone call hadn't come from Spyros Lambrou – it had come from Demiris! He had laid his trap to get him on the ship, and Rizzoli had leaped into it.

The tanker started to sink deeper, faster, and Rizzoli felt the cold ocean lapping at his feet, and then his knees. The bastard was going to let them all die here, in the middle of nowhere, where there would be no trace of what happened.

Rizzoli looked up at the helicopter, and yelled frantically, 'Come back, I'll give you anything!' The wind whipped his words away.

The last thing Tony Rizzoli saw before the ship heeled over and his eyes filled with the burning salt water was the helicopter zooming toward the moon.

Chapter 17

St Moritz

Catherine was in a state of shock. She sat on the couch in her hotel room, listening to Lieutenant Hans Bergman, head of the ski patrol, tell her that Kirk Reynolds was dead. The sound of Bergman's voice flowed over Catherine in waves, but she was not listening to the words. She was too numbed by the horror of what had happened. *All the people around me die*, she thought despairingly. *Larry's dead, and now Kirk.* And there were the others: Noelle, Napoleon Chotas, Frederick Stavros. It was an unending nightmare.

Vaguely, through the fog of her despair, she heard Hans Bergman's voice. 'Mrs Reynolds . . . Mrs Reynolds . . .'

She raised her head. 'I'm not Mrs Reynolds,' she said wearily. 'I'm Catherine Alexander. Kirk and I were . . . were friends.'

'I see.'

Catherine took a deep breath. 'How . . . how did it happen? Kirk was such a good skier.'

'I know. He skied here many times.' He shook his head. 'To tell you the truth, Miss Alexander, I'm puzzled about what happened. We found his body on the Lagalp, a slope that was closed because of an avalanche last week. The sign must have been blown down by the wind. I'm terribly sorry.'

Sorry. What a weak word, what a stupid word.

'How would you like us to handle the funeral arrangements, Miss Alexander?'

So death was not the end. No, there were *arrangements* to be

199

made. Coffins and burial plots, and flowers, and relatives to be notified. Catherine wanted to scream.

'Miss Alexander?'

Catherine looked up. 'I'll notify Kirk's family.'

'Thank you.'

The trip back to London was a mourning. She had come up to the mountains with Kirk, filled with eager hope, thinking that it was, perhaps, a new beginning, a door to a new life.

Kirk had been so gentle and so patient. *I should have made love with him*, Catherine thought. *But in the end, would it really have mattered? What did anything matter? I'm under some kind of curse. I destroy everyone who comes near me.*

When Catherine returned to London, she was too depressed to go back to work. She stayed in the flat, refusing to see anyone, or talk to anyone. Anna, the housekeeper, prepared meals for her and took them to Catherine's room, but the trays were returned, untouched.

'You must eat something, Miss Alexander.'

But the thought of food made Catherine ill.

The next day Catherine was feeling worse. She felt as though her chest were filled with iron. She found it difficult to breathe.

I can't go on like this, Catherine thought. *I have to do something*.

She discussed it with Evelyn Kaye.

'I keep blaming myself for what happened.'

'That doesn't make sense, Catherine.'

'I know it doesn't, but I can't help it. I feel responsible. I need someone to talk to. Maybe if I saw a psychiatrist . . .'

'I know one who's awfully good,' Evelyn said. 'As a matter of fact, he sees Wim from time to time. His name is Alan Hamilton. I had a friend who was suicidal and by the time Dr Hamilton was through treating her, she was in great shape. Would you like to see him?'

What if he tells me I'm crazy? What if I am? 'All right,' Catherine said reluctantly.

'I'll try to make the appointment for you. He's pretty busy.'

'Thanks, Evelyn. I appreciate it.'

Catherine went into Wim's office. *He would want to know about Kirk*, she thought.

'Wim – do you remember Kirk Reynolds? He was killed a few days ago in a skiing accident.'

'Yeah? Westminster-oh-four-seven-one.'

Catherine blinked. 'What?' And she suddenly realized that Wim was reciting Kirk's telephone number. Was that all people meant to Wim? A series of numbers? Didn't he have any feelings for them? Was he really unable to love or hate or feel compassion?

Perhaps he's better off than I am, Catherine thought. *At least he's spared the terrible pain that the rest of us can feel.*

Evelyn arranged an appointment for Catherine with Dr Hamilton for the following Friday. Evelyn thought of telephoning Constantin Demiris to tell him what she had done, but she decided it was too unimportant to bother him about.

Alan Hamilton's office was on Wimpole Street. Catherine went there for her first appointment, apprehensive and angry. Apprehensive because she was fearful of what he might say about her, and angry with herself for having to rely on a stranger to help her with problems she felt she should have been able to solve herself.

The receptionist behind the glass window said, 'Dr Hamilton is ready for you, Miss Alexander.'

But am I ready for him? Catherine wondered. She was filled with sudden panic. *What am I doing here? I'm not going to put myself in the hands of some quack who probably thinks he's God.*

Catherine said, 'I – I've changed my mind. I don't really need

201

to see the doctor. I'll be happy to pay for the appointment.'

'Oh? Just a moment, please.'

'But . . .'

The receptionist had disappeared into the doctor's office.

A few moments later, the door to the office opened, and Alan Hamilton came out. He was in his early forties, tall and blond with bright blue eyes, and an easy manner.

He looked at Catherine and smiled. 'You've made my day,' he said.

Catherine frowned. 'What . . . ?'

'I didn't realize how good a doctor I really was. You just walked into my reception office, and you're already feeling better. That must be some kind of record.'

Catherine said defensively, 'I'm sorry. I made a mistake. I don't need any help.'

'I'm delighted to hear that,' Alan Hamilton said. 'I wish all my patients felt that way. As long as you're here, Miss Alexander, why don't you come in for a moment? We'll have a cup of coffee.'

'Thank you, no. I don't . . .'

'I promise you can drink it sitting up.'

Catherine hesitated. 'All right, just for a minute.'

She followed him into his office. It was very simple, done in quiet good taste, furnished more like a living room than an office. There were soothing prints hanging on the walls, and on a coffee table was a photograph of a beautiful woman with a young boy. *All right, so he has a nice office and an attractive family. What does that prove?*

'Please sit down,' Dr Hamilton said. 'The coffee should be ready in a minute.'

'I really shouldn't be wasting your time, Doctor. I'm . . .'

'Don't worry about that.' He sat in an easy chair, studying her. 'You've been through a lot,' he said sympathetically.

'What do you know about it?' Catherine snapped. Her tone was angrier than she had intended.

'I spoke with Evelyn. She told me what happened at St Moritz. I'm sorry.'

That damned word again. 'Are you? If you're such a wonderful doctor, maybe you can bring Kirk back to life.' All the misery that had been pent up inside her broke, erupting in a torrent, and to her horror Catherine found that she was sobbing hysterically. 'Leave me alone,' she screamed. 'Leave me alone.'

Alan Hamilton sat there watching her, saying nothing.

When Catherine's sobs finally subsided she said wearily, 'I'm sorry. Forgive me. I really must go now.' She rose, and started toward the door.

'Miss Alexander, I don't know whether I can help you, but I'd like to try. I can promise you only that whatever I do won't hurt you.'

Catherine stood at the door, undecided. She turned to look at him, her eyes filled with tears. 'I don't know what's the matter with me,' she whispered. 'I feel so lost.'

Alan Hamilton rose, and walked over to her. 'Then why don't we try to find you? We'll work on it together. Sit down. I'll see about that coffee.'

He was gone for five minutes, and Catherine sat there, wondering how he had talked her into staying. He had a calming effect. There was something in his manner that was reassuring.

Maybe he can help me, Catherine thought.

Alan Hamilton came back into the room carrying two cups of coffee. 'There's cream and sugar, if you like.'

'No, thank you.'

He sat down across from her. 'I understand your friend died in a skiing accident.'

It was so painful to talk about. 'Yes. He was on a slope that was supposed to have been closed. The wind blew the sign down.'

'Is this your first encounter with the death of someone close to you?'

How was she supposed to answer that? *Oh, no. My husband and his mistress were executed for trying to murder me. Everyone around me dies.* That would shake him up. He was sitting there, waiting for an answer, *the smug son-of-a-bitch*. Well, she wouldn't give him the satisfaction. Her life was none of his business. *I hate him.*

Alan Hamilton saw the anger in her face. He deliberately changed the subject. 'How's Wim?' he asked.

203

The question threw Catherine completely off-guard. 'Wim? He – he's fine. Evelyn told me he's a patient of yours.'

'Yes.'

'Can you explain how he – why he – is like he is?'

'Wim came to me because he kept losing jobs. He's something very rare – a genuine misanthrope. I can't go into the reasons why, but basically, he hates people. He is unable to relate to other people.'

Catherine remembered Evelyn's words. *He has no emotions. He'll never get attached to anyone.*

'But Wim is brilliant with mathematics,' Alan Hamilton went on. 'He's in a job now where he can apply that knowledge.'

Catherine nodded. 'I've never known anyone like him.'

Alan Hamilton leaned forward in his chair. 'Miss Alexander,' he said, 'what you're going through is very painful, but I think I might be able to make it easier for you. I'd like to try.'

'I . . . I don't know,' Catherine said. 'Everything seems so hopeless.'

'As long as you feel that way,' Alan Hamilton smiled, 'there's nowhere to go but up, is there?' His smile was infectious. 'Why don't we set just one more appointment? If, at the end of that one, you still hate me, we'll call it quits.'

'I don't hate you,' Catherine said apologetically. 'Well, a little bit maybe.'

Alan Hamilton walked over to his desk and studied his calendar. His schedule was completely booked.

'What about Monday?' he asked. 'One o'clock?' One o'clock was his lunch hour, but he was willing to forgo that. Catherine Alexander was a woman carrying an unbearable burden, and he was determined to do everything he could to help her.

Catherine looked at him a long moment. 'All right.'

'Fine. I'll see you then.' He handed her a card. 'In the meantime, if you need me, here's my office number and my home number. I'm a light sleeper, so don't worry about waking me up.'

'Thank you,' Catherine said. 'I'll be here Monday.'

Dr Alan Hamilton watched her walk out the door and he thought, *She's so vulnerable, and so beautiful. I have to be*

204

careful. He looked at the photograph on his coffee table. *I wonder what Angela would think?*

The call came in the middle of the night.

Constantin Demiris listened and when he spoke his voice was filled with surprise. 'The *Thele* sank? I can't believe it.'

'It's true, Mr Demiris. The coast guard found a few pieces of the wreckage.'

'Were there any survivors?'

'No, sir. I'm afraid not. All hands were lost.'

'That's terrible. Does anyone know how it happened?'

'I'm afraid we'll never know, sir. All the evidence is at the bottom of the sea.'

'The sea,' Demiris murmured, 'the cruel sea.'

'Shall we go ahead and file an insurance claim?'

'It's hard to worry about things like that when all those brave men have lost their lives – but yes, go ahead and file the claim.' He would keep the vase in his private collection.

Now it was time to punish his brother-in-law.

Chapter 18

Spyros Lambrou was in a frenzy of impatience, waiting for the news of Constantin Demiris' arrest. He kept the radio on constantly in his office, and scanned every edition of the daily newspapers. *I should have heard something by now*, Lambrou thought. *The police should have arrested Demiris by this time.*

The moment Tony Rizzoli had informed Spyros that Demiris was on board the *Thele* and was about to sail, Lambrou had notified US Customs – anonymously, of course.

They must have caught him by now. Why haven't the newspapers picked up the story?

His intercom buzzed. 'Mr Demiris is on line two for you.'

'Someone is calling for Mr Demiris?'

'No, Mr Lambrou. Mr Demiris himself is on the line.' The words sent a chill through him.

It was impossible!

Nervously, Lambrou picked up the phone. 'Costa?'

'Spyros.' Demiris' voice was jovial. 'How is everything going?'

'Fine, fine. Where are you?'

'In Athens. What about lunch today? Are you free?'

Lambrou had an important luncheon engagement. 'Yes. That will be fine.'

'Good. We'll meet at the club. Two o'clock.'

Lambrou replaced the receiver, his hands trembling. What in God's name could have gone wrong? Well, he would find out what had happened soon enough.

Constantin Demiris kept Spyros waiting for thirty minutes, and when he finally arrived he said brusquely, 'Sorry I'm late.'

'That's all right.'

Spyros studied Demiris carefully, looking for any signs of the recent experience he must have gone through. *Nothing.*

'I'm hungry,' Demiris said cheerfully. 'How about you? Let's see what they have on the menu today.' He scanned the menu. 'Ah. *Stridia.* Would you like to start with some oysters, Spyros?'

'No. I don't think so.' He had lost his appetite. Demiris was acting much too cheerful, and Lambrou had a terrible premonition.

When they had ordered, Demiris said, 'I want to thank you, Spyros.'

Spyros eyed him warily. 'What for?'

'What for? For sending me a good customer – Mr Rizzoli.'

Lambrou wet his lips. 'You – you met with him?'

'Oh, yes. He assured me that we were going to do a lot of business together in the future.' Demiris sighed. 'Although I'm afraid Mr Rizzoli doesn't have much of a future anymore.'

Spyros tensed. 'What do you mean?'

Constantin Demiris' voice hardened. 'What I mean is that Tony Rizzoli is dead.'

'How did . . . ? What happened?'

'He had an accident, Spyros.' He was looking into his brother-in-law's eyes. 'The way anyone who tries to double-cross me has an accident.'

'I don't . . . I don't understand. You . . .'

'Don't you? You tried to destroy me. You failed. I promise you, it would have been better for you if you had succeeded.'

'I – I don't know what you're talking about.'

'Don't you, Spyros?' Constantin Demiris smiled. 'You will very soon. But first, I'm going to destroy your sister.'

The oysters arrived.

'Ah,' Demiris said, 'they look delicious. Enjoy your lunch.'

Afterward, Constantin Demiris thought about the meeting with a feeling of deep satisfaction. Spyros Lambrou was a man completely demoralized. Demiris knew how much Lambrou adored his sister and Demiris intended to punish them both.

But there was something he had to take care of first. Catherine

207

Alexander. She had called him after Kirk's death, near hysteria.

'It's – it's so awful.'

'I'm so sorry, Catherine. I know how fond of Kirk you must have been. It's a terrible loss for both of us.'

I'm going to have to change my plans, Demiris thought. *There's no time for Rafina now. Too bad.* Catherine was the only remaining link to connect him with what had happened to Noelle Page and Larry Douglas. It was a mistake to let her live this long. As long as she was alive, someone would be able to prove what Demiris had done. But with her dead, he would be perfectly safe.

He picked up a telephone on his desk and dialed a number. When a voice answered, Demiris said, 'I'll be in Kowloon Monday. Be there.' He hung up without waiting for a response.

The two men met in a deserted building that Demiris owned in the walled city.

'It must look like an accident. Can you arrange that?' Constantin Demiris asked.

It was an insult. He could feel the anger rising in him. That was a question you asked some amateur you picked up from the streets. He was tempted to reply with sarcasm: *Oh, I think I can manage that. Would you prefer an accident indoors? I can arrange for her to break her neck falling down a flight of stairs.* The dancer in Marseilles. *Or she could get drunk and drown in her bath.* The heiress in Gstaad. *She could take an overdose of heroin.* He had disposed of three that way. *Or she could fall asleep in bed with a lighted cigarette.* The Swedish detective at L'Hôtel on the Left Bank in Paris. *Or perhaps you would prefer something outdoors? I can arrange a traffic accident, a plane crash, or a disappearance at sea.*

But he said none of those things, for in truth, he was afraid of the man seated across from him. He had heard too many chilling stories about him, and he had reason to believe them.

So all he said was, 'Yes sir, I can arrange an accident. No one will ever know.' Even as he said the words, the thought struck him: *He knows that I'll know.* He waited. He could hear the

208

street noises outside the window, and the shrill and raucous polyglot of languages that belonged to the residents of the walled city.

Demiris was studying him with cold, obsidian eyes.

When he finally spoke he said, 'Very well. I will leave the method to you.'

'Yes, sir. Is the target here in Kowloon?'

'London. Her name is Catherine. Catherine Alexander. She works in my London offices.'

'It would help if I could get an introduction to her. An inside track.'

Demiris thought for a moment. 'I'm sending a delegation of executives to London next week. I'll arrange for you to be in the party.' He leaned forward and said quietly, 'One thing more.'

'Yes, sir?'

'I don't want anyone to be able to identify her body.'

Chapter 19

————◆————

Constantin Demiris was calling. 'Good morning, Catherine. How are you feeling today?'

'Fine, thank you, Costa.'

'You are feeling better?'

'Yes.'

'Good. I'm very pleased to hear that. I'm sending a delegation of our company executives to London to study our operation there. I would appreciate it if you would take them in hand and look after them.'

'I'll be happy to. When will they be arriving?'

'Tomorrow morning.'

'I'll do everything I can.'

'I know I can count on you. Thank you, Catherine.'

'You're welcome.'

Goodbye, Catherine.

The connection was broken.

So, that was done! Constantin Demiris sat back in his chair thinking. With Catherine Alexander gone, there would be no more loose ends. Now he could turn his full attention to his wife and her brother.

'We're having company tonight. Some executives from the office. I want you to act as hostess.'

It had been so long since she had been a hostess for her husband. Melina felt elated, excited. *Perhaps this will change things.*

*

The dinner that evening changed nothing. Three men arrived, dined and left. The dinner was a blur.

Melina was perfunctorily introduced to the men and sat there while her husband charmed them. She had almost forgotten how charismatic Costa could be. He told amusing stories and gave them lavish compliments, and they loved it. They were in the presence of a great man, and they showed that they were aware of it. Melina never got a chance to speak. Every time she started to say something, Costa interrupted, until finally she sat there in silence.

Why did he want me here? Melina wondered.

At the end of the evening, as the men were leaving, Demiris said, 'You'll be flying to London early in the morning. I'm sure you'll take care of everything that needs to be done.'

And they were gone.

The delegation arrived in London the following morning. There were three of them, all of different nationalities.

The American, Jerry Haley, was a tall, muscular man with a friendly, open face and slate-grey eyes. He had the largest hands Catherine had ever seen. She was fascinated by them. They seemed to have a life of their own, constantly in motion, twisting and turning, as though eager to have something to do.

The Frenchman, Yves Renard, was a sharp contrast. He was short and stout. His features were pinched, and he had cold, probing eyes that seemed to see through Catherine. He appeared withdrawn and self-contained. *Wary* was the word that came to Catherine's mind. *But wary of what?* Catherine wondered.

The third member of the delegation was Dino Mattusi. He was Italian, friendly and ingratiating, exuding charm through every pore.

'Mr Demiris thinks highly of you,' Mattusi said.

'That's very flattering.'

'He said you are going to take care of us in London. Look, I brought you a little gift.' He handed Catherine a package with an Hermès label on it. Inside was a beautiful silk scarf.

'Thank you,' Catherine said. 'That's very thoughtful of you.'

211

She looked at the others. 'Let me show you to your offices.'

Behind them was a loud crash. They all turned. A young boy stood there, staring in dismay at a package he had dropped. He was carrying three suitcases. The boy looked about fifteen and was small for his age. He had curly brown hair and bright green eyes, and he was fragile-looking.

'For Christ's sake,' Renard snapped. 'Be careful with those things!'

'I'm sorry,' the boy said nervously. 'Excuse me. Where shall I put the suitcases?'

Renard said impatiently, 'Put them anywhere. We'll get them later.'

Catherine looked at the boy inquiringly. Evelyn explained, 'He quit his job as an office boy in Athens. We needed another office boy here.'

'What's your name?' Catherine asked.

'Atanas Stavich, ma'am.' He was near tears.

'All right, Atanas. There's a room in back where you can put the suitcases. I'll see that they're taken care of.'

The boy said gratefully, 'Thank you, ma'am.'

Catherine turned back to the men. 'Mr Demiris said that you'll be studying our operation here. I'll help you in every way I can. If there is anything at all you need, I'll try to arrange it for you. Now, if you gentlemen will come with me, I'll introduce you to Wim and the rest of the staff.' As they walked down the corridor, Catherine stopped to make the introductions. They reached Wim's office.

'Wim, this is the delegation Mr Demiris sent. This is Yves Renard, Dino Mattusi and Jerry Haley. They just arrived from Greece.'

Wim glared at them. 'Greece has a population of only seven million six hundred and thirty thousand.' The men looked at one another, puzzled.

Catherine smiled to herself. They were having exactly the same reaction to Wim that she had had when she first met him.

'I've had your offices prepared,' Catherine said to the men. 'Would you like to follow me?'

When they were out in the corridor, Jerry Haley asked, 'What

212

the hell was that? Someone said he was important around here.'

'He is,' Catherine assured him. 'Wim keeps track of the finances of all the various divisions.'

'I wouldn't let him keep track of my cat,' Haley snorted.

'When you get to know him better . . .'

'I do not wish to get to know him better,' the Frenchman muttered.

'I've arranged your hotels for you,' Catherine told the group. 'I understand each of you wants to stay in a different hotel.'

'That's right,' Mattusi replied.

Catherine started to make a comment, then decided not to. It was none of her business why they had chosen to stay at different hotels.

He watched Catherine, thinking, *She's much prettier than I expected. That will make it more interesting. And she has suffered pain. I can read it in her eyes. I will teach her how exquisite pain can be. We will enjoy it together. And when I have finished with her, I will send her where there is no more pain. She will go to the Maker or the Baker. I'm going to enjoy this. I am going to enjoy this very much.*

Catherine showed the men to their respective offices, and when they were settled in, she started to return to her own desk. From the corridor she heard the Frenchman yelling at the young boy.

'This is the wrong briefcase, stupid. Mine is the brown one. Brown! Do you understand English?'

'Yes, sir. I'm sorry, sir.' His voice was filled with panic.

I'm going to have to do something about this, Catherine thought.

Evelyn Kaye said, 'If you need any help with this group, I'm here.'

'I appreciate it, Evelyn. I'll let you know.'

213

A few minutes later, Atanas Stavich walked past Catherine's office. She called out, 'Would you come in here a moment, please?'

The boy looked at her with a frightened expression. 'Yes, ma'am.' He walked in looking as though he expected to be whipped.

'Close the door, please.'

'Yes, ma'am.'

'Take a chair, Atanas. It *is* Atanas, isn't it?'

'Yes, ma'am.'

She was trying to put him at ease, and was not succeeding. 'There's nothing to be frightened of.'

'No, ma'am.'

Catherine sat there studying him, wondering what terrible things had been done to him to make him so fearful. She decided she was going to have to try to learn more about his past.

'Atanas, if anyone here gives you any trouble, or is mean to you, I want you to come to me. Do you understand?'

He swallowed. 'Yes, ma'am.'

But she wondered if he would have nerve enough to come to her. Someone, somewhere, had broken his spirit.

'We'll talk later,' Catherine said.

The résumés of the delegation showed that they had worked in various divisions of Constantin Demiris' far-flung empire, so they had all had experience within the organization. The one who puzzled Catherine the most was the amiable Italian, Dino Mattusi. He bombarded Catherine with questions to which he should have known the answers, and he did not seem terribly interested in learning about the London operation. In fact, he seemed less interested in the company than in Catherine's personal life.

'Are you married?' Mattusi asked.

'No.'

'But you have been married?'

'Yes.'

'Divorced?'

214

She wanted to end the conversation. 'I'm a widow.'

Mattusi grinned at her. 'I'll bet you have a friend. You know what I mean?'

'I know what you mean,' Catherine said stiffly. *And it's none of your business.* 'Are *you* married?'

'*Si, si.* I have a wife and four beautiful *bambini.* They miss me so much when I am away from home.'

'Do you travel a great deal, Mr Mattusi?'

He looked hurt. 'Dino, Dino. Mr Mattusi is my father. Yes, I travel a great deal.' He smiled at Catherine and lowered his voice. 'But sometimes travelling can bring some extra pleasures. You know what I mean?'

Catherine returned his smile. 'No.'

At 12.15 that afternoon, Catherine left to keep her appointment with Dr Hamilton. To her surprise, she found herself looking forward to it. She remembered how upset she had been the last time she had gone to see him. This time, she walked into his office filled with a sense of anticipation. The receptionist had gone to lunch and the door to the doctor's office was open. Alan Hamilton was waiting for her.

'Come in,' he greeted her.

Catherine walked into the office and he indicated a chair.

'Well. Did you have a good week?'

Was it a good week? Not really. She had been unable to get Kirk Reynolds' death out of her mind. 'It was all right. I – I keep busy.'

'That's very helpful. How long have you worked for Constantin Demiris?'

'Four months.'

'Do you enjoy your work?'

'It keeps my mind off . . . off of things. I owe a lot to Mr Demiris. I can't tell you how much he's done for me.' Catherine smiled ruefully. 'But I guess I will, won't I?'

Alan Hamilton shook his head. 'You'll tell me only what you want to tell me.'

There was a silence. She finally broke it. 'My husband used

215

to work for Mr Demiris. He was his pilot. I . . . I had a boating accident and I lost my memory. When I regained it, Mr Demiris offered me this job.'

I'm leaving out the pain, and the terror. Am I ashamed to tell him my husband tried to murder me? Is it because I'm afraid he'll think me less worthwhile?

'It isn't easy for any of us to talk about our pasts.'

Catherine looked at him, silent.

'You said you lost your memory.'

'Yes.'

'You had a boating accident.'

'Yes.' Catherine's lips were stiff, as though she were determined to tell him as little as possible. She was torn with a terrible conflict. She wanted to tell him everything, and get his help. She wanted to tell him nothing, to be left alone.

Alan Hamilton was studying her thoughtfully. 'Are you divorced?'

Yes. By a firing squad. 'He's . . . My husband died.'

'Miss Alexander . . .' He hesitated. 'Do you mind if I call you Catherine?'

'No.'

'I'm Alan. Catherine, what are you afraid of?'

She stiffened. 'What makes you think I'm afraid?'

'Aren't you?'

'No.' This time the silence was longer.

She was afraid to put it into words, afraid to bring the reality out into the open. 'People around me . . . seem to die.'

If he was taken aback, he did not show it. 'And you believe that you're the cause of their deaths?'

'Yes. No. I don't know. I'm . . . confused.'

'We often blame ourselves for things that happen to other people. If a husband and wife get a divorce, the children think they're responsible. If someone curses a person and that person dies, he thinks he was the cause of it. That kind of belief is not at all unusual. You . . .'

'It's more than that.'

'Is it?' He watched her, ready to listen.

The words poured out. 'My husband was killed, and his . . .

216

his mistress. The two lawyers who defended them died. And now . . .' Her voice broke. 'Kirk.'

'And you think you're responsible for all those deaths. That's a tremendous burden to carry around, isn't it?'

'I . . . I seem to be some kind of bad luck charm. I'm afraid to have a relationship with another man. I don't think I could stand it if anything . . .'

'Catherine, do you know whose life you're responsible for? Yours. No one else's. It's impossible for you to control anyone else's life and death. You're innocent. You had nothing to do with any of those deaths. You must understand that.'

You're innocent. You had nothing to do with any of those deaths. And Catherine sat there thinking about those words. She wanted desperately to believe them. Those people died because of their actions, not because of hers. And as for Kirk, it was an unfortunate accident. Wasn't it?

Alan Hamilton was quietly watching her. Catherine looked up and thought, *He's a decent man.* Another thought came unbidden into her mind. *I wish I had met him earlier.* Guiltily, Catherine glanced at the framed photograph of Alan's wife and child on the coffee table.

'Thank you,' Catherine said. 'I . . . I'm going to try to believe that. I'll have to get used to the idea.'

Alan Hamilton smiled. 'We'll get used to it together. Are you coming back?'

'What?'

'This was a trial run, remember? You were going to decide whether you wanted to go on with this.'

Catherine did not hesitate. 'Yes, I'll be back, Alan.'

When she had gone, Alan Hamilton sat there thinking about her.

He had treated many attractive patients during the years he had been practicing, and some of them had indicated a sexual interest in him. But he was too good a psychiatrist to allow himself to be tempted. A personal relationship with a patient was one of the first taboos of his profession. It would have been a betrayal.

*

217

Dr Alan Hamilton came from a medical background. His father was a surgeon who had married his nurse and Alan's grandfather had been a famous cardiologist. From the time he was a small boy, Alan knew that he wanted to be a doctor. A surgeon like his father. He had attended medical school at King's College, and after graduation, had gone on to study surgery.

He had a natural flair for it, a skill that could not be taught. And then, on 1 September 1939, the army of the Third Reich had marched across the border of Poland, and two days later Britain and France declared war. The Second World War had begun.

Alan Hamilton had enlisted as a surgeon.

On 22 June 1940, after the Axis forces had conquered Poland, Norway, and the Low Countries, France fell, and the brunt of the war fell on the British Isles.

At first, a hundred planes a day dropped bombs on British cities. Soon it was two hundred planes, then a thousand. The carnage was beyond imagination. The wounded and dying were everywhere. The cities were in flames. But Hitler had badly misjudged the British. The attacks only served to strengthen their resolve. They were ready to die for their freedom.

There was no respite day or night, and Alan Hamilton found himself going without sleep for stretches that sometimes lasted as long as sixty hours. When the emergency hospital he worked in was bombed, he moved his patients to a warehouse. He saved countless lives, working under the most hazardous conditions possible.

In October, when the bombing was at its height, the air-raid sirens had sounded, and people were making for the air-raid shelters below ground. Alan was in the middle of surgery, and he refused to leave his patient. The bombs were coming closer. A doctor working with Alan said, 'Let's get the hell out of here.'

'In a minute.' He had the patient's chest open and was removing bloody pieces of shrapnel.

'Alan!'

But he could not leave. He was concentrating on what he was

218

doing, oblivious to the sound of the bombs falling all around him. He never heard the sound of the bomb that fell on the building.

He was in a coma for six days, and when he awakened, he learned that among his other injuries, the bones of his right hand had been crushed. They had been set and looked normal, but he would never operate again.

It took him almost a year to get over the trauma of having his future destroyed. He was under the care of a psychiatrist, a no-nonsense doctor who said, 'It's about time you stopped feeling sorry for yourself and got on with your life.'

'Doing what?' Alan had asked bitterly.

'What you've been doing – only in a different way.'

'I don't understand.'

'You're a healer, Alan. You heal people's bodies. Well, you can't do that anymore. But it's just as important to heal people's minds. You'd make a good psychiatrist. You're intelligent and you have compassion. Think about it.'

It had turned out to be one of the most rewarding decisions he had ever made. He enjoyed what he was doing tremendously. In a sense, he found it even more satisfying to bring patients who were living in despair back to normal, than to minister to their physical welfare. His reputation had grown quickly, and for the past three years, he had been forced to turn new patients away. He had agreed to see Catherine only so that he could recommend another doctor to her. But something about her had touched him. *I must help her.*

When Catherine returned to her office, after her session with Alan Hamilton, she went in to see Wim.

'I saw Dr Hamilton today,' Catherine said.

'Yeah? In psychiatric social readjustment, the rating scale for death of a spouse is 100 divorce 73 marital separation from mate

219

65 detention in jail 63 death of a close family member 63 personal injury or illness 53 marriage 50 being fired at work 47 . . .'

Catherine stood there listening. *What must it be like*, she wondered, *to think of things only in mathematical terms? Never to know another person as a human being, never to have a real friend. I feel as though I've found a new friend*, Catherine thought.

I wonder how long he's been married.

Chapter 20

—◆▶—

Athens

You tried to destroy me. You failed. I promise you it would have been better for you if you had succeeded. But first I'm going to destroy your sister.

Constantin Demiris' words were still ringing in Lambrou's ears. He had no doubt that Demiris would try to carry out his threat. What in God's name could have gone wrong with Rizzoli? Everything had been so carefully planned. But there was no time to speculate on what had happened. The important thing now was to warn his sister.

Lambrou's secretary walked into the office. 'Your ten o'clock appointment is waiting. Shall I send . . . ?'

'No. Cancel all my appointments. I won't be back this morning.'

He picked up a telephone and five minutes later he was on his way to see Melina.

She was waiting for him in the garden of the villa. 'Spyros. You sounded so upset on the phone! What's wrong?'

'We have to talk.' He led her to a bench in a vine-covered gazebo. He sat there looking at her and thought, *What a lovely woman she is. She's always brought happiness to everyone her life has touched. She's done nothing to deserve this.*

'Aren't you going to tell me what's wrong?'

Lambrou took a deep breath. 'This is going to be very painful, darling.'

'You're beginning to alarm me.'

'I mean to. Your life is in danger.'

'What? In danger from whom?'

He measured his words carefully. 'I think Costa is going to try to kill you.'

Melina was staring at him, open-mouthed. 'You're joking.'

'No, I mean it, Melina.'

'Darling, Costa is a lot of things, but he's not a murderer. He couldn't . . .'

'You're wrong. He's killed before.'

Her face had gone pale. 'What are you saying?'

'Oh, he doesn't do it with his bare hands. He hires people to do it for him, but . . .'

'I don't believe you.'

'Do you remember Catherine Douglas?'

'The woman who was murdered . . .'

'She wasn't murdered. She's alive.'

Melina shook her head. 'She – she couldn't be. I mean – they executed the people who killed her.'

Lambrou took his sister's hand in his. 'Melina, Larry Douglas and Noelle Page didn't kill Catherine. All the time the trial was going on, Demiris had her hidden away.'

Melina sat there stunned, speechless, remembering the woman she had caught a glimpse of at the house.

Who is the woman I saw in the hall?

She's a friend of a business associate. She's going to work for me in London.

I caught a glimpse of her. She reminds me of someone. She reminds me of the wife of the pilot who used to work for you. But that's impossible, of course. They murdered her.

Yes, they murdered her.

She found her voice. 'I saw her at the house, Spyros. Costa lied to me about her.'

'He's insane. I want you to pack up and get out of this place.'

She looked at him and said slowly, 'No, this is my home.'

'Melina, I couldn't bear it if anything happened to you.'

There was steel in her voice. 'Don't worry. Nothing will

happen to me. Costa is no fool. He knows that if he did anything to harm me he would have to pay dearly for it.'

'He's your husband, but you don't know him. I'm afraid for you.'

'I can handle him, Spyros.'

He looked at her and knew that there was no way he could persuade her to change her mind. 'If you won't leave, do me a favor. Promise you won't be alone with him.'

She patted her brother's cheek. 'I promise.'

Melina had no intention of keeping that promise.

When Constantin Demiris arrived home that evening, Melina was waiting for him. He nodded to her and walked past her into his bedroom. Melina followed him.

'I think it's time we had a talk,' Melina said.

Demiris looked at his watch. 'I only have a few minutes. I have an engagement.'

'Have you? Are you planning to murder someone else to-night?'

He turned to her. 'What are you raving about?'

'Spyros came by to see me this morning.'

'I'm going to have to warn your brother to stay away from my house.'

'It's my house, too,' Melina said defiantly. 'We had a very interesting chat.'

'Really? About what?'

'About you and Catherine Douglas and Noelle Page.'

She had his full attention now. 'That's ancient history.'

'Is it? Spyros says you sent two innocent people to their deaths, Costa.'

'Spyros is a fool.'

'I saw the girl here, in this house.'

'No one will believe you. You won't see her again. I've sent someone to get rid of her.'

And Melina suddenly remembered the three men who had come to dinner. *You'll be flying to London early in the morning. I'm sure you'll take care of everything that needs to be done.*

223

He moved closer to Melina and said softly, 'You know, I'm really getting quite fed up with you and your brother.' He took her arm and squeezed it hard. 'Spyros tried to ruin me. He should have killed me instead.' He squeezed harder. 'Both of you are going to wish he had.'

'Stop it, you're hurting me.'

'My dear wife, you don't know what pain is yet. But you will.' He let go of her arm. 'I'm getting a divorce. I want a real woman. But I won't be out of your life. Oh, no. I have some wonderful plans for you and your dear brother. Well, we've had our little talk. If you'll excuse me, I'll go in and change. It's not polite to keep a lady waiting.'

He turned and walked into his dressing room. Melina stood there, her heart pounding. *Spyros was right. He's a madman.*

She felt completely helpless but she wasn't afraid for her own life. *What do I have to live for?* Melina thought bitterly. Her husband had stripped her of all dignity and brought her down to his level. She thought of all the times he had humiliated her, abused her in public. She knew that she was an object of pity among her friends. No, she was no longer concerned about herself. *I'm ready to die*, she thought, *but I can't let him harm Spyros*. And yet what could she do to stop him? Spyros was powerful, but her husband was more powerful. Melina knew with a terrible certainty that if she let him, her husband would carry out his threat. *I must stop him somehow. But how? How . . . ?*

Chapter 21

The delegation of executives from Athens was keeping Catherine busy. She set up meetings for them with other company executives and took them through the London operation. They marvelled at her efficiency. She was knowledgeable about every phase of the business, and they were impressed.

Catherine's days were full, and the distractions kept her mind off her own problems. She got to know each of the men a little better.

Jerry Haley was the black sheep of his family. His father had been a wealthy oil man, and his grandfather a respected judge. By the time Jerry Haley was twenty-one, he had served three years in juvenile detention centers for auto theft, breaking and entering, and rape. His family had finally sent him to Europe to get rid of him. 'But I straightened myself out,' Haley told Catherine proudly. 'Turned over a whole new leaf.'

Yves Renard was a bitter man. Catherine learned that his parents had given him up and he had been brought up by distant relatives who abused him. 'They had a farm near Vichy, and they worked me like a dog from sun-up to sunset. I escaped from there when I was fifteen and went to work in Paris.'

The cheerful Italian, Dino Mattusi, was born in Sicily, to middle-class parents. 'When I was sixteen, I caused a big scandal by running away with a married woman ten years older than me. Ah, she was *bellissima*.'

'What happened?' Catherine asked.

He sighed. 'They brought me home and then sent me to Rome to escape the wrath of the woman's husband.'

Catherine smiled. 'I see. When did you go to work for Mr Demiris' company?'

He said evasively, 'Later. I did many things first. You know – odd jobs. Anything to make a living.'

'And then you met your wife?'

He looked into Catherine's eyes and said, 'My wife is not here.'

He watched her, talked to her, listened to the sound of her voice, smelled her perfume. He wanted to know everything about her. He liked the way she moved and he wondered what her body was like under her dress. He would know soon. Very soon. He could hardly wait.

Jerry Haley walked into Catherine's office. 'Do you like the theater, Catherine?'

'Why, yes. I . . .'

'There's a new musical that's opened. *Finian's Rainbow*. I'd like to see it tonight.'

'I'll be happy to arrange a ticket for you.'

'It wouldn't be much fun going alone, would it? Are you free?'

Catherine hesitated. 'Yes.' She found herself staring at his enormous, restless hands.

'Great! Pick me up at my hotel at seven o'clock.' It was an order. He turned and walked out of the office.

It was strange, Catherine thought. He seemed so friendly and open and yet . . .

I straightened myself out. She could not get the image of those huge hands out of her mind.

*

226

Jerry Haley was waiting in the lobby of the Savoy Hotel for Catherine and they drove to the theater in a company limousine.

'London's a great city,' Jerry Haley said. 'I always enjoy coming back to it. Have you been here long?'

'A few months.'

'You from the States originally?'

'Yes. Chicago.'

'Now there's a great town. I've had some good times there.'

Raping women?

They arrived at the theater and joined the crowd. The show was wonderful and the cast excellent, but Catherine was unable to concentrate. Jerry Haley kept drumming his fingers on the side of the chair, on his lap, on his knees. He was unable to keep his huge hands still.

When the play was over, Haley turned to Catherine and said, 'It's such a beautiful night. Why don't we get rid of the car and go for a walk in Hyde Park?'

'I have to be at the office early in the morning,' Catherine said. 'Perhaps some other time.'

Haley studied her, an enigmatic smile on his face. 'Sure,' he said. 'There's plenty of time.'

Yves Renard was interested in museums. 'Of course,' the Frenchman said to Catherine, 'in Paris we have the greatest museum in the world. Have you been to the Louvre?'

'No,' Catherine said. 'I've never been to Paris.'

'That's a pity. You should go one day.' But, even as he said it, he thought to himself, *I know she won't.* 'I would like to see the museums in London. Perhaps on Saturday we could visit some of them.'

Catherine had planned to catch up on some of her office work on Saturday. But Constantin Demiris had asked her to see that the visitors were taken care of.

227

'All right,' she said. 'Saturday will be fine.'

Catherine was not looking forward to spending a day with the Frenchman. *He's so bitter. He acts like he's still being abused.*

The day started out pleasantly enough. They went first to the British Museum where they wandered through galleries filled with magnificent treasures of the past. They saw a copy of the Magna Carta, a proclamation signed by Elizabeth I, and treaties of battles fought centuries earlier.

Something about Yves Renard was bothering Catherine, and it was not until they had been at the museum for almost an hour that she realized what it was.

They were looking at a case containing a document written by Admiral Nelson.

'I think this is one of the most interesting exhibits here,' Catherine said. 'This was written just before Admiral Nelson went into battle. You see, he wasn't sure he had the authority . . .' And she was suddenly conscious of the fact that Yves Renard was not listening. Realization swept over her: he had paid almost no attention to any of the displays in the museum. He was not interested. *Then why did he tell me he wanted to see museums?* Catherine wondered.

They went to the Victoria & Albert Museum next and the experience was repeated. This time, Catherine was watching him closely. Yves Renard went from room to room paying lip service to what they were seeing, but his mind was obviously somewhere else.

When they were finished, Catherine asked, 'Would you like to see Westminster Abbey?'

Yves Renard nodded. 'Yes, of course.'

They walked through the great abbey, stopping to look at the tombstones of the famous men of history who were buried there, poets and statesmen and kings.

'Look,' Catherine said, 'this is where Browning is buried.'

Renard glanced down. 'Ah, Browning.' And then he moved on.

Catherine stood there looking after him. *What is he looking for? Why is he wasting this day?*

When they were on the way back to the hotel, Yves Renard said, 'Thank you, Miss Alexander. I enjoyed that very much.'

He's lying, Catherine thought. *But why?*

'There's a place that I've heard is very interesting. Stonehenge. I believe it's on Salisbury Plain.'

'Yes,' Catherine said.

'Why don't we visit it, next Saturday perhaps?'

Catherine wondered whether he would find Stonehenge any more interesting than the museums.

'That would be fine,' Catherine said.

Dino Mattusi was a gourmet. He walked into Catherine's office with a guidebook. 'I have a list of the greatest restaurants in London here. Interested?'

'Well, I . . .'

'Good! Tonight I am taking you to dine at the Connaught.'

Catherine said, 'Tonight I have to . . .'

'No excuses. I will pick you up at eight o'clock.'

Catherine hesitated. 'Very well.'

Mattusi beamed. *'Bene!'* He leaned forward. 'It is no fun doing things alone, is it?' His meaning was unmistakable. *But he's so obvious*, Catherine thought, *that he's really quite harmless.*

The dinner at the Connaught was delicious. They dined on Scottish smoked salmon, roast beef and Yorkshire pudding.

Over the salad, Dino Mattusi said, 'I find you fascinating, Catherine. I love American women.'

'Oh. Is your wife American?' Catherine asked innocently.

Mattusi shrugged. 'No, she is Italian. But she's very understanding.'

'That must be nice for you,' Catherine said.

229

He smiled. 'It is, very nice.'

It was not until they were having dessert that Dino Mattusi said, 'Do you like the country? I have a friend who has a car. I thought we might go for a drive on Sunday.'

Catherine started to say no, and then she suddenly thought of Wim. He seemed so lonely. Perhaps he would enjoy going out for a drive in the country. 'It sounds like fun,' Catherine said.

'I promise you it will be interesting.'

'I wonder if I might bring Wim?'

He shook his head. 'It's a small car. I'll make the arrangements.'

The visitors from Athens were demanding and Catherine found that she had very little time for herself. Haley, Renard and Mattusi had had several meetings with Wim Vandeen, and Catherine was amused at how their attitudes had changed.

'He does all this without a calculator?' Haley marvelled.

'That's right.'

'I've never seen anything like it.'

Catherine was impressed with Atanas Stavich. The young boy was the hardest worker she had ever seen. He was at the office when Catherine arrived in the morning, and he was there after everyone else had left. He was always smiling and eager to please. He reminded Catherine of a trembling puppy. Somewhere in his past, someone had badly mistreated him. Catherine resolved to talk to Alan Hamilton about Atanas. *There has to be some way to build his self-confidence*, Catherine thought. *I'm sure Alan could help him.*

'You know the boy is in love with you, don't you?' Evelyn said one day.

'What are you talking about?'

'Atanas. Haven't you seen that adoring look in his eyes? He follows you round like a lost sheep.'

Catherine laughed. 'You're imagining things.'

On an impulse, Catherine invited Atanas to lunch.

230

'In – in a restaurant?'

Catherine smiled. 'Yes, of course.'

His face flushed. 'I – I don't know, Miss Alexander.' He looked down at his ill-fitting clothes. 'You would be ashamed for people to see me with you.'

'I don't judge people by their clothes,' Catherine said firmly. 'I'll make a reservation.'

She took Atanas to lunch at Lyons Corner House. He sat across from her, awed by his surroundings. 'I – I've never been in a place like this. It is so beautiful.'

Catherine was touched. 'I want you to order anything you want.'

He studied the menu and shook his head. 'Everything is too expensive.'

Catherine smiled. 'Don't worry about it. You and I are working for a very wealthy man. I'm sure he would want us to have a good lunch.' She did not tell him that she was paying for it.

Atanas ordered a shrimp cocktail and a salad, and a chicken roast with fried potatoes, and he finished off his lunch with chocolate cake with ice cream.

Catherine watched him eat in amazement. He had such a small frame. 'Where do you put it all?'

Atanas said shyly, 'I never gain weight.'

'Do you like London, Atanas?'

He nodded. 'What I've seen of it, I like very much.'

'You worked as an office boy in Athens?'

He nodded. 'For Mr Demiris.' There was a note of bitterness in his voice.

'Didn't you enjoy it?'

'Forgive me – it is not my place to say it, but I do not think Mr Demiris is a nice man. I . . . I do not like him.' The young boy glanced around quickly as though he might have been overheard. 'He – never mind.'

Catherine thought it best not to pursue it further. 'What made you decide to come to London, Atanas?'

Atanas said something so softly that Catherine could not hear him.

231

'I beg your pardon?'

'I want to be a doctor.'

She looked at him, curious. 'A doctor?'

'Yes, ma'am. I know it sounds foolish.' He hesitated, then went on. 'My family comes from Macedonia and all my life I have heard stories about the Turks coming into our village and killing and torturing our people. There were no doctors to help the wounded. Now, the village is gone and my family was wiped out. But there are still many wounded people in the world. I want to help them.' He lowered his eyes, embarrassed. 'You must think I'm crazy.'

'No,' Catherine said quietly. 'I think that's wonderful. So you came to London to study medicine?'

'Yes, ma'am. I'm going to work days and go to school nights. I'm going to become a doctor.'

There was a ring of determination in his voice. Catherine nodded. 'I believe you will. You and I are going to talk more about it. I have a friend who might be able to help you. And I know a wonderful restaurant where we can have lunch next week.'

At midnight, a bomb exploded in Spyros Lambrou's villa. The blast tore out the front of the house and killed two servants. Spyros Lambrou's bedroom was destroyed and the only reason he survived was because at the last moment he and his wife had changed their plans and decided to attend a dinner party given by the mayor of Athens.

The following morning, a note was sent to his office reading 'Death to capitalists'. It was signed: The Hellenic Revolutionary Party.

'Why would they do a thing like this to you?' asked a horrified Melina.

'They didn't,' Spyros said bluntly. 'It was Costa.'

'You – you have no proof of that.'

'I don't need any proof. Don't you understand yet what you are married to?'

'I – I don't know what to think.'

232

'Melina, as long as that man is alive, we are both in danger. He will stop at nothing.'

'Can't you go to the police?'

'You said it yourself. I have no proof. They would laugh at me.' He took her hands in his. 'I want you to get out of there. Please. Go as far away as you can.'

She stood there for a long time. When she finally spoke, it was as though she had reached a decision of great importance. 'All right, Spyros. I will do what I must.'

He hugged her. 'Good. And don't worry. We'll find some way to stop him.'

Melina sat in her bedroom alone during the long afternoon, her mind trying to take in what was happening. So, her husband had really meant his threat to destroy her and her brother. She could not let him go through with it. And if their lives were in danger, so was the life of Catherine Douglas. *She's going to work for Costa in London. I will warn her*, Melina thought. *But I must do more than that. I must destroy Costa. I must stop him from harming anyone else. But how?* And then, the answer came to her. *Of course!* she thought. *It's the only way. Why didn't I think of it before?*

Chapter 22

CONFIDENTIAL FILE

TRANSCRIPT OF SESSION WITH
CATHERINE DOUGLAS

C: I'm sorry I'm late, Alan. There was a last-minute meeting at the office.

A: No problem. The delegation from Athens is still in London?

C: Yes. They – they're planning to leave at the end of next week.

A: You sound relieved. Have they been difficult?

C: Not difficult exactly, I just have a . . . a strange feeling about them.

A: Strange?

C: It's hard to explain. I know it sounds silly, but . . . there's something odd about all of them.

A: Have they done anything to . . . ?

C: No. They just make me uneasy. Last night, I had that nightmare again.

A: The dream that someone was trying to drown you?

C: Yes. I haven't had that dream in a while. And this time it was different.

A: In what way?

C: It was more . . . real. And it didn't end where it had ended before.

A: You went past the point where someone was trying to drown you?

C: Yes. They were trying to drown me and then suddenly I was in a safe place.

234

A: The convent?

C: I'm not sure. It could have been. It was a garden. And a man came to see me. I think I dreamed something like that before, but this time I could see his face.

A: Did you recognize him?

C: Yes. It was Constantin Demiris.

A: So, in your dream . . .

C: Alan, it wasn't just a dream. It was a real memory. I suddenly remembered that Constantin Demiris gave me the gold pin I have.

A: You believe that your subconscious dredged up something that really happened? You're sure it wasn't . . .

C: I know it. Constantin Demiris gave me that pin at the convent.

A: You said you were rescued from the lake by some nuns who took you to the convent?

C: That's right.

A: Catherine, did anyone else know you were at the convent?

C: No. I don't think so.

A: Then how could Constantin Demiris have known you were there?

C: I – I don't know. I just know that it happened. I woke up frightened. It was as though the dream were some kind of warning. I feel something terrible is going to happen.

A: Nightmares can have that effect on us. The nightmare is one of man's oldest enemies. The word goes back to the Middle English 'niht' or 'night' and 'mare' or 'goblin'. The old superstition is that it prefers to ride after four a.m.

C: You don't think they have any real meaning?

A: Sometimes they do. Coleridge wrote, 'Dreams are no shadows, but the very substances and calamities of my life.'

C: I'm probably taking all this too seriously. Other than my crazy dreams, I'm fine. Oh. There's someone I would like to talk to you about, Alan.

A: Yes?

C: His name is Atanas Stavich. He's a young boy who came to London to study medicine. He's had a rough life. I thought

235

that perhaps one day you could meet him and give him some advice.

A: I would be happy to. Why are you frowning?

C: I just remembered something.

A: Yes?

C: It sounds crazy.

A: Our subconscious doesn't distinguish between crazy and sane.

C: In my dream, when Mr Demiris handed me the gold pin . . .

A: Yes?

C: I heard a voice say, 'He's going to kill you.'

It must look like an accident. I don't want anyone to be able to identify her body. There were many ways to kill her. He would have to begin making arrangements. He lay on his bed thinking about them and found that he was getting an erection. Death was the ultimate orgasm. Finally, he knew how he was going to do it. It was so simple. There would be no body left to identify. Constantin Demiris would be pleased.

Chapter 23

Constantin Demiris' beach house was located three miles north of Piraeus on an acre of waterfront property. Demiris arrived at 7.00 p.m. He pulled up in the driveway, opened the car door, and started toward the beach house.

As he reached it, the door was opened by a man he did not recognize.

'Good evening, Mr Demiris.'

Inside, Demiris could see half a dozen police officers.

'What's going on here?' Demiris demanded.

'I'm Police Lieutenant Theophilos. I . . .'

Demiris pushed him aside and walked into the living room. It was a shambles. A terrible struggle had obviously taken place. Chairs and tables were overturned. One of Melina's dresses was lying on the floor, torn. Demiris picked it up and stared at it.

'Where's my wife? I was supposed to meet her here.'

The police lieutenant said, 'She's not here. We've searched the house and we've looked up and down the beach. It looks like the house has been burgled.'

'Well, where's Melina? Did she call you? Was she here?'

'Yes, we think she was here, sir.' He held up a ladies' wristwatch. The crystal had been smashed and the hands had stopped at three o'clock. 'Is this your wife's watch?'

'It looks like it.'

'On the back is engraved "to Melina with love, Costa".'

'Then it is. It was a birthday present.'

Detective Theophilos pointed to some spots on the rug. 'Those are bloodstains.' He picked up a knife lying on the floor, careful not to touch the handle. The blade was covered with blood.

'Have you ever seen this knife before, sir?'

Demiris gave it a brief glance. 'No. Are you saying she's dead?'

'It's certainly a possibility, sir. We found drops of blood on the sand leading down to the water.'

'My God,' Demiris said.

'Luckily for us, there are some clear fingerprints on the knife.'

Demiris sat down heavily. 'Then you'll catch whoever did it.'

'We will if his fingerprints are on file. There are fingerprints all over the house. We have to sort them out. If you don't mind giving us your fingerprints, Mr Demiris, we can eliminate those right away.'

Demiris hesitated. 'Yes, of course.'

'The sergeant right over there can take care of it.'

Demiris walked over to a uniformed policeman who had a fingerprint pad. 'If you'll just place your fingers right here, sir.' A moment later, it was done. 'You understand it's just a formality.'

'I understand.'

Lieutenant Theophilos handed Demiris a small business card. 'Would you know anything about this, Mr Demiris?'

Demiris looked at the card. It read, 'Katelanos Detective Agency – Private Investigations'. He handed the card back. 'No. Does it have any significance?'

'I don't know. We're checking into it.'

'Naturally, I want you to do everything you can to find out who's responsible. And let me know if you get word of my wife.'

Lieutenant Theophilos looked at him and nodded. 'Don't worry, sir. We will.'

Melina. The golden girl, attractive and bright and amusing. It had been so wonderful in the beginning. And then she had murdered their son, and for that there could never be forgiveness . . . only her death.

*

238

The call came in at noon the following day. Constantin Demiris was in the middle of a conference when his secretary buzzed him. 'Excuse me, Mr Demiris . . .'

'I told you I didn't want to be disturbed.'

'Yes, sir, but there's an Inspector Lavanos on the phone. He says it's urgent. Do you want me to tell him to . . . ?'

'No. I'll take it.' Demiris turned to the men sitting around the conference table. 'Excuse me a moment, gentlemen.' He picked up the receiver. 'Demiris.'

A voice said, 'This is Chief Inspector Lavanos, Mr Demiris, at Central Station. We have some information we think you might be interested in. I wondered whether it would be convenient for you to come down to police headquarters?'

'You have news of my wife?'

'I would prefer not to discuss it over the telephone, if you don't mind.'

Demiris hesitated for only a moment. 'I'll be right down.' He replaced the receiver and turned to the others. 'Something urgent has come up. Why don't you go on into the dining room and discuss my proposal and I'll be back in time to join you for lunch.'

There was a general murmur of agreement. Five minutes later, Demiris was on his way to police headquarters.

There were half a dozen men waiting for him in the office of the Police Commissioner. Demiris recognized the policemen he had already seen at the beach house. '. . . and this is Special Prosecutor Delma.'

Delma was a short, stocky man, with heavy eyebrows, a round face and cynical eyes.

'What's happened?' Demiris demanded. 'Do you have some news of my wife?'

The Chief Inspector said, 'To be perfectly frank, Mr Demiris, we have come across some things that puzzle us. We hoped you might be able to help us.'

'I'm afraid there's very little I can do to help you. This whole thing is so shocking . . .'

'You had an appointment to meet your wife at the beach house around three o'clock yesterday afternoon?'

'What? No. Mrs Demiris telephoned and asked me to meet her there at seven o'clock.'

Prosecutor Delma said smoothly, 'Now, that's one of the things that's puzzling us. A maid at your home told us that you telephoned your wife about two o'clock and asked her to go to the beach house alone and wait for you.'

Demiris frowned. 'She's confused. My wife telephoned me and asked me to meet her there at seven o'clock last night.'

'I see. So the maid was mistaken.'

'Obviously.'

'Do you know what reason your wife might have had for asking you to go to the beach house?'

'I suppose she wanted to try to talk me out of divorcing her.'

'You had told your wife you were going to divorce her?'

'Yes.'

'The maid says she overheard a telephone conversation during which Mrs Demiris told you *she* was going to divorce *you*.'

'I don't give a damn what the maid said. You'll have to take my word for it.'

'Mr Demiris, do you keep swimming trunks at the beach house?' the Chief Inspector asked.

'At the beach house? No. I gave up swimming in the sea years ago. I use the pool at the town house.'

The Chief Inspector opened a desk drawer and took out a pair of swim trunks in a plastic bag. He removed them and held them up for Demiris to see. 'Are these your trunks, Mr Demiris?'

'They could be mine, I suppose.'

'They have your initials on them.'

'Yes. I think I recognize them. They are mine.'

'We found them at the bottom of a closet in the beach house.'

'So? They were probably left there a long time ago. Why . . . ?'

'They were still wet from sea water. The analysis showed that it's the same water that's in front of your beach house. They are covered with blood.'

It was getting very hot in the room.

240

'Then someone else must have put them on,' Demiris said firmly.

The Special Prosecutor said, 'Why would anyone do that? That's one of the things bothering us, Mr Demiris.'

The Chief Inspector opened a small envelope on the desk and took out a gold button. 'One of my men found this under a rug at the beach house. Do you recognize it?'

'No.'

'It came from one of your jackets. We took the liberty of having a detective go to your home this morning to check out your wardrobe. A button was missing from one of your jackets. The threads match perfectly. And the jacket came back from the cleaners just a week ago.'

'I don't . . .'

'Mr Demiris, you said you told your wife you wanted a divorce and that she was trying to talk you out of it?'

'That's correct.'

The Chief Inspector held up the business card that Demiris had been shown at the beach house the day before. 'One of our men visited the Katelanos Detective Agency today.'

'I told you – I never heard of them.'

'Your wife hired them to protect her.'

The news came as a shock. 'Melina? Protect her from what?'

'From you. According to the owner of the agency, your wife was threatening to divorce you, and you told her that if she went through with it you would kill her. He asked her why she didn't go to the police for protection, and she said she wanted to keep the matter private. She didn't want the publicity.'

Demiris rose to his feet. 'I'm not going to stay here and listen to these lies. There's no . . .'

The Chief Inspector reached into a drawer and took out the bloodstained knife that had been found at the beach house.

'You told the officer at the beach house that you had never seen this before?'

'That's right.'

'Your fingerprints are on this knife.'

Demiris was staring at the knife. 'My – my fingerprints? There's some mistake. That's impossible!'

241

His mind was racing. He swiftly ran through the evidence that was piling up against him: the maid saying that he had called his wife at two o'clock and told her to come to the beach house alone . . . A pair of his swimming trunks with blood on them . . . A button torn from his jacket . . . A knife with his fingerprints . . .

'Don't you see, you idiots? It's a frame-up,' he shouted. 'Someone carried those trunks to the beach house, spilled a little blood on them and on the knife, ripped a button off my jacket and . . .'

The Special Prosecutor interrupted. 'Mr Demiris, can you explain how your fingerprints got on that knife?'

'I – I don't know . . . Wait. Yes. I remember now. Melina asked me to cut open a package for her. That must be the knife she handed me. That's why my fingerprints are on it.'

'I see. What was in the package?'

'I . . . I don't know.'

'You don't know what was in the package?'

'No. I just cut the rope around it. She never opened it.'

'Can you explain the bloodstains on the carpet, or in the sand leading down to the water or . . . ?'

'It's obvious,' Demiris shot back. 'All Melina had to do was cut herself a little and then walk out toward the water so you would think I murdered her. She's trying to get even with me because I told her I was going to divorce her. Right now, she's hiding somewhere, laughing, because she thinks you're going to arrest me. Melina's as alive as I am.'

The Special Prosecutor said gravely, 'I wish that were true, sir. We pulled her body out of the sea this morning. She had been stabbed and drowned. I'm placing you under arrest, Mr Demiris, for the murder of your wife.'

Chapter 24

In the beginning, Melina had had no idea how she was going to accomplish it. She knew only that her husband intended to destroy her brother and she could not let that happen. Somehow, Costa had to be stopped. Her life no longer mattered. Her days and nights were filled with pain and humiliation. She remembered how Spyros had tried to warn her against the marriage. *You can't marry Demiris. He's a monster. He'll destroy you.* How right he had been. And she had been too much in love to listen. Now her husband had to be destroyed. But how? *Think like Costa.* And she had. By morning, Melina had worked out all the details. After that, the rest had been simple.

Constantin Demiris was in his study working when Melina walked in. She was carrying a package tied with a heavy cord. She held a large butcher knife in her hand.

'Costa, would you mind cutting this open for me? I can't seem to manage it.'

He looked up at her and said impatiently, 'Of course you can't. Don't you know better than to hold a knife by the blade?' He snatched the knife from her and started to cut the cord. 'Couldn't you have had one of the servants do this?'

Melina did not answer.

Demiris finished cutting the cord. 'There!' He put the knife down and Melina carefully picked it up by the blade.

She looked up at him and said, 'Costa, we can't go on this way. I still love you. You must still feel something for me. Do you remember the wonderful times we used to have together? Do you remember the night of our honeymoon when . . .'

'For Christ's sake,' Demiris snapped. 'Don't you understand? It's over. I'm finished with you. Get out of here, you make me sick.'

243

Melina stood there staring at him. Finally, she said quietly, 'All right. Have it your way.' She turned and left the room carrying the knife.

'You forgot your package,' Demiris shouted.

She was gone.

Melina went into her husband's dressing room and opened a closet door. There were a hundred suits hanging in the closet with a special section for sport jackets. She reached for one of the jackets and tore a gold button from it. She put the button in her pocket.

Next she opened a drawer and removed a pair of her husband's bathing trunks with his initials on them. *I'm almost ready*, Melina thought.

The Katelanos Detective Agency was located on Sofokleous Street in a faded old brick building on the corner. Melina was ushered into the office of the owner of the agency, Mr Katelanos, a small bald man with a tiny mustache.

'Good morning, Mrs Demiris. And what can I do for you?'

'I need protection.'

'What kind of protection?'

'From my husband.'

Katelanos frowned. He smelled trouble. This was not at all the kind of case he had anticipated. It would be very unwise to do anything that might offend a man as powerful as Constantin Demiris.

'Have you thought of going to the police?' he asked.

'I can't. I don't want any publicity. I want to keep this private. I told my husband I was going to divorce him, and he threatened to kill me if I went through with it. That's why I came to you.'

'I see. What exactly is it you wish me to do?'

'I want you to assign some men to protect me.'

Katelanos sat there studying her. *She's a beautiful woman*, he thought. *Obviously neurotic*. It was inconceivable that her husband would harm her. This was probably some little domestic spat that would blow over in a few days. But meanwhile, he would be able to charge her a nice fee. On balance, Katelanos decided it was worth the risk.

'All right,' he said. 'I have a good man I can assign to you. When would you like him to start?'

'Monday.'

So he was right. There was no urgency.

Melina Demiris rose. 'I will give you a call. Do you have a business card?'

'Yes, of course.' Katelanos handed her his business card and ushered her out. *She's a good client to have*, he thought. *Her name will impress my other clients.*

When Melina returned home, she telephoned her brother. 'Spyros, I have some good news.' Her voice was filled with excitement. 'Costa wants a truce.'

'What? I don't trust him, Melina. It must be some kind of trick. He . . .'

'No. He means it. He realizes that it's stupid for you two to be fighting all the time. He wants to have peace in the family.'

There was a silence. 'I don't know.'

'At least give him a chance. He wants you to meet him at your lodge at Acro-Corinth at three o'clock this afternoon.'

'That's a four-hour drive. Why can't we meet in town?'

'He didn't say,' Melina told him, 'but if it's going to mean peace . . .'

'All right. I'll do it. But I'm doing it for you.'

'For us,' Melina said. 'Goodbye, Spyros.'

'Goodbye.'

Melina telephoned Constantin at the office. His voice was abrupt. 'What is it? I'm busy.'

'I just received a call from Spyros. He wants to make peace with you.'

There was a short, derisive laugh. 'I'll bet he does. When I'm through with him he'll have all the peace he'll ever want.'

245

'He said he's not going to compete with you anymore, Costa. He's willing to sell you his fleet.'

'Sell me his . . . Are you sure?' His voice was suddenly filled with interest.

'Yes. He said he's had enough.'

'All right. Tell him to send his accountants over to my office, and . . .'

'No. He wants to meet with you this afternoon at three o'clock at Acro-Corinth.'

'His lodge?'

'Yes. It's a secluded place. It will be just the two of you. He doesn't want word of this to get out.'

I'll bet he doesn't, Demiris thought with satisfaction. *When word does get out, he will be a laughing stock.* 'All right,' Demiris said. 'You can tell him I'll be there.'

The drive to Acro-Corinth was a long one, on winding roads that meandered through the lush countryside, redolent with the odors of grapes and lemons and hay. Spyros Lambrou passed ancient ruins along the way. In the distance, he saw the fallen pillars of Eleusis, the ruined altars of lesser gods. He thought of Demiris.

Lambrou was the first to arrive at the lodge. He pulled up in front of the cabin and sat in the car for a moment, thinking about the meeting he was about to have. Did Constantin really want a truce, or was this another one of his tricks? If anything happened to him, at least Melina knew where he had gone. Spyros got out of the car and walked into the deserted lodge.

The lodge was a lovely old wooden building with a view of Corinth in the distance below. As a boy, Spyros Lambrou had spent weekends there with his father, hunting small game in the mountains. Now he was after bigger game.

Fifteen minutes later, Constantin Demiris arrived. He saw Spyros inside, waiting there, and it gave him a glow of satisfac-

246

tion. *So, after all these years, the man is finally willing to admit he is defeated.* He got out of his car and walked into the cabin. The two men stood there, staring at each other.

'Well, my dear brother-in-law,' Demiris said, 'so we've finally reached the end of the road.'

'I want this madness to end, Costa. It's gone too far.'

'I couldn't agree with you more. How many ships do you have, Spyros?'

Lambrou looked at him in surprise. 'What?'

'How many ships do you have? I'll purchase them all. At a substantial discount, naturally.'

Lambrou could not believe what he was hearing. 'Purchase my ships?'

'I'm willing to buy all of them. It will make me the largest fleet owner in the world.'

'Are you crazy? What – what makes you think I would sell you my ships?'

It was Demiris' turn to react. 'That's why we're meeting here, isn't it?'

'We're meeting here because you asked for a truce.'

Demiris' face darkened. 'I – who told you that?'

'Melina.'

The truth dawned on both of them at the same moment. 'She told you I wanted a truce?'

'She told you I wanted to sell my ships?'

'The stupid bitch,' Demiris exclaimed. 'I suppose she thought that by bringing us together we would reach some sort of agreement. She's a bigger fool than you are, Lambrou. I've wasted a whole afternoon on you.'

Constantin Demiris turned and stormed out the door. Spyros Lambrou looked after him, thinking, *Melina shouldn't have lied to us. She should have known that there's no way her husband and I could ever get together. Not now. It's too late. It was always too late.*

At 1.30, earlier that afternoon, Melina had rung for the maid. 'Andrea, would you bring me some tea, please?'

247

'Certainly, ma'am.' The maid left the room and when she returned with the tea tray ten minutes later, her mistress was speaking into the telephone. Her tone was angry.

'No, Costa, I've made up my mind. I intend to divorce you and I'm going to make it as messy and as public as I can.'

Embarrassed, Andrea set the tray down and started to retreat. Melina waved to her to stay.

Melina spoke into the dead phone. 'You can threaten me all you like. I'm not going to change my mind . . . Never . . . I don't care what you say . . . You don't frighten me, Costa . . . No . . . What would be the point? . . . All right. I'll meet you at the beach house but it won't do you any good. Yes, I'll come alone. In an hour? Very well.'

Slowly, Melina replaced the receiver, a worried look on her face. She turned to Andrea. 'I'm going to the beach house to meet my husband. If I haven't returned by six o'clock, I want you to call the police.'

Andrea swallowed nervously. 'Would you like the chauffeur to drive you?'

'No. Mr Demiris asked me to come alone.'

'Yes, ma'am.'

There was one more thing to do. Catherine Alexander's life was in danger. She had to be warned. It was someone from the delegation that had had dinner at the house. *You won't see her again. I've sent someone to get rid of her.* Melina placed a call to her husband's offices in London.

'Is there a Catherine Alexander working there?'

'She's not in at the moment. Can anyone else help you?'

Melina hesitated. Her message was too urgent to trust to just anyone. But she would have no time to call back. She remembered Costa mentioning a Wim Vandeen, a genius in the office.

'Could I speak with Mr Vandeen, please?'

'Just a moment.'

A man's voice came on the line. 'Hello.'

She could barely understand him.

248

'I have a message for Catherine Alexander. It's very important. Would you see that she gets it, please?'

'Catherine Alexander.'

'Yes. Tell her – tell her that her life is in danger. Someone is
going to try to kill her. I think it could be one of the men who
came from Athens.'

'Athens . . .'

'Yes.'

'Athens has a population of eight hundred six thousand . . .'

Melina could not seem to make the man understand. She hung
up the phone. She had tried her best.

Wim sat at his desk, digesting the telephone conversation. *Someone is going to try to kill Catherine. A hundred and fourteen
murders were committed in England this year, Catherine will
make it a hundred and fifteen. One of the men who came from
Athens. Jerry Haley. Yves Renard. Dino Mattusi. One of them is
going to kill Catherine.* Wim's computer mind instantly fed him
all the data on the three men. *I think I know which one it is.*

When Catherine returned later, Wim said nothing to her about
the phone call.

He was curious to see if he was right.

Catherine was out with a different member of the delegation
every evening, and when she came to work each morning, Wim
was there, waiting. He seemed disappointed to see her.

When is she going to let him do it? Wim wondered. Maybe he
should tell her about the telephone message. But that would be
cheating. It wouldn't be fair to change the odds.

Chapter 25

The drive to the beach house took an hour of actual time and twenty years of memories. There was so much for Melina to think about, so much to recall. Costa, young and handsome, saying, *Surely you've been sent from the heavens to teach us mortals what beauty is. You're beyond flattery. Nothing I could say would do you justice* . . . The wonderful cruises on their yacht and idyllic vacations on Psara . . . The days of lovely surprise gifts and the nights of wild love-making. And then the miscarriage, and the string of mistresses, and the affair with Noelle Page. And the beatings and public humiliations. *Koritsimon! You have nothing to live for, he had said. Why don't you kill yourself?* And, finally, the threat to destroy Spyros.

That was what, in the end, Melina was unable to bear.

When Melina arrived at the beach house, it was deserted. The sky was cloudy, and there was a chill wind blowing from the sea. *An omen*, she thought.

She walked into the comforting, friendly house and looked around for the last time.

Then she began to overturn furniture and smash lamps. She ripped off her dress and let it fall to the floor. She took out the card from the detective agency and placed it on a table. She lifted the rug and put the gold button under it. Next she took off the gold wristwatch that Costa had given her and smashed it against the table.

She picked up her husband's swim trunks that she had taken from the house and carried them out to the beach. She wet them in the water, and returned to the house. Finally, there was only one thing left to do. *It's time*, she thought. She took a deep breath and slowly picked up the butcher knife and unwrapped it, careful not to disturb the tissue paper that covered the handle. Melina held it in her hand, staring at it. This was the crucial part. She had to stab herself hard enough to make it look like murder, and at the same time have enough strength left to carry out the rest of her plan.

She closed her eyes, and plunged the knife deep into her side.

The pain was excruciating. Blood began to pour out. Melina held the wet bathing trunks to her side, and when they were covered with blood she walked over to a closet and shoved them in the back. She was beginning to feel dizzy. She looked around to make sure she had not missed anything, then she stumbled toward the door that led to the beach, her blood staining the carpet a bright crimson.

She moved toward the ocean. The blood was coming out faster now, and she thought, *I'm not going to make it. Costa is going to win. I mustn't let him*.

The walk to the ocean seemed to take forever. *One more step*, she thought. *One more step*.

She kept walking, fighting the dizziness that engulfed her. Her vision was beginning to blur. She fell to her knees. *I mustn't stop now*. She rose and kept walking until she felt the cold water lapping at her feet.

When the salt water hit her wound, she screamed aloud with the unbearable pain. *I'm doing it for Spyros*, she thought. *Dear Spyros*.

In the distance she could see a low cloud hovering over the horizon. She began to swim toward it, trailing a stream of blood. And a miracle happened. The cloud came down to her, and she could feel its white softness enveloping her, bathing her, caressing her. The pain was gone now, and she felt a wonderful feeling of peace steal over her.

I'm going home, Melina thought happily. *I'm going home at last*.

Chapter 26

I'm placing you under arrest for the murder of your wife.

After that, everything seemed to happen in slow motion. He was booked, and fingerprinted again. He had his picture taken, and was placed in a prison cell. It was unbelievable that they would dare do this to him.

'Get me Peter Demonides. Tell him I want to see him right now.'

'Mr Demonides has been relieved of his duties. He's under investigation.'

So there was no one to turn to. *I'll get out of this*, he thought. *I'm Constantin Demiris.*

He sent for the Special Prosecutor.

Delma arrived at the prison one hour later. 'You asked to see me?'

'Yes,' Demiris said. 'I understand you've established the time of my wife's death at three o'clock.'

'That is correct.'

'Then before you embarrass yourself and the police department any further, I can prove that I was nowhere near the beach house at that hour yesterday.'

'You can prove that?'

'Of course. I have a witness.'

They were seated in the Police Commissioner's office when Spyros Lambrou arrived. Demiris' face lit up when he saw him.

'Spyros, thank God you're here! These idiots think I murdered Melina. You know I couldn't have. Tell them.'

Spyros Lambrou frowned. 'Tell them what?'

'Melina was killed at three o'clock yesterday afternoon. You and I were together at Acro-Corinth at three o'clock. I couldn't have driven back to the beach house before seven. Tell them about our meeting.'

Spyros Lambrou was staring at him. 'What meeting?'

The blood began to drain from Demiris' face. 'The . . . the meeting you and I had yesterday. At the lodge at Acrocorinth.'

'You must be confused, Costa. I was out driving alone yesterday afternoon. I'm not going to lie for you.'

Constantin Demiris' face filled with rage. 'You can't do this!' He grabbed the lapels of Lambrou's jacket. 'Tell them the truth.'

Spyros Lambrou pushed him away. 'The truth is that my sister is dead and you murdered her.'

'Liar!' Demiris screamed. 'Liar!' He started toward Lambrou again and it took two policemen to restrain him.

'You son-of-a-bitch. You know I'm innocent!'

'The judges will decide that. I think you need a good lawyer.'

And Constantin Demiris realized that there was only one man who could have saved him.

Napoleon Chotas.

253

Chapter 27

———◄•►———

CONFIDENTIAL FILE

TRANSCRIPT OF SESSION WITH
CATHERINE DOUGLAS

C: Do you believe in premonitions, Alan?

A: They're not scientifically accepted, but as a matter of fact, I do. Have you been having premonitions?

C: Yes. I – I have the feeling that something terrible is going to happen to me.

A: Is this part of your old dream?

C: No. I told you that Mr Demiris sent some men in from Athens . . .

A: Yes.

C: He asked me to look after them, so I've been seeing quite a bit of them.

A: Do you feel threatened by them?

C: No. Not exactly. It's difficult to explain. They haven't done anything, and yet I – I keep expecting something to happen. Something awful. Does that make any sense to you?

A: Tell me about the men.

C: There's a Frenchman, Yves Renard. He insists that we go to museums but when we get there, I can see that he's not interested. He asked me to take him to Stonehenge this Saturday. There's Jerry Haley. He's an American. He seems pleasant enough, but there's something disturbing about him. Then there's Dino Mattusi. He's supposed to be an executive with Mr Demiris' company, but he asks a lot of questions that he should have the answers to. He invited me to go for a drive. I thought I would take Wim along . . . And that's something else.

254

A: Yes?

C: Wim has been acting strangely.

A: In what way?

C: When I come into the office in the morning, Wim is always waiting for me. He never used to. And when he sees me, it's almost as though he's angry that I'm there. None of this makes much sense, does it?

A: Everything makes sense once you have the key, Catherine. Have you had any more dreams?

C: I had a dream about Constantin Demiris. It's very vague.

A: Tell me what you remember of it.

C: I asked him why he was being so kind to me, why he gave me the job here and a place to live. And why he gave me the gold pin.

A: And, what did he say?

C: I don't remember. I woke up screaming.

Dr Alan Hamilton studied the transcript carefully, looking for the unmarked trails of the subconscious, seeking a clue that would explain what was disturbing Catherine. He was reasonably certain that her apprehension was connected with the fact that strangers had arrived from Athens, and Athens was the scene of her traumatic past. The part about Wim puzzled Alan. Was Catherine imagining it? Or was Wim behaving in an atypical way? *I'm due to see Wim in a few weeks*, Alan thought. *Perhaps I will move up his appointment.*

Alan sat there thinking about Catherine. Although he made it a rule never to get involved emotionally with his patients Catherine was someone special. She was beautiful and vulnerable and . . . *What am I doing? I can't let myself think this way. I'll concentrate on something else.* But his thoughts kept returning to her.

Catherine was unable to get Alan Hamilton out of her mind. *Don't be a fool*, Catherine told herself. *He's a married man. All patients feel this way about their analysts.* But nothing Catherine

255

told herself helped. *Maybe I should see an analyst about my analyst.*

She was seeing Alan again in two days. *Perhaps I should cancel the appointment*, Catherine thought, *before I get in any deeper. Too late.*

On the morning she had the appointment with Alan, Catherine dressed very carefully and went to the beauty parlor. *As long as I'm not going to see him again after today*, Catherine reasoned, *there's no harm in my looking nice.*

The moment she walked into his office, her resolve melted. *Why does he have to be so damned attractive? Why couldn't we have met before he got married? Why couldn't he have known me when I was a normal and sane human being? But, on the other hand, if I were a sane, normal human being, I wouldn't have gone to him in the first place, would I?*

'I beg your pardon?'

Catherine realized she had spoken aloud. Now was the time to tell him that this was her last visit.

She took a deep breath. 'Alan . . .' And her resolve broke. She looked over at the photograph on the coffee table. 'How long have you been married?'

'Married?' He followed Catherine's glance. 'Oh. That's my sister and her son.'

Catherine felt a wave of joy sweep through her. 'Oh, that's wonderful! I mean, she . . . she looks wonderful.'

'Are you all right, Catherine?'

Kirk Reynolds had kept asking her that. *I wasn't all right then*, Catherine thought, *but I am now*. 'I'm fine,' Catherine said. 'You're not married?'

'No.'

Will you have dinner with me? Will you take me to bed? Will you marry me? If she said any of these things aloud he would really think she was crazy. *Maybe I am.*

He was watching her, frowning. 'Catherine, I'm afraid we're

256

not going to be able to go on with these sessions. Today will be our last day.'

Catherine's heart sank. 'Why? Have I done something to . . . ?'

'No, it . . . it isn't you. In a professional relationship of this kind, it's improper for a doctor to become emotionally involved with a patient.'

She was staring at him now, her eyes glowing. 'Are you saying that you're becoming emotionally involved with me?'

'Yes. And because of that I'm afraid . . .'

'You're absolutely right,' Catherine said happily. 'Let's talk about it tonight at dinner.'

They dined at a little Italian restaurant in the heart of Soho. The food could have been great or terrible, it made no difference. They were totally absorbed in each other.

'It isn't fair, Alan,' Catherine said. 'You know everything about me. Tell me about yourself. Weren't you ever married?'

'No. I was engaged to be married.'

'What happened?'

'It was during the war. We were living together in a small flat. It was during the days of the Blitz. I was working at the hospital and when I came home one night . . .'

Catherine could hear the pain in his voice.

'. . . the building was gone. There was nothing left.'

She put her hand over his. 'I'm sorry.'

'It took me a long time to get over it. I never met anyone else that I wanted to marry.' And his eyes said, *until now*.

They sat there for four hours, talking about everything – the theater, medicine, the state of the world; but the real conversation was unspoken. It was the electricity building up between them. They could both feel it. There was a sexual tension between them that was overwhelming.

Finally, Alan brought up the subject. 'Catherine, what I said this morning about the doctor-patient relationship . . .'

'Tell me about it at your flat.'

*

257

They undressed together, quickly and eagerly, and as Catherine took off her clothes, she thought of how she had felt when she was with Kirk Reynolds and how different it was now. *The difference is being in love*, Catherine thought. *I'm in love with this man.*

She lay on the bed waiting for him and when he came to her and put his arms around her, all the worries, all the fears of never being able to relate to a man, vanished. They stroked each other's bodies, exploring, first tenderly, then fiercely, until their need became wild and desperate, and they joined together and Catherine screamed aloud with sheer happiness. *I'm whole again*, she thought. *Thank you!*

They lay there, spent, and Catherine held Alan close in her arms, never wanting to let him go.

When she could speak again, she said in a shaky voice, 'You certainly know how to treat a patient, Doctor.'

Chapter 28

Catherine learned about the arrest of Constantin Demiris for the murder of his wife from the headlines. It came as a complete shock. When she got to the office, there was a pall over everything.

'Did you hear the news?' Evelyn moaned. 'What are we going to do?'

'We're going to carry on exactly as he would want us to. I'm sure there's been a big mistake. I'm going to try to telephone him.'

But Constantin Demiris was unreachable.

Constantin Demiris was the most important prisoner that the Central Prison of Athens had ever had. The Prosecutor had issued orders that Demiris be given no special treatment. Demiris had demanded a number of things: access to telephones, telex machines and a courier service. His requests were denied.

Demiris spent most of his waking hours, and much of his dreaming ones, trying to figure out who had murdered Melina.

In the beginning, Demiris had assumed that a burglar had been surprised by Melina while ransacking the beach house and had killed her. But the moment the police had confronted him with the evidence against him, Demiris had realized that he was being framed. The question was, by whom? The logical person was Spyros Lambrou, but the weakness of that theory was that Lambrou loved his sister more than anyone in the world. He never would have harmed her.

Demiris' suspicions had then turned to the gang that Tony Rizzoli had been involved with. Perhaps they had learned what he had done to Rizzoli and this was their way of getting revenge. Constantin Demiris had dismissed that idea out of hand. If the

Mafia had wanted revenge, they would simply have put out a contract on him.

And so, sitting alone in his cell, Demiris had gone round and round, trying to solve the puzzle of what had happened. In the end, when he had exhausted all the possibilities, there was only one possible conclusion left: Melina had committed suicide. She had killed herself and framed him for her death. Demiris thought of what he had done to Noelle Page and Larry Douglas and the bitter irony was that he was now in exactly the same position in which they had been. He was going to be tried for a murder he had not committed.

The jailor was at the cell door. 'Your lawyer is here to see you.'

Demiris rose and followed the jailor to a small conference room. The lawyer was waiting for him. The man's name was Vassiliki. He was in his fifties, with bushy grey hair and the profile of a movie star. He had the reputation of being a first-rate criminal attorney. Was that going to be good enough?

The jailor said, 'You have fifteen minutes.' He left the two of them alone.

'Well,' Demiris demanded. 'When are you getting me out of here? What am I paying you for?'

'Mr Demiris, I'm afraid it's not that simple. The Chief Prosecutor refuses . . .'

'The Chief Prosecutor is a fool. They can't keep me in this place. What about bail? I'll put up any amount they ask.'

Vassiliki licked his lips nervously. 'Bail has been denied. I've gone over the evidence that the police have against you, Mr Demiris. It's – it's pretty damaging.'

'Damaging or not – I didn't kill Melina. I'm innocent!'

The attorney swallowed. 'Yes, of course, of course. Do you – er – have any idea who might have killed your wife?'

'No one. My wife committed suicide.'

The attorney stared at him. 'Excuse me, Mr Demiris, but I don't think that's going to make a very good defense. You're going to have to think of something better than that.'

260

And with a sinking heart, Demiris knew he was right. There was not a jury in the world that would believe his story.

Early the following morning, the attorney visited Demiris again.

'I'm afraid I have some rather bad news.'

Demiris almost laughed aloud. He was sitting in prison facing a sentence of death, and this fool was telling him that he had bad news. What could be worse than the situation he was in?

'Yes?'

'It's about your brother-in-law.'

'Spyros? What about him?'

'I have information that he's gone to the police and told them that a woman named Catherine Douglas is still alive. I'm not really familiar with the trial of Noelle Page and Larry Douglas but . . .'

Constantin Demiris was no longer listening. In all the pressure of what was happening to him, he had completely forgotten about Catherine. If they found her, and she talked, they could implicate him in the deaths of Noelle and Larry. He had already sent someone to London to take care of her, but now it had suddenly become urgent.

He leaned forward and clutched the attorney's arm. 'I want you to send a message to London immediately.'

He read the message twice and felt the beginnings of a sexual stirring that always happened to him before he took care of a contract. It was like playing God. He decided who lived and who died. He was awed by the power he had. But there was a problem. If he had to do this immediately, there would be no time to work out his other plan. He would have to improvise something. Make it look like an accident. Tonight.

261

Chapter 29

━━━◆━◆━━━

CONFIDENTIAL FILE

TRANSCRIPT OF SESSION WITH WIM VANDEEN

A: How are you feeling today?

W: Okay. I came here in a taxi. The driver's name is Ronald Christie. License plate 30271 taxi certificate number 3070. On the way here we passed thirty-seven Rovers, a Bentley, ten Jaguars, six Austins, one Rolls-Royce, twenty-seven motorcycles and six bicycles.

A: How are you getting along at the office, Wim?

W: You know.

A: Tell me.

W: I hate the people there.

A: What about Catherine Alexander? . . . Wim, what about Catherine Alexander? . . . Wim?

W: Oh, her. She won't be working there anymore.

A: What do you mean?

W: She's going to be murdered.

A: *What?* Why do you say that?

W: She told me.

A: Catherine told you she's going to be murdered?

W: The other one.

A: What other one?

W: His wife.

A: Whose wife, Wim?

W: Constantin Demiris.

A: He told you Catherine Alexander was going to be murdered?

W: Mrs Demiris. His wife. She called me from Greece.

A: Who's going to murder Catherine?
W: One of the men.
A: You mean, one of the men who flew in from Athens?
W: Yes.
A: Wim, we're going to end this session now. I have to leave.
W: Okay.

Chapter 30

The offices of the Hellenic Trade Corporation closed at 6.00 p.m. A few minutes before six o'clock, Evelyn and the other employees were preparing to leave.

Evelyn walked into Catherine's office. '*Miracle on Thirty-fourth Street* is playing at the Criterion. It's had great reviews. Would you like to see it tonight?'

'I can't,' Catherine said. 'Thanks, Evelyn. I promised Jerry Haley I'd go to the theater with him.'

'They really keep you busy, don't they? All right. Have a good time.'

Catherine heard the sounds of the others leaving. Finally, there was silence. She took a last look at her desk, made sure everything was in order, put on her coat, picked up her purse and started down the corridor. She had almost reached the front door when the telephone rang. Catherine hesitated, debating whether to answer it. She looked at her watch; she was going to be late. The telephone kept ringing. She ran back to her office and picked up the phone. 'Hello.'

'Catherine.' It was Alan Hamilton. He sounded out of breath. 'Thank God I reached you.'

'Is something wrong?'

'You're in great danger. I believe someone is trying to kill you.'

She made a low moaning sound. Her worst nightmares were coming true. She felt suddenly dizzy. 'Who?'

'I don't know. But I want you to stay where you are. Don't leave the office. Don't talk to anyone. I'm coming to get you.'

'Alan, I . . .'

'Don't worry, I'm on my way. Lock yourself in. Everything will be all right.'

The line went dead.

Catherine slowly replaced the receiver. 'Oh my God!'

Atanas appeared in the doorway. He took one look at Catherine's pale face and hurried to her side. 'Is something wrong, Miss Alexander?'

She turned to him. 'Someone . . . someone is trying to kill me.'

He was gaping at her. 'Why? Who . . . who would want to do that?'

'I'm not sure.'

They heard a knock at the front door.

Atanas looked at Catherine. 'Should I . . . ?'

'No,' she said quickly. 'Don't let anyone in. Dr Hamilton's on his way here.'

The knock at the front door was repeated, louder.

'You could hide in the basement,' Atanas whispered. 'You'll be safe there.'

She nodded nervously. 'Right.'

They moved toward the back of the corridor, to the door that led to the basement. 'When Dr Hamilton comes, tell him where I am.'

'You won't be afraid down there?'

'No,' Catherine said.

Atanas turned on a light, and led the way down the basement stairs.

'No one will ever find you here,' Atanas assured her. 'Don't you have any idea who would want to kill you?'

She thought of Constantin Demiris and her dreams. *He's going to kill you. But that was only a dream.* 'I'm not sure.'

Atanas looked at her and whispered, 'I think I know.'

Catherine stared at him. 'Who?'

'Me.' There was suddenly a switchblade in his hand and he was holding it to her throat.

'Atanas, this is no time to play . . .'

She felt the knife pressing deeper into her throat.

'Did you ever read *Appointment in Samarra*, Catherine? No?

265

Well, it's too late now, isn't it? It's about someone who tried to escape death. He went to Samarra and death was waiting for him there. This is your Samarra, Catherine.'

It was obscene, listening to these terrifying words coming from the mouth of the innocent-looking boy.

'Atanas, please. You can't . . .'

He slapped her hard across the face. 'I can't do it because I'm a young boy? Did I surprise you? That's because I'm a brilliant actor. I'm thirty years old, Catherine. Do you know why I look like a young boy? Because when I was growing up I never had enough to eat. I lived on garbage that I stole from trash cans at night.' He was holding the knife at her throat, backing her toward a wall. 'When I was a young boy, I watched soldiers rape my mother and father and then slash them both to death, and then they raped me and left me for dead.'

He was forcing her back deeper into the basement.

'Atanas, I – I've never done anything to hurt you. I . . .'

He smiled his boyish smile. 'This is nothing personal. This is business. You're worth fifty thousand dollars to me, dead.'

It was as though a curtain had come down in front of her eyes, and she was seeing everything through a red haze. A part of her was outside, looking down at what was happening.

'I had a wonderful plan worked out for you. But the boss is in a hurry now, so we'll have to improvise, won't we?'

Catherine could feel the point of the knife digging hard into her neck. He moved the knife and slit open the front of her dress.

'Pretty,' he said. 'Very pretty. I was planning a party for us first, but since your doctor friend is coming, we won't have time, will we? Too bad for you. I'm a great lover.'

Catherine stood there suffocated, barely able to breathe.

Atanas reached into his jacket and took a pint bottle from his pocket. In it was a pale, pink-colored liquid. 'Have you ever had slivovic? We'll drink to your accident, huh?' He moved the knife away to open the bottle and, for an instant, Catherine was tempted to flee.

'Go ahead,' Atanas said softly. 'Try it. Please.'

Catherine licked her lips. 'Look, I . . . I'll pay you. I'll . . .'

266

'Save your breath.' Atanas took a deep swallow from the bottle and handed it to her. 'Drink,' he said.

'No. I don't . . .'

'Drink!'

Catherine took the bottle and took a small sip. The fierce bite of the brandy burned her throat. Atanas took the bottle back and took another deep swallow.

'Who tipped off your doctor friend that someone was going to kill you?'

'I – I don't know.'

'It doesn't matter anyway.' Atanas pointed to one of the thick wooden posts that supported the ceiling. 'Get over there.'

Catherine's eyes glanced toward the door. She felt the steel blade press into her neck. 'Don't make me tell you again.'

Catherine moved over to the wooden post.

'That's a good girl,' Atanas said. 'Sit down.' He turned away for an instant. And, in that moment, Catherine made a break for it.

She started to race toward the stairs, her heart pounding. She was running for her life. She reached the first step and then the second, and, as she was about to move up, she felt a hand grab her leg and pull her back. He was incredibly strong.

'Bitch!'

He grabbed her by the hair and pulled her face close to his. 'You try that again and I'll break both your legs.'

She could feel the knife between her shoulder blades.

'Move!'

Atanas marched her back to the wooden post and shoved her to the ground.

'Stay there.'

Catherine watched as Atanas walked over to a pile of cardboard boxes bound with heavy cord. He cut two lengths of cord and carried them back to her.

'Put both hands in back of the post.'

'No, Atanas. I . . .'

He slammed his fist against the side of her face, and the room

267

blurred. Atanas leaned close and whispered, 'Don't ever say no to me. Do what I tell you before I slice your fucking head off.'

Catherine put her hands behind the post and a moment later she felt the cord bite into her wrists as Atanas tied them together. She could feel the circulation being cut off.

'Please,' she said. 'That's too tight.'

'Good,' he grinned. He took the second length of cord and tied her legs tightly together at the ankles. Then he got to his feet. 'There we are,' he said. 'All nice and cozy.' He took another swallow from the bottle. 'Would you like another drink?'

Catherine shook her head.

He shrugged. 'Okay.'

She watched him put the bottle to his lips again. *Maybe he'll get drunk and fall asleep*, Catherine thought desperately.

'I used to drink a quart a day,' Atanas boasted. He laid the empty bottle down on the cement floor. 'Well, time to go to work.'

'What – what are you going to do?'

'I'm going to make a little accident. This is going to be a masterpiece. I may even charge Demiris double.'

Demiris! So it wasn't just a dream. He was behind this. But why?

Catherine watched Atanas walk across the room to the huge boiler. He removed the outside plate and examined the pilot light and the eight boiler plates that kept the unit hot. The safety valve was nested in a metal frame to protect it. Atanas picked up a small piece of wood and jammed it into the frame so that the safety valve was inoperative. The heat dial was set at 150 degrees. As Catherine watched, Atanas turned the dial up to the maximum. Satisfied, he walked back to Catherine.

'Do you remember how much trouble we had with that furnace?' Atanas asked. 'Well, I'm afraid it's going to bust open, after all.' He moved closer to Catherine. 'When that dial reaches four hundred degrees, the boiler will blow up. Do you know what will happen then? The gas lines will rip open and the burner plates will set them on fire. The whole building will explode like a bomb.'

'You're insane! There are innocent people out there who . . .'

'There are no innocent people. You Americans believe in happy endings, don't you? You're fools. There are no happy endings.' He reached down and tested the rope that held Catherine's hands behind the post. Her wrists were bleeding. The rope was cutting into her flesh and the knots were tight. Atanas slowly ran his hands across Catherine's naked breasts, caressing them, and then he leaned down and kissed them. 'It's too bad we don't have more time. You'll never know what you missed.' He grabbed her by the hair and kissed her on the lips. His breath reeked of brandy. 'Goodbye, Catherine.' He stood up.

'Don't leave me,' Catherine pleaded. 'Let's talk and . . .'

'I have a plane to catch. I'm going back to Athens.' She watched him start toward the steps. 'I'll leave the light on for you so you can watch it happen.' A moment later, Catherine heard the heavy basement door close and the snap of the outside bolt and then there was silence. She was alone. She looked up at the dial on the boiler. It was rapidly moving up. As she watched, it went from 160 degrees to 170 degrees and kept moving. She fought desperately to free her hands but the more she pulled, the tighter the bonds became. She looked up again. The dial had reached 180 degrees and was climbing. There was no way out.

None.

Alan Hamilton was driving down Wimpole Street like a madman, cutting in and out of traffic, ignoring the yells and blaring of horns from irate drivers. The way ahead was blocked. He turned left and into Portland Place and headed toward Oxford Circus. Traffic was heavier here, slowing him down.

In the basement at 217 Bond Street, the needle on the boiler had climbed to 200 degrees. The basement was becoming warm.

The traffic was almost at a standstill. People were headed home, to dinner, to the theater. Alan Hamilton sat at the wheel of his

269

car, frustrated. *Should I have called the police? But what good would it have done? A neurotic patient of mine thinks someone is going to be murdered? The police would have laughed. No, I have to get to her.* The traffic began to move again.

In the basement, the needle was climbing upward to 300. The room was becoming unbearably hot. She tried to free her hands again and her wrists were rubbed raw, but the rope stayed tight.

He turned into Oxford Street, speeding through a pedestrian lane with two old women crossing. In back of him, he heard a shrill police whistle. For an instant, he was tempted to stop and enlist help. But there was no time to explain. He kept driving.

At an intersection a huge truck pulled out, blocking his way. Alan Hamilton honked impatiently. He leaned his head out the window. 'Move it!'

The truck driver turned to look at him. 'What's the matter, mate, you going to a fire?'

The traffic had become a snarl of cars. When it finally cleared, Alan Hamilton started to drive again, racing toward Bond Street. A trip that should have taken ten minutes had taken him almost half an hour.

In the basement, the needle climbed to 400 degrees.

Finally, blessedly, the building was in sight. Alan Hamilton pulled his car over to the curb across the street and slammed on the brakes. He threw open the door and hurried out of the car. As he started to run toward the building, he stopped in horror. The ground shook as the entire building exploded like a giant bomb, filling the air with flame and debris.

And death.

270

Chapter 31

Atanas Stavich was feeling terribly aroused. Taking care of a contract always did that to him. He made it a rule to have sex with his victims, male or female, before he killed them and he always found it exciting. Now, he was frustrated because there had been no time to torture Catherine or to make love to her. Atanas looked at his watch. It was still early. His plane didn't leave until eleven o'clock that evening. He took a taxi to Shepherd Market, paid the driver and wandered into the labyrinth of streets. There were half a dozen girls standing on street corners calling out to the men passing by.

'Hello, love, would you like a French lesson tonight?'

'How about a little party?'

'Are you interested in Greek?'

None of the women approached Atanas. He walked up to a tall blonde wearing a brief leather skirt and blouse and stiletto-heeled shoes.

'Good evening,' Atanas said politely.

She looked down at him, amused. 'Hello, little boy. Does your mother know you're out?'

Atanas smiled shyly. 'Yes, ma'am. I thought if you weren't busy . . .'

The prostitute laughed. 'Did you, now? And what would you do if I *wasn't* busy? Have you ever made love to a girl before?'

'Once,' Atanas said softly. 'I liked it.'

'You're the size of a minnow,' the girl laughed. 'I usually throw the little ones back, but it's a slow night. Have you got ten bob?'

'Yes, ma'am.'

'All right, love. Let's go upstairs.'

271

She led Atanas through a doorway and up two flights of stairs to a small, one-room apartment.

Atanas handed her the money.

'Well, let's see if you know what to do with it, love.' She stripped off her clothes and watched Atanas undress. She looked at him in astonishment. 'My God! You're enormous.'

'Am I?'

She got into bed and said, 'Be careful. Don't hurt me.'

Atanas moved toward the bed. Ordinarily, he enjoyed beating up whores. It increased his sexual satisfaction. But he knew that this was no time to do anything suspicious or to leave a trail that the police might want to follow. So Atanas smiled down at her and said, 'This is your lucky night.'

'What?'

'Nothing.' He climbed on top of her and closed his eyes and plunged into her, hurting her, and it was Catherine screaming for mercy, begging him to stop. And he pounded her savagely, harder and harder, her screams exciting him until finally everything exploded and he sank back satisfied.

'My God,' the woman said. 'You're unbelievable.'

Atanas opened his eyes and he wasn't with Catherine. He was with some ugly whore in a dreary room. He got dressed and took a taxi to his hotel room, where he packed and checked out.

When he headed for the airport, it was nine thirty. He had plenty of time to catch his plane.

There was a small line at Olympic Airways. When Atanas reached the head of the line, he handed the clerk his ticket. 'Is the flight on time?'

'Yes.' The clerk looked at the name on the ticket, *Atanas Stavich*. He looked up at Atanas again, then glanced at a man standing nearby and nodded. The man walked over to the ticket counter.

'May I see your ticket?'

Atanas handed him the ticket. 'Is anything wrong?' he asked.

The man said, 'I'm afraid we've overbooked this flight. If

you'd like to come into the office, I'll try to straighten everything out.'

Atanas shrugged. 'All right.' He followed the man toward the office, filled with a feeling of euphoria. Demiris was probably out of jail by now. He was too important a man for the law to touch him. Everything had gone perfectly. He would take the fifty thousand dollars and put it into one of his Swiss numbered accounts. Then a little vacation. The Riviera, perhaps, or Rio. He liked the male prostitutes in Rio.

Atanas walked into the office, and stopped, staring. He turned pale. 'You're dead! You're dead! I killed you!' It was a scream.

Atanas was still screaming when they led him out of the room and into a police van. They watched him leave, and Alan Hamilton turned to Catherine. 'It's over now, darling. It's finally over.'

Chapter 32

In the basement, several hours earlier, Catherine had tried
desperately to free her hands. The more she struggled, the tighter
the rope became. Her fingers were getting numb. She kept
looking over at the dial on the boiler. The needle had reached
250 degrees. *When that dial reaches 400 degrees, the boiler will
explode. There has to be a way out of this*, Catherine thought.
There has to be! Her eyes lit on the brandy bottle that Atanas
had dropped on the floor. She stared at it and her heart began to
pound wildly. *There is a chance!* If only she could . . . Catherine
slumped down against the post and stretched out her feet toward
the bottle. It was out of reach. She slid down farther, the splinters
of the wooden post tearing into her back. The bottle was an inch
away. Catherine's eyes filled with tears. *One more try*, she
thought. *Just one more.* She slumped down farther, her back
raked with splinters, and pushed again, with all her strength.
One foot touched the bottle. *Careful. Don't push it away.* Slowly,
slowly, she hooked the neck of the bottle on the rope that bound
her ankles. Very carefully, she pulled her feet in, drawing the
bottle closer. Finally, it was next to her.

She looked up at the dial. It had climbed to 280 degrees. She
was fighting panic. Slowly, she inched the bottle in back of her
with her feet. Her fingers found it but they were too numb to
get a grip on it, and they were slippery with the blood from her
wrists where the rope had cut into them.

The basement was getting hotter. She tried again. The bottle
slipped away. Catherine glanced at the dial on the boiler. *300*
now, and the dial seemed to be racing upward. Steam was
beginning to pour out of the boiler. She tried again to get a grip
on the bottle.

There! She had the bottle in her bound hands. Holding it

tightly, she raised her arms and slid them down the post, smashing the glass bottle down against the concrete. Nothing happened. She cried aloud with frustration. She tried it again. Nothing. The dial was climbing inexorably upward. *350!* Catherine took another deep breath and slammed the bottle down with all her strength. She heard the bottle shatter. *Thank God!* Moving as quickly as she dared, Catherine gripped the broken neck of the bottle in one hand and started to saw at the ropes with the other. The glass cut into her wrists but she ignored the pain. She felt one strand snap and then another. And suddenly her hand was free. She hurriedly loosened the rope on the other hand and untied the ropes binding her ankles. The dial had reached 380. Heavy jets of steam were pouring out of the furnace. Catherine struggled to her feet. Atanas had bolted the basement door. There would be no time to escape from the building before the explosion.

Catherine raced over to the furnace and tugged at the block of wood cutting off the safety valve. It was jammed in tightly. *400!*

She had a split-second decision to make. She ran for the far door that led to the bomb shelter, pulled it open and hurried inside. She slammed the heavy door closed behind her. She lay huddled on the concrete of the huge bunker, breathing hard, and five seconds later there was a tremendous explosion and the whole room seemed to rock. She lay in the darkness, fighting for breath, listening to the roaring flames outside the door. She was safe. It was over. *No, not yet,* Catherine thought. *There's still something I have to do.*

When the firemen found her an hour later and escorted her out, Alan Hamilton was there. Catherine ran into his arms and he held her close.

'Catherine, darling. I was so afraid! How did you . . . ?'

'Later,' Catherine said. 'We've got to stop Atanas Stavich.'

Chapter 33

They were married at a church near Alan's sister's farm in Sussex in a private ceremony. Alan's sister turned out to be a pleasant woman who looked exactly like the photograph Catherine had seen in Alan's office. Her son was away at school. Catherine and Alan spent a quiet weekend at the farm and flew to Venice on their honeymoon.

Venice was a brilliantly colored page out of a medieval history book, a magical floating city of canals and 120 islands, spanned by four hundred bridges. Alan and Catherine Hamilton landed at Venice's Aeroporto Marco Polo, near Mestre, took a motor launch to the terminal at the Piazza San Marco, and checked into the Royal Danieli, the beautiful old hotel next to the Doges' Palace.

Their suite was exquisite, filled with lovely, antique furniture, and it overlooked the Grand Canal.

'What would you like to do first?' Alan asked.

Catherine walked up to him and put her arms around him. 'Guess.'

They unpacked later.

Venice was a healing, a balm that made Catherine forget the terrible nightmares and horrors of the past.

She and Alan went exploring. St Mark's Square was a few hundred yards away from their hotel, and centuries away in time. St Mark's Cathedral was an art gallery and a church, the walls and ceilings lined with breathtaking mosaics and frescoes.

They went inside the Doges' Palace, filled with opulent

chambers, and stood on the Bridge of Sighs, where, centuries earlier, prisoners had crossed to go to their deaths.

They visited museums and churches and some of the outlying islands. They stopped at Murano to watch the glass-blowing, and at Burano to see the women make lace. They took a motor launch to Torcello and dined at Locanda Cipriani in the lovely flower-filled garden.

And Catherine was reminded of the garden at the convent, and she remembered how lost she had been then. And she looked across the table at her beloved Alan and thought, *Thank you, God.*

Mercerie was the main shopping street, and they found fabulous stores: Rubelli for fabrics, and Casella for shoes, and Giocondo Cassini for antiques. They dined at Quadri and Al Graspo de Ua and Harry's Bar. They rode in gondolas and in the smaller *sandoli.*

On Friday, near the end of their stay, there was a sudden downpour and a violent electrical storm.

Catherine and Alan raced to get back to the shelter of their hotel. They looked out the window at the storm.

'Sorry about the rain, Mrs Hamilton,' Alan said. 'The brochures promised sunshine.'

Catherine smiled. 'What rain? I'm so happy, darling.'

Streaks of lightning flashed across the sky and there was an explosion of thunder. Another sound flashed into Catherine's mind: the explosion of the boiler.

She turned to Alan. 'Isn't this the day the jury brings in its verdict?'

He hesitated. 'Yes. I didn't bring it up because . . .'

'I'm all right. I want to know.'

He looked at her a moment, then nodded. 'Right.'

Catherine watched as Alan walked over to the radio in the corner and turned it on. He turned the dial until he came to the BBC station that was reporting the news.

'. . . and the Prime Minister handed in his resignation today. The Premier will try to form a new government.' The radio was crackling and the voice was fading in and out.

'It's that damned electrical storm,' Alan said.

The sound came on again. 'In Athens, the trial of Constantin Demiris has finally come to an end, and the jury returned its verdict a few moments ago. To everyone's surprise, the verdict . . .'

The radio went dead.

Catherine turned to Alan. 'What – what do you think the verdict was?'

He took her into his arms. 'It depends on whether you believe in happy endings.'

Epilogue

Five days before the trial of Constantin Demiris was to begin, the jailor opened up his cell door.

'You have a visitor.'

Constantin Demiris looked up. Except for his attorney, he had been permitted no visitors until now. He refused to show any curiosity. The bastards were treating him like a common criminal. But he would not give them the satisfaction of showing any emotion. He followed the jailor down the hall into a small conference room.

'In there.'

Demiris stepped inside and stopped. A crippled old man was hunched over in a wheelchair. His hair was snow white. His face was a ghastly patchwork of red and white burn tissue. His lips were frozen upward in a horrible rictus of a smile. It took a moment for him to realize who his visitor was. His face turned ashen. 'My God!'

'I'm not a ghost,' Napoleon Chotas said. His voice was hoarse. 'Come in, Costa.'

Demiris found his voice. 'The fire . . .'

'I jumped out a window and broke my back. My butler got me away before the firemen arrived. I didn't want you to know I was still alive. I was too tired to fight you any longer.'

'But . . . they found a body.'

'My houseman.'

Demiris sank into a chair. 'I . . . I'm glad you're alive,' he said feebly.

'You should be. I'm going to save your life.'

Demiris studied him warily. 'You are?'

'Yes. I'm going to defend you.'

Demiris laughed aloud. 'Really, Leon. After all these years,

279

do you take me for a fool? What makes you think I would put my life in your hands?'

'Because I'm the only one who can save you, Costa.'

Constantin Demiris rose. 'No thanks.' He started toward the door.

'I've talked to Spyros Lambrou. I've persuaded him to testify that he was with you at the time his sister was murdered.'

Demiris stopped and turned. 'Why would he do that?'

Chotas leaned forward in his wheelchair. 'Because I persuaded him that taking your fortune would be a sweeter revenge than taking your life.'

'I don't understand.'

'I assured Lambrou that if he testifies for you, you'll turn over your entire fortune to him. Your ships, your companies – everything you possess.'

'You're crazy!'

'Am I? Think about it, Costa. His testimony can save your life. Is your fortune worth more to you than your life?'

There was a long silence. Demiris sat down again. 'Lambrou is willing to testify that I was with him when Melina was killed?'

'That's right.'

'And in return he wants – '

'Everything you have.'

Demiris shook his head. 'I would have to keep my . . .'

'*Everything*. He wants to strip you completely. You see, that's his revenge.'

There was something that puzzled Demiris. 'And what do you get out of all this, Leon?' He studied Chotas warily.

Chotas' lips moved in a parody of a grin. 'I get it all.'

'I . . . I don't understand.'

'Before you turn the Hellenic Trade Corporation over to Lambrou, you're going to transfer all of its assets into a new company. A company that belongs to me.'

Demiris stared at him. 'So, Lambrou gets nothing.'

Chotas shrugged. 'There are winners and there are losers.'

'Won't Lambrou suspect something?'

'Not the way I'll handle it.'

Demiris said, 'If you'd double-cross Lambrou, how do I know you won't double-cross me?'

'It's very simple, my dear Costa. You're protected. We'll have a signed agreement that the new company will belong to me only on the condition that you are acquitted. If you are found guilty, I get nothing.'

For the first time, Constantin Demiris found himself becoming interested. He sat there studying the crippled lawyer. *Would he throw the trial and lose hundreds of millions of dollars just to get even with me? No. He's not that big a fool.* 'All right,' Demiris said slowly. 'I agree.'

Chotas said, 'Good. You just saved your life, Costa.'

I've saved more than that, Demiris thought triumphantly. *I have a hundred million dollars hidden away where no one will ever find it.*

Chotas' meeting with Spyros Lambrou had been a difficult one. He almost threw Chotas out of his office.

'You want me to testify to save that monster's life? Get the hell out of here.'

'You want revenge, don't you?' Chotas had asked.

'Yes. And I'm getting it.'

'Are you? You know Costa. His wealth means more to him than his life. If they execute him, his pain will be over in a few minutes, but if you break him and take everything away from him, force him to go through life without any money, you would be giving him a much greater punishment.'

There was truth in what the lawyer said. Demiris was the greediest man he had ever met. 'You say that he's willing to sign everything he has over to me?'

'Everything. His fleet, his businesses, every company he owns.'

It was an enormous temptation. 'Let me think about it.' Lambrou watched the lawyer wheel himself out of his office. *Poor bastard*, he thought. *What has he got to live for?*

*

281

At midnight, Spyros Lambrou telephoned Napoleon Chotas. 'I've made up my mind. We have a deal.'

The press was in a feeding frenzy. Not only was Constantin Demiris being tried for the murder of his wife, but he was being defended by a man who had come back from the dead, the brilliant criminal attorney who had supposedly died in a holocaust.

The trial was being held in the same courtroom where Noelle Page and Larry Douglas had been tried. Constantin Demiris sat at the defendant's table, cloaked in an aura of invisibility. Napoleon Chotas was next to him in his wheelchair. The State was being represented by Special Prosecutor Delma.

Delma was addressing the jury.

'Constantin Demiris is one of the most powerful men in the world. His vast fortune gives him many privileges. But there's one privilege it does not give him. And that's the right to commit cold-blooded murder. No one has that right.' He turned to look at Demiris. 'The State will prove beyond a doubt that Constantin Demiris is guilty of the brutal murder of a wife who loved him. When you are through hearing the evidence, I'm certain that there's only one verdict you can bring in. Guilty of murder in the first degree.' He walked back to his seat.

The Chief Justice turned to Napoleon Chotas. 'Is the defense ready to make its opening statement?'

'We are, Your Honor.' Chotas wheeled himself in front of the jury. He could see the look of pity on their faces as they tried to avoid looking at his grotesque face and his crippled body. 'Constantin Demiris is not on trial here because he's rich or powerful. Or perhaps it's *because* of that that he has been dragged into this courtroom. The weak always try to bring down the powerful, don't they? Mr Demiris may be guilty of being rich and powerful but one thing I am going to prove

282

with absolute certainty – he is not guilty of murdering his wife.'

The trial had begun.

Prosecutor Delma was questioning Police Lieutenant Theophilos on the stand.

'Would you describe what you saw when you walked into Demiris' beach house, Lieutenant?'

'The chairs and tables were overturned. Everything was all messed up.'

'It looked as though a terrible struggle had taken place?'

'Yes, sir. It looked as though the house had been burgled.'

'You found a bloody knife at the scene of the crime, did you not?'

'Yes, sir.'

'And there were fingerprints on the knife?'

'That's correct.'

'Who did they belong to?'

'Constantin Demiris.'

The eyes of the jury swung toward Demiris.

'When you searched the house, what else did you find?'

'In back of a closet we found a pair of bloodstained bathing shorts that had Demiris' initials on them.'

'Isn't it possible that they had been at the house for a long time?'

'No, sir. They were still wet with sea water.'

'Thank you.'

It was Napoleon Chotas' turn. 'Detective Theophilos, you had a chance to talk to the defendant personally, didn't you?'

'Yes, sir.'

'How would you describe him physically?'

'Well . . .' The detective looked over to where Demiris was sitting. 'I would say he was a big man.'

'Did he look strong? I mean physically strong?'

'Yes.'

'Not the sort of man who would have to tear a room apart in order to kill his wife.'

Delma was on his feet. 'Objection.'

283

'Sustained. The defense attorney will refrain from leading the witness.'

'I apologize, Your Honor.' Chotas turned to the detective. 'In your conversation with Mr Demiris, would you evaluate him as an intelligent man?'

'Yes, sir. I don't think you become as rich as he is unless you're pretty smart.'

'I couldn't agree with you more, Lieutenant. And that leads us to an interesting question. How could a man like Constantin Demiris be stupid enough to commit a murder and leave behind at the scene of the crime a knife with his fingerprints on it, a bloodstained pair of shorts . . . wouldn't you say that was not very intelligent?'

'Well, sometimes in the heat of committing a crime, people do strange things.'

'The police found a gold button from a jacket Demiris was supposed to be wearing. Is that correct?'

'Yes, sir.'

'And that's an important part of the evidence against Mr Demiris. The police theory is that his wife tore it off in the struggle when he tried to kill her?'

'That's correct.'

'So, we have a man who habitually dressed very neatly. A button is ripped off the front of his jacket but he doesn't notice it. He wears the jacket home and he still doesn't notice it. Then he takes it off and hangs it up in his closet – and he still doesn't notice it. That would make the defendant not only stupid, but blind.'

Mr Katelanos was on the stand. The owner of the detective agency was making the most of his moment in the sun. Delma was questioning him.

'You're the owner of a private detective agency?'

'Yes, sir.'

'And a few days before Mrs Demiris was murdered, she came to see you?'

'That's right.'

'What did she want?'

'Protection. She said she was going to divorce her husband and he had threatened to kill her.'

There was a murmur from the spectators.

'So, Mrs Demiris was very upset?'

'Oh, yes, sir. She certainly was.'

'And she engaged your agency to protect her from her husband?'

'Yes, sir.'

'That's all, thank you.' Delma turned to Chotas. 'Your witness.'

Chotas wheeled his chair over to the witness stand. 'Mr Katelanos, how long have you been in the detective business?'

'Almost fifteen years.'

Chotas was impressed. 'Well. That's a long time. You really must be very good at what you do.'

'I suppose I am,' Katelanos said modestly.

'So, you've had a lot of experience in dealing with people who are in trouble.'

'That's why they come to me,' Katelanos said smugly.

'And when Mrs Demiris came to you, did she seem a little bit upset, or . . .'

'Oh no. She was *very* upset. You might say panicky.'

'I see. Because she was afraid her husband was about to kill her.'

'That's right.'

'So, when she left your office, how many of your operatives did you send with her? One? Two?'

'Well, no. I didn't send any with her.'

Chotas frowned. 'I don't understand. Why not?'

'Well, she said she didn't want us to start until Monday.'

Chotas looked at him, baffled. 'I'm afraid you're confusing me, Mr Katelanos. This woman, who came to your office terrified that her husband was going to kill her, just walked out and said she wouldn't need any protection until Monday?'

'Well, yes. That's right.'

Napoleon Chotas said, almost to himself, 'It makes one wonder how frightened Mrs Demiris really was, doesn't it?'

*

285

The Demiris maid was on the witness stand. 'Now, you actually heard a conversation between Mrs Demiris and her husband on the telephone?'

'Yes, sir.'

'Would you tell us what that conversation was?'

'Well, Mrs Demiris told her husband she wanted a divorce and he said he wouldn't give it to her.'

Delma glanced at the jury. 'I see.' He turned back to the witness. 'What else did you hear?'

'He asked her to meet him at the beach house at three o'clock, and to go alone.'

'He said that she should come alone?'

'Yes, sir. And she said if she didn't get back by six, I was to call the police.'

There was a visible reaction from the jury. They turned to stare at Demiris.

'No more questions.' Delma turned to Chotas. 'Your witness.'

Napoleon Chotas wheeled his chair close to the witness stand. 'Your name is Andrea, isn't it?'

'Yes, sir.' She tried not to look at the scarred, disfigured face.

'Andrea, you said that you heard Mrs Demiris tell her husband that she was going to get a divorce and that you heard Mr Demiris say that he wouldn't give it to her, and that he told her to come to the beach house at three and to come alone. Is that right?'

'Yes, sir.'

'You are under oath, Andrea. That's not what you heard at all.'

'Oh yes it is, sir.'

'How many telephones are there in the room where this conversation took place?'

'Why, just one.'

Napoleon Chotas wheeled his chair closer. 'So, you weren't listening to the conversation on another phone?'

'No, sir. I would never do that.'

'So, the truth is, you only heard what *Mrs* Demiris said. It would have been impossible for you to hear what her husband said.'

286

'Oh. Well, I suppose . . .'

'In other words, you did *not* hear Mr Demiris threaten his wife or ask her to come to the beach house or anything else. You *imagined* all that because of what Mrs Demiris was saying.'

Andrea was flustered. 'Well, I suppose you could put it that way.'

'I *am* putting it that way. Why were you in the room when Mrs Demiris was on the telephone?'

'She asked me to bring her some tea.'

'And you brought it?'

'Yes, sir.'

'You set it down on a table?'

'Yes, sir.'

'Why didn't you leave then?'

'Mrs Demiris waved for me to stay.'

'She wanted you to hear the conversation or what was supposed to be a conversation?'

'I . . . I suppose so.'

His voice was a whiplash. 'So, you don't know whether she was talking to her husband on the phone or if in fact she was talking to anybody.' Chotas moved his chair even closer. 'Don't you find it strange that in the middle of a personal conversation, Mrs Demiris asked you to stay there and listen? I know that in my house if we're having a personal discussion we don't ask the staff to eavesdrop. No. I put it to you that that conversation never took place. Mrs Demiris wasn't speaking to anyone. She was setting up her husband so that on this day, in this courtroom, he would be put on trial for his life. But Constantin Demiris did not kill his wife. The evidence against him was very carefully planted. It was planted too carefully. No intelligent man would leave a series of obvious clues behind that pointed to himself. And no matter what else he is, Constantin Demiris is an intelligent man.'

The trial went on for ten more days with accusations and counter-accusations, and expert testimony from the police and the coroner. The consensus of opinion was that Constantin Demiris was probably guilty.

287

Napoleon Chotas saved his bombshell until the end. He put Spyros Lambrou on the witness stand. Before the trial started, Demiris had signed a notarized contract deeding the Hellenic Trade Corporation and all its assets to Spyros Lambrou. A day earlier, those assets had been secretly transferred to Napoleon Chotas with the proviso that it would take effect only if Constantin Demiris was acquitted in his trial.

'Mr Lambrou. You and your brother-in-law, Constantin Demiris, did not get along well, did you?'

'No, we did not.'

'As a matter of fact, would it be a fair statement to say that you hated each other?'

Lambrou looked over at Constantin Demiris. 'It might even be an understatement.'

'On the day your sister disappeared, Constantin Demiris told the police that he was nowhere near the beach house; that in fact at three o'clock, the time established for your sister's death, he was having a meeting with you in Acro-Corinth. When the police questioned you about that meeting, you denied it.'

'Yes, I did.'

'Why?'

Lambrou sat there for a long moment. His voice was filled with anger. 'Demiris treated my sister shamefully. He constantly abused and humiliated her. I wanted him punished. He needed me for an alibi. I wouldn't give it to him.'

'And now?'

'I can't live with a lie any longer. I feel I have to tell the truth.'

'Did you and Constantin Demiris meet at Acro-Corinth that afternoon?'

'Yes, the truth is that we did.'

There was an uproar in the courtroom. Delma rose to his feet, his face pale. 'Your Honor. I object . . .'

'Objection denied.'

Delma sank back into his seat. Constantin Demiris was leaning forward, his eyes bright.

'Tell us about that meeting. Was it your idea?'

'No. It was Melina's idea. She tricked us both.'

'Tricked you, how?'

'Melina telephoned me and said that her husband wanted to meet me at my lodge up there to discuss a business deal. Then she called Demiris and told him that I had asked for a meeting up there. When we arrived, we found that we had nothing to say to each other.'

'And the meeting took place in the middle of the afternoon at the established time of Mrs Demiris' death?'

'That's right.'

'It's a four-hour drive from Acro-Corinth to the beach house. I've had it timed.' Napoleon Chotas was looking at the jury. 'So, there is no way that Constantin Demiris could have been at Acro-Corinth at three and been back in Athens before seven.' Chotas turned back to Spyros Lambrou. 'You are under oath, Mr Lambrou. Is what you have just told this court the truth?'

'Yes. So help me God.'

Napoleon Chotas swivelled his chair toward the jury.

'Ladies and gentlemen,' he rasped, 'there is only one verdict you can possibly reach.' They were straining forward to catch his words. 'Not guilty. If the State had claimed that the defendant had hired someone to kill his wife, then there might have been some small measure of doubt. But, on the contrary, their whole case is based upon so-called evidence that the defendant was in that room, that he himself murdered his wife. The learned justices will instruct you that in this trial two essential elements must be proven: motive and opportunity.

'Not motive *or* opportunity, but motive *and* opportunity. In law, they are Siamese twins – inseparable. Ladies and gentlemen, the defendant may or may not have had a motive, but this witness has proved beyond the shadow of a doubt that the defendant was nowhere near the scene of the crime when it occurred.'

The jury was out for four hours. Constantin Demiris watched as they filed back into the courtroom. He looked pale and anxious. Chotas was not looking at the jury. He was looking at Constantin Demiris' face. Demiris' aplomb and arrogance were gone. He was a man facing death.

289

The Chief Justice asked, 'Has the jury reached a verdict?'

'We have, Your Honor.' The jury foreman held up a piece of paper.

'Would the bailiff get the verdict please.'

The bailiff walked over to the juror, took the piece of paper and handed it to the judge. He opened the piece of paper and looked up. 'The jury finds the defendant not guilty.'

There was pandemonium in the courtroom. People were getting to their feet, some of them applauding, some of them hissing.

The expression on Demiris' face was ecstatic. He took a deep breath, rose and walked over to Napoleon Chotas. 'You did it,' he said. 'I owe you a lot.'

Chotas looked into his eyes. 'Not anymore. I'm very rich and you're very poor. Come on. We're going to celebrate.'

Constantin Demiris pushed Chotas' wheelchair through the milling crowd, out past the reporters, to the parking lot. Chotas pointed to a sedan parked at the entrance. 'My car's over there.'

Demiris wheeled him up to the door. 'Don't you have a chauffeur?'

'I don't need one. I had this car specially fitted so I could drive it myself. Help me in.'

Demiris opened the door and lifted Chotas into the driver's seat. He folded the wheelchair and put it in the back seat. Demiris got into the car next to Chotas.

'You're still the greatest lawyer in the world,' Constantin Demiris smiled.

'Yes.' Napoleon Chotas put the car in gear and started to drive. 'What are you going to do now, Costa?'

Demiris said carefully, 'Oh, I'll manage to get by somehow.' *With a hundred million dollars I can build up my empire again.* Demiris chuckled. 'Spyros is going to be pretty upset when he finds out how you tricked him.'

'There's nothing he can do about it,' Chotas assured him. 'The contract he signed gives him a company that's worthless.'

They were headed toward the mountains. Demiris watched as Chotas moved the levers that controlled the gas pedal and the brake. 'You handle this very well.'

'You learn to do what you have to,' Chotas said. They were climbing up a narrow mountain road.

'Where are we going?'

'I have a little house at the top here. We'll have a glass of champagne and I'll have a taxi take you back to town. You know, Costa, I've been thinking. Everything that's happened . . . Noelle's death and Larry Douglas' death. And poor Stavros. None of it was about money, was it?' He turned to glance at Demiris. 'It was all about hate. Hate and love. You loved Noelle.'

'Yes,' Demiris said. 'I loved Noelle.'

'I loved her, too,' Chotas said. 'You didn't know that, did you?'

Demiris looked at him in surprise. 'No.'

'And yet I helped you murder her. I've never forgiven myself for that. Have you forgiven yourself, Costa?'

'She deserved what she got.'

'I think in the end we all deserve what we get. There's something I haven't told you, Costa. That fire – ever since the night of that fire, I've been in excruciating pain. The doctors tried to put me back together again but it didn't really work. I'm too badly crippled.' He pushed a lever that speeded up the car. They were starting to move fast along hairpin curves, climbing higher and higher. The Aegean Sea appeared far below them.

'As a matter of fact,' Chotas said hoarsely, 'I'm in so much pain that my life really isn't worth living anymore.' He pushed the lever again and the car began to go faster.

'Slow down,' Demiris said. 'You're going to . . .'

'I've stayed alive this long for you. I've decided that you and I are going to end it together.'

Demiris turned to stare at him, horrified. 'What are you talking about? Slow down, man. You'll kill us both.'

'That's right,' Chotas said. He moved the lever again. The car leapt forward.

'You're crazy!' Demiris said. 'You're rich. You don't want to die.'

Chotas' scarred lips turned into a horrific imitation of a smile. 'No, I'm not rich. You know who's rich? Your friend, Sister

291

Theresa. I've given all your money to the convent at Ioannina.'

They were racing toward a blind curve on the steep mountain road.

'Stop the car!' Demiris screamed. He tried to wrest the wheel from Chotas but it was impossible.

'I'll give you anything you want,' Demiris yelled. 'Stop!'

Chotas said, 'I have what I want.'

The next moment they were flying over the cliff, down the steep mountainside, the car tumbling end over end in a grotesque pirouette of death, until finally at the bottom it crashed into the sea. There was a tremendous explosion, and then the deep silence of eternity.